THE STOLEN HEART

Also by Andrey Kurkov in English translation

THE KYIV MYSTERIES

The Silver Bone

FICTION

Death and the Penguin
The Case of the General's Thumb
Penguin Lost
A Matter of Death and Life
The President's Last Love
The Good Angel of Death
The Milkman in the Night
The Gardener from Ochakov
The Bickford Fuse
Grey Bees
Jimi Hendrix Live in Lviv

NON-FICTION

Ukraine Diaries: Dispatches from Kiev
Diary of an Invasion

Andrey Kurkov

THE STOLEN HEART

Translated from the Russian by
Boris Dralyuk

MACLEHOSE PRESS
QUERCUS · LONDON

First published in the Russian language as *Serdce – ne mjaso*
by Folio, Kharkiv, 2021
First published in Great Britain in 2025 by

MacLehose Press
an imprint of Quercus
Carmelite House
50 Victoria Embankment
London W1U 8EW

An Hachette UK Company

The authorised representative in the EEA is Hachette Ireland,
8 Castlecourt Centre, Dublin 15, D15 XTP3,
Ireland (email: info@hbgi.ie)

Map by Bill Donohoe

A CIP catalogue record for this book is available
from the British Library.

ISBN (Hardback) 978 1 52942 653 3
ISBN (Trade paperback) 978 1 52943 106 3
ISBN (Ebook) 978 1 52942 655 7

10 9 8 7 6 5 4 3 2 1

Designed and typeset in Sabon by CC Book Production
Printed and bound in Great Britain by Clays Ltd, Elcograf S.p.A.

FSC
www.fsc.org
MIX
Paper | Supporting
responsible forestry
FSC® C104740

Papers used by Quercus are from well-managed forests and other responsible sources.

The author is sincerely grateful to Yuri Lysenko and Paul Lequesne for their advice and suggestions, as well as to Tatyana Markova and Alexander Markov, who convinced him to deal in detail with the events that unfolded in Kyiv and throughout Ukraine in 1919 and 1920.

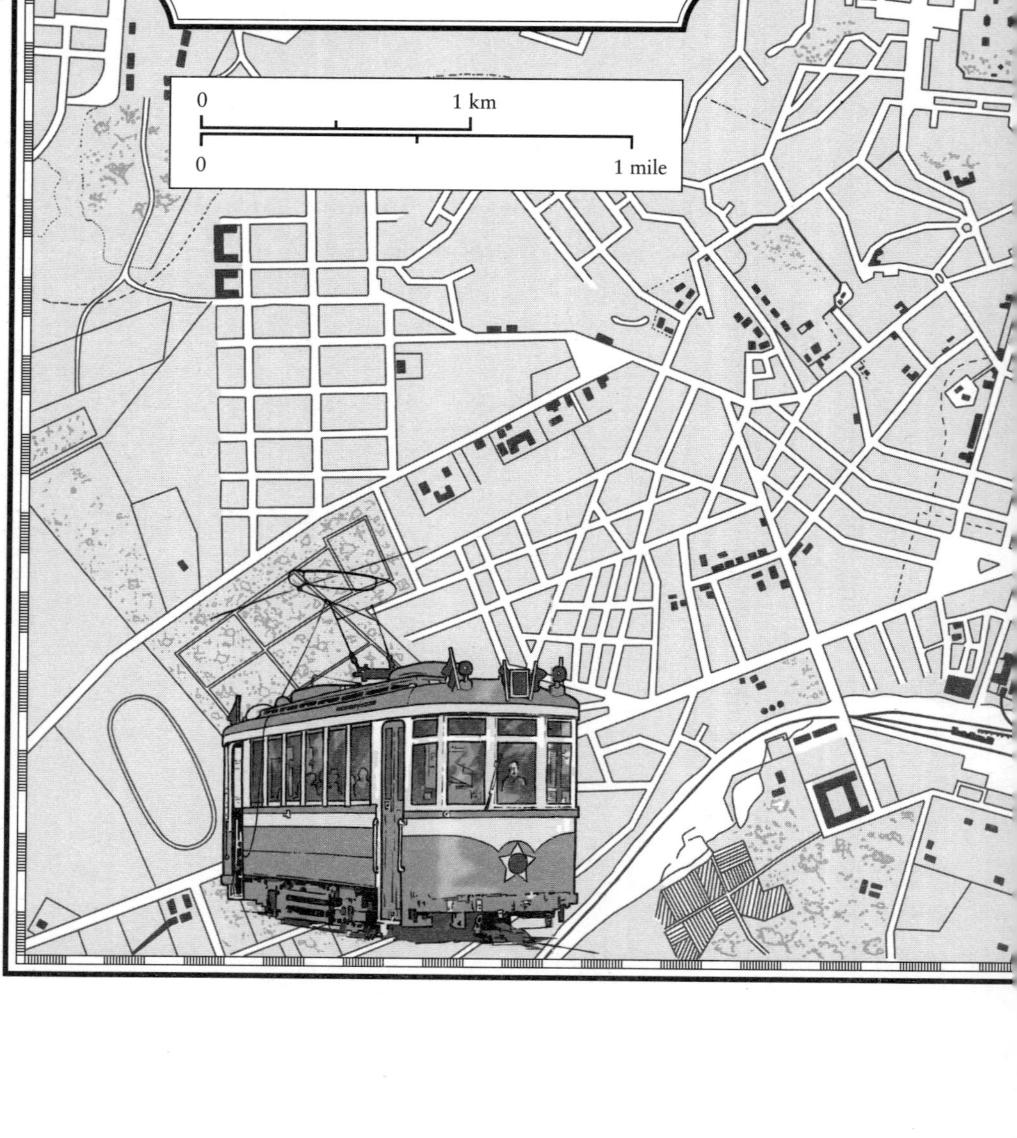
Samson's Kyiv, 1919
0
1 km
0
1 mile

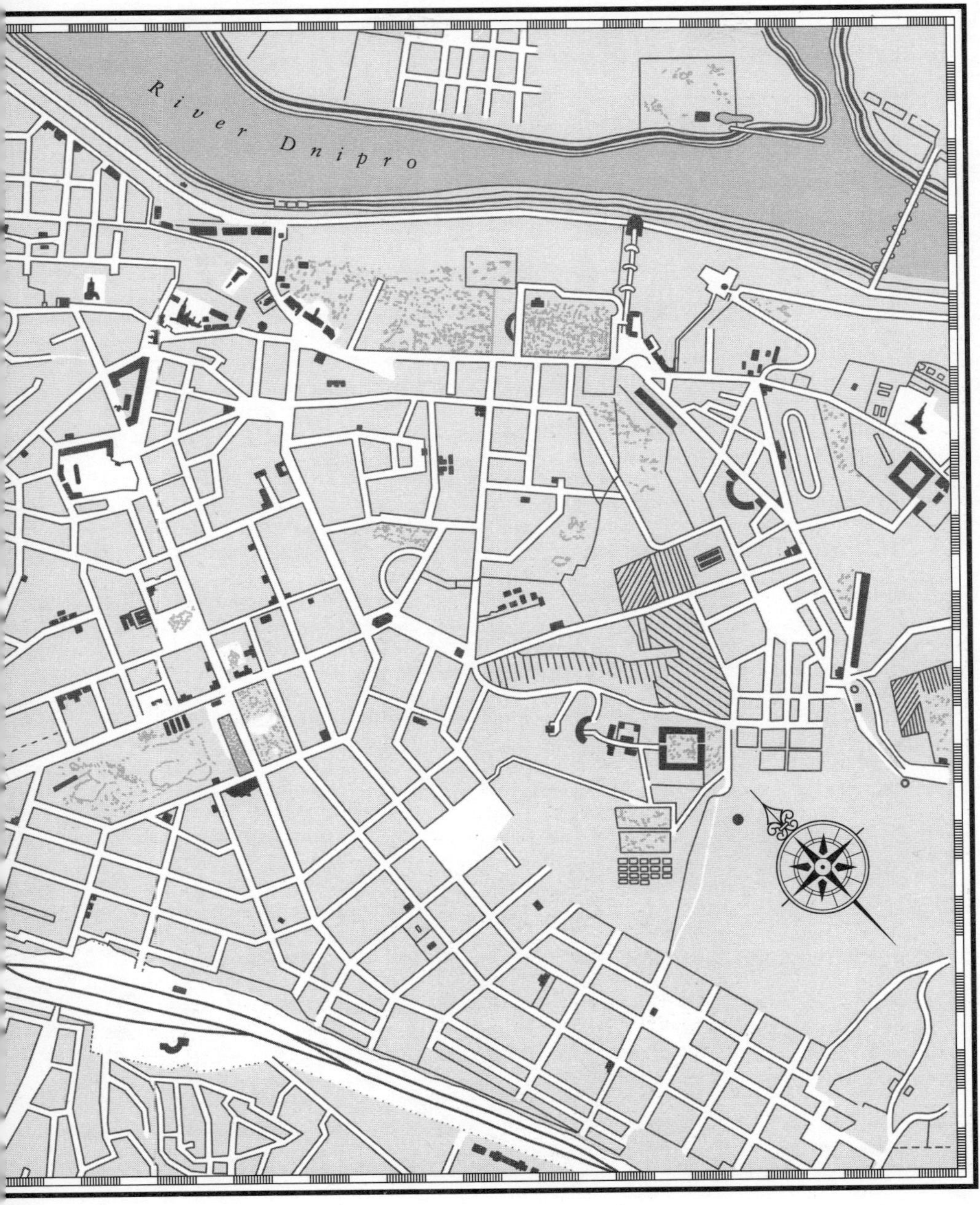
River Dnipro

Chapter 1

The April evening breathed with the soft voices of passers-by. A light wind blended snippets of words and phrases into a melodious mingle-mangle, an eggnog for the ears. There was only one way to imbibe it, this drink – like any music of natural or human origin: through the ears. And it proved altogether pleasant to the taste.

Samson walked to the left of his comrade. His bare right earhole took in all the noises of the world. On occasion, he'd find himself dwelling on the fact that some of the sounds flying into his head from the right were completely inaudible to his left ear. This, of course, was true only of street sounds, which moved unhindered through the air. Street sounds, even when loud, were still quieter than those that resonated in confined spaces. The young investigator recalled the uproar from earlier in the day, which had flown up from the ground floor to assault both sides of his head. For no less than an hour, two Red Army men had pounded the stone floor of the interrogation room with pickaxes in order to extract the iron ring to which the chain that held the stool for detainees in place was attached. It had been decided that the interrogation room should be moved to the second floor, for greater security. This was after a citizen with a Greek surname, detained for banditry, had almost managed to escape after knocking out the soldier on duty with a blow from his fist. They shot the man when he was halfway out of the entrance. At the sound of gunfire, Nayden had come running down from his office, as had Samson. "No more goddamned interrogations on the ground floor!" the commander had thundered, beside himself. "Starting tomorrow, all questioning is to be done on the second floor. Understood?"

There was a tickle in Samson's throat and the sandy flavour of construction appeared on his tongue. He wanted to spit but restrained himself.

Crows cawed overhead and he threw them a questioning glance. Then a woman's voice drew his attention.

"It's such a mess at our place. Whenever that new tenant, Safronin, hits the bottle, he gets all turned around and tries to break down my door," Samson picked out with his left ear as he and Kholodny overtook two young women who were, judging by their pace, strolling with no destination in mind.

The voice appealed to Samson, and he looked round. Glancing at the brunette, with her smoothed hair, he saw a golden tooth flash in her mouth.

Kholodny smiled ironically and shook his head. He and Samson were hurrying off to get a glass of beer after work. The day was quickly receding, leaving no memories behind – save, perhaps, for Nayden's demand, issued for the fifth or sixth time, that Samson remove the tailor's dummy bearing Jacobson's suit from his office. The commander claimed that the dummy was absorbing moisture, causing everyone at the station to develop a nasty cough. Nayden was indeed coughing, but Samson, who sat half a yard away from the thing, remained in good health. Only the two, healing, bullet wounds from the lady's pistol gave him any trouble, yet even these seemed to be unaffected by the dampness Nayden complained of, although the strict surgeon-princess Vera Ignatyevna Gedroits's parting words at the hospital had been: "Avoid damp, cold conditions. Keep your body warm and dry." In any case, the tailor's dummy and suit were now state property, bought and paid for, but pointy-nosed, moustachioed Vasyl, who was in charge of the evidence room, flatly refused to accept them. "The case is closed and I don't need them," he insisted. "Steam the dummy for lice and take it home. You can use it as a hanger."

"I don't think I like this idea of putting up a monument to

Judas Iscariot," Kholodny said, shaking his head and turning to his companion.

"A bit strange, I admit," Samson responded. "A monument to a suicide? People earn monuments by doing brave deeds, persevering. What was Judas's brave deed?"

"Well, he did return the pieces of silver to the high priests," Sergius Kholodny offered, still mulling over his position.

"And then he hanged himself," Samson said. "Betrayed his teacher, repented and committed suicide . . . I see no brave deed in any of it, no death for a high ideal . . ."

At that moment, close behind them, a hoarse male voice rattled like a machine gun: "Get that bitch! Vanya, fire!" Five or six rifle shots followed. Their echo, initially drowned out by the clatter of fleeing passers-by, rolled along the cobblestone pavement like a wheel torn loose from a cab. It rolled, almost visibly, right past Samson and Kholodny, who had stopped mid-step, mid-word. And behind it came a dog, strangely hobbling and jumping, with a white object in its mouth – perhaps a bone. The animal's hind legs suddenly overtook its forelegs and it collapsed on its side. Then two Red Army men appeared, rifles lowered. One, cursing loudly, pierced the already motionless dog's flesh with a bayonet, while the second simply stood there, breathing heavily, as if he had run a mile. The first pulled the bayonet from the dog's side and jabbed it into the piece of pork fat clamped between its teeth.

Kholodny and Samson stared at the scene, motionless. Other passers-by, who had initially jumped back in fright, pressing themselves against the walls of houses, came closer. They realised that this evening would pay off its debt to the Bolsheviks with the life of a dog. The Red Army man was still trying in vain to prise the fat from the dog's mouth.

"Bitch," he growled, and turned to his comrade. "Whatcha waitin' for? Gimme a hand."

The other soldier inserted his bayonet into the narrow part of the jaw opening and looked up at Kholodny.

"Hey, put your foot on the muzzle," he commanded.

Kholodny took a step forward and pressed the dog's face to the pavement with his boot. Then the second soldier pulled sharply at his rifle, as if it were a railway switch lever. There was a crack. Released from the dog's fangs, the fat rose triumphantly into the air atop the first soldier's bayonet. The puncture site was red with blood.

"Let's go," the second soldier barked at the first, looking around warily. The curious crowd clearly made him ill at ease.

The first soldier, too, glanced warily at Samson and Kholodny, who were wearing their leather jackets. Without removing the fat from the bayonet, he threw his rifle over his shoulder.

The Red Army men quickly set off in the direction from which they had emerged in pursuit of the murdered dog.

"I don't understand it myself," Samson said, returning to their interrupted conversation. "He's a traitor, after all. 'Whomsoever I shall kiss, that same is he: hold him fast.'"

"Yes, no doubt, a traitor," Kholodny agreed. "But, for some reason, Comrade Trotsky considers him a revolutionary, a rebel against religious dictates."

"Does this mean that Comrade Trotsky thinks revolutionaries – are traitors?"

"Traitors of the old world." Kholodny nodded. "Seems right. In order to create a new world, one must betray the old one . . . Verily, without the help of traitors, one cannot change the world for the better."

"Still, whatever you say, he did follow Jesus at first. Was it a matter of spiritual blindness?"

"He was searching for someone to follow, driven by a thirst for revolution. He might have believed that Jesus was himself a revolutionary, battling against the old world," Kholodny continued to speculate. "And when he realised that his lord was leading him down the wrong path, he stopped him. So, in effect, Judas represents the deceived masses, a class led astray. Correct?" The policeman bit his lower lip, not entirely sure of his own conclusions.

"It was all his mother's fault," Samson suddenly declared, as if he'd finally grasped something important. "In Hebrew, Judas means 'Praise the Lord'. His mother named him that, long before he met Jesus. That's why he followed him. But then he renounced Jesus, and also renounced himself. That's what suicide is, after all – a voluntary renunciation of life."

Kholodny nodded solemnly. "And how do you know Hebrew?"

"Oh, I don't. But they taught us biblical names in school . . ."

At the pub, they got a glass of Kabinet each and sat down at one of the grimy tables. There were no clean ones left.

Samson took a sip and sensed the sweet taste of blood on his tongue – as in childhood, when one of the neighbourhood boys would bust his lip in a scrap. He took another sip to wash it down. Now, order was restored. The beer was pleasantly bitter. He felt a little drunk already, but he knew it was only his imagination, which had slightly overtaken reality. To get properly drunk, he'd need to down three glasses. Before the revolution, Kabinet had been a weak beer, but now it was different, brewed in a new way.

"They sent a Chekist to replace Pasechny down at the station," Kholodny drawled, licking his thick lips. "Name of Abyazov. Skinny fellow. Unpleasant face, sharp as a razor . . ."

"Is he a good shot?" Samson asked.

"Probably," Kholodny conjectured. "I hear they train on live targets, over there. Nayden and he talked for two hours today. Vasyl brought him a mess of cases. We'll see."

The lights of Khreshchatyk shone through the pub's windows. From time to time, the hooves of cab and cart horses would clatter past, or a tram would glide by like a bright lantern wandering across the ground.

"I'm getting kind of hungry," Kholodny muttered, looking at his empty glass. He raised his head, then lifted his hand and waved. "Another Kabinet," he shouted.

When the waiter brought the beer, Kholodny asked what they had for food.

"We've got sandwiches – pork fat, pickles, or sprats," said the waiter.

"Sprats and pickles, two each," Kholodny ordered. "I don't feel like pork fat . . ."

"Is it bloody, your fat?" Samson asked.

"Why would it be bloody?" the waiter asked. "Today, we've got back and belly cuts. With French mustard."

"Two with belly," Samson said.

"Alright, same for me," Kholodny added, throwing a thoughtful glance at his comrade. "You know," he began again as the waiter walked away, "I would never have thought that the old world would break so easily. Or that fragments of it would survive, pressing on . . ."

"That's because the old world didn't break, it just changed. I mean, a broken world wouldn't work at all. A broken watch doesn't show the right time, does it?"

Kholodny pulled out his pocket watch, opened it, and looked at the hands.

"Yes," he drawled. "I just got this one back from a watchmaker yesterday. It had stopped when I dropped it. The four-eyes fixed it and didn't charge me a thing. He said that my trust meant more to him than money."

"He's right," Samson said with a sigh and finished his beer. "Trust is more important than money."

"No, he's wrong," Kholodny said. "Trust is the same as faith, and faith leads to error. If the watchmaker didn't earn enough for bread yesterday, I'm sure he remembered my visit and cursed me. He must have had faith, in the morning, that he'd earn enough.

I didn't do him any good, while he did me plenty – at his own expense, so to speak. Judas had faith in Jesus and trusted him, even though Jesus did him no good. In addition, Judas had a stomach ache. And, in our ancient tongue, the word for 'stomach' is the same as the word for 'life'. So, he had a life ache, he suffered – and that's why he took those thirty pieces of silver. For food. That is, to heal his soul. And he became a traitor. But then he felt remorse and, as you say, killed himself. Now, if he'd killed someone else, he would have become a revolutionary, but since he only killed himself, he didn't quite make it. So, you're right, Samson – he doesn't deserve a monument."

The waiter lowered a large wooden plate of sandwiches to the table. On thick pieces of black bread lay cuts of pork fat heavily smeared with mustard, dark green circles of sliced pickles and wet, shiny Black Sea sprats straight from the barrel.

Chapter 2

Before closing her bedroom door behind her, Nadezhda glanced once more at Samson, who had just come home, dead tired and smelling of salted sprats and beer. Her glance was critical, the sort that a wife might give her ne'er-do-well husband, but she immediately corrected it. She had remembered that she was his flatmate, not his wife, and had also decided not to put off asking what she'd been meaning to ask until morning.

"Do we have a lot of firewood left in the cellar?" she cautiously enquired.

"Enough," Samson answered, not at all surprised by the question, and gazed into the young woman's eyes with an easily detectable sense of guilt. "Are you cold? Should I go and fetch some and stoke the stove?"

"No, no, I'm not cold. I had something else in mind. Marusya brought some clothes to work – to swap. There's this sundress – so beautiful, green with yellow flowers. She wants three sacks of firewood for it. So, I thought . . ."

"Did you try it on? How does it look on you?"

"Fits like a glove! And just in time. Summer's right around the corner, you know . . ."

"In that case, let's do it," Samson agreed. "Will someone come for the firewood?"

"No, we'd have to take it to her place. But she lives nearby."

"Three sacks?" Samson thought aloud. "I'd better take a cart. What's the address?"

"I'll give it to you tomorrow," Nadezhda promised. She smiled, kissed him on the cheek and disappeared behind her bedroom door.

Later that night, Samson tiptoed into the former bedroom of his parents and slipped the Montpensier tin containing his severed ear under the unused pillow beside Nadezhda's head.

Now, back in his own bed, he could hear the young woman breathing sweetly in the other room. He imagined himself down on one knee, offering her his hand and heart. She must be ready and waiting for his proposal, wondering why he hadn't yet invited her to join him in marital life. After all, she'd asked, "Do we have a lot of firewood left in the cellar?" *We*! Not *you*, not *the building*, but *we* . . .

These pleasant drowsy thoughts were interrupted by a sleep as deep as a river channel full of catfish. And it dragged Samson to its bottom, this sleep, with the force of a 45-pound specimen dragging a greedy fisherman to his watery grave. What remained on the surface, above Samson's sleep, was the warm, even breathing of Nadezhda, on which his ear, detached only physically from its owner, was peacefully eavesdropping.

From the back, skinny Nikanor Abyazov really did look like a fifteen-year-old boy. Small in stature, slightly stooped, he always seemed to be hesitating, both in his words and in his actions. Perhaps he was merely cautious, or perhaps it was the consequence of shell shock from the war.

In any case, when he and Samson met in Nayden's office, Abyazov didn't immediately take the young investigator's outstretched hand. The delay was noticeable – long enough for Samson to throw Nayden an enquiring look. But the commander had withdrawn into himself at that moment and didn't catch the question in his subordinate's eyes. Eventually, Abyazov reached for the hand and asked something unintelligible.

"Excuse me?" Samson responded.

"What is your combat experience?" Abyazov repeated more clearly.

"Only here, on the job. I didn't fight in the war."

"I see," the Chekist assigned "to reinforce" the station said with a nod, then let go of Samson's hand. "No problem. We'll find common ground in due course," he added confidently, preparing to leave the office.

But the door swung open before he could touch the handle.

"They sent us their statements again. A soldier walked right in and dropped them off, like it was nothing," Vasyl almost shouted as he barged into the room, shaking a sheaf of handwritten papers.

He handed them to Nayden.

"Permission to leave?" Abyazov asked Nayden in a military manner.

"Wait!" Nayden barked, without taking his eyes off the papers.

Samson also stayed put, examining Vasyl's indignant face. The station's factotum was rarely in a bad mood and the young investigator had never seen him quite so worked up before.

"Trifling stuff – we won't be wasting our time on it," Nayden concluded after leafing through the papers. "This one may be worth a look." He pulled out a single sheet and, glancing at Samson and Abyazov, handed it to Samson. "I'd like the two of you to go."

"Which of us will take the lead?" Abyazov asked dryly.

Nayden passed another appraising glance over the faces of his subordinates, then sighed and pointed his right index finger at Abyazov. The latter smiled harshly, without parting his thin anaemic lips. His eyes demanded that Samson hand over the sheet of paper.

"Dismissed!" Nayden barked, sending them out the door. Apparently, he wanted to discuss something with Vasyl.

"Did you make it yourself?" Abyazov asked, walking up to the tailor's dummy in Samson's office and fingering the fabric of the jacket.

"No, it's evidence," Samson responded, then, nodding at the paper he hadn't had time to read, asked, "So, what's it about?"

Abyazov sat down in one of the club chairs. His thin lips moved soundlessly as his gaze scanned the letters.

"Looks like homicide," he said after a moment, dismissively, as if he had no particular interest in that category of crime. "But we have to go and check it out. The commander said so."

"Where?"

"Pushcha-Vodytsia: 60 Nekrasovska Street. Shed."

"A shed?" Samson asked, wide-eyed. "Homicide in a shed?"

"This requires understanding," Abyazov said, and – too lazy, it seemed, to relate the sheet's contents – he handed it to Samson. His gaze immediately drifted over to the tailor's dummy again.

Samson fixed his eyes on the statement. The neat handwriting was easy to read. A certain N. V. Elkin reported noticing fresh blood seeping from beneath a shed in the yard of a summer house at 60 Nekrasovska Street, a sight that had unequivocally aroused his suspicions.

Before Samson could reach the end of the statement, the door swung open with a sharp creak. He looked up. Nayden stepped in and immediately threw a sarcastic glance at the tailor's dummy, but this time, apparently, decided to go easy on his subordinate. He simply gave Abyazov two pieces of paper bearing the station's official stamp.

"Take a cab," he said. "And tell those fool cabbies they can't force the vouchers you give them on merchants at the market. They need to exchange them for cash at the station. Tell them to talk to Vasyl."

Samson voiced his doubts. "And will Vasyl give them money?"

"Certainly. True, a while ago, there were vouchers but no money. Now, we have both." Nayden squinted, throwing another sideways glance at Jacobson's suit. "Give that damn scarecrow to Vasyl. He'll find a place for it in the cupboard. It's soaked up enough moisture to give a fellow tuberculosis twice over."

Samson nodded mechanically. When Nayden left, he heaved a heavy sigh.

"You two don't get along?" Abyazov asked.

"We get along fine," Samson assured him. "It's just that his nose is so sensitive. Doesn't take much to make it run, so he senses moisture everywhere."

The cabby who drove them to Pushcha-Vodytsia flatly refused to take their stamped voucher, demanding real money instead – tsarist, Kerensky or new Soviet roubles.

"By God, if you'd told me you planned to pay me in phantoms, I woulda told you to beat it."

"But I swear," Samson tried to persuade him. "The voucher is backed by real money. There's even a list of prices for the routes."

"Where?"

"At the police station. If you just wait – we won't be long – you can drive us back and get money for both rides. I'll take you right up to the desk."

The cabby stared at Samson as if he were a little boy, scratching his bearded right cheek. The gesture made his gaze appear even more dismissive. When the cabby turned to Abyazov, he lowered his hand, and Samson realised that the taciturn Chekist commanded his respect.

"What do you say, chief?"

Abyazov seemed flattered that the cabby had immediately recognised him as the man in charge. "It's true. If you wait, we'll get you paid," he said with a dry smile.

The cabby adjusted his coat and everything he'd stuffed inside it to keep himself warm, then pulled up his belt.

"Alright," he declared. "I'll wait."

The gate to the yard was unlocked.

Abyazov pushed it open and entered, followed by Samson. The wooden house itself stood far back on the property, its window shutters turned out. Closer to the gate, on the left, were three wooden sheds, built hard against the fence separating the yard from the street.

Samson kept his eyes on the Chekist and listened. He heard a cuckoo call. Wind rattled the crowns of nearby pines, and the resulting rustle also filled the sound-space around the men, enriching it. Abyazov, his back bent, examined the first two sheds, then moved on to the third. The ground in front of its door was strewn with yellow sand. The Chekist swept some away with the toe of his boot, bent down for a moment, then looked back at Samson, his eyes gleaming. He straightened his back and adjusted his leather jacket.

"There it is," he said, pointing at a dark spot previously obscured by the sand.

He took hold of the padlock and tugged at it, checking to see if he had the strength to pull it clean off along with the rings around its shackle.

Apparently, he concluded that he didn't. He turned back to the house.

Two wooden steps led up to a door painted the colour of brick.

"Knock," Abyazov ordered.

Samson banged on the door with his fist three times.

"Good, strong," Abyazov said approvingly. "That's the way to do it. You've got to put a scare into suspects from the start. If they're scared, they'll talk."

Footsteps sounded on the other side of the door. Two iron bolts creaked and the door opened to reveal a man with a teacher's face – spectacles, a short wedge-shaped beard. He froze at the sight of his armed visitors in leather jackets. His black trousers needed ironing, while his padded jacket spoke of a poorly heated home. Indeed, there was no trace of coal in the yard, nor was there a well-trodden path between the house and one of the sheds, where firewood might have been stored.

"Surname?" Abyazov immediately demanded.

"Shpakevich. What's this about?"

"You've been accused of murder," the Chekist announced, going on the attack.

"By whom? What murder?" the man asked, his voice quavering. Then he turned back and shouted. "Katya, come quick! They say I murdered someone!"

Behind him appeared the curly-haired head of his wife. She had a broad face with large, slightly bulging eyes that looked like they might easily discharge thunder and lightning.

"Who the devil are you?" she shouted.

"The Soviet Workers' and Peasants' Militia," Abyazov answered, carefully separating and enunciating each word. "Step out and open that shed."

"Which shed?" the woman asked in a mocking tone, shielding her husband.

"The one with blood seeping under the door," Abyazov calmly explained.

Samson did not enjoy playing the role of silent witness, but he felt awkward in Abyazov's presence. The Chekist seemed to radiate some sort of unpleasant wave of subjugation. It wasn't for naught that Nayden had put him in charge.

"Gimme a minute." The woman put on a long grey coat, took a ring of keys from a nail on the wall in the hallway and stepped outside.

She stopped in front of the third shed and looked down at the dark spot swept clean of sand. Using her shoe, she again shifted the sand to conceal what had so excited Abyazov.

The padlock rattled, releasing its shackle on one side. The woman pulled it out of the iron rings and swung open the wooden door.

"Go on, then, look for your murder," she barked defiantly.

Abyazov was the first to enter. Samson followed. The shed was empty. The light that fell through the open door onto the earthen floor was bright enough to bring out a few more dark spots sparingly sprinkled with sand.

"Where did the blood come from?" Abyazov enquired, indicating the spots.

"You ever see a stuck pig that didn't bleed?" she asked in response.

Samson breathed a sigh of relief at the realisation that this wasn't a scene of murder. Now, he and Abyazov could turn right round and go back to the cab.

"You slaughtered a pig," the Chekist said slowly. "A pig belonging to you?"

"Where would we get a pig? It was the neighbour's. He asked us to do it."

"And what did they do with the meat?" Abyazov asked, reluctant to cut off the interrogation.

"He took it."

"Did he pay you?"

"Of course. You don't expect us to exercise our labour for free, do you?"

"How much did you get?"

"Ten pounds of salt."

"Should we make our way back?" Samson interrupted. On top of everything else, he needed to relieve himself.

"If we go back now, we'll need to take one of them with us, for further enquiry," Abyazov said.

"Enquiry into what?" the woman asked.

"Into the illicit slaughter of livestock and violation of the decree of the ExProFooCom banning private trade in meat," Abyazov rapped out.

"Never heard of it," the woman responded. For the first time, her voice carried a hint of doubt, but this didn't make it any less barbed and unpleasant. "Anyhow, we didn't buy or sell any meat," she added indignantly.

"We'll get to the truth of the matter. Fetch your things. You're coming with us," Abyazov said. "Or maybe your husband should come instead, so that we can sort all this without shouting."

"Yes, take my husband," she spluttered, and, pursing her painted lips in displeasure, she rushed back to the house. "Vanya, get out here! You're going with them," she called from the front steps.

The husband's frightened face showed in the doorway. His spectacles, which he must have slipped onto his nose in a hurry, were askew.

"Going where?"

"Into town, with them," she said. Then, turning to the policemen, "You'll bring him back, won't you?"

"Who knows?" Abyazov replied with a shrug. "Depends on what he has to say."

Samson and Abyazov bobbed up and down as the cab made its way along the cobbled road. The detainee sat wedged between them, scared half to death.

"You'll conduct the interrogation. Make sure to record every word," Abyazov instructed Samson, leaning forward. "I have a few matters to attend to."

Samson also leaned forward; he looked at the Chekist and nodded.

Strange thoughts swirled in his head. He himself hadn't heard of any ban on private trade in meat. And it was true that there hadn't been any meat sold.

"But . . . what should I ask? He didn't trade in meat. All he did was slaughter a pig."

"Wherever a pig has been slaughtered, you will find trade in meat," Abyazov responded. "Have you ever seen meat given away for free? What we need to learn is how much was sold, who sold it and to whom. Don't you worry, he'll talk." Abyazov shot a sly look at the pale detainee, who pretended to be dozing. The tension in the fellow's face and the slight adjustment of his ears as the policemen spoke gave him away.

Chapter 3

The transcript of the interrogation of the frightened Pushcha-dweller Ivan Shpakevich took up only half a sheet of paper. Shpakevich indicated the address of citizen Briskin, who had brought him the pig in question, and also admitted that, at Briskin's request, he had already slaughtered four pigs, in exchange for which Briskin had given him about fifty pounds of salt and nothing more. Shpakevich had later exchanged the salt itself for millet and flour at the Jewish Market. He had also kept five pounds of fat from each slaughtered pig. According to him, that fat was long gone – part of it eaten by him and his wife, part of it traded for a piece of woollen fabric from which they planned to have a warm dress made for her.

When the interrogation was over, Samson made Shpakevich sign a sworn statement that he would not leave Kyiv, released him and took the transcript to Nayden.

"Nothing to it," he declared to the commander. "We can close the case and hand it over to the archive. Is killing a neighbour's pig a crime?"

Nayden took the transcript in his hands and read it carefully.

"Yes, Abyazov has already reported to me, in detail." He nodded, pursing his lips. "We can't close the case just yet . . . A violation of the decree of the ExProFooCom—"

"What's this ExProFooCom? We haven't received any documents from them."

"*You* may not have received any, but that's because you're not in charge around here. I am – and I've received my share. I just didn't get to them in time. ExProFooCom stands for Extraordinary

Provincial Food Committee," Nayden explained. "Understand? Extraordinary! Think of it as the ministry of food. In a time of hunger. The army must be fed, and the workers, too. As a Chekist, Abyazov immediately senses when a matter is serious and when it isn't . . ."

Nayden's intonation suggested to Samson that the commander wasn't especially fond of Abyazov, but was showing caution.

"So . . . should I go and question this Briskin, then?" Samson asked reluctantly.

Nayden remained silent for a moment, his tired eyes drilling holes through Samson.

"Yes," he finally breathed out. "Detain him for speculation in meat. We'll go from there."

"May I take Kholodny with me?"

Nayden nodded.

The same cab that had taken them to Pushcha-Vodytsia in the morning was still parked in front of the station, as if the cabby knew that he had another trip ahead of him. Vasyl had paid him in full, albeit grudgingly. Now, there was at least one driver in town who had confidence in the Workers' and Peasants' Militia.

Kholodny was glad to ride through half of Kyiv, and in Samson's company to boot. He had clearly developed friendly feelings towards his colleague.

"Well, what do you make of him?" he asked about Abyazov as he watched the houses of Bibikovsky Boulevard slowly pass by to the rumble of wheels over cobblestones.

"Dry, gloomy," Samson responded.

Then something drew his attention and he turned back. There, walking along the side of the road, was Shpakevich, who had been released from custody an hour ago.

"Stop!" Samson shouted to the driver and immediately stepped onto the right footboard, making the cab lean slightly in his direction. "Over here!" he called out to the Pushcha-dweller, who had by this point noticed him.

Shpakevich ran up to the cab, although his face expressed total fearful bewilderment. But this expression might merely have lingered on his face from the time of the interrogation. Samson moved closer to Kholodny, making room.

"We're on our way to Pushcha, so we can drop you off," Samson explained.

"Why are you going to Pushcha?" Shpakevich asked, puzzled.

"To pick up Briskin."

"Please don't tell him that I told you about the pigs."

"How could I keep you out of it? It's the same case," Samson responded, genuinely surprised. He turned to Kholodny. "Did you hear that?"

Kholodny smiled and nodded.

"As I was saying," Samson said, continuing the interrupted conversation, "Abyazov is also . . ."

But at this Kholodny shook his head sharply, forbiddingly, and nodded towards Shpakevich. Samson understood. It wasn't a good idea to discuss such things in front of strangers.

"The days are warming up," Kholodny said, opening a new topic after a moment of silence. "See? The dirty snow's almost melted away." And then he frowned, as if at a dubious thought, and turned to the new passenger. "Comrade, what is your name?"

"Me?" Shpakevich asked, looking up. "Ivan Stepanovich Shpakevich."

"And what is your profession?"

"I looked after finances."

"At a private estate?"

"No, at a shop. But I haven't worked in two years. Not since they burned the place down."

"Then how do you support yourselves?" Samson asked, looking into Shpakevich's eyes.

"Like everyone, these days." The man shrugged. "Living off savings and growing what we can – some vegetables, a few fruit trees—"

"Understood," Kholodny said, cutting him off. "Listen, do you believe in God?"

"Well, sometimes I do, sometimes I don't."

"And how do you feel about Judas Iscariot?"

"No love lost between us," Shpakevich snapped. "After all, he betrayed God."

"See? There you are," Kholodny said, turning his gaze to Samson. "That's how everyone feels – everyone. And they want to build him a monument!"

"Build whom a monument?" Shpakevich asked, his eyes widening.

"Judas."

"Who wants to do a thing like that?"

"Comrade Trotsky," Kholodny responded.

The former clerk shook his head. He looked like he wanted to say something, but the words seemed to stick in his throat. "Maybe he knows more about Judas than we do?" he finally coughed out, hesitantly. "I'm judging solely by what I've read in Holy Scripture."

"He knows more," Kholodny confirmed. "But the people must first be prepared. Without a proper explanation, they just won't understand."

"So why do they build monuments to tsars without any explanation?" the Pushcha-dweller enquired.

"Used to," Kholodny corrected him. "Tsars used to build monuments to other tsars. They won't be doing that anymore."

They deposited Shpakevich at his gate. Samson reminded him that he should not leave Kyiv.

"What am I, suicidal?" the clerk said humbly. "It's frightening enough over here. Out there, it's sure death."

"In fact, better not to leave your yard," Kholodny concluded, in an altogether convincing voice. "I certainly wouldn't go out, if I were you."

"Right." Shpakevich nodded in agreement.

Reaching the end of Nekrasovska Street, the cab turned right, made its way to Lermontovska and stopped in front of the second suspect's address.

The gate was locked, and behind it a dog of no particular breed but of a very large size overflowed with resonant barking.

"Hey, anyone home?" shouted Samson, his eyes on a wide, portly wooden house with its blue window shutters parted.

A minute or two later, the door opened and an adolescent girl stepped out onto the threshold. She wore a long grey skirt with an astrakhan coat thrown over her shoulders.

The dog looked back at her and fell silent. And, in the ensuing silence, a gentle and friendly female voice asked, "How can I help you?"

"Is Moses Briskin at home?" Samson asked.

"Papa's in town. He should be back soon."

"Could we come in? We'd like to wait inside," Kholodny cut in.

"You'd better wait out there. I won't be able to hold Rex back. He's a biter."

The policemen got back in the cab and prepared to wait. The driver's face expressed displeasure, but his mouth stayed shut. He restricted himself to a couple of sullen glances back at his passengers.

Time ticked away. Dusk began to fall. Pedestrians walked past; carts rolled by. People were coming home, and suddenly Samson wanted to do the same. Just then, he heard the loud rustle of fabric, as if someone were pulling a sheet off a bed. Then came the booming sound of wood being struck, as if something had fallen to the floor, and then the slight screech of metal and a scream. The scream belonged to Nadezhda.

Samson shuddered, jumped to his feet, and leapt down to the

ground. His felt his body tremble all over and grow cold. Now Nadezhda was no longer screaming but crying. What could have happened? Nervousness seemed to tighten like handcuffs around his wrists. He had heard no extraneous voices or any other noises, but this didn't lessen his anxiety. He looked down at his hands and raised them, clenched, to his face. Uncurling the fingers of his right hand, he slid his leather cap to the side and pressed his ear.

"What's the matter with you?" Kholodny called out from the cab.

"I don't feel well," Samson answered.

Then he walked quickly to the closed gate, prompting another burst of barking from the watchdog, took a few steps back and was almost hit by a passing cart.

"Look where yer going, you drunk bastard!" the cart's bearded, fat-faced driver shouted as he looked back, whipping his horse. "Gee up! Gee up!"

Kholodny got out and went up to Samson.

"Are you ill?" he asked, peering into his comrade's eyes. "Maybe you caught typhus?" he suggested aloud and immediately leaned back.

"No, it's not that," Samson said, waving away the idea. "Just nerves. And it got chilly all of a sudden, didn't it?"

"It's evening. Sun's gone. Cold seeps in from everywhere."

Without looking, Samson unfastened the strap that held his holster closed, but, noticing Kholodny's uncomprehending look, hooked the strap over the copper knob again.

Then the men heard the sound of an approaching engine. Both turned round in surprise, because, throughout the whole time they'd spent navigating the streets of Pushcha-Vodytsia and waiting in the cab, they hadn't seen a single motor car drive by.

An elegant black Model T Ford, which looked like an expensive horseless chaise, came to a stop beside Briskin's fence. The goggled driver turned back to his passenger, who then stepped out of the car. The door closed with a beautiful sonorous click, after which the Model T backed up, passed the cab, turned and drove away.

Samson shifted his eyes from the car to the passenger who had emerged from it. The man was thin and wore a black coat and black trousers. He reached over the gate, opened it from the inside, and even managed to step into the yard before Samson took off towards him, shouting, "Stop! Are you citizen Briskin?"

The man turned round.

"And who are you?" he asked.

The watchdog dashed into the space between his master and the gate.

"We're with the police! You'll have to come with us," Samson shouted.

Kholodny also approached the gate.

"Come where, exactly?" Briskin boldly asked in response. "I haven't even had supper."

"You want us to use force?" Kholodny growled. "We've been waiting here for two hours!"

"Look, what's this about?" Briskin asked, taking a step forward to stand next to Rex. "What do you want from me?"

"We'll explain at the station," Samson said.

"You're inviting difficulties," Briskin said calmly. "You do understand, don't you, that ordinary citizens aren't driven home in automobiles?"

"You're returning from work?" Kholodny asked with a note of caution in his voice. "Where would that be?"

"I sit on the Forage Committee."

"Did citizen Shpakevich slaughter your pigs?" Samson asked in a stern voice as he again heard the distant cry of Nadezhda. His lips twisted painfully, giving him a furious look.

"Shpakevich? Who's Shpakevich?" Briskin asked, taking a step back towards the threshold of his home.

Rex immediately jumped up and burst out barking, apparently

sensing fear in his master's voice and realising that the danger had not yet passed.

"Get rid of that dog and come out," Samson pronounced harshly as he unhooked the strap of his holster and drew his revolver.

"Alright, alright," Briskin said, raising his hand in a reassuring gesture. "Down, boy," he commanded Rex. "I hope your supervisor is on duty. I'm sure he'll straighten this out quickly. And then you two will have to bring me right back here."

The last part sounded like a threat.

"Will you just give me one moment to tell my daughter that I'll be gone for a little while?" he suddenly asked politely and, without waiting for an answer, he hurried towards the threshold.

"Tell your wife, too!" Kholodny shouted at his back.

"My wife is long buried." Briskin turned round. "Typhus took her."

He went inside. Five minutes later, he still had not emerged, and Samson and Kholodny looked at each other in bewilderment. Rex, watching them from the yard, pricked his ears and tensed up.

"We'll have to shoot the dog," Kholodny said.

At that moment, the door of the house opened. Briskin made his way to the gate, chewing something as he walked. He smelled of pork fat and onions.

"I couldn't very well go off to jail on an empty stomach," he announced angrily, getting into the cab.

"No-one mentioned jail. You're going to the station," Samson told him. He heard his own stomach growling in hungry displeasure, as if envying the stomach of the detained.

Chapter 4

"The search is more important than the arrest! What are you, morons?" Abyazov shouted in a thin, hysterical voice, shifting the sharp gaze of his small slitted eyes from Kholodny to Samson and back again.

"But we didn't have a search warrant," Samson wearily justified their decision.

"You didn't have an arrest warrant, either – did that stop you?" Abyazov replied, but less aggressively than before. "Don't you know how to backdate a warrant?"

They were standing on the stairs between the ground and first floors. The Red Army soldier on duty had already taken Briskin to the basement, placing him in one of the cells, but the sounds of this workplace squabble were surely loud enough to reach the detainees down there.

Kholodny yawned. The journey back through the dark, which took at least an hour and a half, had shaken them thoroughly. In addition to his fatigue, Samson felt an ache in his hips, and his nerves had been plucked raw by Nadezhda's screams and cries. He stood there, biting his lower lip and staring at Abyazov with a strange mixture of hostility and pity.

"Alright," Abyazov said at last, putting an end to the abusive confrontation. "You're free to go. Have arrest and search warrants made out in the morning, then hurry right back to Briskin's home and turn it upside down."

"What should we look for?" Samson asked.

Abyazov looked at him as a teacher looks at an ignoramus.

"Meat! Look for meat! And money or goods exchanged for meat!"

When he walked out onto Tarasivska Street, Samson felt a shiver in his legs. The street lamps were dark and the air pricked his skin with its cool dampness. His bare earhole felt especially cold, and so Samson pulled his leather cap over it and set off for home with a hasty step.

The reflections of burning candles flickered in a few windows. A Red Army detachment galloped out towards him, striking sparks from the cobblestones. Samson stepped aside and followed them with his eyes. They swept past like a heavy, tired whirlwind, leaving behind them only a trail of noise.

Samson paused for a moment, listening. The Red Army men wouldn't have gone rushing off somewhere without a solid military rationale. The times were growing more and more alarming – so alarming that no-one wanted to talk about them. Nayden and Kholodny never uttered a word about the situation around Kyiv. They were silent, but how could they keep the matter out of their thoughts? Samson, too, thought and thought about it in silence. News of the Red Army's victories might put him at ease for a while, but the sheer number of these victories, all briefly mentioned in the daily *Bolshevik*, created the impression of an endless front, not of some fast-approaching final triumph of Soviet power. War seemed to wander aimlessly through the former Russian Empire, and at times it didn't even touch the Red Army. Battles arose between forces hostile to the Soviet regime, and by their very occurrence they confirmed the notion that there were territories over which the Soviets had no power whatsoever.

At home, Samson didn't have to wait long at the main entrance. Recognising his voice, the yard-sweeper's widow had drawn out the bolts, opened the door and moved aside, expecting the tenant to help her slide both bolts back in, as usual. Instead, Samson rushed up the stairs. He opened his front door, ran into the living room and saw Nadezhda sitting at the table, illuminated by the flames of a three-branch candelabra. She was as motionless as a sphinx, resting her elbows on the tabletop and hiding her face in her hands. The Montpensier tin lay on the floor, its lid some distance away. The powder box that contained Samson's sabre-severed ear was peeping out from under a chair.

Samson held his breath, bent down to the floor and picked up the box. He then lowered it into the tin, which he closed and slipped with difficulty into the left-side pocket of his jacket. After that, he paused for a moment, thinking. Shaking his head, he removed his holster belt and walked back out into the hallway, where he took off his jacket and boots. He returned to the living room, his nose catching a whiff of the sweaty odour that always rose from his feet once they were freed after a long workday.

Nadezhda, who had been sitting in silence, shuddered and began to cry.

"How could you?" She looked at Samson. The puffiness of her eyes seemed to age her. "What did I do to deserve it? No-one has ever frightened me like that . . . I thought you'd put a treat under my pillow – I was so happy! Montpensier – imagine! I even shook the box and it sounded like boiled sweets. But no – it was two bullets – and an ear! Why would you do a thing like that?"

Samson was ready to fall through the floor.

"Forgive me, my dear – for God's sake, forgive me," he whispered, reaching out to take her warm wrists in his hands, pulling them gently towards him, lowering them to the tabletop and covering her palms with his palms. "Do forgive me . . . I'll explain everything. Maybe not now, but soon. I didn't mean to frighten you. Those bullets almost killed me – I keep them to remember. And the ear, too. It's my own."

"But why did you put them under my pillow?" Sighing heavily, Nadezhda pulled her hands out from under his palms and placed them on her knees, under the table. She shook her head dejectedly.

"I'm going to bed," she said in a calmer, but noticeably cold voice. "I've spent half the day in tears. I'm exhausted . . . They let me leave work early. My head hurt. I thought I'd lie down and rest, then make some soup for you. But when I happened to slip my hand under the pillow . . ."

Alone in the living room, Samson stared for a long time at the three candles. He felt uneasy, even a bit pained, as if a needle were stuck somewhere in his uniform, pricking him slightly from time to time. He couldn't sit any longer, but neither would his agitation, mixed with a sense of guilt, allow him to enter the realm of Morpheus.

Fired up by a sudden thought, he left his flat, descended the stairs and knocked on the widow's door.

"What do you want?" she asked as she opened it.

Her moderately drunken gaze revealed that she herself had not yet retired.

"Do you happen to have any Montpensier?" Samson asked. "I would buy them off you. I'm desperate."

"Boiled sweets, eh?" she asked, absently. "Come in, sit a spell."

She led him into her kitchen and sat down in front of a stemmed shot glass. Then, after glancing up at her guest, she got out a second glass and filled it with liqueur.

"Now, what was poor Nadezhda sobbing about? You could hear her through the ceiling."

"She hasn't been feeling well. Came home early. Migraine, probably. That's why I thought I'd treat her to some sweets, but it's late and all the shops are closed."

"Maybe I could chip her off a bit of sugar? I've got plenty. Always put some in my mouth when I get a bad case of heartburn. Helps, you know."

Samson shook his head, sighed and drained his glass. His contorted face expressed the suffering of one who had failed to solve a crucial problem.

"Bitter, eh?" the widow asked sympathetically.

"No, it's not the drink, it's my thoughts . . ."

"On account of the sweets?" The drunken gleam in her narrowed eyes gave way to kind curiosity. "You must really care for her," she pronounced in a wily tone, and seemed to stare even more penetratingly into his face.

"I do," he admitted.

"You know what? I'll help. After all, it was me that got you together," the widow decided, looking down at her glass. "There's one place where you can buy sweets even in the middle of the night. Do you know the synagogue by the Jewish Market?"

Samson nodded, and immediately remembered how, when he was still a student, he and his friends had hidden there, escaping the tsarist police. Not inside, but behind the synagogue. He remembered how the policemen had stopped in front of the Jewish temple, as if rooted to the spot – how they had crossed themselves, spat under the fence and left. They hadn't wanted to hunt for political hooligans on Jewish territory. Must have been afraid of the Jewish God.

"Third lane on the left, after Halytska Square, right?" the widow asked, reminding either herself or Samson. "I mean, right after the synagogue. You go down that lane, all the way to the end, and, on your right, you'll see a long building with a semi-basement. Knock on the second door and say Kaydan sent you. You'll remember that?"

"I will." Samson nodded. "What do I do then?"

"You just tell 'em why you came. But dress like you're in need. And don't you go saying you're with the police, you hear? God forbid."

Inspired by the widow's suggestion, Samson rummaged through the wardrobe that held his parents' clothes. He found an old pair of baggy grey trousers. They were much too big, of course; his father had loved pancakes and, to justify his gluttony, always cited the example of the great fabulist Ivan Krylov, a man also known for his devotion to pancakes – who likely died of indigestion. Samson secured the trousers with a belt, and they immediately gave him the look of a tramp. In the wardrobe he found the simple cotton jacket his mother would wear to the market in difficult, typhus-ridden times – so as not to draw too much attention. The jacket fitted Samson well, snugly, though it was a bit short. He then put on a pair of his father's shoes, which he had also found in the wardrobe, in a sack. They were worn down but sturdy. His mother had intended to donate that sackful of old footwear, but she had never got around to it. The shoes sat loosely on his feet, so Samson stuffed crumpled newsprint behind his heels.

The murk had grown thick outside. None of the street lamps along Zhylianska were lit, and so the sight of the ones on Halytska Square delighted Samson – not so much with their bright lights, but with their friendly communal presence. There were four of them, and they illuminated a solid row of shops and warehouses on the other side of the square. Everything was closed, dead, motionless.

The immobility of this bazaar-like façade bewitched Samson, held him rapt. He stood there staring at it from the opposite side of the square, near the railway station. And the longer he stared, the more contradictions he felt he noticed between what he saw and reality. Smoke from a fire settled on his lips. And incomprehensible human voices reached him from a distance, as if coming from underground. It wasn't just one conversation, but several. Then someone rose right from the ground in front of one of the shops and coughed. The cough rolled across the open space of the square in Samson's direction, bringing him out of his stupor. He took off quickly, reached the western side of the square and turned down the lane the widow had indicated, walking and walking until he came to a set of tracks.

"Damn it," he muttered in frustration, turning back.

This time, he stopped in front of a long, tall, single-storey building, the whitewashed walls of which looked grey in the dark. Its black windows gave no sign of life. He saw an entrance, with a few steps in front of it, and, about twenty yards further, an identical second entrance. There, too, the windows were bereft of life's glow.

Samson climbed up the stone steps and knocked softly, cautiously. There was nothing but silence on the other side of the door.

The widow must have been mistaken, he concluded. But he wasn't upset with her. Perhaps years ago, before the war and revolution, they really had sold sweets here at night. However, this building had clearly forgotten all that long ago.

Samson walked back to Bibikovsky Boulevard, where he spotted, beside a fence, a prone body in an overcoat. The body lay in a strange, unnatural manner, which reminded him of the position in which his father had lain after he was killed, his head split by a sabre.

Samson squatted down. The policeman in him had awakened. He wanted to learn the identity of the victim, and so he reached into the inside pocket of the overcoat, where Red Army soldiers, as well as all other people, kept their important documents and cherished photographs. His hand found either a wallet or a thick envelope. And then the body jerked to life and shouted for the whole district to hear: "Help! I'm being robbed! Get off me, you son of a bitch!"

Startled, Samson jumped aside and took off running, not even looking at his feet. He lost the crumpled paper from behind his right heel and his foot now knocked about inside the shoe, ready to slip out. He slowed to a stop and sat down beside the nearest fence, coughing and trying to catch his breath. Then he placed his palms on the cold, damp earth, thinking he heard footsteps somewhere nearby. It was hard for him to hold his breath, but he tried.

All of a sudden, someone sat down next to him. In the darkness, Samson saw only that the person was smaller than him, skinny and sharp-nosed.

"Tried to roll Koloda, did ya?" a teenage voice sounded.

Samson leaned towards his diminutive neighbour and saw that he was a boy of fifteen or so.

"I thought he was dead," he answered.

"Koloda always looks dead. Don't think I know you."

"And, what, you know everyone?" Samson asked, regaining his courage.

"Everyone around here, I do."

"Where's 'here'?"

"Jewish Market."

"Well, I'm not from here."

"Then you'd better shell out some cash, or I'll whistle. You don't want me to whistle."

Samson realised that he should have taken the conversation more seriously. He got out twenty Kerensky roubles and handed them over.

"Where're you from, then?" the boy asked.

"Oh, from Kaydan," Samson said, remembering the name the widow had urged him to mention.

"Kaydan?" the boy asked, his voice trembling. He handed back the twenty. "Take it. What're you doing here, middle of the night?"

"Wanted to buy some sweets, but there was no-one there."

"You mean there?" the boy asked, pointing towards the corner where Samson had encountered the body that turned out to be alive.

"Yep."

"Come," the boy said, jumping to his feet. "I'll show you."

The boy led Samson to the other side of the same long building, where, at first glance, there were no doors. But then they came to a set of steps, which took them down to a basement entrance.

"They're in there," the boy said, and left.

Samson knocked, just as cautiously as before. The door opened a crack, revealing a kerosene lamp and a woman's round face, steamed red as if fresh from a bathhouse and framed by a kerchief.

"Whaddya need, darlin'?"

"Kaydan sent me. I'd like some sweets."

"Come in, come in."

A scent of sweet brew spilled from the basement, as if someone actually were taking a steam bath with honey.

Once Samson was inside, the solidly built woman examined him more carefully in the light of the kerosene lamp, or rather, examined his strange outfit, paying particular attention to his hands.

"Didn't ya bring a basket?" she asked.

"I didn't," Samson confirmed, not quite understanding the question.

"Suit yourself," she said, waddling along a low-ceilinged hallway into an even thicker, sweeter, hotter atmosphere, and beckoning him to follow.

Chapter 5

Samson would have gladly kept on sleeping, but the door to his bedroom had creaked suspiciously, forcing him to open his eyes. He couldn't close them now. Nadezhda, wearing only a negligee, her face glowing with joy, did not so much enter as float into his night-time quarters. She stopped at the head of the bed, leaned over and planted a hot, assertive kiss on his cheek, as if she were stamping him with a seal.

"That's what you were out all night doing? Looking for sweets to give me?" the young woman asked excitedly. "Let me make you some tea! No, no, you stay in bed! I'll be right back!"

It took Nadezhda perhaps half an hour to make the tea; in the meantime, she had brought a chair from the living room into Samson's bedroom. He had a strong urge to rise and get dressed, so that this whole business wouldn't resemble a bride's visit to her ailing groom in the infirmary. But just when he was about to give in and lower his feet to the cold floor, she returned, proudly holding a tray with two steaming cups. She placed it on the dressing table and – after waiting for Samson to sit up comfortably, with a pillow under his back and the covers pulled up – handed him one of the cups. Then she got her own cup and took a seat in the chair next to the bed. Her eyes still shone with excitement, but now they also looked cheerful, even mischievous.

"Tell me, how did you get them? You didn't rob a sweet shop, did you?" she asked in a jolly tone. "Is that why you went out in those raggedy togs?"

"No, I . . . You won't believe it. First, I found a corpse. I mean,

I thought it was a corpse, but it turned out to be alive and started shouting that I was robbing it . . ."

Samson looked up at the ceiling, recalling all that he'd felt the previous night – a night that had seemed so terrible until that moment, but now, as he recounted its events, struck him as both terrible and terribly funny.

"I'll believe you, I promise! Go on!" she pleaded.

"The widow told me where to go. Turns out they make sweets down there for the whole Jewish Market. They thought I'd buy five dozen, but I wanted only two or three. For you."

"Did they make you buy more? There are over a dozen."

"Yes, they don't sell fewer than two dozen. They also told me that, if I'm ever seen with them at the market, I'll get a beating. So I won't be selling the extras there." He smiled. "You'll have to dispose of them yourself."

"What extras?" Nadezhda asked, opening her eyes wide. "I didn't see any extras. They'll be gone without a trace in two, three days. Polished off with tea."

"Have one now," he suggested.

She shook her head. "I already had three. I feel all sticky inside, and my chest hurts. I'll take two to my parents, one to my chief at work . . . You don't mind, do you?"

"Of course not."

"Now, you're my sweetest hero," she gushed. "You always look out for me."

"And you for me," he replied. "Does this mean you've forgiven me?"

She planted another kiss on his cheek. "Yes, it does. But I have to go to work. We have quite a job ahead of us – I don't know how we'll manage. They ordered us to collect data on all railway workers."

"That makes sense. Railway workers are like gods, these days. They can block all the access routes with empty carriages, so that no-one can enter the city, and no-one can leave. What's the difficulty?"

"Simple – they won't comply."

"They won't provide you with information?"

"They refuse to give their surnames and addresses. All we get are nicknames – Vanya, Styopa . . . We first sent some of our older colleagues to question them, hoping they would show respect, take them seriously – and then we sent the girls. We were sure they'd charm the facts out of them, but no. There are thousands of railway workers in Kyiv, but we've only been able to fill out 136 cards. And we don't even know whether those men gave their actual addresses! Some of them don't even have addresses. They told us they sleep in carriages or in their workshops."

"Did you go and see them as well?"

"No. I'm with a different department, you know."

Samson breathed a sigh of relief.

"I'd better go too," he said, recalling the situation at the station. "They assigned us an auditor from the Cheka. For reinforcement. We've got to show that we don't need any reinforcing. That we can handle everything ourselves."

He kissed Nadezhda on the lips as they parted, and the sweet aftertaste stayed with him as he walked to work.

In front of the station, life was at a heavy boil, like sugar melting in a cauldron. Red Army reserves formed a stern circle around a crowd of frightened detainees. Abyazov, paper in hand, shouted out surnames, forcing the detainees to climb into the back of a truck, one by one. He stopped when he spotted Samson.

"Look in on Briskin," he shouted. "I left him in the interrogation room overnight. Time enough to confess."

Samson nodded, went inside and immediately bumped into Kholodny.

"Where are they taking them?" he asked, tilting his head back at the front entrance.

"To Sadova Street. They say we don't have the specialists to deal with them."

"Whom have they rounded up?" Samson asked, recalling that the detainees in the crowd were dressed decently and wore civilised expressions on their faces.

"They were on a list of those who had refused to fulfill their linen- and furniture-related duties. Say, you did get an exemption, didn't you?"

Samson's startled look answered Kholodny's question.

"Be sure to get one. The Workers' and Peasants' Militia owes nothing to anyone, understood?"

Samson remembered how the Red Army men, who were later arrested, had moved in with him. They also had a piece of paper stating that their host should provide them with clean linen. He had provided it, in accordance with the paper, but they had turned out to be criminals. At least the one in charge, Anton, was dead and buried. Fyodor, he hoped, had returned to work the land in his native region, leaving banditry behind.

The sweet aftertaste on his lips distracted him from these sad recollections, eliciting a smile that seemed to appear specifically in order to counter his thoughts and return his good feelings.

A Red Army soldier with a rifle stood beside the door to the interrogation room. He wasn't especially alert, leaning his back against the wall and letting his sleepy eyes wander. On seeing Samson, he tried to straighten up, but the attempt was awkward, as if undertaken with great reluctance.

"Open it," Samson commanded.

The soldier fished a key from one of the pockets of his overcoat and turned it in the lock.

Inside, a light bulb burned dimly. At the table, with his head resting on his folded arms, slept Briskin.

"On your feet!" the soldier barked.

Briskin twitched, threw back his head and blinked rapidly, fearfully.

"Who? What?" he blurted, fixing his terrified gaze on the soldier.

Samson walked up to the table and saw a blank sheet of paper, a pen and an inkwell. Briskin obviously hadn't touched them at any point in the night.

"Step out and guard the door," Samson ordered the soldier.

The soldier left the room.

"Take that seat," Samson said assertively, indicating the stool with his eyes.

Briskin rose with difficulty and obeyed the order.

Samson removed his holster belt and unbuttoned his jacket. He ran his eyes slowly across each of the room's blank walls. Getting a lungful of the stale, stuffy air, he went over to the door and opened it a crack, directing the soldier outside not to close it until so ordered.

"Well, citizen Briskin?" he addressed the detainee after returning to his seat. "Couldn't get any writing done?"

Briskin remained silent, with his head down. Then he looked under the stool and scrutinised the chain securing it to the floor.

"You don't much like it here, do you? Would you rather we take you to Sadova Street?"

The detainee shuddered, threw up his head and stared plaintively at Samson.

"I can't write," he whispered. "My hands are trembling. I didn't know that trade in meat was prohibited . . . Now, I know . . . Comrade Abyazov explained it all very well . . ."

"I'll be honest. I myself didn't know," Samson admitted. "New orders, decrees and prohibitions are issued every day. You have to keep up with the *Bolshevik*."

"But how will I afford the newspaper if I don't engage in trade?"

"Trade in permitted goods."

"But meat has always been permitted."

"Enough," Samson declared decisively, realising that this excessively friendly banter wouldn't get them anywhere. "Show me your hands. Now."

Briskin looked puzzled but held out his hands.

Samson peered at the detainee's fingers. Their barely perceptible tremor was more likely due to fear rather than illness. Nevertheless, he suddenly felt sorry for Briskin and wanted to show him compassion.

"If illness prevents you from writing, then I'll just have to write for you," he pronounced with a sigh. "I'll pose my questions and write them down, and then I'll write down your responses. At the end, you'll add your name, attesting that everything is correct. Do you agree to proceed? Put your hands down."

Briskin hesitated, but eventually nodded.

Samson dipped the nib of the pen in the inkwell, and, when he withdrew it, he realised that the ink was red. He noticed that Briskin's eyes, too, were fixed on the bloody red droplet that momentarily hung suspended from the tip of the pen before falling back into the inkwell.

"Strange," Samson exhaled, trying to remember if he had ever seen a record of interrogation or any other document made out in red ink.

"English," Briskin said firmly.

"What?"

"The ink is English. The kind that Perelman used to sell," the detainee elaborated.

"Used to?" Samson asked, raising his eyebrows.

"His goods were confiscated a month age. Then he was found dead."

"Who confiscated them?"

"How do I know? Perhaps your people. He was killed at home. They say he walked in and found a gang of thieves going through his things. Thieves are meaner, these days. They'll kill you at the drop of a hat."

"Understood," Samson nodded. "Let's get to it. What is your full name?"

"Moses Zelikovich Briskin."

Samson wrote slowly, looking closely at the red ink, which at first seemed too watery but soon began to dry on the paper.

"Year of birth?"

"1886."

"Social background?"

"Bourgeois. Of Jewish extraction. Not Jewish."

"What was your occupation under various governments?"

"Trade."

"With which government did you sympathise?"

"Whichever was in power. These days, I sympathise with yours."

"Hold on," Samson said. He didn't want to hurry, but he couldn't keep up without pauses. "How long have you been trading in meat?"

"Two months."

"How much meat have you sold?"

"How would I know?" Briskin responded with evident surprise.

"Well, how many carcasses, and of which animals?"

"Only pork. But why count in carcasses?" Briskin asked cautiously, clearly suspicious. "Will I be tried separately for each one?"

"I really can't say," Samson admitted.

"In that case, I won't talk," Briskin declared, his face suddenly turning hard and losing all trace of fear.

Samson looked down at the detainee's fingers. They no longer trembled.

"So, you'd rather be taken to Sadova Street," Samson said calmly but coldly, inserting the pen into the inkwell to suggest he had finished writing.

Briskin began to breathe rapidly, as if he were preparing, in defiance of his own fear, to cause a scene by launching into a rude tirade.

"Just tell me about the last carcass. Forget about the others," Samson suggested. "We know that the Shpakeviches slaughtered at least four pigs for you in their shed."

The detainee relaxed and his breathing steadied. "What can I tell you about it?"

"Where you got it. Who bought the meat and at what price. If it was bartered, then for what. Names and addresses."

"I'd have to think, remember," Briskin complained.

"Yes, you have to remember."

"I don't know the exact addresses, or the names . . . I could tell you by sight . . ."

Samson took out a blank sheet of paper, then rose from the table with the sheet he had filled with writing.

"Take that seat and write down everything you remember. You can indicate the addresses visually. I'll be back in one hour. If the sheet is still blank at that time, you'll continue this conversation with Comrade Abyazov."

As Samson left the interrogation room, Briskin remained on the stool. He sat more limply than before, as if his spine had been removed. His head hung low and his lips were parted, but his hands lay stiff in his lap, the fingers clasping his knees as if he feared that someone was going to tear his legs off at the joints.

"Should I close the door now?" the Red Army man asked.

Samson nodded and marched off to his office.

Chapter 6

By noon, the sun was peeping out from behind the clouds in the sky over Kurenivka.

"Look," said Kholodny, the defrocked priest, clapping Samson on the shoulder. "It's crept out. Must have heard our prayers."

Samson reluctantly poked his head out from under the hood of the cart.

"I didn't pray to see it," he muttered, still dissatisfied with the pointless searches of Briskin's and Shpakevich's properties. All they had found were what looked like pig bones in the doghouse in Briskin's yard.

"Just a figure of speech. A slip, out of happiness," Kholodny explained, his spirits dampened by his comrade's foul mood. "You were ill-humoured yesterday, too – it isn't good for you. Doctors say internal malice irritates the stomach and leads to ulcers."

"I had every reason to feel upset yesterday," Samson answered in a conciliatory tone, but decided not to go into details. "Yesterday was awful. Today – it's just a shame is all—"

"Whoa!" the driver suddenly yelled, and the cart's sharp deceleration nearly sent Kholodny and Samson tumbling forward, right under the wheels.

It turned out that an old woman was crossing the road with a stubborn goat. The goat had stopped right in front of their cart, giving the driver a fright.

The wheels of the cart rolled on, though at a lower speed than before, but the conversation that the forced stop had interrupted did not continue. Samson's face did brighten slightly – not because of the sun, but because his thoughts drew him away from the memory of the futile searches. He watched the houses and huts pass by. Soon, the huts receded into alleys and dead ends, and a mix of two-storey wooden and brick houses lined the street. The wooden ones, with their wet black-and-brown façades, evoked a degree of pity, while the brick ones, on the contrary, elicited cosy feelings and thoughts. One could almost feel their warmth.

It occurred to Samson that, if people were lined up like buildings, they too would alternate in this manner: sickly, healthy, sickly . . . Then he noticed a sign on one of the brick façades: BUTCHER. And in front of the entrance to the shop he saw three stray dogs warming themselves in the sun on the bare ground.

"Stop!" Samson shouted to the driver.

The cart halted.

"I'll only be a minute," Samson loudly informed both the driver and his comrade, then jumped down to the ground.

"What can I do for you?" the butcher said, greeting him with a forced smile.

Samson did not respond. Instead, he inspected the six-foot-wide oak block for chopping meat, running his hand over it to check whether it had recently been used. The rough, fibrous surface, which had been stained with blood over and over, was dry. Samson glanced at the empty counter and at the greenish copper scales – one suppressed by a dozen weights, the other empty.

The smile on the butcher's face gave way to a tense expression. He kept his eyes on Samson's wooden holster.

"Where's the meat?" Samson asked, looking up at the butcher.

"What meat? Ours is a cooperative shop, not state-owned. We can't be selling meat."

"So, you know about the decree on meat?"

"Certainly, certainly. They went around announcing it, stopped at every butcher's shop in town. Whatever anyone had on their hooks, they took it. I was lucky – happened to sprain my ankle and showed up late. When I reached the shop, I saw the decree stuck to the door. I'm no fool – went right down to the cellar and took all the meat off my hooks."

"Where did you take it?"

"Wherever I could – family, mostly. Gave it away for free. No trade."

"Was there a lot?" Samson asked, with a note of sympathy.

"I'd say so, yes," the butcher answered, nodding sadly.

"Then why is the shop open?"

"So that I can explain to my regular customers why there isn't any meat. Otherwise, they might think I'd died – or, worse, that I'd been shot by the state, for nothing."

Samson's gaze rested on a diagram of pork cuts that hung on the wall.

"May I step behind your counter and take a closer look at that picture?" he asked.

The butcher moved aside, freeing a narrow passageway between the block and the counter.

Samson went up to the wall and peered at the properly dissected pig carcass. His lips moved as he whispered the words printed on the diagram. To him, each word sounded like the name of a nation separated by borders from its neighbouring word-nations.

"Loin, ham, sirloin . . ."

The whispering of these words apparently drew a thin string of saliva from the corner of Samson's mouth. Embarrassed, he quickly wiped it away and looked back to check whether the butcher had noticed.

"Maybe you'd like half a pound of back fat?" the butcher asked in an unexpectedly friendly tone. The look in his eyes suggested that he had in fact noticed the saliva.

"How?" Samson responded in surprise. "It's forbidden . . ."

"Trade is forbidden, but not gifts. There's no law against giving gifts."

"No, but thank you," Samson said, shaking his head, and then again looked up at the proper pork cuts.

He returned to the cart with a large sheet of thick paper rolled up into a tube.

"What's that?" Kholodny enquired.

"A butcher's diagram," Samson explained, sounding lively. "I have an idea how we might get the truth out of Briskin!"

"An idea. Good." Kholodny nodded.

The first thing Samson did back at the station was to stick the diagram up on the wall. To clear the space in front of it, he moved the tailor's dummy into a corner and suddenly noticed that it was naked. Jacobson's suit was gone. He went out into the corridor, looking for Vasyl. Who else could have taken it? Vasyl was in charge of the evidence room, and Samson didn't doubt that Nayden had complained to him of the dampness emanating from the suit. But Vasyl was nowhere to be found, as if he'd been swallowed up by the earth. While, from the floor below, came the sharp voice of Abyazov, who was lecturing one of the Red Army men, saying that it was inappropriate to speak politely with detainees – that it was, in fact, inappropriate to speak with them at all. He underscored that one should absolutely refrain from telling them about oneself and one's family. When the Chekist's voice died away, Samson looked down the flight of stairs and suddenly remembered that he had left Briskin in the interrogation room.

"He didn't leave the room, did he?" he asked the soldier sternly guarding the door.

"Of course he did. Under escort, to the latrine out in the yard. Then they brought him back."

Samson pushed open the door. Briskin was asleep at the table, his head resting on his folded hands. The dim bulb that hung from the ceiling flickered, its light too weak to illuminate the paper Briskin had pushed aside. The flow of power was, as before, characterised by inconstancy, much like everything else in Kyiv, including the weather, which might summon you into spring only to douse you with cold autumnal rain.

Standing directly under the bulb, Samson took one of the sheets from the table. He was delighted to see it covered with red scribbles, but he couldn't decipher them. The effort made his eyes water. He went out into the corridor and positioned himself near a window. Now, there was no need to strain his eyes.

The red English ink had dried, taking on the colour of solid brick. Briskin had indeed failed to list a single exact address in his statement, putting down only first names and streets, sometimes adding indications like, *third house from the corner*.

On returning to the interrogation room, Samson shook Briskin by the shoulder. Then he picked up the pen and inkwell and led the detainee up to his office. Obeying instructions, the Red Army man followed them up the stairs, but waited in the corridor.

The sun shone outside the office windows, so the inconstant flow of power was of no consequence to Samson in the daytime. He took Briskin over to the butcher's diagram.

"See that?" he asked. "It should make things easier. Take the pen and write down a customer's name on each piece you sold."

"But the pig is . . . in profile," Briskin said thoughtfully. "I see the left legs, front and back, but not the right ones."

"Draw a line, like a fraction. On the top, mark who bought the left back leg; on the bottom, who bought the right – and the same for the front legs."

Briskin nodded. The sight of the diagram had clearly perked him up. He even reached out and ran his fingers over the dissected carcass, emitting a light, dreamy sigh.

"Get to work," Samson commanded, handing Briskin the pen and inkwell. Without taking his eyes off the detainee, he sat down at his desk.

For a few moments, Briskin looked like an artist before his

easel. With meticulous strokes, he applied several names to the cuts of pork. Then he paused, sinking into thought, and placed the inkwell on the wide windowsill beside him. Evidently, he was trying to remember more names, making a serious mental effort, now scratching his temple, now the back of his head.

The door to the office opened and Vasyl's anxious face appeared in the crack.

"You were looking for me?"

Samson quickly raised his index finger to his lips, silently asking him not to enter. Vasyl disappeared, quietly closing the door behind him.

"I need a little time," Briskin said, turning around. The look in his eyes, at once thoughtful and uncertain, confirmed his sincerity.

"Have a seat, take your time," Samson said, pointing to the nearest chair. Then he ducked out and asked the soldier at the door to find Vasyl and ask him to bring two glasses of tea.

Only on the way home did Samson recall that he'd neglected to ask Vasyl about Jacobson's suit. Why had he taken it but not the dummy? Especially since, as Samson discovered when he sniffed it, the dummy really did smell of damp. Samson hadn't noticed the smell before – probably thanks to the suit, which kept it from entering the atmosphere. Here was proof, if any were needed, of the high quality of Yorkshire wool. Of course, a leather jacket would also have contained the dampness, Samson thought, smiling and glancing at his own.

Near number 28 Zhylianska, when he had almost reached his home at number 24, Samson was overtaken by a truck that splashed him with filthy water from a puddle. He stopped to run his palm down his jacket and immediately felt that the left leg of his trousers was soaked through. The unpleasant feeling of unjustified humiliation was so powerful that, as his eyes followed the truck, his hand rose all by itself to rest on the wooden cover of his holster. He couldn't show himself to Nadezhda in such a state and mood, and so he decided to stop by the widow's flat. There, he could heat up her iron on the kerosene stove and dry his trousers.

This plan, however, was thwarted by unforeseen circumstances.

He spotted the widow in front of his building, speaking loudly and indignantly with their neighbour. Samson quickened his pace. When the pair saw him, they fell silent. Yet the widow's face retained its funereal expression.

"What happened?" Samson asked.

"Someone stole our firewood, must have been last night," the yard-sweeper's widow prattled. "Thought I was dreaming, heard a noise through the window, cartwheels – wasn't no dream."

"And what's really shocking is that they did it now, in the springtime," the neighbour added in an astonished tone. "Perhaps they thought we'd be watching the cellar in the winter, and that now our guard was down."

"They took all of it?" Samson asked with sudden interest, having at first not taken all this to heart precisely because, with the sun gaining strength day by day, he had found himself using less and less wood to heat his flat. But now he remembered that he needed three sacks of firewood to exchange for Nadezhda's sundress, and his face darkened. "Did they leave any behind? Even a little?" he asked, staring intently into his youthful neighbour's eyes.

"No, they didn't take all of it – but at least half is gone. They probably couldn't fit any more into their cart," he answered.

"That means they'll be back," the widow declared confidently. "Back to pinch the rest!"

Samson peeled his left trouser leg away from his thigh. The feel of the wet fabric against his skin was irritating in the extreme.

"You should track them down," the widow said, staring at the young investigator.

It seemed to Samson that she was looking at his right temple. He pulled his leather cap over his bare earhole and cleared his throat.

"Make out a complaint and I'll take it to the station," he said, shifting his gaze from the widow to the neighbour.

"I will," the neighbour responded with a nod.

Forgetting about his plan to stay at the widow's until his trousers were dry, Samson went up to his flat. Nadezhda was still out. He boiled some water and made tea. Then he stoked up the stove closest to his and Nadezhda's bedrooms with what remained of his unused firewood, hung his wet trousers on the back of a chair and placed the chair against the stove's wall, which had not even begun to warm up. His legs and feet were cold, so he pulled on a pair of long underwear, put on his slippers and waited for warmth. Sitting down in the chair he'd pushed back against the stove, he sipped his tea and thought about work – specifically, about the fact that some of his colleagues radiated warmth, while others seemed to give off the same chilly air that now prevailed in his living room. Warmth most often wafted from Vasyl and Kholodny. At this thought, a smile stretched across the entire breadth of Samson's face. Kholodny's surname, after all, was derived from the Slavic root for "cold". A paradox. Now imagine if someone with a surname derived from the root for "hot" were to show up at the station – some Goryachev or Goryachy. People would gasp and laugh. Were these sorts of contradictions quirks of nature or quirks of human perception? In any event, what a wonderful couple of characters that would be . . . Noah would surely have taken them aboard his ark, if only to keep himself entertained during the Flood.

The burning logs slowly warmed the stove's wall. Samson felt the heat and stroked the tiles with his hand. He held his palm in that place near the back of the chair where the tiled surface seemed warmest, and, because his thoughts had rested on Noah's ark, he accepted this warmth as a form of salvation. He remembered that, when God had ordered him to build an ark, telling him how, Noah was already five hundred years old. God had allowed him to involve his wife, as well as his three sons and their wives, in the construction project. They were the only people who remained alive after the Flood, and they followed God's command to "Be fruitful, and multiply, and replenish the earth, and subdue it: and have dominion over the fish of the sea."

So, it's not from Adam that we descend, thought Samson, but from Noah and his sons. Rogues and ruffians come from Ham, whom Noah cursed, while honest, kind, meek people come from Shem and Japheth.

Dismissing these religious superstitions, which had been hiding in his head since childhood, Samson redirected his thoughts back to Kholodny. He imagined them sitting there together, talking over mugs of hot tea in an aura of warmth and human sympathy. Another smile stretched across his face. He rose to his feet, placed the empty mug on the table and glanced first at the darkness outside the window, then at the barely glowing bulb suspended from the ceiling. There had been no power for several evenings, but now here it was, released, coursing through the wires.

But where was Nadezhda? The realisation that she wasn't yet home startled him, and he threw a worried look at the door that led into the hallway.

The clock showed that it was half past ten. The trouser leg was dry and the tiled wall was hot, although the firewood had burned away. It was quiet behind the stove's cast-iron door – quiet and hot, the embers still glowing.

Samson pulled his trousers over his long underwear and began to feel more comfortable. Then he stuck his feet into his boots and put on his jacket. He left the holster belt on the floor, went downstairs, stepped out of the building and peered in the direction of Nadezhda's workplace, the Provincial Bureau of Statistics. Zhylianska Street looked dead. It seemed to bear no relation to the noises of city life that reached Samson from afar. For some reason, there were no carts of any sort, no automobiles, no pedestrians and no-one on horseback – only silence and the motionless murk, punctured by faint light in a couple of windows of the house opposite.

Nervously, Samson bit his lower lip, thinking that he really should go to the Bureau of Statistics and find out from the soldier on guard duty whether anyone was still inside. After all, they were tackling a major project, a census of the railway workers, which required collecting information from those who didn't wish to share any. First, he had to tell the widow to bolt the front door behind him, otherwise, God forbid, thieves might get the rest of the firewood, leaving Nadezhda and him with nothing to barter in exchange for the sundress.

Chapter 7

Samson returned to his flat near dawn. He was shivering and his lips were blue. Without undressing, he crouched in front of the stove and broke several matches before managing to light an old newspaper, which then transferred its flame to the woodchips beneath it. Trying to suppress, by sheer will, the tremor in his hands, he laid logs over the chips and closed the cast-iron door. Then he sat down on the floor, leaned back against the stove and began to wait for warmth.

The sleepless, hectic night he had spent running around the city made itself felt. Anxiety over Nadezhda's fate had first given way to fear, then to cold – not external, but internal cold. The Red Army man had not let Samson enter the Bureau of Statistics, despite the fact that the young investigator had presented him with a pass permitting unhindered passage through Kyiv at all hours. "The boss is sleeping, not to be disturbed. Gave me orders. There's no-one else in there," the soldier declared, and yawned without covering his mouth. The infrequent black teeth in the man's mouth proved more memorable than any other feature of his nondescript earth-coloured face. There was something sinister, even diabolical in that yawn. It was as if the abyss itself, with its bottomless cynicism and indifference to human destinies, had gazed into Samson's eyes. It occurred to him at that moment that the abyss looked into a person's face precisely with its teeth – its rotten, terrible teeth – rather than with its eyes.

From there, he had taken off to Podil, now running, now walking. The streets were nearly empty. Occasionally, soldiers on patrol turned to look at the lone hurrying man, but, noticing his leather jacket and cap, didn't shout for him to stop and continued on their way.

He woke up Nadezhda's parents, desperately clinging to the possibility that she might have decided to spend the night at home, in her own bedroom. She wasn't there. Trofim Sigismundovich wanted to join in the search for his daughter, but his wife expressed such fear at being left alone that, in the end, he gave in. And, of course, Samson promised to muster the entire police force.

In truth, he didn't know where to go from there. His feet led him homeward. He paused near the dry Fountain of Samson, catching his breath, and looked his namesake in the face. It appeared as if the statue had filled its mouth with water and was just about to spit it out.

And here again Samson remembered Nadezhda's words about the railway workers resisting the census. Something told him that her disappearance could be connected with this fact. Biting down on his lower lip to reinforce his determination, he set off quickly towards Andrew's Descent.

It must have been close to two in the morning. When the few lit street lamps went out, Samson realised that two had struck. By that point, he had already reached the government buildings and even entered Sophia Square, where he stopped in confusion precisely because of the sudden onset of total darkness. He had lost his sense of place. Usually, he was able to indicate a particular direction with his hand even in the dark. But now, apparently owing to his anxiety, his spatial intuition had deserted him. He turned back and listened. The distant hum of an engine told him nothing. So he simply began to walk forward again, a bit more carefully than before. Indeed, in such a situation, no matter where one goes, one is in fact going forward.

A few dozen steps led him up to the gloomy hulk of the monument to Hetman Bohdan Khmelnytsky. Soon, he reached the walls of St Sophia Cathedral, where his intuitive vision awoke, rectifying his internal compass. He came out onto Reitarska and, quickening his pace, continued towards Stolypin Street.

Arriving at the Jewish Market on Halytska Square in the middle of the night, Samson noticed that the darkness here wasn't quite so complete and frightening. It seemed to him that he saw rows of wooden storehouses and shops to the right of him, receding towards Dmytrivska Street. At the same time, staggering with the drunkenness of fatigue, he no longer fully trusted his eyes, which might only be conjuring up what he had seen here quite recently, when his night-time search for Montpensier sweets had led him first to the synagogue, then to the basement saturated with the scent of melted sugar. Yes, he thought, his eyes could easily be sabotaging him, pretending to see while slipping him a picture of another night drawn from the past.

As he reached the corner of his native Zhylianska and Stepanivska, he froze for a moment, remembering with horror how the entire area around the railway station had been transformed a year earlier by the Spanish flu. Wherever in the city he would find himself back then, the scent of warm quicklime and iodine might reach him on the wind from the direction of these one-storey wooden barracks. The beautiful, Gothic old station had been dismantled in 1913, and the builders had just managed to lay the foundations for the more expansive and pompous replacement when war broke out. The project never progressed past those foundations. At first, the role of the station was played by a wooden pavilion just past the end of Stepanivska, right next to the platforms, but then the pavilion disappeared, and the cashiers and other personnel took up their posts in these long buildings, which sat a little further from the platforms, along the street. The row of barracks resembled a train. Even before flu struck, the characteristic scent of rooming houses and hospitals for the poor moved about the place. Failing to find a latrine, peasants would relieve themselves behind the barracks. Drunks were often confused with corpses, corpses with drunks.

And so it went until 1918, when the Germans arrived and forced the locals to shovel out all the rubbish, all the trash from the area, and gave them money to scrape from the floors all the snot expelled from dirty noses, all the filth that could only be left behind by a person who had descended to a stage of banal indifference towards everything, or who'd been born and raised in this indifference.

Had the Germans stayed, they would probably have completed the construction of the new station. But they left, and now their short Kyivan era felt like a passage from *The Tale of Igor's Campaign*, that old medieval epic. It seemed as distant from the present and as murky as the ancient chronicles of Rus', with their descriptions of events that might or might not have happened.

Up ahead, apparently beside the last of the barracks, a fire was burning. Approaching it, Samson slowed down, trying to make out who had started it to warm themselves. When he saw the flame illuminate oriental features beneath Red Army caps, he regained his confidence and stepped livelier.

The Red Army soldier Li Yin Jun, whom Samson had already encountered on patrol, gave him a friendly smile. The melodious conversation in Chinese ceased and the crackling of the fire sounded louder. The other two soldiers stared at Samson warily, their cheekbones twitching a bit, as if they were chewing something.

"Show me your papers," Li Yin Jun said.

Samson nodded and handed him the entire stack of folded papers from the inside pocket of his jacket.

Li Yin Jun squatted down and unfolded the uppermost document in the light of the flames. "How have you been?" he asked, without taking his eyes off the pass authorising Samson to walk the streets of Kyiv at any time of day or night.

"Not well," Samson admitted. "My wife is gone."

"Left you?"

Samson shook his head, but immediately realised that Li Yin Jun wasn't looking at him. "No, I think she's been taken, kidnapped."

"Who was it?" the soldier asked, and Samson was taken aback by the calmness of his tone.

But then Li Yin Jun got to his feet, returned the papers and posed the question a different way: "Who took her?"

Samson indicated the long wooden barracks of the temporary station with a nod.

Li Yin Jun looked at the building and sighed. He said something to the other men in Chinese, which seemed to startle them. They unslung their rifles from their shoulders.

"Let's go," Li Yin Jun said to Samson, and moved towards the entrance of the barracks.

Samson wanted to stop him, to explain that he didn't have this specific building in mind, but then he was visited by a completely useless intuition: what if Nadezhda really was somewhere here?

The door creaked open. Behind it gaped profound darkness, and Samson understood the futility of taking another step. At that moment, however, pools of light spilled on the ground before him. He looked back. Two of the Chinese soldiers held burning brands in their hands, apparently having pulled them out of the fire.

"They'll light the way. You look," Li Yin Jun explained. "If she's here, we'll find her."

The search of the long building, with its several separate rooms, was fruitless. The creak of the wooden floors still echoed in Samson's head as the men returned to the fire outside. All they had found in the barracks were a dozen peasants asleep on the floor, atop their ratty fur coats and padded jackets. They had bribed the guard, who was himself sound asleep on an iron cot in one of the rooms. He hadn't even woken up when Samson and the torch-bearing soldiers had entered the little room and examined it. Under the guard's cot lay a plywood case with a big red medical cross painted on the lid – likely a vestige of the recent pandemic. The case was too small to arouse dark suspicions in Samson's mind.

"Alright, I'll go and check over there," Samson said dejectedly, nodding in the direction of the platforms.

"You'd better not," Li Yin Jun warned, looking him in the eyes. "It's dangerous. They have their own patrols . . . Might get shot."

"Their own patrols?" Samson asked incredulously. "Without Red Army men?"

"That's right," the soldier said. "We've had problems with them . . . At night. During the day, everything's fine, but at night they put out patrols."

"What kind of problems?"

"They don't trust us . . . They have their own territory – their own empire. Wherever there are rails, they're in charge. More than two thousand of them were killed and shot last year, for sabotage and disobedience."

"Who killed them?"

"The Cheka and the Red Army. The authorities," Li Yin Jun said calmly. "But they deserved it. Now, they take their revenge when they can. They take revenge on us, and they fear us . . ."

"Oh . . ." Samson drawled in an understanding tone.

"What?" the soldier asked.

"Now I see . . . Nadezhda told me that the railway workers were sabotaging the efforts of the ProvStatBuro . . ."

"What's the ProvStatBuro?"

"The Provincial Bureau of Statistics," Samson explained. "A Soviet institution. They count everything – especially people."

Li Yin Jun nodded. "So, your wife came down here to count them?"

Samson heaved a sigh.

"Here, eat," Li Yin Jun said, shoving a little bundle of newspaper that contained something crunchy into Samson's hand.

Samson crammed the bundle into a side pocket of his jacket.

"I'm going over there to find out," he said firmly, and, without saying another word to his Chinese comrade, he walked off towards the railway.

There was no-one beneath the long canopy covering the platforms. Samson could see that much even in the darkness. The fact that this darkness wasn't total, only relative, seemed inexplicable, until he identified within it individual points of light. These turned out to be candles burning behind the small windows of wagons and carriages on the rails.

While walking towards the nearest window candle, he passed by several short wagons that stood separately and showed no signs of waking life. At one point, he had to walk between two such lifeless wagons, as if along a narrow street between two houses. And then he found himself in a slightly freer section of interweaving rails, which seemed to gleam dully here and there, and over which he had already learned to step easily, without stumbling. Ten steps ahead of him, in the only window of what looked to be a postal wagon, shone the flame of a candle.

Samson stopped to listen closely, even moving his cap to expose his right earhole, just in case. All the worthless noise the cap usually blocked now gushed into his head like milk poured from a larger can into a smaller one. In came muffled conversations, distant honking and a hard metallic grinding, perhaps of rails, rising from the ground. There wasn't a single gunshot, but even without gunfire the noises were enough to frighten, conveying as they did to all living beings the bad news – news of the unpredictability not only of this night, but also of the following morning, the following day, and of a great many nights to follow.

"Hands up!" The words were followed by the click of a rifle bolt, and Samson understood that he had better obey.

He raised his hands.

A man wearing a padded jacket and a fur hat with the earflaps down skilfully unfastened and removed Samson's holster belt.

"Wanted to get in there?" The man nodded towards the wagon with the lighted window. "Well, go on, then. Let's have a talk."

He ordered Samson to climb the three metal steps to the wooden door and knocked thrice, shouting, "Open up! It's me, Miron! We've got an uninvited guest."

The narrow door slid aside and someone raised a kerosene lantern to Samson's face.

"A commissar, by the looks of it," a voice sounded. "Bring 'im in."

The wagon felt roomier inside than it appeared to be from the outside, perhaps due to the poor lighting. All that Samson saw was the centre. The walls, wherever they were, had been engulfed by darkness. In the middle of the floor stood a pot-belly stove, crackling with fire and spreading its heat. Its shoulder-high chimney was pointed at the wall opposite the door and smoked away into the murk. By the window, at a table that held the candle, sat two heavyset men. Two fans of cards, face down on the wooden tabletop, suggested that a game had been interrupted.

"Here on duty, or what?" one of them asked, looking at Samson. "Gimme your papers."

Samson lowered his stack of identifications and passes onto the table.

"I have the right—" he began.

"Your rights end at the Jewish Market," the same man cut in rudely but without malice. "Once you hit Stepanivska, you're out of rights. Got it?"

He rustled the papers, slipped a pair of spectacles onto his nose and pulled the candlestick closer.

"Workers' and Peasants' Militia!" he pronounced loudly, barely concealing the irony in his voice. "At least it ain't the Cheka. What brings you?" he asked, lifting his eyes from the papers. "The transport policemen come to us sometimes, but we send them to the river station. They can roam free over there. Not here. We're our own police."

"What kind of police are you?"

"Our own. Here we are," the man said, glancing at his partner in the card game. "We're linemen, signalmen and now policemen. Listen, what's this about?"

"My . . ." Samson began, but stopped when he heard his voice trembling. He didn't want to speak in a trembling voice, especially with men who had illegally disarmed him.

"Your what?"

"My wife works at the Provincial Bureau of Statistics, counting the population . . . She's gone missing. She said the bureau was conducting a census of railway workers, and that the workers were sabotaging the effort . . . So, I've come looking for her."

"Uh-huh," the second card-player exhaled. "And what right do they have to count us?"

"It's a Soviet institution – they have the right to count everything," Samson declared with greater confidence. "You too are a Soviet institution—"

"We're no institution," the same man cut him off. "We're responsible for the safety of the tracks, even if the train riding along them is full of Denikin's men, or Petliura's."

"What happened to your ear?" asked the first man. "What are you, a cavalry man?"

"What does my ear have to do with it? I'm looking for my wife!" Samson snapped back indignantly and felt his interlocutors changing their attitude towards him.

"Looking for you wife . . ." the second repeated, soothing Samson with his deep, velvety baritone. "Show us a photograph, then. We'll tell you if we've seen 'er."

"A photograph? I don't have one . . . But her name is Nadezhda . . ."

"Miron, go ahead and search this Workers' and Peasants' policeman," the first man ordered. "Who goes looking for his wife without a photograph? Mighty strange. Look, here's my wife."

The man pulled an oval photograph of a curly-haired woman from his pocket and held it out.

"Ivan, show 'im your Masha," he told his partner.

"Why should I?" the man resisted.

"Go ahead and show 'im. Prove to 'im a true, faithful husband always carries a photo of 'is wife."

Ivan pulled an envelope from his pocket, then drew a photograph from the envelope. He examined it by the light of the candle, then reluctantly showed it to Samson.

In the meantime, Miron had removed the newspaper bundle from the side pocket of Samson's leather jacket and, from the other pocket, two stamped cab vouchers and four meal vouchers for the Soviet cafeteria. He had also found a few Kerensky and two hundred Soviet roubles.

The first card-player unfolded the newspaper, brought the crispy contents close to his nose and sniffed them.

He reached inside the unfolded bundle with thick fingers and took out something thin and black.

"Nasty stuff you've been eatin', policeman," he said with a grimace.

"What is it?" Samson asked.

"Looks like rotten pigs' ears," the man answered in disgust.

"The Chinese treated me."

"So, you're friends with the Chinese, are ya?" the second man, Ivan, commented.

"Tell us what you're doing here." The first man re-entered the conversation. "Clearly you ain't lookin' for your wife. You know what happens to snoops around here, don't ya?"

"What?"

"All sorts of things. Sometimes a fella gets crushed by coal and no-one finds what's left of 'im for a year. Sometimes a fella stumbles over a rail and falls under a locomotive . . ."

"But I really am looking for my wife! I've got no other business with you."

"Tie 'im up, Miron, and take 'im over to the third prison wagon. Let the chief conductor sort him out in the morning. He's got a nice heavy hand, the conductor does – he'll figure out what kinda wife this fella's lookin' for."

Chapter 8

The heavy door slid aside, then rumbled shut behind Samson's back. He found himself squatting against the inner wall of a wagon, in weighty, viscous silence. A lump of hunger rolled up to his throat, while his fingers clenched into a fist all on their own so as not to tremble from the cold dampness. From time to time, despair seeped into his thoughts, transforming them into rubber and pulling at them as at the strings of a Romani guitar; their verbal meanings were stretched into mere sound, into a groan, a nervous rattle that twisted Samson's lips, expressing pain. He wanted to distract himself from this inner noise, this nervousness, this fear that seemed to send him tumbling into the black railway pit above which the entire sky was crosshatched by tracks. He wanted to distract himself, to forget, but he couldn't. Fear bound him as a bog binds one's legs, preventing them from taking a free step towards salvation.

He tried to think about his father; called up a memory of him and it willingly appeared. The memory told him in a sweet inner voice of how his father had taken him to the station when he was still very small – the old station, built of yellow brick, huge and sprawling like a strongman with his arms outstretched. To little Samson, the station looked like a royal palace. He had held his father's hand, afraid to let go, as if some irreparable harm might come to him if he did. Even St Volodymyr's Cathedral hadn't seemed to the boy so frighteningly grand, so overwhelmingly powerful as the interior of the old station. How had they ever managed to take it apart, Samson now wondered, trying to imagine millions of hands, each pulling a single brick out of the wall. Whatever their method had been, the deed was done. They had dismantled it in order to build a new, even larger station. But once the old station was dismantled, the era of construction and creation suddenly ended. Another had begun – the era of wars and revolutions.

What did they do with the bricks, Samson wondered. But this question didn't save him from an even sharper, more unpleasant awareness of his deplorable situation – especially since he didn't have an answer.

His hands felt frozen. He shoved them into his jacket pockets, yawned and heard the crinkle of the newspaper bundle. He remembered Li Yin Jun's warning not to enter the station at night. Should he have listened to him? No, not when Nadezhda might be sitting in some fifth or tenth prison wagon, held captive by unknown, census-averse railway workers. Samson shook his head and drew the bundle from his pocket, unfolded the twisted top, reached inside and pulled out something thin and hard, which felt like the angel-wing biscuits he used to wash down with tea in cheap cafés back in his student days.

Then someone nearby coughed, hoarsely and painfully. Samson winced.

"Who's there?" he asked in a whisper.

In answer, he heard a rustle, then a sigh, from both the left and the right. The outer silence seemed to vanish in an instant. Or was it merely that the strings of the Romani guitar had finally ceased to vibrate in his head?

"Who are you?" Samson asked a little louder.

"All sorts of people," he heard a man whisper, very close. "I, for instance, am an engineer. More precisely, a timber cruiser."

"What's that?" Samson asked.

"An engineer of timber . . . I inspect forests . . ."

Samson digested the information. "Ah, a forest inspector."

"And who are you?" the invisible interlocutor whispered.

"Me?" Samson asked in response, suddenly afraid to say who

he was. After all, some actual criminal might be sitting there in the dark. "I'm . . . unemployed . . . Why are you here?"

"I live nearby, in the Cadet Grove. The best path home leads through the station, but they forbid us crossing the tracks in the dark. This is the third time they've caught me. You're walking along, looks like no-one's there, but as soon as you raise your foot over the rail, someone shouts, 'Hands up!'"

"What then? Do they beat you?"

"Why would they? They know me! In the morning, they'll bawl me out and turn me loose. What use have they got for me?"

"What's your name?"

"Kapytin. Svyatoslav Kapytin."

"I'm Samson. Samson Kolechko."

Samson brought what he had pulled out of the bundle up to his nose and sniffed it. Although the railway men had called it nasty, he found its smell to be unusual, but not repellent. It was a pig's ear, either cured or dried. Samson hesitated for a moment, then stuck the sharp edge into his mouth, clamped it between his teeth and broke the rest off with his fingers. A sour-salty taste appeared on his tongue – a bit like that of cold, stale cracklings, he decided.

"Who else is here?" he whispered to the invisible Kapytin.

"There's someone here, that I know. The railway men hustled me in when it was already dark . . . I asked, 'Who's there?' But whoever it is didn't answer. They might be gagged."

The last comment made Samson freeze. He realised that Miron hadn't fulfilled his superiors' orders: his hands remained unbound, which was the only reason he had been able to put at least some food in his mouth.

"What is that you're eating?" Kapytin asked.

"Pigs' ears," Samson admitted. "The Chinese treated me to them."

"May I have one?"

Samson drew another one from the bundle and held it out towards his interlocutor.

"Here."

"Would you mind bringing it up to my mouth? My hands are tied."

Samson moved closer to the invisible timber cruiser, pressing his left shoulder against the man's right.

"Is that you?" he asked.

"Yes," the man assured him.

He felt his interlocutor's face with his hand, then inserted the Chinese treat into the open mouth.

The timber cruiser bit down with a crunch and began to chew loudly, as if he hadn't bothered to close his mouth.

"Try to be quiet," Samson told him. "Someone might be sleeping."

"In this cold?" Kapytin asked, his whisper shot through with irony and followed by loud crunching.

"Do you like it?" Samson asked, after a pause.

"Can't say," the timber cruiser replied. "Smells like ears."

"What ears?" an unfamiliar, hoarse voice suddenly cut in.

Outside, there was a noise, a knock, a squabble. The iron padlock creaked as someone took hold of it and pulled it to the side, as if it were a lever. The wagon door slid open heavily and light burst in – dim, pre-dawn light – and with it the acrid smell of burnt coal.

Samson turned to Kapytin and, out of the corner of his eye, noticed several more people sitting and lying by the wagon's wooden walls. One of them was blue in the face. He looked dead.

"Well, lil' fishies?" barked a man in an unbuttoned sheepskin coat girded by a holster belt, as he climbed into the wagon.

A lump formed in Samson's throat. The belt, wooden holster and revolver were his.

"That damned forester again," the man growled, staring at

Kapytin with a venomous smile. His unshaven cheeks added still more venom to the smile. "Get up and get the hell out. We catch ya again, we send ya home barefoot, ya hear?" he added, shifting his gaze to the timber cruiser's solid calfskin boots.

Kapytin breathed a sigh of relief, then rose to his feet with some difficulty. His legs, Samson thought, must have grown stiff and numb from the cold.

"Will you untie my hands?" he asked the man in the sheepskin coat.

"Your wife can do that for ya. Now git!"

"Can you run over to Tarasivska?" Samson whispered to Kapytin from the floor. "Tell my . . . friends . . . that I'm here?"

"No, I'm afraid I can't," Kapytin whispered in response, shaking his head. "I've got to get home, then back to work."

Then he leapt out of the wagon, his hands still tied behind his back.

The man in the sheepskin coat took a step towards Samson, bent over slightly and sized him up from cap to boots. Then he reached out, removed the cap and peered at the bare earhole.

"Cavalry man, are ya?" he asked, a bit more respectfully.

"No, I'm with the police . . ."

"Which police?"

"The Workers' and Peasants' Militia. Municipal force of Kyiv. Lybid station."

"Fancy that! What the hell you doin' here, then?"

"Searching for my wife. She's disappeared. I thought she might be here."

The man in the sheepskin coat straightened up and ran his burgundy tongue over his dry lips.

"Have you got a document?"

Samson handed him his pass and a couple of other pieces of paper.

"Got a whole lot, I see," the man said, somewhat surprised. His face softened as he took Samson's documents in his rough hands. Then he shifted his gaze to a young man sitting by the wall opposite, who wore a grey padded jacket and grey trousers, as well as a pair of shoes too light for such a spring. "Can you read?"

The young man nodded.

"Read this, then," the man in the sheepskin coat said as he handed him one of the papers.

The young man unfolded it and read: "It says, 'Comrade Samson Theophilovich Kolechko is authorised to walk the streets of Kyiv at any time of the day or night. He is permitted to carry bladed weapons and firearms.' There's a signature belonging to Commissar Konstantin Nayden, and a stamp."

"Wife's disappeared," the man in the sheepskin coat muttered, shifting his gaze back to Samson. "She pretty, at least?"

Samson nodded.

"Let's have a look at a photo."

"Don't have one. They took it away," Samson lied.

"I'll tell ya something – if she's pretty, you won't find 'er . . . This 'ere's a bad place for pretty women. Ya know yerself what sorta rubbish goes wanderin' by the tracks at night, lookin' to get away. For these 'ere rats," he said, nodding towards the men sitting and lying in the wagon, "it's all the same, stealin' wood or bendin' a woman and chokin' the life outta her. They don't care. But if she ain't that pretty, you might find 'er. Go off and look. Go now – before the chief conductor shows up. He's always awful sore in the mornings. Only simmers down after poundin' someone's face in. He's nice after that, downright pleasant."

"What's his name?"

"What's it to you?" the man asked suspiciously. "It's Claudius. Claudius Porfirenko."

"Is he responsible for that?" Samson asked, indicating the motionless blue-faced man with a glance.

"Anyone coulda done that. Wood thief. Caught 'im three times, now."

"Where did you get that belt?" Samson asked, rising to his feet.

"You'd better git before I take yer boots. And yer jacket. Dismount!"

Samson walked over to the doorway and leapt down to the ground. He was again overcome with fear, as if the muzzle of a gun were staring fixedly at his back. Without turning, he went round the wagon and took off at a half-run, half-walk, jumping over the rails and trying not to stumble. He hurried as if a bog were undulating beneath his feet, promising to break open and swallow him whole.

Only when the tracks were behind him did he realise that he had gone the wrong way. In front of him, past a few railway workshops and some kind of small factory, lay the Cadet Grove, half of which had already been cut down for firewood.

Chapter 9

On the way to his office, Samson lingered outside Nayden's door: Abyazov's voice sounded louder than the commander's. One might conclude that power had shifted at the station. Abyazov spoke clearly, as if he were senior in rank. But then Nayden began to holler and Samson, assured, proceeded to his office.

There was a smell of damp in the air, and it must have been this that directed Samson's gaze to the tailor's dummy, which now stood to the left of the window.

Why had Vasyl taken the suit and left the dummy, he wondered again and frowned, realising that he had forgotten to ask the tea-serving old fellow about this.

His gaze glided smoothly over to the diagram of pork cuts. The sight of this pig that had been turned into a map of meaty nations gladdened Samson, because a couple of words had been added to each of its domains. He had managed to force Briskin to give up his customers.

However, his joy at the sight of these scribbles, which were illegible from five or six paces away, turned out to be short-lived, because his hand, out of habit, had tried to rest on the cover of his wooden holster, and had failed.

He realised with horror that he would have to report the loss of his revolver. And, at that moment, an even more nightmarish vision flashed through his imagination: Nadezhda's murdered body on the wet ground, her head beside the tracks.

He shuddered, suddenly craving a stiff drink. But there was no vodka in the office. Then another thought sought to give hope. It occurred to him that he hadn't been home since last night, and now it was morning. Perhaps Nadezhda hadn't gone to see the railway workers at all. Perhaps she had merely stayed late at the house of a friend – say, the girl to whom she'd offered firewood in exchange for the sundress.

Samson looked at the door, listening, then quickly left his office, flew down the stairs and nearly leapt out into the street. Then his legs seemed to buckle. Maybe they actually did, fatigued as he was after the cold sleepless night. But he stayed upright and, like a drunkard steeling himself for the road home from the tavern, took a few hasty steps forward, his hands searching for balance in the air. They found it. He straightened his stooped back and pulled down his jacket, which hung oddly, like a sack, without the help of his belt.

The faces and eyes of the oncoming passers-by looked unjustifiably fresh to him. He was oblivious to the fact that it was early, only barely eight in the morning. For him, the previous night had never ended, outlasting the dawn. Morning meant opening one's eyes after a restorative night in bed, but he hadn't been to bed. He had experienced fear, wariness and doubt, but not sleep. Instead of sleeping, he had chewed an ear in the dark – a pig's ear, cured or dried, with some sort of Chinese flavouring. That taste was still in his mouth as he hurried along Zhylianska Street, looking down at his feet to keep from reeling.

The front door to the building opened easily. Samson didn't know whether the yard-sweeper's widow locked and unlocked it at set hours or in peasant fashion – that is, when the sun rose and set.

There was no-one in his flat, and he was again confronted with a damp, musty scent. In springtimes gone by, his family would stoke up the stoves all the way until the Day of Rejoicing, when people remembered those who had passed away. On this day, which usually fell in late April or early May, Samson's father had always allowed himself a glass of walnut liqueur, for the repose of his cousin, who had perished while defending Port Arthur. Warmed by the stoves, the walls would repel all dampness. And just a couple of weeks later, summer would approach – cautiously at first, furtively, looking back at spring with apprehension.

Samson walked over to his parents' wardrobe, which now stood between the windows facing the street. He looked in the mirror and didn't immediately recognise himself. More precisely, he didn't wish to recognise himself. On the table he saw seven rooster-shaped sweets on sticks. He went to the kitchen, brought out Nadezhda's teacup and inserted the sweets like flowers into a vase. Then he pulled out one of the roosters and licked at it nervously, driving away the taste of the dried pig's ear with sugary sweetness.

He laid the bundle of pigs' ears on the table and, after a moment, unwrapped them in order to draw one out and examine it in the light. It was wispy, hardly weighed a thing, but when he held it between his eyes and the window, no light shone through.

Something made him raise his fingers to his left ear. It wasn't much thicker than this piece of pork, and it was warm to the touch, its living cartilage crackling a bit in response to the compression of its edges.

These unusual considerations and movements gave Samson sufficient respite to gather his strength and decide on a course of action.

He reached the Provincial Bureau of Statistics in only a couple of minutes and aggressively made his way past the Red Army soldier on guard, proceeding directly to the office of Nadezhda's chief, Valerian Sergeyevich Poddomov.

The chief sat behind a desk littered with folders and papers. He looked bewildered and his lip was split. At first, he didn't recognise Samson and leapt to his feet. When the visitor introduced himself, Poddomov sank back into his chair and sighed with what sounded like relief.

"I came to enquire about Nadezhda," Samson informed him. "She didn't come home last night and wasn't with her parents."

Poddomov nodded, then shrank back as if from a blast of cold air, glanced behind him and picked a yellow blanket up from the floor, throwing it over his shoulders on top of his coarse black shirt.

"Where is she?" Samson demanded.

"She's been captured. Taken hostage. Together with two of her co-workers . . ."

"Who has her? The railway men?"

Poddomov nodded. "I was there, too," he added. "But I managed to get away. Not before they split my lip."

"Have you contacted the police?" Samson asked nervously. "Or the Cheka?"

"I was afraid to involve the Cheka. They were the ones who'd ordered the census in the first place, and we've failed them . . ."

"How about the police?"

"What can the police do?" Poddomov asked, giving his visitor a plaintive look.

"What do you mean, 'what'?" Samson shot back, outraged. "Where did they take her? Did you see them?"

Poddomov nodded.

"Let's go," Samson ordered him sharply. "Get up."

"Where?" There was fear in Poddomov's voice.

"To Tarasivska. The station. You'll tell us and write down everything you know."

"I was just wondering where you were," Nayden exclaimed as a panting Samson pushed a pale, unshaven citizen wearing a short grey coat and no hat into the commander's office. "And who's this?"

"Uh," Samson began, then took a step to the side and filled his lungs with air. "This is Poddomov, from the Provincial Bureau of Statistics. The railwaymen captured three of his subordinates at night and got him too. He escaped, but he didn't report the crime. My Nadezhda is still there."

"Is that right?" Nayden burst out and his face seemed to grow sharper. He fixed his eyes on the citizen in the grey coat. "How come?"

"Didn't have the strength," Poddomov murmured. "I ran straight to work, didn't even go home – and then my nerves gave out – lost the use of my legs, arms . . ."

"And of your head, it seems," Nayden added, annoyed. "Sit," he said, indicating his desk with a nod.

Poddomov took his seat and looked up at the man issuing orders.

Nayden then slipped him a sheet of paper, an inkwell and a pen. "Write out a statement about the crime. In detail."

Poddomov, a man accustomed to writing, immediately set to work.

"I went over there myself," Samson said, attracting Nayden's attention. "They disarmed and arrested me. In the morning, one of them found out that I was with the police and released me."

"What in the world were you thinking?" Nayden asked. "That territory is covered by the transport police."

"I was looking for Nadezhda. Thought she might be there . . ."

"Vasyl!" Nayden shouted in the direction of the door.

"Here," they heard, as the door opened slightly and the face of the keeper of material evidence appeared in the crack.

"Make some tea."

The door closed.

"Go to your office and write a report about the loss of your weapon," Nayden commanded.

Samson, who suddenly craved tea, reluctantly did as he was told.

The light bulb in his office shone brighter than usual. He approached the diagram of pork cuts. On the hind leg, he read, *43 Volodymyrska Street, no. 4*. Then, beneath the line, *Rostyslavska Street, house behind the blue fence*. His gaze drifted over to the front leg: *Kristina, 15 Stolypin Street, first floor*. Beneath the line: *Tatarska Street. Yeast factory. Prokhor Temin, foreman.*

It occurred to him that he'd much prefer to take up this meat affair than to describe his night-time misadventures. But, of course, the commander's orders were the commander's orders.

He sat down at his desk, prepared the blank back of some old document and lifted his pen over the inkwell, waiting for a drop of red ink to fall back in.

Meanwhile, he feverishly considered the question of how best to title what he was about to write. Confession, report, communiqué, denunciation? How could he denounce himself?

Samson's hand brought the pen to the head of the sheet. Creaking as it touched the paper, the nib wrote out in red ink: *Statement*.

From the perspective of the victim, the statement flowed easily, albeit with rancour. This rancour swelled the size of the letters. Samson realised that he would soon run out of space for all he had to say, and so he forced himself to continue in a smaller hand.

When he returned to Nayden's office, he found the commander reading Poddomov's statement about the kidnapping. Poddomov himself stood beside him, expectantly, and kept shooting wary glances at Abyazov, who stood on the other side of Nayden, reading over his shoulder.

The Chekist offered no word or gesture of greeting to Samson. Instead, he immediately grabbed the paper from his hands and narrowed his eyes at it, as if forgetting that he had just been engrossed in Poddomov's statement.

The door opened and Vasyl entered with two mugs of tea, which he placed on the edge of the desk.

"Don't go burning yourselves," he warned. "Hot as can be."

"Where's Kholodny?" Nayden asked, looking up from the paper.

"Downstairs, questioning a detainee."

"Send him up," Nayden commanded.

"Any more tea?"

Samson swallowed his saliva, understanding that neither of the two mugs was intended for him.

Nayden noticed this. "Bring another mug," he said. Then he turned to Abyazov. "How do you see it? A matter for the transport police, no?"

The Chekist shook his head. "A matter for us," he declared. "We've got to exterminate these locomotive bastards like bedbugs, nits. They feel they can get away with everything, no matter who's in charge. You won't find a single communist among them, not with a lantern in the daytime, but their pockets are stuffed with certificates of exemption from eviction, requisitioning, mobilisation and public works . . . I know how to handle them."

Nayden raised his eyebrows. "You know what? Go ahead," he said. "Need help?"

"I'll take this one," Abyazov said, nodding towards Samson. "Also, Kholodny. And five Red Army men."

Chapter 10

The drizzling rain drove pedestrians off the streets, into homes and shops. Abyazov decided that they would walk to the railway station, so as not to attract undue attention. Samson had been temporarily issued with a rifle. Looking back at the Red Army soldiers walking behind him, he felt humiliated. Together with this humiliation, he felt not resentment, but anger – anger at himself. It was so thick and intense, this anger, that it seemed to spread over the skin of his arms and legs.

As soon as they moved away from the police station, the Red Army men unleashed a chorus of metallic clanging as the heel taps on their boots struck the cobblestones. They were used to walking in step this way, loudly, as if their stepping were itself a weapon to scare off enemies. Only after Abyazov's third shout did they adopt a less brain-rattling, synchronised gait, which sounded unsteady, even timid. In addition, they now kept looking around as they walked, as if suspecting hidden dangers. A couple of times, Samson shot them disapproving glances, all the while trying to understand Abyazov, who had somehow included these clumsy soldiers in his Chekist plan. He certainly did have a plan, or his little eyes wouldn't be burning with such determination and righteous malice.

When they reached the railway station, Abyazov ordered the soldiers to halt and wait beside an exceedingly long one-storey building that itself resembled a railway carriage Then he nodded to Kholodny and Samson, signalling that they should follow him, and walked over to the nearest door. Inside the building, female voices murmured nervously. A motley crowd bustled by the ticket window, with nearly every person holding out a stamped piece of paper.

The door was to the right of the window. Abyazov pulled it towards him, but it didn't give. He knocked.

When the door opened, a clean-shaven man in black trousers and a military tunic stuck out his head and asked, "What?"

Abyazov pushed him so hard that he fell backwards onto a tattered couch pressed up against the wall opposite the entrance. Before he could get up, the three visitors stepped inside and latched the door behind them.

Samson noticed that a revolver had appeared in the hand of the man rising from the couch. Before he could warn Abyazov, he realised that Kholodny had already drawn his Mauser pistol.

"Who's in charge around here?" Abyazov asked the clean-shaven man, unfolding his identification in front of his nose.

"In what branch? At the ticket office?" the man asked nervously.

"In general. Who's in charge?" the Chekist repeated, emphasising the last word, nearly shouting it.

"In general, Panas Zharko, People's Commissar of Railways."

"Don't play the fool," Kholodny cut in, his voice sounding less hostile than Abyazov's. "Where's Porfirenko? Who else gives orders?"

"Porfirenko is the chief conductor, Sashinsky's in charge of the telegraph operators and we deal with the passengers," the clean-shaven man answered a bit more calmly, his revolver still pressed into Abyazov's belly.

"I should shoot you where you stand, non-Party scum," the Chekist grumbled, looking down at the revolver, and then he turned to Samson. "Let's go over to the tracks."

"Do you have a pass permitting access to the tracks?" the chief of the ticket office asked caustically.

"What sort of pass?" Kholodny asked, narrowing his eyes and glaring at their unpleasant interlocutor.

"A pass like this," the clean-shaven man said, putting away his weapon and taking out a square of pink paper bearing a stamp and four red-ink signatures.

"'Pass for unhindered entry into Kyiv station and access to tracks issued to chief of ticketing Avtandil Kariesov. Head of the railway police . . .'" Kholodny muttered aloud, then tore his eyes away from the paper.

"You'll be arrested without one – or maybe even shot where you stand," the clean-shaven man commented. "For sabotage."

"We'll see about that," Abyazov declared as he snatched the pass from the ticketing chief's hands and pulled Kholodny by the shoulder, signalling that they should hurry. "You'll get it back later," he added.

It was still raining outside. Samson straightened his leather cap and pulled it down to cover his bare earhole. The Chekist looked round and fixed his eyes on a man in an old railway uniform approaching the end of Stepanivska Street from the direction of the tracks.

"Let's go," Abyazov commanded Samson and Kholodny.

They took the railway worker by surprise. He even flinched when Abyazov appeared in front of him and the two policemen flanked him on either side.

"Over to the fence," the Chekist ordered, showing his identification papers to the befuddled man.

"What'd I do? Didn't do nothing," muttered the railway worker, a man of about fifty with a reddish beard and a moustache obscuring his upper lip. "Just taking a break to get a bite—"

"Quiet," Abyazov cut him off. "Listen, either you tell us everything or we shoot you down for sabotage, right on the spot."

"What sabotage?" the man asked, properly frightened now. "I man turnout post number five . . . There aren't any trains coming through, so I was going to grab a bun."

"You abandoned your post?" Abyazov asked with greater gruffness, and the man grew still more frightened.

"Guilty," he offered, and immediately tried to turn back towards his post, but Kholodny stopped him.

"Where do you keep the hostages?" Kholodny asked directly into the railway worker's right ear.

"What hostages?"

"The ones taken on the tracks."

"Ah. That's over there, closer to the Cadet tram."

"Lead the way," Abyazov commanded.

"Can't. Don't have a pass for that side."

"I'll give you a pass you'll never forget," Abyazov snapped.

The bearded man looked round imploringly at the three men surrounding him. The wrinkles at the edges of his eyes deepened piteously, taking on the appearance of lines drawn with an indelible pencil.

"For God's sake, have mercy. I've got to work here – if they kill me, my family will starve."

"Nothing to fear. You can point from a distance," Abyazov said, showing compassion.

"Let's go along the side, alright? Not straight down the path," the railway worker suggested.

Abyazov beckoned the Red Army soldiers to come closer.

"Listen up, men," he said, pronouncing each word distinctly. "Stay twenty paces behind us. When we come out onto the tracks, remain on the side. If the enemy pursues us, open fire."

"How will we know who the enemy is?" one of the younger soldiers asked.

"The ones chasing after us will be the enemy," the Chekist explained. "If they're armed and shooting, aim at their heads and chests. If they're unarmed, at their legs. Is that clear?"

The soldiers nodded.

Coming out to the tracks and leaving the passenger platform, with its long wooden canopy, on their left, the four men set off along a well-trodden path, slippery from the rain. A familiar brick building appeared to their right, and Samson realised that they were passing the basement in which sweets were boiled for the Jewish Market at night. He even lifted his chin, perhaps hoping to get a whiff of that thick, warm, sugary aroma. Instead, burnt locomotive coal, which had grown heavy in the humid air, settled still more thickly in his nostrils. Samson blew his nose towards his feet and immediately looked round in embarrassment, wondering whether the soldiers marching behind them had noticed his faux pas.

Three separate freight wagons appeared to their left.

"What's in those?" Abyazov asked the railway worker.

"Nothing. They ain't guarded."

Samson peered at the cars as they walked – one was green, the other two brown – and tried to recall whether he had seen them the previous night. But then his gaze drifted a little further and it seemed to him that he recognised the figure of a man standing in front of another wagon, no fewer than fifty paces away. Samson squinted, trying to determine whether the holster belt girding this man's sheepskin coat was his own.

"There – I think they kept me in that one," he told Abyazov.

The group stopped.

"Yes," the bearded man confirmed in a half-whisper. "They have prisoners in that one, and in two up yonder, on the right. You'll see 'em – long, painted blue with large numbers, jolly."

"Why jolly?" Kholodny asked.

"That's what they call mail and luggage wagons," the bearded man explained. "Let me go, now?" The plea gleamed in his narrowed eyes again. "Otherwise, I'll get killed here with you."

"Hold it." Abyazov took a step forward and positioned himself close to the man, face to face. The Chekist was half a head shorter, but he stood ramrod straight and looked intimidating enough. "You'll answer my questions, then go. Understood?"

The bearded man nodded.

"How many of your men are guarding the prisoners and the chief conductor?"

"Not many," the railway worker replied, then thought for a moment. "Six or seven. But there are fifty or more in the workshops behind the tracks. With two machine guns."

"And, if they hear shots, they'll run out?" Abyazov asked, trying, not altogether successfully, to conceal his nervousness.

"You bet. They're the reserve. Whoever ain't drunk will run out."

"Will anyone come from anywhere else?" The Chekist continued the line of questioning.

"Some might come from over there," the man responded, pointing to the left, towards the passenger platform. "But that's a long way to run."

"I see. You're released. Go get your bun, and don't come back here in the next hour."

The man nodded, turned round and ran off. He tried to stop in front of the soldiers and almost fell. Soon, he disappeared round the corner of the white brick building in which sweets were boiled at night.

After walking a bit further, Samson, Abyazov and Kholodny froze as they drew level with the third prisoner wagon. Now, Samson was certain they were in the right place, and he definitely recognised the man in the sheepskin coat in front of the sliding door. This was the man who had released him in the morning.

"There's the outhouse," Abyazov said, pointing. "Let's position ourselves behind it."

The blue-painted wooden outhouse was wider than usual, by the length of two latrines. Leaving the Red Army soldiers under an old, crooked willow, which had, very conveniently, grown near the spot, Samson, Abyazov and Kholodny ran to the outhouse and hid behind its wall.

"We'll wait. This is the best place for an effective interrogation,"

Abyazov said with a grin, then fixed his gaze on Samson. "Fix your bayonet. Might need it."

After fulfilling the order, Samson did not return the rifle to his shoulder, lowering its butt onto the tracks. It seemed to him that he heard the measured monotonous clatter of a train approaching from afar.

"Is there something coming our way?" he asked uncertainly.

Kholodny looked round. At that moment, a sliding door clanged nearby.

Abyazov raised his finger to his lips. All three froze. The sound of footsteps reached them – now loud, when the soles of the boots fell on the rails; now quiet, when they fell on the wet ground between the tracks. The outhouse door creaked open. They heard a grunt inside, and the rustle of clothing.

"You stay here. If anything goes wrong, open fire," Abyazov ordered Kholodny. Then he looked hard into Samson's eyes and the young investigator understood everything, raising his rifle.

"Turn it butt up," whispered Abyazov, indicating the weapon with his eyes. "It's tight in there."

They burst into the outhouse and shut the door behind them. The man, who had been holding up the hem of his unbuttoned sheepskin coat with both hands as he balanced his rear end over the hole, was knocked backwards by the shock and, had he been of a slimmer build, would definitely have fallen right in. But a cushy life on the rails had made his figure resistant to such misfortunes. His ample backside simply plugged up the hole, while his face turned purple, expressing a mixture of fear and fierce anger.

"Quiet! Quiet!" commanded the Chekist, looking at the victim's open mouth.

Abyazov shot a lightning glance at Samson. Samson brought the bayonet close to the man's chest and the butt of the rifle touched the back of the wooden door. The young investigator looked back and accidentally pricked the man, who placed his hands on the floorboards and abruptly moved to the side.

"Where are you keeping the women from the Provincial Bureau of Statistics?" growled Abyazov.

"The spies?" asked the round-faced man, immobilised by both the bayonet and the situation. "They're in the jolly wagon, number five—"

"Where is it?" the Chekist demanded.

"Over there," the man said, swinging his head to the right. "It's green. Standing apart."

"How many guards?"

"Just one. Zhorik. He likes the dames. Volunteered."

"Is he inside? In the car?" cut in Samson, frightened anew for the nearly rescued Nadezhda.

"I don't keep track of 'im," the man growled. "Let me up or I'll start hollerin'."

"I'll give you hollering," Abyazov growled, pointing the muzzle of his revolver at the man's face.

"Brothers!" the man suddenly shouted as he tried to jump up, which he didn't quite manage to do because his trousers were down to his knees.

"Stick him!" Abyazov commanded.

Samson pushed his rifle forward and a terrible wheeze filled the outhouse. The man twitched, arched his back and began to gasp for air with his big mouth.

"You fool," the Chekist said, shaking his head and turning to Samson. "Leave him. Let's go get the women."

It was only at that moment that Samson realised the tip of his bayonet was still inside the wheezing man's chest.

They leapt out of the outhouse and ran towards the green wagon, which really was standing to the right. Kholodny hurried after them.

A railway worker in a padded jacket and cap was stationed by the door. Seeing the armed men running towards him, he froze and began to throw frightened glances from side to side.

"Stay where you are, Zhorik!" Abyazov shouted.

On hearing his name, the railway worker took off towards the kerosene warehouses.

"Should I fire?" Samson asked.

The Chekist shook his head.

Running up to the wagon, Samson and Kholodny slid open the door and climbed up the iron steps. Seeing the men burst in, three young women with bruised faces pressed their backs even more firmly against the cold wooden wall. They were sitting on a bench, their hands bound.

"Don't be afraid," Kholodny said.

He took out a penknife and quickly cut the ropes around the captives' wrists. Samson knelt down before Nadezhda, tears streaming from his eyes.

"My God," he whispered. "I found you."

Shots rang out close by.

"Let's go," Kholodny commanded. "Quick."

As they were jumping out of the wagon, a bullet hit the sliding door and got stuck in it.

"Behind the wagon!" Abyazov shouted. "Everyone!"

The young women were unable to run quickly, and occasionally stumbled and fell. Samson helped them up, his efforts hampered by the heavy rifle in his right hand. Kholodny kept shooting back at the railway men, although the main exchange of gunfire sounded a little further away, where the Red Army soldiers were gathered beneath the willow.

"Faster, faster – hurry!" Abyazov shouted.

At last, they climbed onto a low embankment, slippery with rain, and ran past Megel's kerosene warehouses towards the Brest-Litovsk Highway.

When they had made it onto the highway and stopped to catch their breath, Samson heard crying. He turned to Nadezhda, thinking it was her. But no. She was breathing rapidly and her hands, which were raised to her face, trembled. But she wasn't crying. That was another young woman, who wore a marsh-coloured quilted cotton coat and had a black scarf on her head.

"Dusya, don't, don't." The third young woman tried to comfort her.

The gunfire on the tracks continued, and because of that the group didn't immediately hear the tram approaching from the direction of Sviatoshyn. The little red wagon was flying towards them at what seemed to be great speed. Abyazov ran out onto the rails and raised his pistol into the air, as if he wanted to kill the sky with one shot. The screech of the tram's brakes drowned out the gunfire. The wagon stopped. The elderly driver behind the windscreen was stock-still, clearly frightened to death.

The group leapt aboard and some of the passengers immediately moved to the back. The screech of the metal wheels continued to ring in Samson's head, but he still heard Abyazov's cry: "Go! No stopping until Gymnasium Street! No, Volodymyrsky Passage!"

The tram drove off. But now it seemed to Samson that it was moving too slowly, as if out of spite – as if the driver wanted the railway men to catch up with them.

In confirmation of Samson's fears, Abyazov again shouted to the driver, "I said, go! Make tracks!"

"I'm going, I'm going," the driver answered in his thin, elderly voice. "Can't go any faster."

The passengers waiting at Halytska Square stared with surprise at the number-6 tram that passed them without stopping.

Kholodny appeared to sense the hostile glances of the passengers gliding over him. Abyazov too, it seemed, had begun to feel awkward, or maybe he had simply calmed down.

"You can start making stops, now. Understand?" he called to

the driver, who turned round, as if wanting to make sure that he had heard right.

"Stepanivska!" the driver shouted as his left hand pushed the brake handle away from him by fifteen degrees.

Chapter 11

Samson desperately wanted to take Nadezhda home right away, but Abyazov wouldn't allow it. When the group arrived at the station, the Chekist ordered each of the released captives to write out a statement. Dusya, the young woman in the black scarf, continued to cry, and her statement, written in neat, even letters in spite of her state, was generously stained with tears. Samson led Nadezhda to his office and seated her at his – or, rather, his father's – desk. He sat down in the chair opposite, offering silent support by gazing at her with sympathy and tenderness.

"But what should I write? What?" she asked in a trembling voice. Her face was uncharacteristically pale, and now Samson could clearly see the abrasion on her cheek.

"Don't worry. Just write down exactly what happened."

She gathered her strength and the pen began to move with ever greater confidence.

Samson looked at her lowered face, at her moving, occasionally quivering lips, and reflected on the fact that she was sitting at his father's desk. There was a thread in this, he thought – a thread connecting not only the two, but the three of them, because the desk remembered his father's hands, remembered their warmth, remembered the clicking of the abacus as his father had worked on his accounts.

It occurred to Samson that his father would have blessed his and Nadezhda's union.

His mind drifted further into his store of filial memories. But then the main and final memory of his father – that of their fatally unsuccessful trip to the tailor – struck him cold. It even seemed to

Samson that both his ears were burning with frost, crying out for help. He raised his hands to shield and warm them.

His left palm really did feel a cold ear, while the right simply lay flat against his temple, its heel resting on his cheekbone.

Samson decided to go to the cemetery, and then to the Church of St Macarius, where he would leave a memorial note asking the priest to pray for the repose of his father.

From the corridor came the sound of footsteps and general hubbub. A door was slammed.

Samson peeped out and saw Red Army men entering the commander's office. This was surprising.

When Nadezhda had finished writing, he picked up her statement, found Vasyl and asked him to bring her tea, then went to see Nayden. The commander was seated at his desk, staring disdainfully at the soldiers.

"Not a single one of you is literate?" he asked angrily.

"I can write, but only with a pencil," one of the older men replied. "Can't use a pen. Nib keeps snappin'."

"Listen here. Go down and get a pencil and paper from the officer on duty. Then record your own witness testimony and that of the others, briefly and clearly: who shot at whom and the like. Under each statement, write, 'Taken down correctly from my words', and let them sign. Dismissed!"

Now, Samson and Nayden were alone.

"You've certainly mucked it up," the commander pronounced, shaking his head. "Two soldiers killed, along with five of theirs, the chief conductor among them. It's a good thing the plan was Abyazov's, not yours. His pals from the Cheka have already taken him back to Sadova Street. Chances are we won't be seeing him again."

"You mean they might shoot him?" Samson asked with fear in his voice.

"Who knows? He made quite a mess of it."

"But the young women had been unlawfully detained and beaten, and my weapon had been confiscated . . ."

"You'd better not mention that yet," Nayden responded with a condescending smile. "If I send up your confession about the loss of your weapon, you'll find yourself on Sadova too."

"Understood," Samson said, nodding sadly.

"You have three days to recover the revolver."

At home, as Samson helped Nadezhda take off her shoes, he noticed how her fingers were trembling. She was still pale and could hardly stand. When she finally took a seat at the table, she began to sob, covering her face with her hands.

"I was so scared," she said through her tears. "Scared witless. I was sure they would kill me."

Samson kept pouring her fresh cups of tea. He tried to persuade her to take one of the sweets, but she refused.

He boiled some potatoes and managed to convince her to eat a little. After that, she went off to bed without uttering a single warm word to him.

He cleared the table and poured himself more tea. Then, he went down to the cellar, brought up a large armful of birch logs and stoked up the stove. He retrieved the Montpensier tin from the bedroom and took out his ear, which looked as fresh as any living thing. With the candle's flame behind it, it proved slightly translucent. He then drew a pig's ear from the newspaper bundle and held the two organs in front of him, comparing them. The pork had a strong smell, while his own ear gave off a barely perceptible spicy odour, like a fresh basil leaf.

He remembered how the Cossack's sabre had flashed for a second time over his head and how the ear had flown off to the side. The tiniest drops of blood had misted the air, as if they'd been squirted from an eau-de-Cologne atomiser. In retrospect, he was awed by the desperate dexterity with which he had caught the severed ear – had caught it, clenched it in his hand and fallen to the ground.

How had he managed it? And then he remembered how his already dead father's hand had shoved him aside, away from the Cossack's sabre. If it weren't for that hand, the blade would have cleaved his head just as it had his father's . . .

Warmth wafted from the stove's cast-iron door. Samson took the tin with the ear into his father's study, placed it among the books in the bookcase and returned to the living room.

Nayden's voice echoed in his mind: *You have three days to recover the revolver.*

Samson bit his lip. His sense of guilt kept growing. How would he recover the thing? He'd have to go back there, arrest the men who had held him and conduct a search. Yet that meant more gunfire, more killing . . .

He sighed, then put on his jacket, cap and boots.

The yard-sweeper's widow was still awake.

"Where are you off to, this late in the evening?" she asked, catching him on the threshold.

"Work," he answered dryly.

Already moving away from the house, he heard the bolts clanging behind him, locking the front door.

Nayden wasn't surprised to see Samson peering into his office.

"Come in," he said from behind his desk. He held a magnifying glass in his hand, and in front of him lay a sheet of paper covered with minuscule handwriting.

"I'm here to discuss the matter of the revolver," Samson began. "I don't see us resolving it without gunfire. They don't seem to leave their territory very often – only to get a bun, sometimes."

"They have no territory," Nayden responded, vigorously shaking his head. "There is only our Soviet territory. As for gunfire, we aren't the army, we're the police. We have to use our wits, lure them out of their holes and hiding places, trap them like rats." Nodding at the scribbled sheet, he added, "Here's a real riddle. An agent reports that the ban on private trade in meat wasn't accompanied by a ban on the sale of pies. Now, some merchants at the Jewish Market are stuffing pies with ground dog, cat and rat meat. They're mixing it with horseradish, to stifle the unfamiliar smell, so consumers don't get suspicious. What can we do? The sale of pies isn't prohibited, and, if we nab the merchants, they'll say there's no meat in there. They have a point: are dogs, cats and rats really meat? By the way, did you close that meat case?"

"The one concerning the shed and the pigs? Not yet," Samson responded, tensing up. "That's why I came in, actually – thought I'd subject Briskin to a night-time interrogation . . ."

The look in Nayden's eyes was condescending and faintly sympathetic, suggesting that he knew Samson was lying, but didn't wish to reprimand him.

"Go on, then. Interrogate," he said.

Samson flipped on the light in his office, approached the diagram of pork cuts and stared at it as though at a treasure map.

After some thought, he decided to transcribe the information about Briskin's customers, so that he might at least have another document to include in the case file. He spent half an hour going back and forth between the desk and the diagram, making out a beautiful list: cuts in one column, names and addresses in the other. As he read and reread the list, something kept nagging at him, until he realised that the diagram and, consequently, the document, lacked some essential elements – namely, the intestines, the liver, the kidneys and, finally, the heart. He appended these to the end of his list, then ordered the soldier on duty to go down and fetch Briskin.

Briskin looked like a pitiful dandy. His clothes were still in decent shape, but his face had grown thin and there was dried blood on his left eyebrow.

Samson was about to order him to sit down, but he stopped himself. A club chair seemed too plush a seat for a detainee.

Briskin hiccupped and coughed.

"Cold down there?" Samson asked.

He hiccupped again. "Cold, among other things," he answered gloomily.

"I've made a list, according to the diagram." The investigator got down to business. "Some things don't add up. There's no mention of internal organs. Also, there appears to be a single buyer for each large cut. Is that possible?"

"There aren't any organs named on the diagram," Briskin responded, looking up at the wall. "I can supply that information."

"Well, have a seat, then. While you're at it, check what I've copied down. There may be more to add."

Briskin sat down at the desk, carefully read the list, then reached for the pen in the inkwell. The nib creaked across the page. He hiccupped again.

"Indigestion?" the investigator asked with some concern in his voice.

"No, no," the detainee responded. "My daughter brought me some eggs. I have a heart condition that requires me to eat hard-boiled eggs every day. Another fellow down in the basement wanted to take them away from me, so I had to eat them fast, shell and all. Seems the shells got stuck somewhere." Briskin hiccupped again, loudly, then heaved a sigh and continued to run the pen across the paper.

A few minutes later, he stopped and raised his head.

"Will you arrest my customers as well?"

"I don't imagine we will, no," Samson replied. "Don't know for sure, but I don't imagine so."

"It would be better if you used your imagination," the detainee exhaled. "They're people, just like you."

"We'll see about that. If they're the same as us, then they have nothing to worry about," Samson assured him. And then a thought flashed in his eyes. "Do any of your customers bake pies for the Jewish Market?"

"With meat, you mean?" Briskin asked thoughtfully. "Yes, pies and cutlets . . . Antonina from Kryvy Lane sells them at the Jewish Market."

"Antonina?" Samson asked, surprised, and he walked over to the diagram. "There's no Antonina here."

"She buys the intestines, and a bit of fat," Briskin answered, pointing to the bottom of the piece of paper. "I added her."

Samson leaned over the desk. "What about the heart?"

"Don't remember," Briskin muttered.

"You don't remember the heart?" Samson asked with doubt in his voice. "How could that be? It's the chief internal organ."

"Perhaps in a person, but not in a pig. A pig's chief organs are its fat, its legs, its loin and its shoulders."

"Go on, give it a try," Samson urged. "Who bought the heart? I've been ordered to close this case as quickly as possible."

Briskin heaved another heavy sigh, then twisted his mouth as if recalling something unpleasant.

"I sold the heart to Shura," he half-whispered, almost romantically. "You can even say I gave it to her as a gift . . . Hardly took any money for it . . ."

"Well, then, write down her address and we'll wrap this up."

Briskin again drew the pen from the inkwell and shook off a dangling drop of red.

"And you haven't forgotten about anyone else?" Samson asked, having waited for the detainee to return the pen to the inkwell.

"No," Briskin sighed, defeated.

*

Samson summoned the Red Army man on duty, who took the prisoner back to the basement.

Left alone with the tailor's dummy, which again smelled of damp, Samson thought about his lost revolver and holster belt. He didn't feel like sleeping, and, even if he had, the station was every bit as noisy as it was in the daytime. There were footsteps outside the door.

He decided to go to the Jewish Market, hoping to come up with something there.

At that moment, the door opened cautiously, revealing Vasyl's questioning face.

"Can't sleep, eh?" he chuckled, then smiled and asked, "Want some tea?"

"Yes," Samson responded, nodding decisively. "And I wanted to ask you something." He looked round, his gaze pausing for a moment on the dummy. "You took the suit but left this . . . Yes?"

"I didn't touch that suit," Vasyl replied, almost indignantly. "I haven't got any more space for your evidence."

"So, who took it, then?"

"No idea. Maybe someone who liked it – someone it fits. I'll be back with the tea."

The door closed and Samson turned his unhappy, puzzled eyes back to the dummy.

Vasyl's phrase, *someone it fits*, echoed in his mind, and he shook his head. Suddenly, his hands began to tremble and his gaze drifted over to the upper left-hand drawer of his desk, in which he kept another important piece of evidence, a silver replica of the Belgian swindler Jacobson's left femur, *os femoris*.

The drawer had remained unsealed for some three days. Samson hardly ever bothered about clerical rules concerning the sealing and unsealing of desks and cabinets.

He pulled the drawer open and couldn't believe his eyes. The silver bone was gone. In its place lay a thick bundle of Kerensky roubles.

Samson's eyes again rose to the dummy, only now they burned with a combination of resentment, anger and fear – fear of the consequences of his negligence: the loss of the revolver, of the suit and of the heavy silver item of evidence.

Chapter 12

No-one answered the knock at the door, nor did the widow's sleepy face, illumined by a candle, appear in her window, as usually happened in these rare situations. Samson felt a painful vigour uselessly draining his body of its last reserve of strength. The time was too early rather than too late. There couldn't have been more than an hour and a half of darkness left before dawn.

Samson looked round and heard a faraway noise, something like the whistle of a locomotive. The noise could very well have been a figment of his imagination, conjured up by his thoughts, since only half an hour ago he had been standing in front of the wooden barracks on Stepanivska, speaking with Li Yin Jun, who was again on duty with his comrades on the outskirts of the railway station. Now, Samson knew that the Chinese Red Army patrol had been positioned there for a reason, not by chance. Non-Chinese soldiers tended to find a common language with the railway workers and to venture onto their territory for drinking sessions – sessions that sometimes ended in the loss of weapons, sometimes in clumsy deaths. The Chinese, on the other hand, tended not to violate orders and regulations, and were therefore assigned to the most critical posts and patrol routes.

Even before he had seen that the soldiers were Chinese, Samson had caught the familiar scent of the pigs' ears to which Li Yin Jun had treated him, and so he approached the patrol more boldly, without stopping. He told Li Yin Jun about the holster belt and described the man in the sheepskin coat whom he had seen wearing it. Li Yin Jun promised to keep an eye on the railway workers who went to the Jewish Market at night for food and drink.

"If I see him, where will I find you?" the soldier asked.

"The Lybid police station, at the end of Tarasivska," Samson answered.

"Lybid. I know it," Li Yin Jun confirmed.

The appearance of a candle in the kitchen window of the yard-sweeper's flat distracted Samson from his recollections. He waved his hand, assuming that the widow was just now trying to determine who was banging on the front door so early in the morning.

In the hallway, Samson tried to pull his boots off his feet as quietly as possible, then hung up his jacket. Stepping into the living room, he saw Nadezhda. She sat the table, fully dressed, her head resting on her folded hands in front of a guttering candle. Although she seemed to be asleep, her shoulders occasionally trembled.

He approached her on tiptoe, listening closely to her breathing.

"Nadezhda?" he whispered. "Are you asleep?"

She raised her head.

"I don't feel well," she breathed out weakly. "My knees and elbows are cold, and my head's ringing. It gets closer, then further away . . ."

"My God," Samson said. "We need to get you a doctor. Go and lie down, and I'll make you some tea."

The young woman obediently rose to her feet and went into the bedroom.

Samson helped her get into bed, covered her up with a blanket and placed his hand on her forehead. It felt cold and moist, adding to his fear.

"I'll be right back. Try and go to sleep," he said, hurrying out to the kitchen.

By the time he returned with a cup of hot tea, Nadezhda was already dozing.

Back in the living room, he sat down on the chair she had warmed and moved the candle closer. Its flame, soon to be extinguished by the melted wax, flickered with all its remaining strength.

He took a sip of tea and felt the fatigue pressing down on his shoulders. He too wanted to lie down.

Late in the morning, he took Nadezhda to see Dr Vatrukhin, into whose home office he had burst in search of salvation on that fateful day, clutching his severed ear and spattered with his and his father's blood.

Nadezhda put up no resistance. She looked weak and pale, and complained of a migraine and joint pain. The sun shone over Zhylianska Street, its rays lending a radiant, joyful aspect to the faces of certain passers-by. As soon as these people stepped out of the sunshine, however, their faces resumed their usual expressions of anxious expectation. Perhaps one or another of them really was happy this morning, going off to work? It seemed to Samson that, at present, the dark side of Kyivan existence easily overpowered the joy-giving power of the sun's rays, generally interfering with any attempts to see life as bright and joyful. Indeed, the fact that these sunlit pedestrians kept glancing fearfully at those around them revealed their true state of mind.

"They didn't . . ." Samson began to ask, but he couldn't find the right word. "You weren't tortured, were you?"

Nadezhda didn't seem to hear him. Her attention was turned inward, focused on her own thoughts and pains.

Samson recalled what one of the railway workers had told him – that, if his wife was pretty, he wouldn't find her. That they might "bend" her and kill her.

"You know," Samson said suddenly, his voice so filled with emotion that Nadezhda turned to face him, "when I was searching for you, I told everyone that you were my wife."

A smile, faint but distinct, appeared on her lips.

"But they didn't believe me. You know why? Because I didn't have a picture of you. We'll have to go to a photographer's studio as soon as possible."

"I have a photo at home, at my parents' house. I'll give it you,"

Nadezhda promised, and her face seemed to brighten, regaining its beauty.

"He's actually an eye doctor." Samson spoke again a few minutes later. "But he can deal with all sorts of ailments, just specialises in eyes. He was of great help with my ear."

Samson's attention was drawn to an unusual wordless wooden sign to the right of Dr Vatrukhin's door. In black paint, it depicted a triangle, pointing up like a pyramid, inside of which hovered an eye.

At least he's designated his medical practice somehow, Samson thought, and, looking back at Nadezhda, he knocked on the door with his fist.

Nikolay Nikolaevich Vatrukhin first opened the door only as far as the chain would allow, but when he recognised the visitor, he immediately closed it again, then swung it wide open. A benevolent smile enlivened his face, lifting the tips of his neat moustache, which Samson was seeing for the first time. Altogether, he looked unprecedentedly well groomed and polished. The soft, purple smoking jacket he wore was a bit baggy, yet it had an almost solemn appearance, as did his blue woollen trousers. His feet were shod in grey felt boots lined with snow-white sheep's wool.

"It's been too, too long," Vatrukhin said in greeting, stepping aside to let in his guests.

Taking off Nadezhda's sheepskin coat, Samson introduced her and briefly described the misfortune that had befallen her.

"Let's have a spot of linden tea and talk things over," the doctor suggested.

The doctor's living room was also unusually clean and orderly. Samson would likely have spent a great deal of time in search of an explanation for the sudden improvement of both Vatrukhin and his living quarters, but at that very moment a beautiful young woman emerged from the kitchen, bearing a samovar. She had on a long, heavy black skirt and a fluffy blue blouse with a standing collar, which emphasised the clean lines of her face.

"Dunya, dear, we still have some gingerbread in the sideboard," the doctor said, helping her place the samovar on a copper tray in the centre of the oval table.

"Yes, Nikolay Nikolaevich." She nodded. "And quince jam, too."

"You have a new housekeeper, I see," Samson said approvingly, with slight envy.

The doctor dismissed the suggestion. "A housekeeper? At a time like this? Not a chance. No, Dunya is my wife."

"Congratulations," Samson declared, widening his eyes and turning to Nadezhda.

"Yes, congratulations," she echoed. "So wonderful!"

"Oh, don't be silly," the doctor said, shaking his head and placing Nadezhda's cup under the samovar's spigot. Then he looked at Samson and switched to a whisper, "A veritable feast in plague-time . . . The main thing is for the plague not to notice." Turning back to Nadezhda, he declared, "Your complexion troubles me. I'd have referred you to Dr Feykus, but he left for Berlin some time ago. It's a matter of nerves – a mental disorder, so to speak. I recommend a regimen of bubbled milk, according to the method of Dr Pasternatsky. He's a student of Botkin's – a physician of genius. Go over to Martsinchik's chemist and ask them whether they have a Pasternatsky device for carbonating milk. If not, just mix some milk with Narzan mineral water and shake the solution until bubbles form."

"But where can we buy Narzan water?" Samson enquired with a sigh.

"Pharmacists are a thrifty bunch. They stock up. These days, one doesn't buy goods, one begs for them. Once you get it, it will be half a glass of milk and half a glass of Narzan, four times a day, perhaps even five."

The gingerbread with quince jam melted slowly and pleasantly on Samson's tongue. He was especially pleased with Nadezhda's unexpected appetite. There was even a blush on her cheeks. The doctor also kept glancing at Nadezhda, but the clearly medical interest in his eyes did nothing to arouse Samson's jealousy. Vatrukhin's wife never did join them at the table.

"She's in mourning," the doctor explained after she disappeared behind one of the doors leading off the spacious living room. "Her brother is missing. Together with his wife. They simply vanished, leaving all their possessions and documents in their flat. She's worried, doesn't know where to look for them."

"She should go to Sadova Street, to the Cheka," Samson advised.

"She's already been," the doctor replied. "They aren't there."

After tea, Vatrukhin led Samson and Nadezhda to his office. He asked her to take off her stockings and he examined her knees. Then she rolled up the sleeves of her blouse so he could examine her elbows.

"As I suspected," he said and nodded. "Neurosis. A month of carbonated milk treatments and you'll be right as rain. By the way," he added, gazing intently into Samson's eyes, "I recently recalled your silver bone. Do you read German?"

Samson shook his head. A German medical journal appeared in the doctor's hands. He leafed through it, folded it so that it would be easier to hold, then showed it to Samson.

"Here, in the November 1912 issue, is an interesting article on diseases of the bone. At the end, the author mentions a number of surgeons who advise replacing diseased bones with ones made of silver. Among them is a doctor in Kyiv – Trattner!"

"Is that so?" Samson asked, his curiosity piqued. "What else does it say?"

"It says that he has successfully used silver ribbon wire to reinforce osteoporotic bones. There's also a substantial article about Vera Ignatyevna Gedroits, concerning military surgery. In fact, she gave me the journal, and I decided to read it cover to cover. You know, reading in German seems to soothe my soul, restoring order to my mind. In any case, that was how I came across this article about silver bones."

Seeing off his guests, Vatrukhin also stepped out of the house.

"I see you're taking patients again," Samson said, indicating the sign with a glance.

"A few, one by one." The doctor nodded. "One has to make a living somehow."

On the way back along Zhylianska, which had been bustling since morning, Nadezhda stopped in front of the entrance to the Bureau of Statistics.

"May I go up for a second?" she asked Samson. "Tell them I'm ill?"

"Of course. I'll wait," he agreed.

He waited a quarter of an hour before Nadezhda stepped out onto the street again.

"You know what? I'm feeling better already," she told him. "The doctor has such warm hands. Maybe he healed me with his touch? I'll stay a while, help the other girls. They've just received statistics concerning Kyivan livestock – they won't manage without me. Each number is of three or four figures. And this evening they're bringing rations for all the employees."

Samson shrugged.

"Of course," he consented. "Just don't strain yourself. And later, let's take the firewood to your girlfriend and pick up the sundress. Summer's almost here."

Nadezhda smiled, gave him a playful kiss on the cheek and disappeared behind the bureau's door.

Chapter 13

"Will you dance?" Nayden asked with a sly grin on his unshaven face.

"Why should I dance?" Samson asked, confused.

He had just arrived at the station and his mind was still occupied with his plans for the evening. He couldn't conjure an image of the sundress Nadezhda had fallen in love with, but he could already see her happy round face, red-cheeked and brightened by a sunny smile. All they had to do was take three sacks of firewood to the dress's current owner. As these thoughts were swirling in his head, he was approaching the diagram of pork cuts, and then Vasyl peered into the office to say that Nayden demanded his presence, urgently.

"I don't care what you dance," the commander chuckled. "The hopak, the Kamarinskaya – as long as you put your heart into it!"

He turned back to his desk, picked something up and tossed it lightly to Samson. The young investigator took half a step back, but he extended his hands and caught the object – a leather belt. The heavy wooden holster dangling from it slammed painfully against his knee.

"Yours?" asked Nayden, at once sternly and almost cheerfully.

Samson opened the holster, pulled out the revolver and examined it. His face beamed with joy.

"Mine," he confirmed, and added, "How did you get it back?"

"A Chinese soldier brought it in, told us it was for you. Obviously a friend of yours. Left some sort of bundle for you, too," Nayden said, nodding towards the table.

"So quick . . . How?" Samson marvelled, shrugging his shoulders and relishing the pleasant sense of relief.

"Ask Vasyl. He spoke to the soldier. This was before dawn, and I had just lain down for some shut-eye. Say, how did you adapt that Mauser holster for a revolver?"

"That too was Vasyl, probably. When he first gave it to me, the revolver was in the holster. So, what happens to my report about the loss of the weapon?"

"Nothing," Nayden responded with a wink. "I'll tear up what you scribbled and we'll leave it at that. Now, go wrap up that meat case. I want a verdict and sentence in two days."

"Do I have to write them out myself?"

"Why yourself? The two of us will sit down with Vasyl and write it over a few mugs of tea," Nayden declared.

"What about Abyazov? Have you heard anything?" Samson asked, his expression growing serious.

"Nothing yet. He was assigned to us for reinforcement, you know – seconded. Had he been one of ours, I might have been able to make enquiries . . ."

"Understood." Then Samson immediately returned to the previous topic of conversation. "I have a list with about a dozen of Briskin's customers," he said, peering into the commander's eyes with the penetrating gaze of a good student. "They aren't a gang – more like witnesses, no? Or are they accomplices?"

"Those who didn't know of the ban will be considered witnesses, and those who did, accomplices. You'll figure it out. If the person in front of you is clearly a malicious buyer of meat, record them as an accomplice, but don't tell them. Let them testify first."

Back in his office, Samson tightened the belt around his leather jacket and straightened the holster so that it hung precisely on his thigh. This action reminded him of the way Abyazov had always taken great care with his appearance. Pricked by a sense of guilt, the young investigator shook his head. He knew perfectly well that, if not for the kidnapping of Nadezhda, Abyazov would now be sitting here in a club chair, likely giving him instructions regarding the interrogation of witnesses in the meat case. Instead, he had been taken back to the Cheka, probably as a prisoner.

In order to distract himself from the guilt and other related feelings, Samson sat down at his desk and picked up the list of pork buyers. There was no point in bringing them all here for interrogation. The entrance to the station couldn't admit everyone at the same time, and every day there seemed to be more and more people gathered outside; some just stood around, waiting – perhaps for news about arrested relatives – while others wanted to get inside, and still others were being brought in by force. Samson hadn't seen such crowds since his school days. The relative proximity of the Jewish Market contributed to the mess. Every now and then, a Red Army soldier or an ordinary Kyivan would catch a pickpocket or petty thief, give him a drubbing and drag him to the station, hoping that the police would take matters further and permanently remove the miscreant from the paths of honest citizens.

Judging by the addresses Briskin had written down, many of his customers also lived fairly close to the market, which meant that it was as native a ground for them as for the aforementioned pickpockets and thieves. It was strange that Briskin hadn't included any of his neighbours in Pushcha-Vodytsia or Horenka. The farthest any of them lived was Priorka and Kurenivka. Apparently, he didn't like delivering pork to the suburbs. It was true that the residents of these outlying settlements always had less money than those who lived closer to the centre of town.

Samson's eyes came to rest on the address of a certain Krystyna, who lived on the first floor at 15 Stolypin Street. At that very moment, he felt an attack of hunger and remembered that near that address was a Soviet cafeteria where he had often eaten, paying with the stamped vouchers he'd received from Vasyl. He decided that he ought to go to Stolypin Street straight away, first to question Krystyna, then to have lunch.

Krystyna Orzechowska turned out to be a young fair-haired Polish woman with a languid look in her brown eyes. She lived in a spacious flat that she had not yet been forced to share with anyone, but which was filled with the sour odour of cheap tar soap.

"You live here all by yourself?" Samson asked, unable to hide his surprise, as she, not at all surprised at the arrival of a policeman, escorted him to the kitchen, where she seated him at a rough wooden table, the top of which, with its notches and dents, had clearly only been used to prepare food, never to serve it.

"Now I do, yes. But at one point our home bubbled with life." She sighed and looked round at the walls, gazing with special tenderness at a calendar for the year 1913. It hung open in a glass-fronted frame, and its upper part depicted children throwing snowballs in front of a Christmas tree.

Her visitor nodded with sympathy and looked down at the briefcase he had lowered to his knees.

This brown leather item, which he had asked Vasyl to release to him from the evidence room, had been confiscated in the arrest of a bank teller. Samson found it easy and pleasant to walk down the street holding the briefcase in his left hand, not only because it contained just one light folder, but also because it created a sense of balance – although, of course, the holstered revolver on his right thigh was considerably heavier.

Samson ran his palm over the workaday tabletop, felt its roughness and relative cleanliness, and only then pulled out the folder, placed it on the table and removed from it two sheets of paper and a pencil.

"I came to pose some questions regarding the case of Moses Briskin," he finally informed his hostess, shooting a glance at the malachite brooch that adorned her white, fluffy woollen blouse.

Noticing the glance, she straightened the brooch, then pulled her blouse down further towards her heavy blue woollen skirt.

"Who is this Moses?" she asked, her face taking on an expression of inscrutability. "A prophet?"

To Samson, her thin, pointed nose looked like that of a doll, not a living human being. It seemed too white for her generally lively, pink face. An effect of face powder, he suddenly realised, then he looked her in the eyes.

"You recently bought pork from him."

"Ah, so that's his real name!" Krystyna exclaimed cheerfully. "He gave me a different one."

"What name?" asked Samson, but then he lowered his eyes to the paper and pencil. "Hold on, you'd better write it down. Here." He handed her a clean sheet.

"What should I write, exactly?"

"First, across the top, 'Witness Statement'. Then the details: how long you've known Briskin, what he called himself, how many times he visited and how many times you bought meat from him."

"So, he's under arrest?" Krystyna guessed.

Samson nodded.

"On what charges?"

"Meat-related. You do know that the private trade in meat has been forbidden, don't you?"

"Is that so?" she asked, her surprise seemingly genuine. "When did that happen?"

The last question caught Samson off guard. He realised that he didn't know the exact date – and he hadn't actually read the ban itself.

"Recently," he replied after a short pause. "Two weeks ago."

"Ah, so I should write about the meat I've purchased from your Moses in the last two weeks?"

"Yes, but also about Briskin – how you became acquainted with him, how long you've been in touch, what you spoke about."

Krystyna Orzechowska stared at the thick, roughly sharpened pencil.

"Might you have a pen?" she asked.

"I'm sorry, I didn't bring one," Samson answered. "You know, with briefcases, inkwells are a devil of a problem, always spilling."

"I have one," she announced with a smile. "May I use it? Your pencil is too thick for my fingers."

Samson turned his attention to her truly unusually delicate fingers, for which even the piano would be too crude an instrument.

She left the kitchen and returned with a stationery tray, on which, in addition to a blotter, sat a porcelain inkwell in the form of a tree stump. There was also a bronze cup attached to the tray, with several pens sticking out of it.

"This was my father's," she explained, setting down the tray some distance from her chair, so as to leave space for the sheet of paper.

While his hostess was busy writing, Samson listened closely to the sounds of the flat. He had the sense that, beyond the confines of the kitchen, there was someone else present – walking, breathing, moving something.

"Do you really live by yourself?" he couldn't help asking when he heard, quite clearly, the shuffling of feet.

She looked up at her visitor.

"Yes, except for the dog," she said, and she looked so intently at Samson's right temple, with its bare earhole, that he began to feel uneasy. "These days, a single woman can't do without a dog. But dogs require meat."

"You mean to say that you used Briskin's pork as dog food?"

"Correct! Did you think it was for me? I don't eat meat at all," she responded, almost indignantly.

"Forgive me," Samson whispered. "Do finish the statement. I'll go and have a look at the dog."

He got up, propped his briefcase against the leg of the chair and left the kitchen.

"His name is Crimea! We bought him as a puppy in Gurzuf. But don't try to pet him – he doesn't like strangers' hands!"

Opening the door to the living room, Samson froze. Crimea turned out to be a broad-chested British bulldog. The animal stood in his way and clearly had no intention of letting him pass. Samson squatted down, but Crimea's growl brought him back upright.

Having read what Krystyna Orzechowska had written, Samson recorded her answers to a number of additional questions on another sheet of paper, asking her to sign below the phrase *Taken down correctly from my words.*

"You don't still have any of Briskin's meat, do you?" he asked at the end.

"No, I'd have nowhere to store it. Our cellar was requisitioned. It's now a workshop for revolutionary artists."

"Do they make monuments?" Samson asked, perking up.

"No, posters. Utterly lacking in taste. I even told them so. They protested that they were only given three colours to work with – yellow, red and black."

Samson took a corner table at the Soviet cafeteria. He ate his borscht and millet porridge with gravy quickly, but decided to savour his fruit compote, the way he used to do at cheap Polish-owned student cafés or, sometimes, at Bernard Semadeni's famous establishment on Khreshchatyk. He took a sip from the mug, set it aside to the left and opened the folder before him, fixing his gaze on the testimony of the fair-haired Krystyna Orzechowska:

I first met the person whom you call Moses Briskin aboard a steamer, under the following circumstances. I was sailing to Khodoriv, to visit my aunt. Suddenly a man of decent appearance approached me on the deck, demanding to review my documents. The only document I had in my possession was the steamer ticket. Then one of the other passengers came up and showed the officious man his identification, declaring that he knew me and that I wasn't the person they were looking for. The officious man left, and the one who had intervened introduced himself as Matvey. He went ashore with me at Khodoriv and accompanied me to my aunt's gate. As we walked, he told me that he worked in food supply and would be happy to help me obtain meat. I gave him my address and he really did help me, five times, once on credit. I know nothing more about the person whom you call Moses Briskin.

Samson wondered what identification Briskin had shown, and whether the whole scene had not been staged in order to secure a customer.

This last thought struck him as humorously naive, and he shook his head in disappointment. He slipped the sheet back into the folder and picked up the next one, which he himself had filled out in pencil.

Krystyna Orzechowska, citizen of Poland, born in 1894. Social origin: Bourgeois. Faith: Catholic. Occupation: Housewife, under all regimes. Marital status: Widow. Political orientation: Sympathises with workers and peasants.

And then someone plopped down next to Samson with a plate in his hands. The edge of the plate hit the tabletop and a drop of borscht splashed onto the young investigator's neat handwriting.

"Sorry about that," said a familiar voice.

Samson threw up a displeased glance and recognised Kholodny. He wore a new brown leather jacket, cinched by a hostlerless belt.

"Oh, am I glad to see you!" Samson smiled and held out his hand. "I'm working on the meat case. Nayden ordered it closed, and quick – but I have a dozen people to question," he complained, then, gazing appraisingly at the jacket's stiff collar, which lent it an even more stern and resolute look, he added, "Is that new?"

"Yes." Kholodny sighed. "Mine disappeared. Good thing Vasyl had a spare."

"What do you mean, 'disappeared'?"

"Just vanished, from the office. I went down to the basement to interrogate a speculator – was gone half an hour at most – and when I got back, no jacket."

"So, it was stolen," Samson concluded, staring thoughtfully at the plate of borscht.

"God knows it was," his comrade confirmed with a nod. "But, on Vasyl's advice, I wrote that it went missing. If I had written *stolen*, I'd have had to open a case, hunt for the thief. But if it's missing, it's missing. Besides, every cloud has a silver lining. The old jacket had holes in the pockets. Anyhow, what's this case with a dozen people?"

"That same one, the case of the murdered pig. I should say, of speculation in meat."

"Ah! Well, I'm happy to help," Kholodny offered. "We'll do the rounds together. I could use a bit of fresh air. Back at the station, it's interrogate this one, interrogate that one – well, I'd like to make an arrest for a change. Let someone else do the interrogating."

"Alright, then," Samson agreed. "I'll tell Nayden. But, to be clear, we're not out to arrest anyone. Our mission it to collect evidence of guilt. Now, if we establish that one or another of the customers is an accomplice, that's different."

The prospect of spending two days travelling round the city seemed to buoy Kholodny's spirits. He looked down joyfully at his borscht and pressed together the thumb, forefinger and middle finger of his right hand, raising them towards his broad forehead, as if he were about to cross himself, by force of old habit, before the meal. But he didn't complete the gesture, and instead lowered his fingers to the spoon, the handle of which was stamped with a five-pointed star.

So, he wasn't the only victim of theft at the station, Samson thought mournfully, recalling Jacobson's suit and the silver bone. He shook his head, glanced at the borscht-stained paper, then licked his finger and touched the stain. It turned lighter, more translucent.

"Well, I'll be going, now," he told Kholodny. "Stop by my office later. We might go right out and get started."

Chapter 14

In the evening, although later than he had originally planned, Samson took three sacks of firewood to the address Nadezhda had given him, and, in exchange, received a paper box containing a sundress from a young woman with an ample bosom.

When he returned, he found Nadezhda, who had already drunk her last glass of carbonated milk for the evening, yawning wearily. However, after she pulled the green sundress with its dense pattern of yellow flowers from the box and shook it out, giving it the opportunity to take on an airy shape, all signs of fatigue vanished from her eyes and her lips regained their liveliness. To his incredible joy and amazement, Samson felt her hot kiss on his right cheek.

She changed in the bedroom and fluttered out like a dragonfly or a grasshopper. It appeared to Samson that she had undergone an extraordinary transformation, had grown lighter, younger – that she had come to look more like an adolescent than like a youthful yet strict and responsible employee of the Provincial Bureau of Statistics.

Realising that, despite the late hour, Nadezhda was overcome with joy, he offered her tea, but the happy owner of the green, flowered sundress asked instead for something a bit stronger – that is, for wine or brandy. This desire of hers also surprised Samson to the very depths of his soul. It seemed so unlike the Nadezhda he knew. Of course, he much preferred a Nadezhda with such desires to one without them. And so he went downstairs to see the yard-sweeper's widow, as she would certainly be able to help.

"She asked for it herself?" the widow marvelled, throwing up her hands in celebration.

Taking a seat at a kitchen table piled with dirty dishes, Samson nodded in the affirmative. The widow pulled up her sagging grey woollen skirt, tightened the rope-belt around her waist, pulled down and straightened her burgundy jersey, then reached into the sideboard for a green bottle plugged with a wadded piece of newspaper. She placed the bottle on the table and the flame of the nearby candle set its surface sparkling playfully.

"Never you fear, I'll give you the good stuff, but do have a glass of this bitter liqueur with me first. I'm your matchmaker, after all."

"It would be my pleasure," Samson responded. "You also came to my rescue with the boiled sweets. But let's be quick!"

She filled two shot glasses to the very top.

"How about some pork rinds?" she asked, raising her eyes to Samson's.

"Pork rinds?" he repeated, licking his lips. "Gladly!"

The salty food made the bitter liqueur taste almost sweet.

"Two of you getting married, then?" she asked pryingly.

"Likely not in church, but yes," Samson answered.

"How can you, if not in church?" the widow said rather than asked, refilling the shot glasses.

Her guest grew nervous. "I should go; Nadezhda's waiting."

"Then we'll have one last drink on our feet." The widow rose, pushing the unwashed dishes even further from the candle and the bottle, to the very edge of the table. "I wish you and Nadezhda all the happiness in the world! Lord forbid she should wind up like me, widowed in the prime of her life."

Samson, who had already taken a sip, as his heart was speeding him onwards, almost choked.

He went up to his floor with a bottle of cherry brandy and salty lips. The widow had also poured a handful of walnuts into the pocket of his leather jacket, saying they were just the thing to nibble on when quaffing brandy.

As soon as Samson placed the bottle on the table, the room

seemed to brighten. He looked up at the light bulb, unable to tell whether it had been infused with greater than usual power or whether his eyes had merely lit up with inner joy, causing them to illuminate whatever they touched like the lanterns of a carriage.

"You truly are my trusty eagle. Wherever I send you, you bring back a prize," Nadezhda intoned, approaching him especially slowly, so as to give him another good look at her sundress.

"Sit down, sit down," he told her, indicating one of the chairs with a nod. "I'll get the glasses."

"Have you noticed how bright the light is tonight?" she asked, sitting down. "Evidently Soviet power is gaining strength!"

Samson threw another glance up at the tall ceiling, realising that his eyes weren't responsible for the extra illumination.

He laid the walnuts on the table, fetched a nutcracker and set out two shot glasses. Then he thought about the pork rinds he'd eaten at the widow's and, realising that they'd need more than nuts for a proper celebration, remembered the pigs' ears to which Li Yin Jun had treated him. As he unfolded the bundle, it occurred to him that Nadezhda might find the ears less than appetising in their current form, so he cut them into strips with a pair of scissors and arranged them on a porcelain plate.

"To the sundress!" he exclaimed, lifting a glass filled with bright red liquid. "Now, let the summer come soon!"

"Well, it's just a few weeks away," Nadezhda said with a smile. "That's soon enough!" Then she took a sip, returned her glass to the table, picked up a piece of pig's ear and brought it to her mouth in a slightly mannered fashion. "Fish?" she asked.

"No, meat. A gift from my Chinese comrades."

"Interesting taste, like apple-smoked duck."

"Very accurate," Samson said, praising her gustatory discernment. "I wouldn't have been able to describe it so well."

"That's alright – you're able to do lots of other things. Firing a pistol, for instance."

"I haven't really done too much shooting," Samson admitted. "But my methods of interrogation are improving by the day."

"Whom have you been interrogating?"

"I got a meat speculator to give up his customers over the course of a few days. Today, Comrade Kholodny and I took witness statements from three of them, and even requisitioned a pork shoulder. Kholodny insisted on that – I wouldn't have taken it, myself. The meat had begun to go bad, which must be why the fellow let us have it without raising a fuss. But our Red Army men came to the rescue."

"To whose rescue?" Nadezhda asked.

"The shoulder's. It had a bad smell. But one of the soldiers said that was nothing – easy to deal with. He had us burn birch logs until we had half a bucket of charcoal. Then we stuck the shoulder into another bucket, thick end down, added water and dumped in the embers. The thing steamed like a bathhouse! When we pulled out the shoulder, the smell was gone."

"And did you eat it?"

"According to the law, we couldn't, but Nayden commanded us to cut it into small pieces and distribute it to the soldiers. He gave me a piece, too, but a dog began to follow me as I was walking home. It occurred to me that dogs have a keener sense of smell than we do, and so this one must have picked up the bad scent, even if I myself couldn't detect it. I tossed it the meat. To tell the truth, I wasn't so eager to dine on physical evidence."

"I understand," Nadezhda said, and her hand again reached for the plate. "We're going ahead with the census of railway workers," she added firmly and decisively. "They'll send us a detachment of Chekists for reinforcement. Whoever refuses to provide us with information will be arrested."

Samson turned serious, sober. For a moment, he felt that the green sundress looked excessively frivolous, even vaudeville-like on Nadezhda. It was so terribly incongruous with the heavy responsibility she had taken upon her shoulders.

He refilled his glass and drained it, then placed a strip of pig's ear into his mouth and commenced chewing it diligently, forcing out its savoury, hunger-quelling juice.

"Maybe you, too, should learn how to shoot?" he asked cautiously.

"I will," she answered fervently. "The day after tomorrow, on Friday, they're taking us to the firing range. From now on, we won't be sent out unarmed. So, you didn't even try that stale meat?"

Samson shook his head.

That night, Samson and Nadezhda fell asleep in each other's arms. It took them a long time to drift off. They clung to their sense of unimaginable closeness, refusing to slacken their embraces, the hot breath of each inflaming the other's passion. And when they finally did drift off, an obsessive buzzing crept into Samson's bare earhole, now coming nearer, threatening to penetrate to the very centre of his head, now moving further away. Only in the morning, his mind rather foggy after the sultry night, did Samson realise where the noise might have been coming from. He walked barefoot into his father's study and saw, in the grey light of dawn, a weary but still buzzing June bug beside the Montpensier tin. He scooped up the bug and carried it to a narrowly opened window. A pleasant, cooling breeze struck his face, and he set the bug free. From the street came the clatter of hooves. He leaned against the glass and spotted several horsemen with rifles over their shoulders. This mounted Red Army patrol was proceeding in the direction of Halytska Square and the Jewish Market. After a couple of minutes, silence resumed its reign and the day's first sunbeam reached the roof of the house opposite.

Chapter 15

Nayden must have got out of the wrong side of bed, Samson sensed straight away, as soon as he edged his way inside the station, without waiting for the guards to lead out to the truck all the detainees who were being transferred to the Cheka.

"The fleas have jumped all the way up to the first floor!" he heard the commander shout at someone. "You may be used to them, but I won't stand for it – fleas and detainees belong down in the basement! They can't be allowed to go crawling all over the place!"

Climbing the stairs, Samson bumped into another detainee whom Red Army soldiers were leading down from the first floor.

"Up against the wall," one of the soldiers barked at the man as the young investigator approached.

Samson took two steps at once as he passed them, to prevent the fleas that had so enraged Nayden jumping over to his jacket or trousers.

Pushing open the door to his office, Samson immediately took a step back. At first, he thought he had made a mistake, but then he caught sight of the familiar tailor's dummy in the left corner and the diagram of pork cuts on the wall between the windows, and he again took a step forward. He now clearly saw that someone had not only moved the furniture, but had also decisively, drastically divided his workspace. His father's desk was far to the left of the room, the chair behind it flush against the wall. On the far right, as if in a mirror's reflection, stood another desk – a cheap clerkish one. Both club chairs were gone, and a large map of Kyiv hung on the wall.

Samson tried to sit down but couldn't squeeze his legs between the desk and chair. His face showed irritation. Sighing angrily, he first moved the end of the desk closest to the door some three inches from the wall, then straightened out the other end, after which he took off his holster belt, unbuttoned his jacket and sat down. At that moment, the door creaked. He looked up and noticed another innovation: in the right corner, behind the door, stood a four-hook wooden coat stand.

"Greetings!" a familiar baritone sounded.

Kholodny walked over to the poor newcomer of a desk and put down his black briefcase.

"They really laid into Nayden last night. A commission arrived – two carfuls. Rakovsky's deputy, Supinov, someone from the Cheka and some old man from the department for the sensible organisation of revolutionary offices. Apparently, we're short twelve investigators and have failed to archive our cases properly, the cells in the basement are overcrowded and unsanitary, and our records of weapons and material evidence are incorrect. In a word, enough sins for three executions! Nayden turned blue . . . That's why they've put me here," Kholodny said, nodding down at his desk. "They said there's room for four more investigators. And the extra detainees are on their way to Sadova Street—"

"Sadova?" Samson interrupted. "But they're detained for our investigations, not the Cheka's—"

"Most of them aren't being investigated for anything. The soldiers bring in anyone who rubs them the wrong way. What they say goes."

"Wait a minute, so my Briskin may also be taken away?" asked Samson, springing up and rushing to the door.

"He's probably gone!" he heard behind him.

Stopping at the threshold of the station, Samson saw a Red Army soldier yelling at the detainees to make more space inside the back of the truck. Five more detainees stood waiting, their faces flushed with confusion and fear. Among them was Briskin.

"Stop!" Samson shouted, addressing no-one in particular, simply trying to bring this whole situation to a halt.

It worked. Everyone froze and stared at the young policeman. When his eyes met those of the soldier in charge of loading the detainees, he commanded, "Return detainee Briskin to the basement!"

"Which one of you is Briskin?" the Red Army man asked, turning to the detainees.

"Me, me! I'm Briskin!" the meat speculator announced, raising his hand and even jumping up a bit to make it easier to distinguish him from the others.

"Two steps back!" the soldier commanded.

Briskin looked round uncertainly, searching for the best direction in which to take two steps back, and finally took them towards Samson.

"Follow me, Briskin," Samson commanded, trying to sound as stern as possible. He didn't want to spend another second under the scrutiny of the soldiers and detainees.

He led Briskin back into the station.

"To the basement, then?" the meat speculator asked with relief.

"Yes. Sit there quietly."

"Thank you, Comrade Investigator," Briskin said, momentarily flashing a pained smile.

"Did you know where you were going to be taken?"

Briskin nodded.

Climbing to his floor, Samson again heard Nayden's voice. The commander's door must have been open.

"Take them wherever you want. See which of the fighters is more competent and assign them to those courses. Understood?"

"Understood," Vasyl replied, barely audibly.

A door slammed and the voices disappeared. The station felt unusually quiet after the morning's commotion.

"Let's go," Samson said to Kholodny. "Time to work the meat case."

"Where to first?" the former priest asked, rising eagerly. He took his brand-new leather jacket from the coat stand, pulled it on and cinched it with his holster belt.

"Not far: 7 Zolotoustivska. Could you sneak over to Vasyl's room and grab five cab vouchers?"

The dapple-grey horse harnessed to the cab appeared too well bred or well groomed for so lowly a job. The cabby too differed from his colleagues. He was rather short and thin, and the clothes he had on seemed unsuited to his position: brown hussar-style breeches and a shabby, tattered doublet of the kind that important servants in manor houses used to wear. The horse pulled the cab uncertainly, shying away from oncoming wagons and carriages, for which she would immediately receive a lash and a shout from the cabby. His voice grated on the ear. He didn't sound ill or drunk, but rather extremely fresh and youthful, and excessively sonorous. The one good thing about the cab was that its rubber tyres were in unusually decent shape, so that it didn't shake too much when the horse veered to the right or the left.

"She needs blinkers!" Kholodny shouted, leaning forward.

"That would only make things worse," the cabby answered, half-turning. "She's a purebred, not a simple workhorse."

"She used to pull bourgeois carriages, did she?" Kholodny asked.

"She was a racehorse. Belonged to the Potocki family, before they went off to Paris. Now, she has to work for her supper," the cabby responded without turning at all.

An image formed in Samson's mind, one from much earlier, before the revolution and the war – an image of a festive procession along Khreshchatyk, with the jockeys of the Pechersk Hippodrome riding along beautifully in light two-wheeled chariots painted gold.

"Are you from the Syrets Hippodrome, or from the Pechersk?" Samson entered the conversation.

"Pechersk. We only have about four dozen horses left. They say they're closing us, turning the track into an airfield, just like Syrets."

The cab slowed down on Halytska Square, which was crowded with people and carriages.

"Pies! Pies!" a female voice cried nearby, and Samson's mouth began to water. Then he heard a more distant male cry: "Knives, axes, brass knuckles! All your self-defence needs! Broad pig-skin belts! Knives, axes, brass knuckles!"

Samson tensed up at the mention of the belts, now realising that pigs, in addition to meat, also provided leather for briefcases and belts. He wondered whether the private trade in leather items had also been put under a ban. After all, the hide is separated from the meat only after slaughter, and private slaughter had been banned. So how could private traders be selling leather?

Plunged as he was in these reflections, which led to no clear conclusion, Samson didn't notice the cab making its way through the seemingly road-like but probably pedestrian part of the Jewish Market and rolling out onto Zolotoustivska Street.

Number 7 turned out to be a two-storey private home with an attached wing, which had maintained a neat and tidy appearance even in these drab times. The brick single-storey wing had a separate entrance, which Samson and Kholodny now approached. The door opened at the first knock, revealing an ancient woman in a tattered, faded housecoat. She was barefoot, and her tousled hair clearly hadn't been touched by a comb in ages. In short, she looked like a madwoman, and her gaze corresponded to this appearance.

"Whaddya want?" she asked. And then she began to mutter mournfully, "Fimka ain't home, been gone three years, and you all keep comin' and comin' . . ."

"Who is Fimka?" Samson asked.

"My son. Ain't around no more. Can't give nothin' back. And you won't get nothin' from me."

Samson and Kholodny exchanged glances.

"Did you buy meat from Briskin?" Samson asked cautiously.

"Meat?" she repeated, genuinely surprised, and both investigators understood that she hadn't eaten meat for a long time. Her teeth didn't look like they were up to the challenge, no matter how long the meat was boiled.

"I see. We apologise," Samson said. "Our mistake. But this is 7 Zolotoustivska, isn't it? Someone here did buy meat."

"Gotta be that one," she said, throwing back her head. "Gotta be."

"Whom do you mean?" Kholodny asked, fixing her with his eyes.

"Asmodeus – he owns the place."

"Is that his first or family name?" Kholodny asked.

She stared gloomily at her questioner, her face registering disgust, which made her look even more mad and repulsive.

"That's the name of one of Lucifer's assistants," Samson explained to Kholodny as they approached the front door. "You were a priest, weren't you? You should know that."

"It's not in the Holy Scripture, otherwise I would have remembered it," Kholodny offered in his defence. "I remember Satan and his demons, but not Asmodeus."

Samson knocked politely at first, then began to bang on the door, but no-one answered for a long time. Just as they were about to leave, and Kholodny was already beckoning to the jockey-cabby, a woman's voice sounded behind the door.

"What do you want?"

"We're with the police. Here to see the owner. You are obligated to open up," Samson, who was tired of knocking in vain, pronounced sternly.

"Go round to the other side. There's a back door."

They went round and found a nondescript wooden door, with no decorative carvings and painted the dullest brown.

"Look at that." Kholodny chuckled. "Like an old blood stain."

Samson glanced at his friend in surprise, but then the door creaked open. Before them stood a man of about forty, in light grey trousers and a white shirt. He had his stomach drawn in and his chest puffed out. It was clear from his posture that he didn't intend to let them inside.

"Did you buy meat from citizen Briskin?" Samson began.

"What kind of meat? What Briskin? Do you know where you're standing right now?" the man shot back rather sharply, but his tone was less menacing than his posture.

"This is number 7 Zolotoustivska. Citizen Briskin gave us your address and informed us that you bought pork sirloin," Samson continued, adding notes of steel to his voice.

"My cook might have bought some. So what?" the man countered with a shrug.

"We need to talk to the primary occupant," Kholodny said, scowling, and tried to take on a more belligerent look.

"So, you don't even know who lives here," laughed the man, blocking their way. "The master of the house is a person who is not obligated to answer you. He is untouchable – exempt from all duties, requisitions and divisions of living space."

"What is he, a railwayman?" Samson suddenly barked, growing angry, and the man in the white shirt changed his expression and took a cautious half-step back.

"Albert Veniaminovich won't talk to you anyway," he pronounced more carefully. "Do try to understand, it is unthinkable for a person of his rank to speak to the police about meat. The only people he sees without an appointment are men of the cloth."

"Priests, you mean?" Kholodny asked, perking up.

"Yes, holy fathers."

"Well, then, he should speak to me," Kholodny said, a smile creeping onto his face.

The man guarding the door twisted his lips and haughtily looked

Kholodny up and down, from cap to boots. His gaze settled on the leather holster hanging from the former priest's belt.

Kholodny unbuttoned the top of his leather jacket, undid the collar of his tunic and reached in, slowly pulling out into the light a heavy, thick, palm-sized silver cross on a chain. The cross was clearly not meant to be worn. It was nothing like the type a priest hangs around a baptised baby's neck.

Samson opened his mouth. The silver flashed in his eyes, and at the same moment something changed in Kholodny's face. It grew more noble, somehow, more sublimely strict.

"And now you're . . ." the man in the white shirt muttered, also unable to tear his eyes away from the cross. "You're serving with the police?"

"Wherever the good Lord directs me to serve, there I shall serve," Kholodny declaimed in a churchy baritone. "Will the master of the house see me now?"

"I'll ask. Wait here."

The door closed. A crow cawed overhead. Samson looked round. The yard had an unsightly appearance and was cut off by a wooden fence that had collapsed in two places. At the left end of the fence stood a slightly lopsided clapboard outhouse. Its door opened and out came a large woman, apparently a merchant from the Jewish Market. She straightened her skirt and set off with a rough manly step along the path towards Halytska Square.

"It they let me in, what should I ask?" Kholodny enquired, drawing Samson's attention away from the outhouse.

"Find out who he is, his family name. I suspect we'll have to send a detachment of Red Army men in order to continue the conversation in the interrogation room."

The back door opened and the man in the white shirt beckoned Kholodny inside.

"I'll wait in the cab," Samson said before his partner disappeared.

Chapter 16

"You know, this carbonated milk works wonders," Nadezhda said that evening. "My elbows don't hurt anymore."

She sat at the table with her cup of medicine. Samson himself drank tea, from time to time thoughtfully chewing his lips. The room was unusually bright, due to the city's generous supply of electricity. Soviet power really must have been gaining in strength, the young investigator concluded, glancing up at the ceiling.

"You look a bit sour today," Nadezhda said, shaking her head and smoothing down a fluffy pink sweater that wasn't new – probably a hand-me-down from her mother. "Bad day at work?"

"Not especially," Samson answered, emerging from his thoughts. He looked into her eyes lovingly, tenderly, but at the same time could not hold back a heavy sigh. "But I'm worried about Kholodny. He went into that house and never came out. I waited a whole hour, then lost my patience and returned to the station."

"Why didn't you knock again?"

"I did, I did. But they wouldn't let me in. They said I had no cross – that Kholodny was drinking and talking with the master of the house, and that he'd asked me not to wait."

"Maybe he did. After all, what could have happened to him if they knew that you were right there, waiting outside?"

"Yes," Samson agreed. "Highly unlikely that anything terrible happened. Nevertheless, he was in there drinking with a suspected buyer. A clear criminal violation of standard procedure. Did he intend to extract important evidence from this drunken palaver?"

"He probably did extract it," Nadezhda assured him before taking a sip of milk.

"I'm worried about something else," Samson continued, heaving another sigh. "We have an interrogation course in the morning. What if he overdid it and can't get out of bed? What if he forgets everything that he managed to find out?"

"Oh, *I* almost forgot," Nadezhda exclaimed, throwing up her hands. "I have a course tomorrow as well – marksmanship. They're taking us there straight from work."

"Where?"

"Somewhere in Priorka."

"I know the place," Samson replied buoyantly. "The former Society for Proper Hunting." His mind called up the sight of the beautiful, stern-looking women in uniform who had fired at the humanlike plywood targets with enviable accuracy before Kholodny and he took their turns.

The evening ended on a warm note, about twenty minutes later, when Nadezhda kissed Samson on the cheek and went off to bed. He stepped into his own bedroom, stood before the window, which revealed nothing in the darkness, and thought about Kholodny for a while. Eventually, he climbed under the covers.

In the morning, he hurried to work, waking up on the go and frequently patting the wooden holster on his right, to make sure it was still there. When he turned from Zhylianska onto Tarasivska he found himself staring directly into the sun, which at that time was almost level with the horizon. He had to squint, which made him feel childishly playful. Then, suddenly, he heard shouting, a commotion, the clatter of hooves and the rumble of wheels. He barely had time to widen his eyes and jump to the left before a cab drawn by a dun horse hurtled past. The face of the young driver was distorted with fright and seemed to be calling for help, but no-one could help him. The horse raced ahead, though the driver, having risen from his box, kept pulling at the reins with all his might and shouting, among a string of curses, commands the animal should have understood: "Whoa!" and "Stop, goddammit!" This twinned noise, which had partly swept past and partly remained in Samson's head, was then augmented by a ringing metallic note. He stopped, turned his back to the sun and, like all his fellow pedestrians, directed his gaze towards the runaway horse. It occurred to him that those who hadn't taken that particular cab were very lucky indeed, but before he could even finish that thought, a tram drove out from the direction of Halytska Square into the sunlit intersection with Mariinsko-Blagovishchenska Street and the horse slammed into its side. Samson couldn't believe his eyes: the tram seemed to vanish. It took him a moment to realise that only its red side had disappeared. The tram had overturned, and its black underside and wheels had to some extent blended into the cobblestones. The horse's piercing neighs soared over the rooftops. The din subsided, but human cries rose from the site of the collision. Pedestrians who were closer to the intersection rushed towards it, and very quickly Samson saw a crowd gather around the toppled tram, as well as the horse and, surely, the cabby lying on the cobblestones. A desire to go and see the aftermath for himself flashed through his mind. But he was too close to the police station. He was seized by a special sense of responsibility and discipline, by the magnetism of his job, which sometimes made him think of it even in the middle of the night. He hurried to the station, realising that it was much more important to appear in Nayden's office on time, before Kholodny and he were driven to Yekaterininska Street, where someone – probably a former specialist – would instruct the young investigators and other competent policemen in the art of interrogation, without which the disclosure of any crime, however simple, might prove impossible.

Up on the first floor, Samson heard a familiar voice from inside the evidence room. Surprised, he pulled the door towards himself and saw – amid the boxes, chests and clumsily made shelves piled with objects that didn't go together in ordinary life – Vasyl and

Kholodny sitting on stools at a small card table, which Samson had never noticed before. Kholodny's face was bluish, and he held a mug of tea in his hand. Both men now had their eyes on Samson, who had interrupted their conversation. Vasyl's gaze was friendly and enquiring, while Kholodny's spoke of guilt.

"Thank God," Samson exhaled. "I was afraid you hadn't made it out of there."

"I made it out, alright," Kholodny said, and shrugged. "Then the trouble started. You didn't wait for me and didn't even leave a voucher for a cab . . . It's a good thing Vasyl sleeps here," he continued, nodding towards the station's chief tea-maker. "I woke him up so that I could pay the cabby . . ."

"Well, what did you find out?" Samson asked.

"I'll tell you later. Nayden's waiting. I didn't want to show up without you."

In Nayden's office, Samson and Kholodny saw three rookie policemen, apparently selected from the Red Army soldiers seconded for arrest and guard duties. The expression on the commander's face made clear that he wasn't completely satisfied with this selection, but the tone of his voice suggested that he had made his peace with it.

"There you are," he said, turning to the two investigators. "Have you wrapped up the meat case?"

"Not yet," Samson responded. "We need two more days, not counting this one."

"Two days?" Nayden echoed. "And that will be the end of it? I have your word?"

Samson suddenly realised that he couldn't actually promise what he essentially just had promised, especially in the presence of the rookies, in whose eyes he probably looked like a seasoned professional.

"We'll do our best," he said, and tried to adopt a hard, soldierly smile.

"Alright," Nayden assented, then glanced behind Samson and Kholodny. "Vasyl, you here?"

"Here!" replied Vasyl, stepping through the half-open door.

"Get them some vouchers for the baths. When's our turn?"

"In two days, early morning. At the Halytska bathhouse, right down the street. I say we give them the vouchers right before they go, otherwise they'll lose them, or, worse, swap them for tobacco."

"You know best," Nayden agreed, and tensed up, staring behind Vasyl's back at the not fully closed door. A noise rose behind it – the clatter of feet – growing louder and louder with each moment, like an avalanche of stones rolling along the wooden floor towards the office.

The door swung open with force, and someone resolutely shoved aside Vasyl, who had just managed to look behind him. A loud gasp for breath escaped the mouth of a tall Red Army soldier. His chest heaved rapidly under his tunic.

"What happened?" Nayden exclaimed.

"Accident . . . many killed . . . need police . . ." the soldier got out through his gasps, and, half turning round, he pointed back with his hand. "Tram," he added, regaining control of his breathing. "Turned over at the corner of Tarasivska and Mariinsko-Blagovishchenska."

"Down the stairs, go, go," Nayden commanded, and he began to push the hesitant rookies towards the door. "On the double!"

There was a truck with blue wooden sides parked in front of the station, with a driver in military uniform behind the wheel.

When the entire station had emptied out into the street, Nayden rushed over to the truck.

"Down to the intersection, quick!" he shouted to the driver, indicating the way. "An overturned tram – many dead and injured – get the survivors to any hospital that can take them."

The driver lowered his window. "What are you shouting about?" he asked.

"I order you to drive down there, immediately!" Nayden barked. "There's been a crash – many injured!"

"I'm not obligated to take your orders," the driver responded in an astoundingly cool manner. "I've come to pick up policemen scheduled for a course in interrogation."

Nayden obviously wanted to swear, very loudly and profanely, but, with a huge effort of will, he restrained himself. Instead, he spat under the truck, turned round and set off running down the street after the rest of the soldiers and policemen.

Samson was struck by the size of the crowd surrounding the overturned tram. It had been a long time since he'd seen so many people huddled together so tightly in one place.

"Disperse, everyone! Disperse!" Nayden shouted, but almost no-one paid any attention to him. Then he fired his revolver into the air. The crowd, which hadn't expected a gunshot, began to scatter, disintegrate. Cracks formed in it – slim passageways – and these slowly widened, expanded.

"Disperse, everyone! Disperse!" Nayden kept shouting to the people hesitating near the site of the accident. He was almost hoarse, gazing around with despair in his eyes.

Samson spotted several dead citizens on the cobblestones near the tram. Caring pedestrians had already folded these people's hands over their chests, so that the nurses and everyone else could easily see that nothing in life would disturb them any longer. An injured old man sat on the side of the road, moaning. Next to him lay a stuffed sack, its neck tied with a rope, and the man held the knot tightly with one hand, so that his possessions wouldn't be stolen. A woman squatted beside him, either comforting him or propping him up.

"Kolechko! Kholodny!" called Nayden, looking around in all directions.

Both investigators rushed up to him.

"Stop anyone you see with a cart – force them to pick up the bodies and take them to the nearest morgue. Which one is that? The one on Fundukleev Street?" Nayden asked.

"They're full," Kholodny stated confidently. "A friend of mine told me yesterday. They refused to accept his grandmother. He had to take her to the morgue at the Oleksandrivska Hospital."

"Send them there, then," said Nayden. "See those? Stop them! Go!" he commanded, pointing at two carts that had entered the intersection from the left.

"Hey, you, there! Stop!" Kholodny shouted as he made his way towards the carts.

He ran slowly, heavily. Samson felt sorry for him and set off in pursuit, to help.

Both the drivers were villagers from near Kyiv. They were frightened of the policemen, and for this reason seemed not to listen very carefully to what they were told about compensation. The rookies helped Samson and Nayden load the bodies onto the carts: three on one, four on the other.

"You mean you ain't comin' with us?" one of the drivers asked.

"No, we have to attend a course. Take the bodies to the morgue, get a receipt from the orderly, then take it up there, to the station. Ask the officer on duty for Vasyl. Hand him the receipt and the vouchers, and he'll give you the money," Samson explained.

Three young women with first-aid kits ran up to the injured, whom Samson and Kholodny had not managed to count. Samson didn't care who had summoned these aid-givers or how. Nayden left one rookie at the site of the accident to interview witnesses and record in detail what had occurred, ordering the rest to return to the station. Those assigned to the interrogation course were to board the truck without delay.

As they were heading back up Tarasivska, two men – obviously journalists – came running towards them with heavy wooden photo-cameras in their hands.

"This will be all over the papers tomorrow," Kholodny pronounced, following them with his eyes.

The driver took them to Yekaterininska, to a building next to the Cheka headquarters. He handed them over to the soldier on duty, who escorted all five of them up to the first floor and led them into a hall that looked like a theatre, containing red chairs and a stage. A military man of short stature, wearing spectacles with round lenses, was speaking from the stage. Catching sight of the latecomers, he abruptly interrupted his remarks and gestured towards some empty seats.

Samson noticed that the other participants, who looked back at them, all had notebooks on their knees and were taking down in pencil whatever the lecturer said. He realised that he hadn't brought anything to write on, or with. But then another military man ran up and handed each of the newcomers a notebook and a very short pencil. Kholodny and Samson sat down next to each other, and the rookies hurriedly crashed into the neighbouring chairs, so that the whole team from the Lybid station was grouped together.

Samson examined his stubby writing implement, concluding that it was actually just a third or even a quarter of a real pencil, which had been neatly sawn off and sharpened.

"Order!" the lecturer roared. "Let's continue, comrades. I'll briefly summarise what we've covered for the latecomers: a proper interrogation is carried out by means of the exertion of psychological and physical pressure upon the suspect, in order to obtain from said suspect the operational information and evidence required by the investigator. The subject of your attention, and therefore of the pressure you apply, should be not only the detainee, but also those witnesses who provide testimony that serves to shield or to exonerate the detainee."

"Can you explain that a little?" someone from the second row called softly.

"Explain it a little?" the lecturer echoed ironically. "Let me reiterate: you are to write down everything I say, and to reread it before going to bed until you understand. You are here to learn. To learn means to become more intelligent – in your case, to become more intelligent and more experienced. So, write! The subject of your attention, and therefore of the pressure you apply . . ."

Samson wrote quickly, at the same time thinking over what he had heard. He also felt joy come alive in his mind – a joy independent of his thoughts – like a little flame. It lit the way towards new knowledge. His spirits rose, as if he were a student again. Back then, he had had his freedom and his studies, and one did not interfere with the other, because they were in fact interconnected: he had been free to choose what to study.

He recalled his friends and comrades from those days. Why hadn't he seen any of them in the last month? Not even by chance. It used to be that he couldn't step out onto Khreshchatyk or into Nikolaevsky Park near the university without bumping into someone he knew.

"Now, put down your pencils and listen," the lecturer said, distracting Samson from his thoughts. "The psychological pressure you exert on the detainee determines the success or failure of the interrogation. As soon as you start flashing smiles at them, flattering them, they grow bold, and you won't get anything out of them. Therefore, the first thing you must do before starting the actual interrogation is to instill fear and uncertainty in the detainee. How does one go about this? Simple. You have to be rude, but not excessively rude. Always keep your distance. Detainees are the enemies of our ideas, the enemies of our future, the enemies of the order we have established, and they are therefore your personal enemies. If the person in front of you is a man, immediately order him to empty his pockets and to place the contents on the table. Take away his tobacco, pipe or cigarettes. Take away the photos of his loved ones, along with everything related to his family – letters, lockets with portraits. Hide the tobacco, pipe or cigarettes in a drawer or somewhere else. Move the photos or objects reminding the suspect of his loved ones and relatives away from him, but make sure he can still see them. Understand?"

The participants, Samson and Kholodny among them, nodded in unison.

"Write down what was said in your own words, briefly. Then we'll continue," the lecturer commanded.

Samson wrote, and what he wrote reminded him that he still had no photograph of Nadezhda. Several times, he had thought of asking her to go to a photographic studio with him. Many studios were cropping up these days, turning out photos of Red Army soldiers and Soviet employees.

"Done? Moving on," the hard voice sounded again, with its undertone of ringing metal. "After you've taken the steps I've just outlined, do not start posing questions. No. There is no need to hurry. Instead, take out your cigarettes, light one and stare at the detainee in silence, stonily, for as long as possible. You could even finish one cigarette and light another. When the detainee grows visibly more nervous, lean towards him and blow a cloud of smoke in his face. You need to learn to do this expressively, at just the right moment. Let's devote some attention to it. Take out your cigarettes."

The participants reached into their pockets. The hall resounded with the rustle of cardboard packs and the clicking of cigarette cases.

"Light up!" the lecturer ordered.

Not every participant had matches, but almost every second one did. Those who had come equipped struck theirs, throwing up little flames, and shared the fire with those in need.

Samson turned to Kholodny, who had taken out a pack of Joy cigarettes.

"But I don't smoke," Samson whispered.

"Apparently," Kholodny replied in a lower whisper, indicating the lecturer with a glance, "that isn't an option here. Take one."

Samson pulled out a cigarette. Kholodny shared his flame after lighting up himself.

"Get them going good," the lecturer ordered.

Samson coughed and immediately caught the lecturer's eye.

"Are there non-smokers in attendance?" the lecturer asked.

Samson raised his left hand, since he held the cigarette in his right.

"You'll have to learn. After all, you're no lady," the lecturer said to him directly, adopting the voice of a caring mentor.

Samson nodded and immediately drew in another deep puff.

He managed to restrain the cough that threatened to escape his throat.

"On to the key step," the lecturer continued. "After you've lit your cigarette, inhale as much smoke as possible . . . Done? Good. Now, imagine that a detainee is seated in front of you. Blow."

A cloud of dove-grey smoke rose over the red chairs. Someone coughed.

"Now, turn to the person sitting next to you. Blow smoke into their face and let them do the same. You must understand what a person feels when smoke is blown into their eyes."

"Me first," Kholodny warned.

Samson faced his comrade and squinted.

"If the person undergoing interrogation closes his eyes, you must order him to open them," the lecturer continued.

Chapter 17

The flavour of pearl barley struck Samson as strange and not especially pleasant, but hot porridge never tastes truly bad.

"What's this gravy?" he asked Nadezhda.

The light above them shone brightly again. Outside the window reigned the evening of a tense day. Perhaps this tension had been universal, draining the strength not only from the city of Kyiv and its inhabitants, but also from the sky and the air. Hence the darker than usual darkness – but then, the flow of electricity was now more intense than usual. If the lamp shone bright, then there was clearly enough firewood at the power plants, and if that was the case, then the societal panic of winter was over, along with the theft of wood – at least until autumn, when the weather would again turn cold.

"My co-worker Masha taught me," Nadezhda confessed, scooping up the remnants of barley from the bottom of her plate with a silver spoon. "It's herring. When the fish is past its prime – I mean, out of the barrel for a week or so – you just mash it up, sprinkle in some pea flour and cover it in boiling water. Let it brew for two days on the windowsill, then strain it through a cheesecloth, to get the bones out."

"Herring?" Samson echoed in surprise, searching his tongue for the taste of the fish. "Couldn't have guessed that," he declared, shaking his head. "I thought it was fermented offal. And where did you get the pea flour?"

"Don't you wonder where I got the herring?" Nadezhda asked with a smile. "At work – both the herring and the flour. They gave us an entire pound of the latter! A special ration, separate from the regular one, which we'll receive tomorrow."

Samson licked his lips when he heard "ration", and at that very moment he finally detected the taste of herring, softened by peas.

"And why haven't you asked about the marksmanship course?" Nadezhda continued, changing the subject but retaining her smile. "Aren't you the least bit interested?"

"Of course I am!" Samson blurted out anxiously. "Of course! Well, how did it go?"

"According to the instructor, superbly well!" Nadezhda boasted.

"What weapon did you use?"

"A revolver! And you know, he told me he'd never seen anyone aim so gracefully."

"He must have been sweet on you," Samson objected.

"Perhaps – still, I never missed."

"Well, maybe that's why he was sweet," Samson backtracked. "I would have much rather gone shooting myself, instead of taking that interrogation course. I'm not a smoker, you know, but now I have to learn how to blow smoke in people's faces . . ."

"What do you mean?" Nadezhda asked, bringing the last spoonful of barley to her mouth.

"Just that – cigarette smoke. I had to light up. Turns out it's an important part of preparing a detainee for interrogation."

"What did you smoke?"

"Kholodny brought cigarettes and let me have one."

"We were given a lecture after the shooting exercise," Nadezhda said, perking up at the memory. "About the future! Very interesting stuff. This writer-planner from St Petersburg told us that it was only possible to change one's attitude towards labour by changing one's way of life, which includes where and how one lives and eats. In future houses and flats, there will be no kitchens – no-one will spend creative time on cooking. Meals will be organised by the authorities, through Soviet cafeterias, of which many more will be established – one in each residential building. And we'll be issued meal vouchers at work—"

"I already have some! Look," Samson cut in, reaching into his trouser pocket and pulling out three stamped vouchers, each of which bore the words *One Lunch*.

"But those are only for lunch," Nadezhda responded condescendingly. "And only for those in the first category. I don't receive them. What about breakfast? Dinner? This?" she asked, nodding at the two already-empty plates from her parents' dinner set, with their blue borders and small blue watermills.

"Don't get me wrong, I'm all for the cafeterias. But breakfast, lunch, dinner – it adds up to a lot of walking," he explained.

"But what if it's close to home? Or inside the building, right downstairs?" Nadezhda asked.

Samson nodded. Concluding that they had exhausted the topic of food, he yawned, covering his mouth with his hand.

"I don't know," he began again, somewhat anxiously. "On the way over to the lecture, the fresh recruits from the Red Army were whispering about Hetman Hryhoriv's gangs. They spoke of piracy, of Soviet personnel being killed in the villages. The impression I have is that there's one sort of life here in Kyiv, with electricity," he said, glancing up at the lamp, "and an entirely different life outside the city limits – no electricity, no order. So, I think we ought to build cafeterias in the villages first, to feed the peasants. Maybe then they wouldn't be so eager to join gangs, wouldn't eye us in Kyiv with such suspicion."

As he uttered these last words, Samson's anxiety was transmitted to Nadezhda, who sighed heavily and grew more serious.

"We have two more days of lessons before the end of the month," she said softly. All enthusiasm seemed to have vanished from her voice, but this may have been merely a sign of fatigue after an eventful day.

"Same with us," Samson replied, but then immediately corrected himself, so that she wouldn't misunderstand. "Three more lessons in interrogation, I mean. Did you have your carbonated milk yet?"

"Oh, I forgot," Nadezhda confessed. She rose to her feet and went into the kitchen.

Samson followed her, holding their plates, which he would rinse in a bowl of water, dry and put away in the cupboard.

The following morning at the station began with an argument. Kholodny entered the office some time after Samson, took off his brown leather jacket and hung it on the coat stand. Then he pulled a small booklet, no thicker than a pinkie finger, from one of the jacket's pockets.

Samson pushed the open meat-speculation case file to his left and raised a doubtful gaze at his comrade. That gaze followed Kholodny across the office, and, when the latter sat down at his own desk, the investigators' eyes met. Kholodny looked guilty.

"Sssergius," Samson began, deliberately drawing out the first syllable. "You still haven't written out the testimony of the meat buyer at 7 Zolotoustivska Street, whom you questioned without me."

"But he and I didn't touch on meat," Kholodny breathed out with a shrug.

"You mean you didn't even ask him about meat – or about Briskin?" Samson enquired angrily.

"Of course I did. But he'd never heard of Briskin, and he himself never buys meat."

"Well, then, write everything down in detail. The whole conversation. Your impressions of him. Is he the type to lie, or does he strike you as honest?"

Kholodny grimaced, as if there were a bitter taste in his mouth. It was clear that he didn't wish to comply.

"He's honest," the former priest averred. "And he's certainly not the type to lie."

“Nayden ordered us to wrap up the case, and you see how thin it is?” Samson asked, indicating the open file with a glance.

“A thin slice of meat is better than none,” Kholodny quipped, trying to joke his way out of trouble.

“We need to issue a verdict and sentence tomorrow, or, at the latest, the day after tomorrow,” Samson said, still more cantankerously. “And there are only eight sheets of paper in here.”

Kholodny thought for a while, scratching his plump right cheek. He looked back at the map of Kyiv behind him, then turned his gaze to the diagram of pork cuts between the windows. Suddenly, his eyes lit up.

“Say, why don’t we take that thing down, fold it six or eight times and stick it in the file? That would thicken it right up! Nayden will be pleased.”

“Nayden will pull out the diagram and there’ll hardly be anything left,” Samson objected. “Go on and write, will you? The more the better.”

The former priest frowned, heaved a sigh, took a sheet of paper from his desk drawer, moved his inkwell and pen closer and asked, “So, what should I write?”

“Everything, from the very beginning – from the moment we arrived. How they wouldn’t let us in at first, and then how they let you in by yourself.”

“Even about the cross?” Kholodny asked, a ring of fear in his voice.

“Certainly – how could you leave that out?” Samson shot back, but then he reflected on the matter for a moment. “You could put it like this: ‘Having learned that I was formerly a clergyman, they allowed me to enter the premises.’”

“Perfect!” Kholodny exclaimed.

He lifted the pen, held it aloft until its excess ink dripped back into the inkwell, and then, after bringing it down to the paper, picked up the pinkie-thick booklet with his left hand and extended it to Samson.

"Here, enjoy. A gift from that very Albert Veniaminovich, by the way – 'a body-warming album of pleasures', he called it."

Samson had to leave his desk in order to free Kholodny's left hand and give him the opportunity to concentrate on his writing.

While Kholodny's pen squeaked across the paper, Samson slowly leafed through the book, which turned out to be a photo album containing images of lovely half-naked ladies in hats. The women were seated in seductive poses, their bare breasts apparently brimming with desire. The hats gave them a coquettish look, while their long skirts hinted at the fact that, in ordinary life, they pretended to be paragons of chastity and decency. One of the ladies, it seemed to Samson, bore a resemblance to Nadezhda. He shuddered, brought the album closer to his face, then noticed that Kholodny, whose pen kept squeaking, was glancing at him from beneath his brows and grinning. Samson put down the booklet and nervously slammed it shut.

It couldn't be her, he thought, then looked at his colleague and asked, "Well, did you get a lot down?"

"I'm still at it," Kholodny muttered, without taking his eyes off the paper. "The conversation was long, and he treated me to food."

"Yes, make sure to describe that in detail." Samson raised his right hand, as if he wanted to wave or make some other gesture. Then he lowered it awkwardly and added, in a softer tone, "Especially if it was meat."

Kholodny nodded, his eyes still on the paper, which was already nearly full.

The door to the office swung open as if from a strong gust of wind. Nayden came in, clutching a sheaf of papers of various sizes, all covered with writing.

"Busy?" he asked, looking first at Kholodny, then shifting his gaze to Samson.

"Yes, closing the meat case," Samson responded.

"That's what I like to hear. Reports of new crimes are nipping at us on all sides, like bedbugs in the barracks," Nayden added in an entirely friendly tone. "I'd put two more desks in here, but we don't have any. It would be nice to plant two amateurs at your sides, so they could learn how it's done." He chuckled.

"We ourselves are only learning," Samson replied in confusion. "Look how long this case has taken us."

"Such are the times," Nayden sighed. "Apprentices teaching apprentices. We'll issue the verdict on the meat case tomorrow, then? And you'll move on? We get dozens of new cases every day, you know," he added, shaking the papers in his hands.

"No, not tomorrow," Samson said cautiously, and he gazed at Kholodny in search of support.

"We need two more days. Some witnesses have turned up, real characters," Kholodny chimed in, nodding at the scribbled sheet of paper in front of him.

"Is that so?" Nayden asked, perking up. "Bring that to my office later. I'd like to give it a read."

"The whole file?" Samson asked fearfully.

"Just the interesting part," Nayden responded, jabbing a finger at Kholodny. "And don't forget about the bathhouse – day after tomorrow, five in the morning."

"Why?" Samson asked, befuddled. "Did something happen there?"

Nayden laughed. "Our station's turn to wash up. Did you forget?"

Kholodny and Samson nodded guiltily.

"Well, now you'll remember."

The door closed, leaving Kholodny and Samson alone in the office. The former priest turned over the sheet in front of him and his pen began to squeak again.

*

At lunchtime, they walked to the Soviet cafeteria at the corner of Karavaevska and Nazarivska streets. Kholodny had already sampled their offerings a number of times, but this was the first time that Samson had decided to accompany him.

The cook-dispenser took their meal vouchers and examined them in the light, moistening a finger with her tongue and running it over the stamps.

"What are you doing that for?" Samson asked, taken aback. "You can see that we're armed and in uniform."

"Anyone can buy a uniform," she answered, nevertheless casting a respectful glance at their holster belts. "And we've been getting as many as ten forged vouchers a day. My chief hauls me over the coals for accepting them . . ."

Reassured, she lowered the vouchers onto a spike that stuck out of a wooden stand, then served each policeman a bowl of oatmeal soup and a plate that held a small heap of pearl barley covered with a brownish liquid.

"No meat today?" Kholodny asked, frowning.

"Only fat. We haven't had a meat delivery in two days," she replied.

"Where's the fat, then?" Kholodny asked, scrutinising the barley.

"In the gravy. It's rendered."

"Ah," Kholodny said, and nodded.

The choice of tables wasn't great, but it was varied: no two were the same. And the smell in the air was strange, not so much gastronomical as mechanical.

As the tables by the windows were occupied, they sat down next to a blank wall.

Samson sniffed loudly.

"This used to be a printing house," Kholodny said, having guessed the cause of his comrade's confusion, then he immediately dipped his spoon into the soup. "No good without meat," he pronounced after ingesting two spoonfuls, squinting at the barley.

"Indeed," said Samson. "It seems Abyazov was right. Speculation in meat is a serious crime, and the decree wasn't in vain . . ."

"It leads to the starvation of the working class, the army and the police," Kholodny added.

"Did you finish the report on 7 Zolotoustivska?" Samson asked, looking up at his soup-slurping comrade.

"I most certainly did – three sheets, front and back," Kholodny responded proudly.

"What's the gist of it? The main point?"

"Read it and see for yourself. I didn't write all those words for nothing, did I?"

"Then what's the main thrust of what you left out?"

Kholodny reflected for a moment.

"Probably the fact that this Albert Veniaminovich is about to be appointed to the position of consul. By the way, what kind of position is that – consul?"

"A diplomatic one," Samson explained. "A consul is a representative of his country abroad. So, he's going abroad? To handle foreign affairs?"

Kholodny finished chewing another spoonful of the thick soup, thought a while and then shook his head.

"No, he's staying. He showed me the hall where he'll be hosting consular receptions – with champagne – and promised to invite me, but only if I come dressed as a priest. Took my address and everything. Said the invitations would be sent by courier."

"So, he'll serve as a foreign consul? Of which nation?"

Kholodny sank into thought again.

"He said he's deciding between India and Argentina. But, in all honesty, I didn't quite know what he meant," the former priest admitted. "Or even understand at all . . ."

Samson chuckled and started on the barley.

"I'll read it later," he said, almost without opening his mouth. "Once we're done here, let's ride over to Sophia Square, where some citizen named Nikolay bought eight pounds of sirloin. We'll take his testimony, and that will leave us with exactly two days of work to do."

"I mean, if we believe that Briskin told us the whole story."

"I think he did," Samson countered. "He even provided the name of the former – or perhaps the current – object of his affection, a certain Shura, emphasising that he gave her the meat for next to nothing . . ."

"The bastard!" Kholodny exclaimed.

Samson looked up at his comrade in surprise.

"He could have given it to her for free," Kholodny elaborated. "What kind of person asks a loved one to pay for meat?"

Samson breathed a sigh of relief. He'd feared that Kholodny had called Briskin a bastard for having given up his beloved to the police.

Chapter 18

On returning home in the evening, Samson spotted in the hallway a pair of dirty men's shoes next to Nadezhda's, as well as an unfamiliar yellow leather bag. A wave of anxiety led him to unfasten the cover of his holster. He walked as quietly as he could towards the door to the living room. Luckily, it was slightly ajar, and through the crack he saw Nadezhda sitting at the table. Opposite her, with his back turned to the hallway, sat a man he could not identify. Boldly, with loud step, he entered the living room. The man at the table turned at the sound. It was, to Samson's great surprise, Dr Vatrukhin.

"Nikolay Nikolaevich! To what do we owe the pleasure?"

"I came to pay my respects," said the doctor. "After all, I shouldn't be the only person in town expected to receive people all the time – someone ought to receive me for a change."

Samson shook the doctor's hand and smiled at Nadezhda, then took a chair from the table and carried it to the corner of the room closest to the hallway. He sat down, removed his boots and footwraps, and took off his holster belt and jacket. Leaving everything on the chair, he walked into the kitchen, soaked a rag in a bucket of water, wiped his sweaty feet, dried them off and slipped them into a pair of slippers.

While he was tending to his feet, Nadezhda went into the kitchen and took a cup from the cupboard.

"I must ask for your help," admitted the doctor, when Samson, in domestic attire, sat down beside him and took a sip of freshly poured tea. "They're trying to conscript me."

"Which front?" Samson asked cautiously, conscious of the fact that the Red Army was now fighting all over Ukraine – here against Denikin, there against Petliura, elsewhere against Hetman Skoropadskyi.

"Moscow."

"But there's no front in Moscow," Samson replied in bewilderment.

"They don't need me at the front. Not long ago, a lad from the Provincial Bureau of Statistics showed up at my door, accompanied by a Red Army soldier. He wanted to ascertain whether I was indeed a doctor. Earlier, you know, I had identified myself as a doctor to the census-taker. Then, they came again and said that I was to report for duty on 24 April. Doctors and medical workers are being mobilised. The wounded and sick from all fronts are brought to Moscow, you see, but there's no-one there to treat them . . ."

"You ought to go and treat them, then," Samson said, throwing a somewhat disapproving glance at the doctor. "And come back when you're done."

"Samson, are you really still blind to reality?" Vatrukhin asked indignantly. "Am I to leave my wife? And my flat, which someone will no doubt occupy straight away? And am I to travel – who knows how – across three or four front lines? Do you actually believe that it's possible to get to Moscow, these days?"

"If the authorities have declared mobilisation, then surely they've made the necessary arrangements," Samson objected, though he sounded anything but sure. "I understand, of course, that it would be difficult . . ."

"Do you know that these military comrades believe that an eye doctor can inflate a gouged eye and insert it back into its socket? And if he doesn't do it, then he must be a counter-revolutionary? Up against the wall with him! Do you know that?"

Vatrukhin grew so agitated that his face turned red. Samson noticed that his fingers were trembling.

"Yes, I remember." Samson nodded and extended his hand, gesturing for his guest to calm down. "I remember when the Red Army men robbed you for medical purposes, making off with the artificial eye."

"Oh, I have something to go with the tea!" Nadezhda exclaimed a little too brightly, clearly aiming to defuse the tension. She hurried out and returned with three little pies on a dish. "I went past the Jewish Market today. They were too cheap to resist!"

At the sight of the pies, Vatrukhin seemed to go limp, placing his hands on the table and bowing his head.

"Help yourself," Samson directed, indicating the dish with a glance. "I'll think about how I might help," he added, then immediately bit his lip, regretting the promise.

The doctor reached for a pie. His fingers still trembled in the air, but when they grasped the food, the tremor vanished.

"Stuffed with meat," Nadezhda said, nodding at the pies, while straightening her pink blouse and pulling it down.

Samson, suddenly feeling quite hungry, also reached for a pie. His tongue detected the taste of intestines and rotten onions, yet, despite this less than exquisite combination, he was glad to have the food in his mouth. He chewed the pie thoroughly, longer than usual, as if he were reluctant to part with it – to dispatch it into those depths of the body that were unable to distinguish between sweetness and bitterness.

A painful silence settled over the table. Nadezhda yawned. All the tea had been drunk.

"Now, I have nowhere to go." Vatrukhin sighed in utter defeat, gazing at Samson like a caged bear.

The look disturbed the young investigator.

"Where is your wife? Dunya?" he asked, anticipating, with barely concealed trepidation, a tragic response.

"I sent her off to Fastiv, for the time being. She has a cousin there. After all, it isn't her fault that I'm a doctor."

"Stay with us, then," Samson whispered. "We'll think of something."

"I won't overstay my welcome, I promise. As soon as the mobilisation is completed, I'll go home," Vatrukhin said, tears glinting in his eyes. "Unless my flat is requisitioned in the meantime."

"Don't worry," Samson assured him, glancing at the sideboard that concealed the door to his late sister Verusya's room. "We have the space. As for food . . ."

"I have a ration card, fourth category, and can go to get food any time," the doctor babbled defensively.

"How can you go when you're hiding out?" Samson asked, adopting the gaze of a policeman. For a moment, he imagined Vatrukhin as a detainee. He even saw himself blowing smoke in the doctor's face. "Besides, those in the fourth category hardly receive a thing."

"That's not true," the doctor responded, sounding confused. "I've been given barley groats, soap . . ."

"Are you a smoker?" Samson asked all of a sudden.

"No, but I have cigarettes. Do you smoke?"

"No, but I'm supposed to start," the young man answered sadly.

The doctor pulled out a pack of cigarettes from his jacket pocket and held them out.

"I'll just take one," Samson said, reaching for the pack.

"Take the whole thing. I have more at home. Wouldn't want to be caught empty-handed by a soldier or one of the desperate characters at the Jewish Market. All you hear down there is, 'Gimme a cig.' Really grates on the ear." Noticing Samson shudder at that, Vatrukhin glanced at the intact left ear his host had directed towards him. "Forgive me. A poor choice of words."

The next morning, when the previously concealed door to his deceased sister's room creaked open, Samson turned round in fright and nearly choked on his tea. The doctor's face spoke of insomnia and guilt.

"I'm sorry to ask," he began, hoarsely. "But may I wash my face with your water?"

Samson, already dressed, led the doctor to the bathroom, but on hearing the sounds of Nadezhda freshening up inside, asked the guest to wait. He also explained to him that he should use the water in the basin first, then check the tap. If it worked, then he should refill the basin to the brim.

"I know," Vatrukhin nodded. "It's the same at my place. I used to take baths, but now there's never enough water. Three buckets' worth at most."

Samson and Nadezhda left the flat together, and the doctor saw them off with a smile and a slightly ingratiating look, like a servant or housekeeper.

"I'll stay right here," he assured them in a gentle tone. "You can trust me to keep an eye on things."

Samson arrived at the station long before Kholodny. He removed the mastic seal from the door and sat down at his father's desk to pore over his comrade's report on his meeting with the mysterious consul living at 7 Zolotoustivska. The only mention of meat was at the very end: *He doesn't know where his cook buys her meat. He gives her money for grub, but she decides what to plump for on her own. The only thing he cares about is that his uninvited guests have enough vittles to cram down their gullets.*

Strange, thought Samson. If Kholodny had taken down the man's actual living words, then this consul-to-be didn't sound well bred or wealthy. "Grub", "vittles" – these were terms used by those who hadn't finished secondary school. But if this Albert Veniaminovich was really going to be named a consul, then he would have graduated not only from high school, but from a university.

The door swung open so forcefully that the resulting gust sent two pages of the report flying from the desk onto the floor.

The young investigator had never seen Nayden look so sullen.

"My office, now!" the commander barked, and instead of leaving the door open, to make things easier, he slammed it shut with such a bang that a gust again struck Samson's face.

Vasyl was already standing in Nayden's office, looking confused and gloomy. Nayden, who had just collapsed into his chair, cast an angry glance at the old man – apparently not for the first time that morning. To his surprise, Samson saw Kholodny sitting in a chair against the wall. He, too, seemed dispirited, and hadn't taken off his jacket. Nayden must have intercepted him on the stairs.

"Present, as you requested," Samson said. "Is this about the meat case?"

"To hell with meat!" Nayden shouted.

Kholodny shuddered. Vasyl didn't stir. Samson didn't even have time to be afraid.

"This is the third theft from my office in two months." Nayden had switched to a muffled tone, as if he didn't want anyone outside to overhear. "One – my pocket watch from the desk. Two – the undershirt I slept in at the station. And tonight, while I was asleep right here, the tea mug that had accompanied me on three front lines. Explain," he said, again fixing Vasyl with a piercing gaze.

"Well, I can't keep track of everything, can I?" the old man stammered. "Someone's always stealing clothes from the evidence room, too. Though, now that it's warmer, they've slowed down a bit."

"And what about you?" Nayden asked, his gaze moving first to Kholodny, then resting on Samson. "Do they steal from you?"

Samson's breathing grew rapid, heavy. He threw a nervous glance at Vasyl, but the old man didn't notice.

"The suit. That disappeared," Samson admitted. "And then the silver bone – from my desk."

Nayden's look was withering.

"They took silver," he exhaled, then turned to Kholodny. "How about you? What did they take?"

"Nothing," the former priest said with a shrug. He seemed discomforted to be answering in the negative. "I have nothing worth stealing . . ."

"Nothing worth stealing," Nayden repeated, then heaved a sigh. "Then I'm putting you in charge of this mess. Open a case – but no date, no number. Let's find the bastards and teach them a lesson ourselves, without any verdicts. The shame of it all! Thefts at a police station . . . Gather evidence and collect statements from the victims," the commander ordered, pointing first at Samson, then at Vasyl, and then at his own chest. "I want a quick investigation. Understood?"

Back in their own office, Samson looked incredulously at Kholodny.

"Are you sure no-one stole anything from you? What about the leather jacket?"

Kholodny gave his stubbly cheek a scratch and grimaced at an unpleasant thought.

"Yes," he sighed. "But I couldn't . . . I just couldn't confess . . . What if he asked me why I hadn't reported it earlier?"

"I hadn't reported my thefts either," said Samson, who also felt uncomfortable. "And neither had Nayden, before someone took his mug. No-one said anything."

"Right . . . And now I've got to go sniffing around for all these mugs and silver bones?"

"I don't think you'll track them down too quickly. Let's wrap up the meat affair first," Samson said, giving his comrade a firm, convincing look. "If the thieves are here at the station, they're not going anywhere. Whereas Nayden will come knocking in an hour or two, asking about the meat case."

"Alright, but will you lend me a hand with the thefts later?" Kholodny asked.

"Of course. We'll crack the meat case, then catch our thief."

"A smoke first?" Kholodny suggested.

"Without a detainee?" Samson asked in surprise.

"Yes, just a smoke for its own sake." Kholodny took a cigarette case from his pocket, opened it with a click and walked over to Samson's desk.

Samson took a cigarette and his gaze fell, perhaps by chance, perhaps not, on Kholodny's report.

"Wait a minute," he said, noticing the box of matches in his comrade's hand.

He rose, went out into the corridor and ordered the soldier on duty to bring up Moses Briskin.

While the order was being carried out, Samson rearranged the chairs in the office, placing one with its back against the wall, directly under the diagram of pork cuts, and the two others, pulled out from behind the desks, opposite the first.

Soon, the Red Army man shoved Briskin through the door. The detainee looked pale, unhealthy. He had a cough.

"Have a seat," Samson said, pointing to the chair by the wall, then he looked at the detainee more closely. "You haven't caught consumption, have you?"

"No, no, I'm fit as a fiddle!" Briskin hastened to answer. "It's just the eggs. My daughter brought more this morning and I had to eat them fast again, shell and all. Scratched my throat."

"Are the other detainees still determined to take them away from you?" the young investigator asked sympathetically.

Briskin shook his head. "No, one of the soldiers . . . Impudent fellow. He steals from the packages meant for detainees. Sometimes, he even decides what to keep for himself right in front of your eyes."

Samson and Kholodny exchanged glances.

"Point him out to us later," Samson said. "Now, sit down. Do you have cigarettes?" he asked sternly.

"No. I quit smoking."

"Photos of loved ones?" Kholodny demanded.

The detainee reluctantly reached into the inside pocket of his jacket, retrieved a stuffed envelope and held it out.

Samson extracted three thick cards: the detainee's daughter in a sundress, an oval portrait of his late wife, and the detainee with the wife on a sofa, beside a palm tree planted in a wine barrel.

Having reinserted the photo-cards, Samson tapped the envelope on his leg, then turned and threw it onto his desk.

"Number 7 Zolotoustivska," he began, staring into Briskin's eyes. "The residence of Albert Veniaminovich. He told us it was his cook who bought the meat from you, not him personally. Is that true?"

"I don't know any Albert," the detainee responded. "There was a cook, yes, and another man, probably a servant."

"Short and skinny?" Kholodny asked.

Briskin nodded.

"Let's go over the list one more time," Samson said, turning round and picking up the case file from the edge of his desk. He drew out the list of buyers copied down from the diagram and supplemented by the detainee in his own hand.

A match flared. Kholodny lit his cigarette, then extended it to Samson. Clumsily, Samson used his comrade's cigarette to light his own, which he held in the fingers of his left hand. Then he took a puff and exhaled a cloud of smoke into the detainee's face. Kholodny followed suit.

Briskin leaned back, pressing his head against the wall. There was fear in his eyes.

"I told you everything I knew," he sputtered. "I'm not hiding anyone – I even gave you Shura!" At this, tears sparkled in his eyes. "I can't take this anymore . . . My feet are freezing . . ."

"Alright, alright," Samson interrupted, trying to calm him. He handed his cigarette to Kholodny to free his hand. "Let's just go over the list."

Briskin's memory proved excellent. Each time Samson read him the name or address of a buyer, the detainee immediately identified the part of the carcass purchased and its weight. Before long, they reached the final entry on the list, but Samson didn't utter Shura's name, fearing that it might once again trigger an attack of nerves and tears.

"What about the photo-cards?" Briskin asked. "Will I get them back?"

Samson considered the question.

Here, Kholodny gestured subtly at the door and his comrade understood his meaning. They stepped out of the office.

"Let's send for a photographer," Kholodny suggested excitedly. "He'll take snapshots of Briskin's face, front and side views, and we'll stick them in the case file. That ought to plump it up!"

Samson liked the idea. He found Vasyl and asked him to take a cart to Khreshchatyk and find a photographer at one of the studios. Vasyl seemed to rejoice at the opportunity to get some fresh air. A smile appeared on his thin, moustachioed face.

"At your service," he pronounced precisely, tensely, and he hurried down the stairs towards the entrance.

Returning to the office, Samson found Briskin examining the diagram.

"Do you recall something else?" he said, addressing the detainee's back.

Briskin turned round and confessed, "No, I'm just hungry."

At these words, Kholodny licked his lips, pulled out a round watch from his trouser pocket, flicked open its lid and checked the time.

Chapter 19

Samson didn't sleep well that night. One might even have said that he didn't sleep at all, if it weren't for those brief periods – no more than a minute or two – when his thoughts, which gave his mind almost no rest, would suddenly die away and sleep would cautiously, timidly creep into his head, taking advantage of the silence. But this sleep was extremely timid indeed, because at the first inner sound of an emerging thought it would not even hide, but simply vanish from the abode of dreams in a puff.

Meanwhile, Dr Vatrukhin had lain snoring next door, in the bedroom of Samson's late sister. In the room beyond that, dear Nadezhda slept sweetly. And next to that room was a small vestibule leading to Samson's father's study, where the man's restless spirit likely still hovered, anxious and confused by his inability to play with the abacuses hanging on the walls – his inability to calculate algebraically the results of his own life.

What really hindered Samson's sleep was the excitement of the preceding day and the anticipation of the following evening, when he, as agreed upon with the photographer, would take Nadezhda for a walk along Khreshchatyk and casually drop in at the photographic studio of one Leon Vishnevsky. It was from there that Vasyl had fetched the photographer, who had brought with him a large box camera on a tripod and a dangerous device for emitting a flash of light, which was intended to make his images sharper and clearer. Vishnevsky, a short, bearded old man, had positioned Briskin's face at an angle, the rightness of which only he could determine. He instructed Kholodny to hold the device – a horizontal metal tray on a handle the length of a forearm – and poured into it a strip of powder from a blue cardboard tube. Having uncovered the lens and made a few more adjustments to the camera, he lit a long kitchen match and ignited the powder. Samson would never forget what happened next. A bright explosion of light dazzled everyone present, especially the detainee. Briskin even leapt in the direction of the tailor's dummy and began to brush himself off, although Samson hadn't seen a spark landing on his clothes. One did land on the dummy, however, burning a hole in it. This they only noticed when cottony grey smoke rose from the figure. Vasyl, who was present more out of curiosity than to render aid, managed to grab Samson's unfinished mug of tea, then pushed the dummy onto its back as if it were a living person and poured the hot drink into the smoking hole.

The flash had also shocked Kholodny. He turned pale and scratched his stubbly left cheek.

"It burned," he muttered. "Look, it's a burn, isn't it? It really burned. What in the world are you doing?" he asked, glancing at the completely calm photographer. "Why would you set off a charge of gunpowder inside a closed room?"

"It's not gunpowder," explained the photographer. "It's magnesium with potassium chlorate. An English recipe."

"Same damned thing . . . Strong enough to propel a projectile out of a cannon," Kholodny murmured.

"Did the full face come out?" Samson asked, when the turmoil had subsided.

"Of course it did. I've been in the photographic business for thirty years now. Let's get the profile."

Briskin obediently turned sideways, but he also asked the photographer and Kholodny to take two steps back.

"Can't do that," the photographer replied. "You don't want to be too small in the picture."

Having sent Briskin downstairs with the soldier on duty, Samson enquired about the price of photographs.

"You mean I'm to be paid?" the photographer asked in delight. "Well, then, eight roubles. I charge institutions a higher rate than I do individuals. And I had to leave the studio, too."

"When will the photographs be ready?" asked Vasyl.

"Tomorrow evening."

"Then I'll come in the evening," Vasyl said.

"No," Samson interjected. "I'll pick them up myself."

"As you wish," Vasyl responded with a shrug, but his face showed disappointment.

Samson then volunteered to help the photographer carry his camera out to the cart, and, on the way, he asked if the man would be willing to take pictures of him and his wife the following evening.

"Certainly," the photographer responded, turning round on the stairs ahead of Samson. "Dress up as if it were a holiday."

And now, recalling in detail the entirety of the preceding day, Samson rejoiced at the thought of the evening to come, which was, of course, still off in the distance. Yet this distance was so relative, so unimportant – a small, lonely cloud in a clear springtime sky.

Samson yawned sweetly, as before a good night's sleep. And he did finally close his eyes, though without pausing his dreamy thoughts, in which he pictured tomorrow's photography session with Nadezhda. They would pose for separate images, which he would carry on his person to meet quotidian needs, as well as for an image together, to be placed in a wooden frame behind a thin sheet of glass. He even tried to pick out a place for this photo on the walls of the living room. But then a sharp noise resounded in his head, as if a glass street lamp had fallen from a pole and crashed onto the cobblestones. The ringing was so loud that Samson squeezed his already closed eyes more tightly, painfully shut. The sound took him by surprise, scared him. He immediately threw back his head to look at the window, as there was no other glass in the bedroom, but the curtain blocked his view. He got up, staggering a bit, turned on the light, moved the curtain aside and saw his reflection in the glass. It was intact. At that point, he realised where the ringing might have originated. He went out barefoot into the living room, in his nightshirt, and tiptoed across the wooden floor towards his father's study. He opened the door carefully, so as not to frighten away the silence with a creak. Although, the silence wasn't exactly silence; his head was still ringing. On entering the room, he spotted shards of glass on the floor, illuminated by the moon. He looked up at the window and saw in it a hole no smaller than a soup bowl, with sharp edges. Then he noticed a stone under the bookcase – black, one third the size of a cobblestone. Trying not to step on the glass, he approached the window. The hole was level with his face.

To his amazement, he saw a man right in the middle of the pavement, staring straight at him.

"Whatcha gawkin' at, eh?" the man shouted, an echo picking up his voice and carrying it over the roofs of the sleeping city. "Tell Nyura to get down here – I gotta see her!"

Samson half-consciously took hold of the handle of the window and turned it to the horizontal position. He heard the brass catches slide out of the upper and lower slots. But, as soon as he pulled the window towards himself, a piece of broken glass still hanging from the frame made a gnashing sound, as if it were about to fall out.

Having located the loosened piece with his eyes, Samson leaned a little closer to the hole and shouted to the night-time bandit, "There's no Nyura here!"

"This here's number 18, ain't it?" the window-breaker shouted back.

"No, it's number 24," Samson answered.

"Your own damn fault!" shouted the window-breaker. "Serves you right for takin' the numbers off the houses." The man looked round for a moment, wondering where he might find his Nyura now, then tramped off in the direction of Kuznechna Street.

After this incident, Samson lost all desire for sleep. His thoughts focused on the curfew, which no patrols on Zhylianska seemed to be enforcing that night.

At half past four, without having slept a wink, Samson went out into the street. He closed the front door, but he chose not to wake the yard-sweeper's widow so that she could bolt it from the inside. It was unlikely, he concluded, that the criminal element would be roaming the streets at such an early hour. Before setting out on foot towards the Halytska bathhouse, he confirmed that the house number, as well as the sign with the street name, were indeed missing from the building's façade. He remembered hearing that tenants were purposely stripping their homes of identifying markers, to make it more difficult for bandits to carry out robberies and for the authorities to carry out requisitions at specific addresses. As he walked, he noted that the street signs and numbers had also been removed from the building next door, the two beyond it and the house opposite.

As agreed, he first came to the station and left his revolver and documents in his office. Then, accompanied by three dozen other familiar and semi-familiar faces, he walked along Karavaevska Street. After turning right at Mariinsko-Blagovishchenska, they soon found themselves at the entrance to the bathhouse.

Nayden lined everyone up in front of the door.

"I demand you all observe and maintain the customary order of the bathhouse," he said dryly. "Follow the instructions of the senior attendant and do not sit idly in the steam. Dirt doesn't come off by itself, and one wash won't do it, either. Soap yourselves up and scrub yourselves down as many times as it takes. Hand over all your clothes, including underwear, to the changing-room attendant, in exchange for a numbered token. Tie the token to your hand, not to the handle of your washtub – and try to remember the number, too. I have a whistle." He raised a black metal whistle on a string. "When I blow thrice, it's time to get dressed."

"Why naked? No underwear?" someone asked.

"Hand it all over. There are no women in the bath," the commander replied.

"What if they lose it?" another voice asked.

"That shouldn't happen."

Samson was one of the first in line for the changing room. He undressed on the go and handed his tunic, trousers and undershirt to the elderly attendant, along with his boots, into which he had stuffed his footwraps. In exchange, he received an unevenly cut medal disc stamped with the number 34. A length of twine was threaded through a small hole above the number. He tied the token to his wrist and, while walking away, saw that Kholodny was last in line.

"What are you doing?" he asked as he approached him. "Go right up there."

"No," Kholodny muttered. "I'll let the others go first . . ."

Samson shrugged his bare, skinny shoulders and took a couple of steps back towards the wall, where he would wait for his comrade to undress and get his token. His gaze fell on an announcement posted on the wall: *The private steam rooms open at 9 in the morning.*

"Meet the senior attendant, Uncle Karp. He'll tell you what you need to know," Nayden said, five minutes later, introducing a man of heavy build.

Uncle Karp's bare legs and feet shod in wooden sandals showed from beneath the hem of a thick white coat that had clearly been laundered many times over. The coat's sleeves were rolled up to his elbows.

"Let's go," Uncle Karp commanded, and the throng of naked policemen and Red Army soldiers followed him along the wide corridor.

They stopped in the anteroom. Here, the senior attendant gave each man a metal washtub and a bar of brown soap.

Samson noticed that, when Kholodny received his tub, he dropped into it something wrapped in a handkerchief. He sidled up to the former priest – not out of curiosity, just so they could bathe together.

"Look at that," Kholodny said, turning his attention to the two bluish bullet marks on Samson's forearm. "All healed up?"

"Yep," Samson said, nodding.

In front of the entrance to the steam room, in a hall lined with wooden benches, Uncle Karp pointed out a row of taps sticking out of the wall. Above the taps were hooks, from which hung frayed bast wisps the colour of soaked wood.

"Here you soap up, rub down and wash off. Do not enter the steam room without washing off, or the soap will burn your eyes," he instructed.

The clanging of the metal tubs was drowned out by the sound of pouring water. Human voices sounded odd amid this noise, also somewhat like gurgling. Naked co-workers from the station bumped into each other without apologising or looking one another in the eye. Their nakedness seemed to rob them of personal identity, replacing it with uncertainty and vulnerability. And this vulnerability put them on edge. Samson, who had already twice been pushed away from the wall with the taps, now felt ready to answer rudeness with rudeness, brute hostility with brute hostility. Noticing the change in his comrade's gaze, Kholodny shoved a naked Red Army soldier away from the nearest tap and inserted Samson into the vacated space. Filling their tubs with hot water and each removing one wisp from the wall, they made their way to the other side of the hall and the last of the benches. Here, they soaped themselves up and scrubbed each other's backs.

"What do you have there?" Samson asked, nodding at the object in the empty tub.

"My cross," Kholodny said. "Forgot to take it off at home.

Wouldn't want anyone to swipe it. I'll put it on in the steam room, where it's too foggy for anyone to notice."

"Do not discuss official business in the bathhouse!" the stern voice of Nayden sounded nearby.

The two investigators turned round. It was strange for Samson to see the commander in the nude, but the diagonal sabre scar across his chest elicited respect.

"We're just washing up," Kholodny told him, lathering the wisp again. "All we're talking about is the bath."

"Correct. Bath talk at the bathhouse, job talk on the job. Scrub hard. Who knows when we'll get our next turn," Nayden said approvingly and walked away.

The steam room was filled with hot fog.

"Let's get up higher," Kholodny suggested, looking back at Samson.

"But you forgot your cross – it's in the tub, back there," his comrade responded worriedly, nodding in the direction of the wide wooden door through which they had just entered.

"Forgot, my foot! What am I, a fool?" The ex-priest chuckled and, turning to show his chest, he displayed the heavy silver crucifix hanging around his neck.

They sat on the upper benches.

"Feels mighty good," Kholodny exhaled.

Samson liked it up there too, but he didn't want to talk about it. When he felt good, he liked to linger in his thoughts.

He was thinking about Nadezhda. As he imagined the evening to come, a smile spread across his face. It pleased him to know the steam concealed this expression of his feelings from everyone in the room, with the possible exception of Kholodny. And then another playful thought came to mind.

It must be said, the thought was appropriate to the setting. He imagined himself and Nadezhda in the bathhouse – not here, in the public steam room, but in one of the private ones that opened at nine in the morning. These were meant for couples – and they, after all, were a couple. He enjoyed picturing the two of them in such a room, but he couldn't complete the picture. All he saw were their heads and faces. In truth, he could easily imagine himself naked, but he couldn't bring himself to imagine her. Something interfered with the effort. Perhaps it was a kind of shyness, a sense that someone might sneak into his thoughts and imaginings by means of their own thoughts and imaginings. He let out a sigh.

"What's the matter? You hot?" Kholodny asked, glancing at his comrade.

"I am," Samson confirmed. "But I like it."

"It's cooling down," Kholodny added critically. "The steam, I mean. It'll settle if they don't put on more."

Indeed, the fog began to dissipate and the naked people sitting below them began to exchange displeased glances. Samson realised that everyone could see everything – and that included his face, from which he now removed all indications of his feelings.

"More steam!" shouted Kholodny.

He used his right hand to conceal the silver cross from prying eyes.

"Hey, who's in charge down there? Put on more steam!" he shouted again.

Others too began to murmur. Someone even opened the door and shouted into the hall with the taps. Almost immediately, in response, came a dull, booming noise, which sounded like firewood being tossed into a capacious stove. Then, Uncle Karp arrived with two buckets of water.

"Quit your shouting!" he boomed. "Here's your steam!" He nodded at the buckets and emptied one after the other into the wide mouth gaping at the naked men from the tiled brick wall.

A wave of steam drew a groan of approval from those sitting closest to the wall, then rose and enveloped those above them.

"Oh, that's nice," Kholodny sighed, letting go of the cross. "Hot as hell, this thing!" he added, and shook his hand in the air. "This feels even hotter!"

The next time the steam began to settle, Samson noticed that the crowd in the room had grown thicker. And one of the new heads – although he only saw its back and the very edge of a cheek and temple – seemed familiar to him. But then the attendant poured two more buckets into the mouth of the stove, and the fog painted everything a greyish white.

"Would be great to follow this up with a visit to a barbershop," Kholodny commented, lifting up the hair on his head with outstretched fingers, as if checking its length. "Nothing better than a barbershop after the bathhouse – to get a good whiff of cologne. Then a pint of beer, with a bit of dried roach . . ."

"Keep dreaming." Samson chuckled. "And, after the beer, a boat down the Dnipro," he intoned, mimicking the voice of his comrade. "And then we'll disembark on an island, go straight to the local pub . . ."

"When we get dirty again, we'll come here some Sunday by ourselves and proceed with that exact plan," Kholodny said, nodding.

"If it's to be a Sunday, then we'd better go to the bathhouse on Karavaevska. There aren't so many thieves at that one," Samson opined.

"True," agreed Kholodny. "That one is better. But I don't believe they put on the steam on Sundays."

"They didn't used to," Samson corrected him. "It was the same here, on Sundays. Only Tuesdays, Thursdays and Saturdays."

"They still don't do it every day, only when there's firewood," Kholodny added.

Three whistles cut through the steamy fog, softly and plaintively, and were followed immediately by the sounds of movement. Some of the steamed policemen and Red Army soldiers got up reluctantly, and the door began to slam open and shut.

"On the double," someone muttered. "Don't let the steam out."

Looking back from the door, Samson realised that quite a few people remained on the benches. A momentary hole had formed in the fog, and he again searched the crowd for the man he thought he recognised.

And again the face, this time in profile, seemed familiar. Yet Samson's thoughts, overheated by the steam, somehow fled in another direction, towards Nadezhda.

"Permission to soap up again?" Samson asked Nayden.

"One more time, while the others are cooling down and drying off."

Samson scooped some water into his tub, lathered himself up with a wisp and then, when everyone had gone to dry off, washed off the soap and returned to the steam room. He tried to forge a path through the steam towards the familiar face, but he tripped over someone's foot and fell on the wet stone floor, his body making a splashing sound like a fish frolicking along a stream.

"Hey, what's the big idea?" someone shouted overhead.

Samson got up and backed away towards the door, rubbing his bruised side. Once out of the steam room, he doused himself with hot water and hurried to catch up with his colleagues.

The thigh that had hit the floor ached, and a bruise was already forming.

"Anyone need their corns cut off? Over here!" someone shouted nearby.

Samson looked round. The round Tatar face of the corn-cutter, in his white coat above bare legs, did not inspire confidence. In his hand, the man held a wide knife with a short blade.

"Anyone need their corns cut off? Over here!" he shouted again. "One corn – one rouble!"

Having exchanged the token for his clothes and boots, Samson dried himself with the shared towel that hung on a nail and began to dress. He took his time, trying to focus his mind on the seemingly familiar face he'd glimpsed through the fog.

At long last, as he was pulling on his right boot, it came to him: the face belonged to Jacobson! He immediately thought of the missing suit, and of the silver bone stolen from his desk drawer.

He returned to the locker-room attendant, pushing aside some workmen who were handing over their uniform shirts of coarse blue cloth, black trousers, underpants and boots.

"Has anyone given you a black and brown striped suit?" he asked in a demanding tone, since he was already in his police clothes.

"I don't see any suits before nine o'clock," the old man told him. "All work shirts and tunics. We only serve institutions at this hour. The suits come later, when people pay for entry."

"And what institutions are you serving at this moment?" Samson demanded again.

"A military vehicle repair unit, and the railway workshops. And these fellows are from Michelson's brick factory." He nodded at the workers waiting to turn in their clothes.

"Michelson's long gone," the first worker in line corrected the old man.

"Don't you think I know he's dead?" the old man asked. "Ten years dead. But the factory's still standing, ain't it?"

"Tell me," Samson said, switching to an intimate whisper and clearly asking not as a police investigator, but as a citizen, "is it possible to take a private steam with your . . . sweetheart?"

"Take whomever you want. Sweetheart, sailor, Chinese soldier. There's a special separate refreshment room, too."

Out on the street, Samson saw the backs of policemen and Red Army soldiers heading towards the Lybid station.

Kholodny was bringing up the rear. Samson caught up and walked alongside him.

"Got burned," Kholodny whispered to him on the go. "Badly burned."

"How?" asked Samson.

"The cross," his comrade whispered. "It got so hot that it burned itself into my skin. Hurts like the devil. And I can't very well go and see a doctor with an injury like this."

"Why can't you?" Samson asked in a surprised tone. "I know of one who'd be glad to treat you. He probably wears a cross himself."

"Where does he live?"

"At my place, for now. We'll go there at lunch."

"Thank you, my friend. You know burns – if left untreated, they get infected. Could be fatal," Kholodny said, looking down at his feet.

Chapter 20

As a result of the communal bath, the scent of soap hovered in the air of the station and everyone was in high spirits. Everyone, that is, except Samson, who kept rubbing his bruised thigh, and Kholodny, who winced every time his undershirt stuck to his burn due to some ill-considered movement.

Having no desire to take a cab and make the rounds of the still unquestioned meat-buyers, they instead took up the case of thefts at the station. Briskin, after all, had given them a suspect: the Red Army man.

This soldier's name, they discovered, was Trofim, and he, it turned out, was not a person with whom one can have a quick and meaningful conversation. When they called him into the interrogation room and sat him on the chained stool, he sized them up with his hostile brown eyes and squeezed his rifle even tighter in his hands, pressing its butt into the floor. For a long time, he ignored the order to surrender his weapon to the other two Red Army men present, merely mumbling, "What for?" Finally, he complied.

"Light up," Samson told Kholodny, as he himself didn't wish to smoke.

While Kholodny was lighting a cigarette, Samson ordered the soldier to empty his pockets of tobacco and to hand over any photographs he might have on him. All this material migrated to the table, after which Kholodny blew smoke into Trofim's face.

"We know you've been stealing," the former priest said in an unfriendly tone, trying to look this awkward and obviously not very bright fellow directly in the eyes.

Trofim fixed his gaze on the floor and remained silent.

"What do you have to say for yourself?" Samson picked up the questioning.

"What can I say?" Trofim asked, looking up at the former priest, or rather, at his unshaven cheeks, ruddy after the bath. "Requisitions from our enemies are allowed, so sometimes I requisition what I need, or what I want."

"What, for example, have you requisitioned at the station? And from whom?" Samson asked.

"From whom," the soldier muttered. "Detainees, of course. And what could I requisition from them? Just grub. Their kin bring it, you know – eggs, pork fat. And who's gonna bring me anything? All my kin are in the ground or in Siberia . . ."

"And aside from the detainees?" Kholodny pressed him. "Things have been going missing on every floor. A suit from the evidence room, a tea mug, a leather jacket."

"What are you talking about?" Trofim asked, taken aback. "I don't even set foot upstairs, 'less I'm asked. You got your own thieves up here."

"How dare you?" Kholodny shot back, indignant. "What do you mean, 'your own'?"

"Just what I said. Commissars, bosses . . . What would I need a suit for? Wouldn't even know how to put it on. Never worn one in my life."

Samson sighed. He realised that Trofim wasn't lying: he had no need of a suit. And the investigator knew who did need it. He had caught a glimpse of the man through the break in the bathhouse fog. Jacobson.

"Do people ever come up to you in the street and ask for something?" Samson continued.

"You bet," Trofim said, nodding. "Sometimes, boys'll run up and ask me to fire my rifle. And folks ask me for smokes."

"But has anyone ever asked you to get them something from the station?" Samson followed up, guiding Trofim towards the hypothesis that now took precedence in his mind.

"From the station?" Trofim thought aloud. "Well, that they don't do in front of everyone – they take me aside and whisper."

"What have they whispered?" Kholodny asked, re-entering the conversation. Then he mechanically puffed on his cigarette and again exhaled the smoke in the soldier's face.

Trofim didn't seem to notice.

"We have one comrade," he suddenly remembered. "He can stand on his head. Said he was born in a circus. His ma and pa had an act, doing magic, but the Gypsies took him away and the circus burned down . . . Well, that's what he said, anyway . . . He's capable of stealing anything, that's for sure. Can bend every which way. I seen him climbing through a tiny open window with my own eyes! Only took him a second."

"What's this acrobat's name? And where is he now?" Samson asked, having finally managed to look Trofim in the eyes.

"Right down there. Name's Boris Kosyakin."

"Tell us about him," Kholodny cut in. "What's he like?"

"Like I said, he bends easy. They know him, too," Trofim replied, indicating the two soldiers standing at the door beside his confiscated rifle.

"You do?" Samson asked, turning to them.

"Yes," one breathed out. The second nodded.

"Bring him up at once, and take away his rifle," Kholodny ordered. "You can give his back," he added, pointing at Trofim.

Samson respectfully returned Trofim's pack of cigarettes and envelope of photographs.

"You can go. But don't breathe a word about this conversation to anyone," he said in a weighty tone.

Trofim gave a barely perceptible nod.

The Red Army men left the room. The investigators were alone.

"You'll smoke, this time," Kholodny said with a pained smile, gazing at his comrade and extending the pack.

Boris Kosyakin, who was brought into the room about five minutes later, looked frightened, and this encouraged Samson. The soldier was short and thin. His tunic, which was tightened with a belt because of its larger than necessary size, was gathered into ruffles below his shoulders. His belt buckle, with its tsarist double-headed eagle, shone like a brand-new gold piece.

Samson pointed Kosyakin to the stool and sat down on one of the two chairs opposite him. The second chair was immediately taken by Kholodny.

"Tobacco and photographs," the former priest commanded and held out his hand.

"I don't smoke," Kosyakin said quietly. "Got no photographs, either. I'm an orphan."

"Search him," Kholodny ordered one of the guards.

The guard handed his rifle to his comrade and skilfully went through Kosyakin's pockets. He pulled out everything he found, laid it on the table and returned to his place.

Samson peered at the table and stood up. His attention was drawn to an amber cigarette holder, which lay among papers and documents, silver tsarist coins, Kerensky roubles and two packs of playing cards wound with twine.

He picked up the cigarette holder, brought it closer to his eyes and sniffed it. The scent of tobacco, laced with sweet perfume, hit his nostrils. Samson sat back down, lit a cigarette, inserted it into the holder, inhaled as deeply as he could, to the point of choking, then quickly pulled the holder out of his mouth and exhaled the smoke into Kosyakin's face. As soon as he did so, he began to cough. The cough shook him, as if he were seriously ill. And it rang in his head with such force that it was as if a whole choir were coughing, or a detachment of soldiers. It seemed entirely too loud.

It was only a few moments later that he realised he and Kosyakin were both coughing. For the soldier, the smoke had triggered some sort of attack.

Kholodny leapt out of the interrogation room, dashed over to the common drinking bucket, scooped up a mugful of water and ran back. First, he gave Samson a sip. When his comrade had calmed down, he passed the mug to the soldier.

"Where'd you get the holder?" Samson asked. "I thought you didn't smoke."

"I used to. Still carry it with me . . . Expensive item, you know," the soldier stammered, his voice nearly rising to falsetto at the end, as if someone had stepped on his tail.

Samson expressed his scepticism with a sigh and turned to Kholodny, who shot a glance at the cigarette burning idly in the holder between his comrade's fingers. The young investigator got the hint, shook his head in displeasure and again raised the holder to his mouth. This time, when his lips touched the item, he detected an odd, not quite masculine taste. He took a puff, held back a cough and blew another jet of smoke into the soldier's face.

Now, only Kosyakin coughed, but he did so loudly and convulsively, trembling as if from a seizure.

"Tell me the truth – what did you steal from the station? Your comrades fingered you," Kholodny pronounced coldly, leaning towards the coughing soldier.

"What comrades?" Kosyakin asked after the fit had passed, staring at Kholodny. Then he turned his gaze to the two Red Army men who had brought him. They both shook their heads.

"Not these," Samson confirmed. "Others. Well, do you confess? Shall we start with this cigarette holder?"

"Don't worry about us putting you away for this," Kholodny said, trying to smile, but his hand immediately rose to his burn, hidden behind his tunic and undershirt. "Let me tell you, we haven't even opened a case. Our orders are just to find out what happened. So, you have nothing to fear. Speak up! Unburden yourself."

"But I didn't steal anything!" Kosyakin exclaimed, glancing sideways at the smoking cigarette in the holder. "By God, I swear it!"

"You believe in God?" Kholodny asked sternly.

The detainee hesitated to answer. Kholodny winced again and reached up to unbutton the collar of his tunic, as if desperate to let the cool air soothe his wound.

Samson was also silent. He didn't want to hear the detainee's cough again, to say nothing of his own. Nor did he understand what had come over Kholodny to make him unbutton his tunic. His comrade parted it down to his waist, then stretched the opening of his white undershirt apart – but the opening was apparently too narrow for his purposes, so he pulled at both sides with a sharp movement and the garment seemed to scream as it tore. Turning and leaning forward, Samson peered at his comrade's bare chest. He saw what looked like a cross of living flesh, covered with a thin layer of white foam and with drops of blood forming at its edges.

Kosyakin, too, stared dumbfounded at Kholodny's burn, not comprehending that it was indeed a burn.

"It hurts!" Kholodny moaned, still tugging at his torn shirt and his tunic.

The detainee's face was contorted with horror.

"I do believe, I do," he uttered plaintively. "I believe in God! And if I did something wrong, let Him punish me! I didn't do it for myself alone . . . I always shared everything with my comrades." He cast a glance at the Red Army men by the door, looking for confirmation. One of the two nodded. "And it's not like I took so very much! Only did it twice, maybe three times at most! Like the others . . . We don't get money for tea or a proper hot meal – and, as for soldiers' rations . . . Well, you know—"

"Hold on," Samson said, cutting off Kosyakin's lamentations

and raising the cigarette holder to eye level. "Where did you get this, then?"

"Some lady . . . Stuck it in my hand herself, for returning her purse."

"What purse?"

"You know, a lady's purse – whaddya call it, a reticule? It was up in that room, there, where we keep the stuff from the dead folks and the killers."

"So, it was material evidence?" Kholodny asked.

"I mean, it was made of material."

"And who asked you to steal the suit from the office?" Samson tossed out quickly. He held his breath, gazing at the detainee.

Kosyakin froze, as if caught red-handed.

"Well?" Samson urged, excitement surging in his chest.

"I don't know him," the Red Army man began, matching the volume of Samson's voice, as if resigned to the disclosure of his crimes. "Some Latvian with a game leg. Said he had nothing to wear. And it's true, the fellow was in rags. Said the suit had been taken away by mistake. Suit and boots—"

"What boots?" Samson asked in surprise.

"Calfskin. There was only one suit in there – took it right off the scarecrow. For the boots, he gave me an insole, so that I could find the right pair—"

"Where were they?"

"In that room, with the purse. There's a whole pile of boots in the corner—"

"Did you also take a silver bone from the desk in the office where you found the suit?" Samson asked, his voice quavering, as if he were afraid of the answer.

"No," the detainee said, shaking his head. "Took a steel one – definitely not silver."

"How do you know it was steel?"

"That's what the Latvian said. Told me to look for a big steel bone."

"What about a black leather jacket? On a hanger? Same office as the suit?" Kholodny broke in, distracting himself from his pain and letting go of his undershirt. He sounded angry.

"No, I didn't take any jackets. He didn't ask for one," Kosyakin said, shifting his gaze to the questioner and again lowering his eyes to the mark of the cross on his chest. "Swear to God, I didn't."

"And what did he give you in return for the bone, the suit and the boots?" Samson asked.

"He hasn't paid up yet. Probably sick. He was coughing when we first met. Promised me pork fat and bread, five pounds of each. Said he'd bring it to the station and took down my name, to ask for me."

Samson smiled.

"Did you also take a mug from the commander's office?" he asked more cheerfully.

"I did," the detainee admitted and hung his head. "On a bet. With Fyodor."

"What did you two bet?" Samson asked.

"A pound of sugar. He says Nayden never sleeps, and I says he does – he has to. There used to be people around who didn't need to sleep, but not no more. So, I says to Fyodor, I'll sneak in there and take something, so's to prove Nayden was asleep. And I saw the mug on the edge of the desk—"

"Where is it now?"

Kosyakin moved his chin sideways and used it to indicate the floor.

"Downstairs?" Kholodny asked, somewhat surprised.

"Yep. In the guards' room. We use it for tea."

"Take him downstairs and give him back his rifle," Kholodny ordered the Red Army men at the door. "Then bring us the mug.

And you," he said, turning to Kosyakin. "If you ever steal anything again, I'll shoot you down like a dog! Understood?"

"Swear to God, I won't," the soldier blurted out as he rose from the chained stool. "And if I see someone else stealing, I'll come running to tell ya, I swear! Can I have my stuff back?" he asked, indicating the contents of his pockets on the table.

Samson nodded. The first things Kosyakin picked up were the packs of cards. The cigarette holder remained in the possession of the young investigator. The soldier didn't ask for it back, although he did cast a final parting glance at the amber object.

"Alright," Kholodny said, turning to Samson as soon as they were alone. "We'll bring Nayden his mug and consider the case closed. Then we'll go back to your flat to see the doctor – I can't take this pain any longer."

Chapter 21

Nadezhda was delighted at the suggestion of a walk along Khreshchatyk. It was a pleasant evening, and a breeze still warm from the afternoon sun blew in gusts, playing with the hem of her green sundress.

Afraid to catch cold, she had put on a blouse to cover her arms and shoulders, but she didn't button it. The colour matched the sundress. Samson, for his part, had come out in uniform, armed – partly because he had an official reason to visit the photographer's studio, and partly to scare away whatever minor perils might present themselves along the way. His leather jacket and bulky wooden holster instilled fear and respect not only in common townsfolk, but also in bandits and pickpockets. In fact, this walk struck Samson almost as a return to a former reality, when tsarist officers used to promenade along Khreshchatyk, elegantly and imposingly, with ladies on their arms. The officers' ladies had always seemed to him much more charming than those who accompanied civilians, and the sense of superiority he now felt was probably akin to the feelings of those real officers, whose proud faces and portly figures he remembered so well from his student days. As he called up those memories, his shoulders squared themselves, which made his healed bullet wounds sting. And that brought to mind the face of Jacobson in the bathhouse fog.

Either by accident or on purpose, Nadezhda suddenly clung to Samson, pulling his elbow close, and the wooden holster was for a moment sandwiched between their thighs. He turned towards her, and they gave each other smiles. The distance between them increased just a bit, releasing the holster from captivity.

It occurred to him that, if it hadn't been for his leather jacket, he would have felt the warmth of her hand.

A beautiful black car drove past, and a man who looked like Christian Rakovsky cast an attentive glance at Nadezhda. Samson tensed up, afraid that the car would stop and the man would get out and express his interest in her. Perhaps he would invite her for a ride, ignoring Samson altogether as a man of junior rank. Such a thing was all too possible, these days. No wonder the commandant of Zhytomyr had supposedly forbidden women from riding in military and official automobiles. And, of course, there really were no automobiles of any other kind on the road.

Thankfully, the beautiful black car disappeared without slowing down. Samson didn't even look back after it had passed them, merely sighing in relief. The time was one of worry; it didn't tick idly on the watch face of life, even when strolling arm in arm. No, it was a restless, dangerous, hungry time, when weapons were more important than military uniforms. And yet, just as they turned onto Khreshchatyk, they saw two couples walking towards them arm in arm – not workers or peasants or Red Army soldiers, but calm, old-regime types. They walked somewhat hesitantly, uncertainly, and this uncertainty was evident in their eyes and on their lips. It was clear that they weren't out to have a good time, but rather to test their fate. Samson, on the other hand, was enjoying his stroll with Nadezhda. Then again, perhaps these couples weren't out strolling at all. Perhaps they were attending to business, or maybe hurrying back from, or to, the homes of their friends. Khreshchatyk, with its lavish signboards and festive generosity, attracted townsfolk most strongly on Sundays, a little less so on Saturdays, while on weekdays they tended to bypass it entirely, preferring to take quiet Pushkinska or the even quieter Levashovska, if they were going from Pechersk to Pankivshchyna or further still. Even in a cart, it was still better to avoid Khreshchatyk on weekdays. Although, now, one saw fewer of them on the street than before the war and revolution, villagers were still out there with carts full of various goods and firewood, reining in their horses and trying to figure out where exactly they were and where to turn. They'd spot a tram, as if for the first time in their lives, and stop their cart right in front of it, thinking about which way to direct their horse: right or left? Impatient cabbies rush at such carts on purpose, to frighten both the horse and the driver. And then they reprimand the villager with the choicest foul words, proving their superiority both as drivers and as hurlers of verbal abuse.

"Did you hear about the tram accident?" Nadezhda asked, drawing Samson's attention away from Khreshchatyk, but not before he noticed a tram driving towards them down the middle of the street.

"I saw it happen as I was walking to work."

"Was there a lot of blood?"

"No, hardly any. Only on the dead and injured. We took charge of the scene, making sure the injured were taken to hospitals, the dead to morgues . . . Ah, almost there!" Samson said, stopping and turning back to count the buildings from the corner of Bibikovsky Boulevard. "We're the fourth building from the corner, just past Marcinczyk's pharmacy. There should be a sign on the second floor – 'Kaufman, Notary'." Samson raised his head and checked for the sign, then looked down at the display window of the tobacco shop on the ground floor. "Yes, it should be here, on the first floor – the studio of Leon Vishnevsky."

The front doors of the three-storey building stood out on Khreshchatyk due to their nondescriptness and their particularly unpleasant yellowish-brown coloration. The wooden staircase, however, retained its former chic thanks to a red carpet fastened to each step with a dull bronze rod. The middle of the carpet was thoroughly worn, but the edges had kept their original colour.

Samson knocked on the door, over which arched, in the form

of a drooping moustache, first in black paint, then, on top of that, in gold, the inscription PHOTOGRAPHIC STUDIO.

The lock clicked, the door opened and the photographer's face appeared in the crack.

"Ah, young man, you've come for the photographs," Leon Vishnevsky said, letting the visitors inside and locking the door behind them. He led them into a reception room that was fit for a professor of medicine or even a general: the walls were hung with framed photographic portraits of important male faces and ladies in hats or with elaborately arranged hair. On the floor lay a carpet depicting burgundy roses on a blue background. A heavy yellow curtain veined with glittering golden threads draped the window. In the corners stood ficus in large wooden pots. There was one glaring eyesore amid all the elegance: an iron pot-belly stove, its pipe poking through the wall. The room was neither too cold nor too hot, and the smell was pleasant, domestic, unmarred by the stove – which meant it hadn't been stoked up in a long time.

On a heavy bog-oak desk, plywood boxes of various sizes held stacks of photographs. The old man went behind the working side of the desk and, without sitting down on the brown leather chair, leaned over one of the boxes. He flicked through the photographs so gracefully that Samson looked round in search of a piano; the movements of the photographer's fingers suggested that he was no stranger to the ivories. But there was no instrument in the room.

"Here's your little criminal darling," the old man announced, holding out a long piece of cardboard on which were pasted two high-quality photographs – full face and profile.

"Thank you." Samson nodded with satisfaction. "Have you been paid?"

"Oh, certainly, and more than I had expected." The old man chuckled. "Honestly, I hadn't expected anything," he added, looking slyly into Samson's eyes. Then, he turned his gaze to Nadezhda. "What a charming companion you've brought. Why not take advantage of the opportunity? My camera is all set up, and the power has been remarkably reliable of late, so we could use a lamp instead of a flash."

Samson gave Nadezhda an enquiring look. So far, everything was going smoothly, all according to his and the photographer's scheme. They just had to wait for her reaction.

"Oh, if I had known, I would have at least combed my hair," she said bashfully.

"Ah, you're in luck!" the old man exclaimed. "I have the finest comb, and there's a mirror in the studio." He pointed to an archway covered with a colourful Chinese silk curtain. "A truly wonderful mirror! Red Army men wanted to carry it off and smash it, but then I showed them a photograph of Isaac Schwartz, head of the Cheka, which gave them quite the scare. They left straight away. Citizen Schwartz wanted a half-length portrait, with his revolver. What do I care? Bouquet, book, rifle – all the same to me. Come, come, I'll give you the comb. Tortoiseshell, nice and soft."

In the centre of the studio, on a tripod, stood the already familiar apparatus. Its lens was aimed at a couch upholstered in red plush. On the left were two imposing armchairs, a vase on a high table and a low card table. Standing by the wall on the right were two folding screens of Chinese silk – one blue with white birds, the other green with yellow bamboo shoots. Behind the screens was a living palm tree in a wooden tub.

Nadezhda pulled off her blouse, revealing the whole of her sundress, and carefully examined herself in the mirror. She picked up the tortoiseshell comb but never touched her curls with it, and instead simply tweaked them a bit with her fingers.

"Would you prefer full-length or close-up?" the old man asked Samson.

"You know, I'd like a separate close-up of my Nadezhda's face, then one of mine, and then us together in . . . a romantic photo?"

"With doves?" the old man asked after a moment's thought.

"If you had told me earlier, I would have gladly provided them. We have a terrific dovecote in our yard, and the owner is easy to persuade. But I can do it without doves. Let's capture the young lady first."

Samson had never seen Nadezhda's beautiful round face adorned with as lovely a smile as the one she now showed the camera. The photographer was also extremely pleased.

"I don't even need to talk you through it," he praised her. "It's as if you have your photo taken every day. Have you ever posed for magazines?"

"Oh, surely you're joking!" she responded coquettishly.

The old man had more trouble with Samson. He didn't like the look on the young investigator's face.

"Could you adopt a jollier expression? Otherwise, you won't like the results. I'll put you into an oval, but your face will be sharp, angular, as if someone had just dropped something on your foot. You know what, let me put your young lady right here, next to me. You just look at her – then, when I raise my hand, look here, into the lens, but don't change your expression until I lower my hand."

And that's what he did. At the sight of Nadezhda, Samson's face softened, grew joyful. The old photographer knew exactly how to get what he wanted from his subjects.

"Now, a picture of us together?" Samson asked.

"You know what?" the old man responded, his voice sounding cautious, as if he were about to ask for a loan. "You might want to change your attire. Who needs romance with a revolver when you've got a charming young lady at your side?"

"But I haven't brought a change of clothes," Samson said nervously.

"I have what you need," the old man said, making a soothing gesture with his hand. "Photography is like the theatre, full of costumes. I have all sorts here. And you're the right size."

The photographer went over to a plywood door, pulled it towards himself and revealed a wardrobe filled with suits, uniforms and dresses on padded hangers.

"Here, try this! I'm sure it's a perfect fit," he declared, handing Samson a loose red flannel shirt of the kind Apache dancers wore in the Paris slums.

"But this – this is for poets and gamblers," Samson protested weakly.

"What are you talking about?" The photographer chuckled. "Or do you mean to say that the police don't dress like this? Well, you won't be posing as a policeman. You'll be posing as a young man in love."

He waited a few moments, thinking – wrongly, it turned out – that Samson might respond to his words, then continued, shifting to a half-whisper: "You yourself know how many times power has changed hands here in Kyiv. Better not to immortalise yourself in an outfit linked to a specific government. Who knows what's coming tomorrow? In this shirt, you're merely a citizen – simply a Kyivan. And that will never be a punishable offence."

The old man sat Samson in the red shirt and Nadezhda in her sundress on the couch, forming them into a loving, though slightly timorous, couple – a couple who allowed their shoulders to touch but were afraid to give free rein to their hands.

"Pick it up in three days," the photographer said when they returned to the reception room. "I know what to do with the oval portraits, but what size would you like for the photo of you together?"

Samson turned to Nadezhda. "I would like to frame it, put it up on the wall," he ventured hesitantly.

"Understood." The old man nodded. "And don't forget this." He handed Samson a long brown envelope. "Remember that I'm available any time. There are a great many people arrested today, but they're photographed a lot less often than under the tsar, when there were far fewer of them."

A tram came ringing past them on Khreshchatyk, heading towards Bibikovsky Boulevard. Samson noticed two Red Army men, armed with rifles, on the footboard at the back.

"We'll have to show the photograph to your parents," Samson said to Nadezhda.

The young woman nodded.

She seemed happily excited and walked with a hasty step, as if in a hurry. Samson quickened his pace to keep up. It proved impossible to walk arm in arm at such speed, so Nadezhda let go.

"I'm rather hungry," Samson admitted.

"We still have some oatmeal kissel." Nadezhda gave him a tender look. "Enough for two. And bread and tea."

At the corner of Bibikovsky, they let three sack-laden carts heading in the direction of Halytska Square go past, then crossed.

At home, a surprise was in store. First, in the hallway, they stumbled upon two large plywood suitcases. And, although Samson immediately guessed that their presence was somehow related to Dr Vatrukhin, the discovery that awaited them in the living room could not but puzzle the young investigator.

The light shone brightly in the living room, and in the far left corner, on the wall, hung a strange poster, which had not been there before. About five yards away from it, an unfamiliar grey-bearded citizen sat on a chair that had been pulled out from the dining table. In front of the poster stood Dr Vatrukhin, holding a pointer. He wore a white gown, which contrasted sharply with his yellow trousers and yellowish-brown gaiters.

"Oh, terribly sorry," he said at the appearance of the flat's owner. "We're almost done."

The doctor's elderly patient began to rise from his chair, but the doctor placed a caring hand on his shoulder.

"Andrian Evseich, don't worry, there's no need to rush. These are the master and mistress of the house, the kindest of people," Vatrukhin said, looking back at Samson, then turning his gaze to Nadezhda, whose face expressed no disapproval. "I recommend Daigaku eye drops, from Japan."

"But where am I to get them? At Marcinczyk's?"

"If he doesn't have them, then try Potapenko at the Oleksandrivska Hospital. I'll help."

"Thank you, doctor." The patient calmly rose to his feet, bowed to Samson and Nadezhda, pulled out a leather wallet and handed the doctor a blue tsarist five-rouble note.

"Forgive me, please, but I didn't wish to be a parasite, living off your largesse, like a louse stuck to a Red Army soldier," the doctor explained, after escorting the patient out of the flat. "That's why I went home to fetch everything I needed. And I can't very well abandon my regular patients, can I? I took the Hippocratic oath."

"Do you have many regular patients?" Samson asked cautiously, more at ease now that the stranger had left his flat.

"Not too many. Some have left the country, others have died, others still were shot by the Cheka. I'd say there are about two hundred."

Samson sighed heavily, unfastened and removed his belt, pulled off his jacket and looked back at Nadezhda.

"I will, of course, immediately stop receiving patients if you don't approve," Vatrukhin said, also looking imploringly at Nadezhda. "But this way I can contribute to our household budget. Here, take my fee," he insisted, handing the tsarist banknote to Nadezhda.

She took the five roubles and cast an uncertain glance at Samson, along with a barely perceptible smile.

"Let's have some supper," she said in a conciliatory tone.

"Yes, let's!" the doctor exclaimed, delighted, and he began to pull off his gown, which, it turned out, he'd put on over a yellow three-piece holiday suit.

Samson grinned at the sight of this outfit, so inappropriate both for the season and for the political atmosphere.

"I also have the honour of treating you to herring from my ration," Vatrukhin announced proudly. "Although I'm in the fourth category, this time your leaders proved more generous than usual," he added, nodding at Samson.

He stepped out into the hallway, leaving the door to the living room ajar. Samson and Nadezhda heard a suitcase's locks click open.

"But those in the fourth category never get herring," Samson said, somewhat confused.

"That's true," the doctor's voice reached them from the hallway. "But one of the men in charge of making out the ration cards is a patient of mine, and the fellow distributing the food is an illiterate peasant. Know what he said to me? 'Comrade Vatrukhin of the fourth category, here's your grub.'"

Samson shook his head and walked over to the poster on the wall. It displayed rows of incomplete circles, similar to the letter C, the openings of which were variously turned upwards, downwards, left and right.

"Those are Landolt's rings," explained Vatrukhin, who had returned holding a bundle of newspapers that, presumably, contained a herring. "We use them to check visual acuity. Have a seat," he directed, indicating the chair recently vacated by his elderly patient, then he went over to the table and picked up the long wooden pointer.

Chapter 22

"Why are you so down in the mouth?" Kholodny asked, casting yet another concerned glance at Samson, who sat beside him in the cab.

They were on their way to Kryvy Lane to question Antonina, the buyer of intestines. She was the third to last on their list of unexamined witnesses, yet Samson felt they'd been inching towards her for a week now, unable to reach her.

"So, he'll sit for a while. What's the big deal? They won't do anything to him," Kholodny kept on.

"But we promised they wouldn't touch him. You made a personal promise," Samson answered at last, heaving a sigh.

"My promise didn't mean anything. We had no right to make any promises," Kholodny said, making a dismissive gesture with his hand. He was momentarily distracted by the sight of a lady, in a light fox-coloured coat, walking along the edge of the Brest-Litovsk Highway. "All dolled up, eh?" he let slip as he turned back to his comrade. "If Nayden had assured him, that would be different. He has the right. But who are we to make promises?"

The cabby kept turning his right ear to the passengers. Perhaps it was his good ear. He must have been curious about the content of this conversation between two armed policemen. Kholodny pointed at the driver's head, then touched his ear with the same finger. Samson got the message and lowered his voice.

"I didn't expect him to blow his top like that when he found out the thief was one of the soldiers," Samson almost whispered. "I mean, we recovered his mug, didn't we?"

The cab ran over a stone and the passengers got a good shaking. Samson pressed his leather briefcase to his knees.

"Don't worry, it won't fly away," Kholodny chuckled. "And they won't hurt Kosyakin," he insisted again. "After all, he's of the worker-peasant class."

"Of the circus class," Samson corrected him.

"Alright, *circus* worker-peasant," Kholodny said. "Don't you know how badly people are exploited in the circus? I won't even mention the animals, trained with a whip . . ."

The cab drove out onto Borshchahivska Street and, about a quarter of a mile later, turned onto Kryvy Lane.

"Which house from the end?" the driver turned and asked.

"We don't know yet," Kholodny responded.

"Well, then, get off here, right in the middle."

Kryvy Lane was shaped like a leg bent at the knee. The wooden single-storey houses looked lonely as orphans behind their unpainted fences, as if they'd all been abandoned. When they reached the knee, where the lane turned left, a small but sonorous mutt barked at them from behind a closed gate.

"Probably here." Kholodny stopped walking. "Where there are dogs, there are bones, and you can't have bones without meat," he added, chuckling.

"But she bought intestines," Samson objected, poking a hole in his comrade's reasoning.

"Let's find out," Kholodny suggested. He went over to the gate and began to mug at the mutt teasingly.

The path from the gate led straight to the house's door, a window on either side of which looked out onto the street across the yard. The curtain of the left window moved slightly. Soon, the door opened and a stooped elderly woman emerged to peer at the strangers.

"Who's there?" she shouted.

"We're with the police!" Kholodny shouted in response.

"That the truth?"

"God's honest! Open the gate!"

"It's open!" she called back in the slightly hoarse voice of a habitual smoker.

"Well, then, get this dog under control and we'll come in! We've got a few little questions for you!"

Samson was surprised at the playfulness of Kholodny's intonation. He took his identification out of his pocket and unfolded it. "Here, have a look!" he shouted.

"I believe ya!" the woman responded. "Little Flea don't bark like that for nothin'! She can't stand the police!"

"Why's that?" Kholodny enquired, now gazing at the small dog with apprehension.

"We sell pies over at the Jewish Market, she and I! If she sees a good customer comin', she wags 'er tail – but, if one of yer fellas comes round to check my licence, she starts barkin' so that everyone turns and looks! Knocks the chutzpah right out of 'im!"

"You're telling us you sell pies without a licence?" Kholodny asked in a deliberately stern voice.

"What a godless thing to say!" Antonina tossed back her head and gave the questioner an indignant look. "Of course, I got me a licence!"

"Show us!" the former priest demanded, evoking Samson's respect with his masterful dramatic rendering of a rapidly changing mood.

"Come on in and I will!"

"What about the dog?" Kholodny asked, pointing at the little mutt.

"Flea!" the woman squealed. "In the doghouse! Git!"

The mongrel named Flea obeyed her mistress, tucked her tail between her legs and scurried into her shabby abode, which sat to the right of the threshold. Samson and Kholodny entered the yard.

"Why did you call her that?" Samson asked the woman as they approached, feeling resentment on behalf of the guard animal, which worked honestly, desperately, to fulfil its duty of keeping strangers at bay.

"Ya see how she jumped up and down?" Antonina grinned, opening the door.

There was a musty, spicy smell inside. Hay lay on the wooden floor of the anteroom, right in front of the door. The hostess herself mechanically stamped her slippers on it, although she hadn't gone outside and couldn't have tracked any dirt into the house. Samson also wiped the soles of his boots on the hay, but Kholodny simply stepped over it.

The living room smelled of kerosene, and its walls were hung with paper icons in heavy wooden frames. The two windows provided sufficient light. On a scuffed oval table, atop a yellowed lace tablecloth, stood a kerosene lamp and a large hourglass. Samson's attention was drawn to a couch with worn red upholstery, its back against the wall opposite the windows. In the corner to the left of it, through an open blue door, he could see the edge of an iron bed.

"Do you live alone?" Kholodny enquired as he sat on a chair, which immediately made a cracking sound. The former priest quickly looked down at the chair's legs, but neither his eyes nor his ears noticed anything suspicious, and he returned his attention to their hostess.

She also sat down at the table. Seeing that there was no third chair in the room, Samson sank onto the couch. He took out a pencil and a folder that held blank sheets of paper, then turned the briefcase over so that its lock wouldn't stick out, but he still felt that it would make for a poor writing surface.

"Sergius," he said, turning to Kholodny, "why don't you keep the record? My briefcase isn't smooth enough."

"Why do you have so little furniture?" asked Kholodny, who clearly didn't wish to write, as he glared at the hostess.

"'Cause you all took it away!" Antonina shot back bitterly.

"What do you mean, we took it?" Kholodny asked, his eyes wide.

"Back in March, this was. Some fatty in a sheepskin coat showed up with a crew of Red Army men. Flashed some decree in front of my face, about how much furniture a person's allowed to have. Had to give up everything else. I live alone, ya know, and the paper said one bed and one chair for each person, with one more chair for family or guests. So, they took away two of my chairs."

Kholodny reluctantly rose to his feet.

"Come over here," he said to Samson. "You write, and I'll sit on the couch."

They changed places. Unfortunately, Samson was still forced to use his briefcase; the lace tablecloth, with its holes and patterns, turned out to be an even worse writing surface, with the pencil piercing the paper before the young investigator could even finish titling the document. He smoothed out the hole with his fingers, lined up the sheet with the edges of the briefcase and raised his eyes to the hostess.

"What is your name?"

"Antonina Pokhabkina," the woman answered, and, without waiting for the next question, she added, "forty-seven, from the peasantry."

"From the peasantry?" Samson repeated in a surprised tone.

"That's right. Grandfather was a peasant from the Radomyshl District, village of Kamenny Brod."

"Have you been questioned like this often?" Samson asked, amazed at Antonina's readiness to speak about herself in so brisk and official a manner.

"Hundreds of times," she replied. "I trade at the market, you know, and there you're either a witness, or a criminal, or a victim every other day. Kyiv ain't no village."

"Alright," Samson said, cutting off her disquisition. "Let's get to the point. Do you know Moses Briskin?"

"I do," she answered, nodding.

Samson carefully took down his question and her response.

"How many times have you purchased meat from him?"

"Not meat, intestines," she corrected him. "'Bout ten times."

"When was the last purchase made?"

"Don't remember. I must have bought seven times since then."

"How? From whom?" Kholodny's voice came from the direction of the couch.

"From sellers," she said, looking back at the distant investigator. "Who else?"

"Do you know about the decree of the ExProFooCom banning private trade in meat?" Samson asked her sternly.

"Well, like I said, I don't buy meat." She shrugged. "I buy intestines. Can't afford meat. And who has the money to buy meat pies? Can barely unload the ones I stuff with intestines."

"But can you still find meat at the market?" Samson enquired, narrowing his eyes thoughtfully.

"You can find anything at the market," Antonina answered eagerly, "meat included. Only, they sell it in small batches, on the sly."

"So that the police won't get them?" Kholodny asked from the couch.

"So that the thieves won't," she answered. "Meat's expensive, so the sellers chop it real fine, to keep the price of the pieces down. A piece that small, anyone could grab it and run off. Who's gonna chase after 'im? So, folks sell it on the sly – cover the tray with a cloth and, if the buyer's well dressed and groomed, like, show the meat. If it's some good-for-nothing, they give 'im the boot."

"Do you cover your pies?" Samson asked.

"With a newspaper," Antonina replied. "To keep dust off, not eyes. The first row's out in the open, the others are covered. They're cheap – why would I hide 'em! The faster I sell 'em, the sooner I can throw the next batch into the oven."

*

Samson and Kholodny walked to the Brest-Litovsk Highway. There were no cabs on Borshchahivska, let alone on Kryvy Lane.

"What a headache this case is," Samson sighed. "How will we ever track down all the meat-sellers? The woman didn't even tell us where she gets her intestines now, just kept saying that intestines aren't meat."

"Yes," Kholodny agreed, nodding as he walked. "There are murders all around us, while we're out here investigating trade. This is all Abyazov's fault. If the Chekists care about meat so much, let them look into it."

"It would be easier to conduct a census of all livestock in the city and then to check each address: is the pig still alive or not?" Samson continued his comrade's train of thought.

He stepped over a ditch dug in the road to drain away water. They finally came out to the highway and Kholodny immediately saw a cart drawn by a familiar horse from the Pechersk Hippodrome."

"Greetings, brother!" he shouted to the cabby, taking a step forward and waving his hand.

The diminutive former jockey seemed to recognise them as well. He raised his hand in response, then quickly lowered it and pulled at the reins.

The sun shone over the Brest-Litovsk Highway. A light breeze blew from the south, and crows cawed merrily in the crowns of the roadside poplars. Three trucks loaded with Red Army soldiers drove slowly in the opposite direction from the city centre.

Back at the station, Samson and Kholodny reviewed all the evidence pertaining to the meat case. The number of documents had grown, but not enough for them to march boldly into Nayden's office and report.

"When will we have Briskin's photographs?" asked the former priest.

"I have them right here."

"Why aren't they in the file, then?"

Samson retrieved the envelope with the photos from a desk drawer and slipped it into the file. It looked fatter.

"See?" Kholodny said, nodding contentedly.

A surprise awaited Samson at home.

"What is that?" he burst out as soon as he entered the living room and saw the copper bucket on the table.

"Come closer, dear fellow, and have a look," the doctor answered enigmatically. His medical gown again bulged over his summer suit.

"Nadezhda isn't home yet?" Samson asked, looking around.

Vatrukhin shook his head.

"I could tell," Samson said with a sigh. "There's mud out there," he added, indicating the hallway. "She would have cleaned it."

"Oh, forgive me! *Ma faute! Ma faute!* I'll see to it now," the doctor stammered, hastening out into the hallway with a guilty expression on his face.

Samson approached the table. Inside the bucket, red apples were soaking in brine. His hand reached out for the nearest one all by itself, but Samson stopped it in time. Yet the taste of soaked apples, which he hadn't eaten for two years, appeared on his tongue. Memory was working its magic.

He remembered how, one time, in the good old days, his family had decided to celebrate the year's first snowfall with soaked apples from their summer house. He recalled the wonderful crunch of the apples, wet and juicy, on everyone's teeth. This unusual quartet sounded for some five minutes. They all stood at the left window of the living room, looking out into the street. Snowflakes as big and fluffy as chicken feathers came floating down to the pavement. And the people below – everyone dressed beautifully back then, and no-one was ever in any hurry, no-one was ever afraid – occasionally lifted their faces to the sky, as if wanting to greet the falling snow with their eyes, to have it melt on their cheeks, foreheads and noses. It was all so cheerful, so easeful, like a fairytale. He was only a boy, and he was drawn down to the street, but this special activity – eating these crunchy, sweet-and-sour apples with his family – held him rooted to the spot in front of the window, beyond which the snowfall grew thicker and thicker.

"May I use this rag?" Vatrukhin asked, peering in from the hallway with something purple in his hand.

"Probably," Samson responded.

"Would you get a cup from the cupboard?" the doctor requested, approaching with an ordinary bucket half-filled with water. "Add a cup of brine to this, and, when Nadezhda returns, the hallway will not only be clean, but also fragrant," he explained solemnly.

A minute later, Samson was alone, but from the hallway came the rhythmic noise of a wet rag gliding across the floor, as well as the joyful muttering with which the doctor accompanied his work.

The shiny copper bucket again attracted Samson's attention. He examined it from all sides and noticed a plate bearing the tsarist double-headed eagle. Beneath the eagle was an embossed inscription: MEASURING BUCKET. HOLDS 10 MUGS, 100 CUPS, OR 200 SHKALIKS.

Samson shook his head in surprise, wondering how many apples it would hold.

Nadezhda came home a full hour later and immediately began to ask about the smell in the air. The doctor proudly showed her the bucket of apples. Then they sat down to eat the apples with tea, and the sweet, moist crunching once again brought a smile of remembrance to Samson's face.

"Fees come in various forms, these days," the doctor explained, also smiling with self-satisfaction, even pride. "An old patient brought them. Glorious, aren't they?"

Nadezhda nodded.

"Did he bring the bucket too, or is it yours?" asked Samson.

"Bucket too. Come to think of it, I forgot to ask him whether I should transfer them into some other container . . ."

"A beautiful object," Samson said, stroking the copper. "And it isn't a plain bucket, it's for measuring – see?" He pointed to the eagle, then turned the bucket so that Nadezhda could see better.

"That was before the revolution," Vatrukhin commented. "Now, they say we'll follow the Germans in adopting the metric system. Say goodbye to eggs by the dozen. We'll be buying them in tens, at the same price."

"You have to admit that the metric system is easier," Nadezhda objected, though her face expressed playfulness rather than a desire to argue. "Even under the tsar, we had hundred- and ten-, but not twelve-rouble notes."

"That's not quite right," Vatrukhin continued. "We had three-rouble notes, didn't we? Still do. And what's that? A quarter of a dozen. So, take four three-rouble notes – and there are your twelve roubles." Then, looking tensely and somewhat fearfully at Samson, he changed the subject. "I meant to ask . . . Would you mind if I indicated, outside the door, that I also live here? Temporarily, of course! And not outside the main entrance, only at the door to the flat."

"I don't see why not," Samson replied, shrugging.

"My patients sometimes get lost, you understand, and knock on other doors. I wouldn't want your neighbours to think that we're holding secret meetings here. God forbid they should report it to the Cheka – then we'd all be in trouble."

Samson shuddered at the mention of the Cheka and trouble, but he quickly calmed himself. Just in case, he looked into Nadezhda's eyes, checking for any strong objection to his granting the doctor permission to indicate his residence outside the door. Nadezhda had either missed the doctor's request altogether or had deemed it unworthy of a noticeable response. And so the young investigator again turned his gaze to Vatrukhin, giving him another amiable nod.

Chapter 23

The next morning, Zhylianska Street struck Samson, who was hurrying off to work, with its noisy boisterousness. The sun's rays touched up houses scuffed by the revolutionary era, reviving their faded façades. Indeed, Kyiv as a whole seemed to have perked up, as if someone had wound it up with a special little key, causing everything on the streets and boulevards – cars, carts, pedestrians – to spin, to move faster than usual. All the participants in this general *pas de basque* were able to sustain the exaggerated pace, which meant that Samson too had to walk faster, having become an integral part of wound-up Kyiv. Behind him, the driver of a shiny black car blew his horn, wanting to pass a cab carrying two men in clerkish clothes with stoic peasant faces. One of them looked indignantly at the car. Yet there was also fear in the driver's eyes; he seemed afraid that the car would hit the cab. The cabby's ear hadn't even twitched at the squeak of the horn, indicating that he had no intention of yielding to his motorised competitor. Of course, both vehicles easily overtook Samson, as well as all the other pedestrians hurrying about their business. The sun shone up above and the air was already warmer, already saturated with the scent of fresh horse manure. The approach of May was felt most keenly in the mornings – mornings like this one. Samson also felt the approach of May Day, because at the corner of Zhylianska and Velyka Volodymyrska streets he overtook three skinny bohemian-haired young men carrying a light, apparently plywood, life-size monument to a Red Army soldier. Actually, Samson was surprised at his ability to discern a Red Army man in the large and not especially detailed structure, which bore no hint of a face, nor even a human form. In one place, however, a sharpened wooden rod stuck up from the thing, looking very much like a rifle with a bayonet. And when Samson scanned this plywood monument in a certain way – namely, from the tip of the bayonet-rod to the very bottom, where the trio held the structure – he immediately understood what it was. Probably, it still needed a few finishing touches, the application of lines and contours which would make this temporary work of monumental art familiar and understandable to representatives of any class.

His feet turned onto Tarasivska, and Samson immediately felt that he had stepped out of the stream, leaving the noise and marching rhythm of life behind him, as if he had climbed onto the bank of a river that had carried him downstream to the point he needed to reach, from which he could advance on his own. It occurred to the young investigator that the street itself was a kind of vehicle, carrying people and cars from their points of departure to their points of arrival like an endless non-stop tram.

Tarasivska surprised him with its silence only in contrast to Zhylianska's excessive loudness. However, approaching the station, Samson noticed movement at the front entrance. Policemen, soldiers and people who, though they wore civilian clothes, exhibited an impossible-to-conceal military bearing, were going in and out. And, in this movement, which was by no means Brownian, but rather apian, because the majority of its participants were rushing into the station, as bees into a hive, he also noticed an element of immobility: an adolescent girl in a long blue skirt and black blouse, her short chestnut-coloured hair slicked back in a manner more likely to repel than to attract attention. She had a bundle containing something light. From time to time, the bundle would wobble. When Samson came closer, she raised the hand that held it in order to scratch her nose with her index finger. Her face seemed familiar, but Samson's feet carried him past her into the station. He had been captured by the energy of entering the building in which he was tasked with writing down, in his own hand, the meaning of his actions, the meaning of his very existence in the present.

Climbing up the stairs, he stopped abruptly. His memory had found and brought to his conscious mind proof of his acquaintance with the girl at the entrance. He returned to the street and approached her.

"Are you Briskin's daughter?" he asked.

The girl nodded.

"You've brought him hard-boiled eggs, is that right?" Samson guessed.

Another nod.

"Come with me," he said. "I'll arrange a brief visit."

In a state bordering on shock, the girl obediently followed him into the station. Samson took her up to the interrogation room and ordered the soldier on duty to fetch Moses Briskin.

As soon as the detained meat-merchant entered the room, he stopped, dumbfounded, his eyes fixed firmly on his daughter.

"Alright, you sit down in your usual place," Samson told him, indicating the chained stool with a glance. "And you," he continued, turning to the girl. "Remind me of your name?"

"Sophia."

"And you, Sophia, sit here, at the table. Here's a newspaper," he said, unfolding an old issue of *The Bolshevik* in front of her. "Peel the eggs so that your father can eat them in peace. I'll step out."

And he did, closing the door behind him and ordering the soldier not to let them out of the room. Next stop was Nayden's office.

The commander received him in a not very friendly manner. Sleep lines on the left side of his face spoke of a short night. Samson stared thoughtfully at the depression in the padded leather of the couch's right armrest. That must have been where Nayden had tried to get some rest.

The recovered mug stood on the desk in front of the commander, sending up steam.

"Maybe it wasn't worth sending that petty little thief to the Cheka?" Samson asked, not taking his eyes off the mug of hot tea. "After all, we wanted to keep this quiet, didn't we?"

"They know how to deal with his type," murmured Nayden. "What's the latest on the meat?"

"Nearly wrapped up," Samson assured him. "We've already added photographs of Briskin to the file, and now all that remains is to interview two more witnesses. Then, we can issue our verdict."

"Keep this in mind," Nayden began, with a note of threat in his voice. "The Cheka can demand to review the case. And, if you and Kholodny cut corners or try to pull something, you can imagine the consequences. They think we're too gentle as it is. If I were you, I'd prepare the speculator for a harsh sentence."

"What can they review?" Samson asked cautiously.

"The witnesses. They think the police often protect criminal accomplices from punishment by classifying them as witnesses."

"I see." Samson nodded thoughtfully. "So . . . they might re-interview the witnesses?"

"They might," Nayden confirmed.

After stopping by his own office and greeting Kholodny, Samson went back to the interrogation room.

His arrival interrupted the conversation between father and daughter. They both froze, mouths open. Then Briskin hiccupped.

The number of shell fragments on the newspaper told Samson that the detainee had eaten two eggs. This time, thank goodness, they had been peeled.

"I would—" Briskin began, but hiccupped again. "I would be grateful for a drink."

Samson stepped out again and returned with a mug of water from the common bucket. Briskin drained it in one gulp. An unhealthy pink blush coloured his face. Almost mechanically, Samson shifted his gaze to the daughter, as if he wanted to determine the degree of family resemblance. The only resemblance he could find was that her eyes were set a bit too close to the bridge of her nose, just as her father's were, as if they were of some different race. But what really drew his attention was her pallor, the bloodlessness of her thin lips. The girl was clearly starving.

After letting them say their goodbyes, Samson escorted Sophia outside and, in parting, handed her a meal voucher with a purple stamp.

"You can use it in any Soviet cafeteria," he said in response to her surprised look. "But I'd recommend the one on the corner of Stolypin Street and Chekhov Lane – they always offer two courses with tea. The only thing this won't get you is bread."

Samson himself skipped lunch, choosing instead to restore his vigour and refresh his thoughts by taking a walk to the Jewish Market. Having made sure that the contents of his pockets were at a depth inaccessible to pickpockets, he entered the throng that had formed immediately past the Halytska bathhouse. This initial throng turned out to be of the pushing-and-shoving variety: people crowded around whichever vendor stuck out his goods most forcefully. This person was immediately encircled by a mass of bodies, which a casual passer-by would never be able to divide into vendors, buyers and thieves. These clusters would disperse and regroup, flowing one into another, so that it wasn't terribly difficult to wend one's way between them. Further on, the market became more geometrically comprehensible. The vendors stood in rows, like houses on a street, and buyers and thieves walked along these living streets, occasionally stopping. Unable to surround any of the vendors from all directions, they sometimes suggested that a vendor step aside. But the seasoned hawkers of goods refused, maintaining the orderliness of the arrangement.

Squeezing through the pushing-and-shoving part of the market, Samson aimed for the street-like part. For some reason, his thoughts now made a new kind of sense of this welter, which he'd witnessed so many times before, offering an explanation for the life and self-organisation of the sprawling, diverse body mercantile. He now understood why his feet seemed to lead him, all by themselves, towards the living street of vendors. He understood why intelligent vendors wouldn't wander around with their goods in their hands, opting instead to stand firm, in a row. For a vendor, to be surrounded on all sides by a clasping crowd was to offer oneself in sacrifice, to become a willing victim. When surrounded by a crowd, a single person – with or without goods – is a victim, even if the crowd has no plans to trample or rob him. Perhaps some vendors wish to look like victims, hoping to arouse pity in others, a desire to buy something in order to help them survive. But the faces of most of the wandering vendors expressed fear and self-doubt. On the other hand, those who stood in rows, like houses on a street, appeared to be in the mood to fight, argue and haggle. They had banded together in order to hold out, to occupy their personal, albeit temporary and in no way designated, plot of the market, to dig in their heels until they sold something or reached the point of utter exhaustion.

Samson entered the nearest street of vendors. On the right, beyond two more such streets, there was a wide passage to the wooden shops and storehouses. Beyond that were about a dozen wheelbarrows standing idle with their operators. Their work was usually in full swing in the morning, when they were tasked with unloading goods from carts and delivering them to places the carts themselves couldn't reach. In front of the shops, here and there, were portable wooden counters, at which the permanent vendors guarded their goods with their hands and searched for buyers with their eyes. These eyes were sharp, and they latched on easily. If one met their gaze, it was almost impossible to pass by without stopping and chatting. Samson remembered this from childhood.

Someone bumped into Samson, distracting him from his market memories and meditations. Into his earhole burst a great noise, a proper din, of which he, strangely, had been ignorant until that moment. A man's sorrowful voice rose above the uproar, half-singing, half-shouting a dramatic song.

The young investigator stopped. Beside him, a woman in a gypsy headscarf was trying to sell a lacquered wooden box. A little brass key protruded from the lock in its lid.

After a brief pause, the market singer shouted something and started in on his next number:

Vanya came to the stable that morning
and harnessed his horse to his cart,
then he took him a big swig of vodka,
hopin' to get a good start.

The life of our cabbies ain't easy,
they drive in the snow and the rain
to make just a few measly roubles –
I tell ya, it ain't worth the pain.

Samson moved towards the song and heard the singer's voice a bit more clearly with every step. The din in his head grew louder too, however, as if it were accumulating there, pouring freely, without barriers, into his earhole. On the way, Samson turned his head to the right, appearing to be more interested in the goods on that side of the market street. Now, his intact left ear was better able to discern the words of the song, with less general noise to drown them out.

The singer continued, his voice taking on, it seemed to Samson, more plaintive notes with each verse:

Day before, late in the evening,
leaving his labours behind,
Vanya brawled with a pal over nothin' –
tanning that poor fella's hide.

All that night, his pal couldn't sleep –
thoughts of vengeance ate at his heart.
He was tossin' and turnin' and itchin'
to tear our Vanya apart.

So, he snuck right into the stable
to feed henbane to his horse.
The creature sleepily chewed it,
the poison running its course.

Vanya came to the stable that morning
and harnessed his horse to his cart,
then he took him a big swig of vodka,
hopin' to get a good start.

The living street of vendors ended. Samson stopped as if he'd emerged into a forest clearing. There appeared around him a kind of loosely defined human crossroads, extending eight or ten yards in all directions. In front of him, a crowd of onlookers were listening to the market singer. To the right were lady vendors in scarves, a counter on which goods lay covered with a newspaper and, beyond that, the shop-shed of a tool sharpener. Suddenly, from the opposite direction, came a cry: "Sharpen your knives, axes, scissors!"

Samson looked back and saw a peasant with a grinding wheel on his shoulder.

Meanwhile, the song went on:

He took his cab out on the road,
lookin' to pick up a fare.
The evening's brawl was forgotten –
our Vanya, he just didn't care.

He weaved between wagons and chaises,
passed Oleksandrivsky Park,
then suddenly turned towards Yamska,
the sun shining bright at his back.

He sped down Tarasivska, headlong –
the horse was out of control.
He pulled at the reins like a madman,
but faster and faster he rolled.

At that moment, out came a tram,
wheel after heavy wheel.
Seeing that horse rushin' at 'em,
folks aboard, they started to squeal.

"*Zhu-er-duo! Zhu-er-duo!*" A sharp, almost boyish voice suddenly cut through the song. "*Zhu-er-duo! Zhu-er-duo!*"

Samson turned round in annoyance and saw a Chinese man shouting the strange word, two dozen paces away. He was standing behind a counter covered with newspapers and, continuing to shout, cast glances to the right and left. At some point, he apparently sensed the policeman's gaze on him, fell silent and looked back at Samson. Samson raised his hand and shook his finger.

The song, now freed from unnecessary interruptions, continued.

But the shouting, it didn't matter –
didn't matter a damn.
Unleashing a deafening clatter,
the horse slammed into the tram.

The tram was torn asunder.
Blood stained the cobblestones.
Bodies thrown hither and yonder –
seven were killed at once.

Twenty sat injured, moaning.
People gathered to stare.
Seems even the rev-tribunal
was this time caught unawares.

Samson felt his heart skip a beat. The noise seemed to vanish from his head, while the song remained. He looked again at the nearby counter and didn't even try to guess what lay beneath the newspaper. Instead, he recalled the tram accident he had witnessed the other day. The song recounted exactly what he'd seen: how the cabby had lost control of his horse, fruitlessly shouting and pulling at the reins, and how the cab had slammed into the tram, pushing it over. Only the song seemed to have more to say about the cabby than about the tram. And it went on:

Vanya lay dead on the road,
crushed by his own dead horse.
Now, he would never know
that he'd been the tragedy's cause.

Now, he would drive no more,
would never drink vodka again.
He had made his pal awful sore.
And never would he make amends.

He'd never bring back the dead
or comb his horse's mane.
Kyiv would soon forget 'im,
but that scene will stay in our brains.

Folks'll stay off the trams,
but only a couple of days.
Then life'll grow better, brighter,
returnin' to its old ways.

Samson's head felt hot, for some reason. He looked up at the sky and saw the sun shining. He touched his leather cap; it was scorching and he removed it. It occurred to him that he had already changed his leather jacket for a tunic, but he still wore the cap – largely to protect his bare earhole. By pushing the cap to one side, he could shield himself from excess noise, from the wind and from annoying philistine curiosity.

The crowd that had been listening to the song began to thin out. Samson peered at it, assuming that, once the onlookers left, he would see the singer. The man, he imagined, must have been standing on a stool, to make himself more audible and visible.

The crowd soon dispersed, but there was no sign of the singer.

The young investigator went up to a counter covered with a newspaper.

"Care for a pie, darlin'?" asked a round-faced woman with a blackened, slightly swollen right eye. "Still warm."

"What kind do you have?" Samson asked, his appetite whetted.

"Cabbage."

"What about intestines? Or meat?"

"Tonya's got the intestines," she answered, nodding to the right.

Samson turned in that direction and saw Antonina Pokhabkina, whom he and Kholodny had questioned only the day before.

"Are her pies good?" he asked, returning his gaze to the round-faced woman.

"Who knows what she stuffs 'em with," she said, shrugging her shoulders. "If onions were cheap, that would be one thing. But there ain't no onions for sale, and salt – that'll cost ya plenty. Without onions or salt, intestines smell of dung. Ya gotta wash 'em for a week straight, soak 'em in milk."

Having bought a cabbage pie from the vendor, Samson walked over to the counter of Antonina Pokhabkina. As he approached, he noticed that her goods were also covered with a newspaper – entirely, not just the back rows, as she had claimed.

Chapter 24

In the evening, as Samson sat at the round table with Nadezhda and Dr Vatrukhin, enjoying oatmeal and the pies he had bought from Antonina Pokhabkina at the Jewish Market, he kept returning to the song he heard there. It wasn't the melody that haunted him – a melody reused thousands of times by street singers – but the story, with whose origins Samson, one might say, had a personal, highly memorable acquaintance. Even now, as if it were happening again, he saw the cab rushing down Tarasivska, the cabby trying to rein in his horse, the tram emerging into the intersection of Tarasivska and Mariinsko-Blagovishchenska, the dead passengers, the injured waiting for help. All this – the song, the recollection – were now woven together into a single whole, in which the material of memory and the material of the lyrics complemented each other as a suit's satin lining complements its Yorkshire wool exterior; they could exist separately, to be sure, but they only became a suit when sewn together.

Samson's thoughts automatically transitioned to Jacobson's vanished suit, which had its own peculiar, hard-to-believe story. First, the patterns for the suit were stolen by Red Army men, then the German tailor from whom they'd been stolen refused to acknowledge them as his own, then another tailor made the suit for a fee paid by the Workers' and Peasants' Militia and, finally, the criminal identified by the suit managed to bribe another Red Army man to steal it from the police station.

Samson brushed off these thoughts of Jacobson, albeit with difficulty. Yet, the suit had managed to drag behind it a bitter reminder of the stolen silver bone, with its stunningly beautiful Latin name, *os femoris*. Still, the impressions he had formed earlier that day, crowned by the song, overpowered these painful memories. The intestine-stuffed pies also enriched the meagre pleasure provided by the somewhat flavourless porridge, although both lacked salt. But there was a general shortage of salt, and also of sugar. Therein lay the bitter truth about these troubled times, which could indeed in no way be salted or sweetened.

"Your mind appears to be elsewhere," Vatrukhin said, having decided to break the unusual silence at the table. "You aren't in pain, are you?"

"What?" Samson asked, emerging from his reflections. "No, not at all. It's just hard to collect my thoughts, these days."

"Well, your Nadezhda certainly knows how to concentrate," the doctor responded, flashing a smile at the young woman. "You should be proud of her."

Samson looked blankly at Nadezhda.

"What's to be proud of?" she asked, a bit embarrassed by the attention.

"Quite a lot, quite a lot," the doctor insisted. "After all, you were given a special ration *en récompense*."

"*En récompense*?" Samson asked, surprised that Vatrukhin still employed language from the bygone era of Francophilia.

"Yes, as a reward. That says a lot!"

"What's in the ration?" Samson immediately regretted this expression of banal, hungry curiosity. "I mean, in reward for what?"

"Not at work, at the bureau. At the firing range. For accuracy. Two herrings and over a pound of pickled radishes."

Samson stopped chewing. "They took you all shooting again?"

"Not everyone. Only me and four others who were good at it," Nadezhda explained, not without pride. "We have a new instructor now, a Latvian. He's young, but he's already been wounded, so he limps a little. Such a lovely accent . . . You know, these pies taste . . . a bit odd," she added, shifting her gaze to the one she had just started – her second or third. Then she took another bite.

"A lot of onions," Samson explained. "And they're old, from last autumn. They might have frozen in the winter."

"And how are you faring, doctor?" Samson asked, changing the focus of the conversation.

"I too am trying to the best of my ability," Vatrukhin began, somewhat evasively. "Today, I went out and notified three more patients about the new address. Two came by. So, I will happily make my humble contribution to the family budget. Did you happen to notice the sign?"

Samson shook his head. "You know, under the weight of my thoughts, I barely even lifted my head," he admitted.

"Oh, I also visited my flat," the doctor continued. "I'm surprised it hasn't been looted. I brought a few things back, but they're already in my room. By the way, may I hang my clothes in there?" he asked, glancing at the bulky wardrobe that now stood between the windows overlooking the street.

"It still holds my parents' clothes," Samson said, alarmed. "I wouldn't want to disturb them."

"No, no, of course not." The doctor nodded. "In that case, may I use the empty chest in my room?"

"Yes, please do," the master of the flat answered readily.

When the meal was over and the tea that followed it was drunk, the doctor took his leave. While Nadezhda was carrying the dishes to the kitchen, Samson stepped outside with a lighted candle in his hand. To the left of the door to the flat now hung the same wordless sign that had only recently adorned the façade of the doctor's residence: a pyramidal triangle containing an eye.

Vatrukhin's words over dinner sounded again in Samson's mind: *I will happily make my humble contribution to the family budget.*

The young investigator wondered, without a hint of indignation, whether the doctor had actually come to consider them his family.

*

Soon, he was in bed, but sleep wouldn't come. The song about the tram accident sounded again in his memory, causing slight anxiety.

If the horse had struck the tram because it had been poisoned with henbane as an act of revenge, then this was no accident, Samson concluded, looking up at the ceiling. It was a crime. Murder. Yet, if everyone believed it to have been an accident, then this horse-poisoner, this murderer, would go unpunished.

Samson understood that the more he thought about this song, the less chance he had of getting sufficient sleep, or of falling asleep at all. He rolled onto his side, closed his eyes and tried to empty his mind. But the song still sounded, softly, but clearly enough for him to make out the words. He could even discern the voice of the market singer.

Having tried a number of positions and still failing to drive away the memory, he sat up in bed. Eventually, he rose to his feet, adjusted his nightshirt and walked up to the window. The darkness that had spilled beyond it was accompanied by silence. The gate of the building's courtyard was tightly shut.

He went out into the living room and pressed his ear to Nadezhda's door, listening close. He pulled at the handle gently and the door opened without a creak.

Cautiously, he sat down on the edge of the Nadezhda's bed. The springs made a timid, quiet sound, which proved strong enough to half-awaken Nadezhda. She reached out to him, touching his bare knee.

"Come, lie down," she whispered. "You're so helpless today."

He got into bed and embraced her. In a whisper, he told her about the crash, the song and his suspicions.

"Samson, dear," she said, her fingers running tenderly through his ginger hair. "Don't take offence at this, but I've been meaning to say it for a long time . . . You're sort of – scatterbrained. You think about everything at once, when what you need to do is to concentrate on the main problem. What is your main problem, at the moment?"

"The meat case," Samson admitted.

"And what are you thinking about?"

"About the tram. And Jacobson's suit. And Abyazov, who was taken back to the Cheka for having helped to free you from the railway workers. And about Kosyakin, the Red Army man – Kholodny had promised him he wouldn't be punished, but then . . . And also about our doctor . . ."

"See?" she breathed warmly into his left ear. "There's too much on your mind. You need to concentrate. And besides, singers and poets make up songs on the topic of the day, but it's reporters who write the actual truth for the newspapers. Go on and read what the papers say about the crash. That's where you'll find the facts."

Nadezhda's gentle, velvety voice began to lull Samson to sleep. Drifting off, he realised that she was right. Songs weren't newspapers. They weren't proof. A song was merely a shout – a cry from the soul to evoke feelings in other souls.

At eleven in the morning, Samson found himself walking down Karavaevska on his way to Khreshchatyk from Tarasivska. His feet were carrying him to the building where ficus and palm trees decorated the interiors of Leon Vishnevsky's spacious photographic studio on the first floor, and where the aged, grey-haired photographer himself lived either behind one of the studio's inner doors or on the floor above it. Amid the exotic greenery and boxes of photographs, Vishnevsky was the head of his own invented state, which had absolutely nothing to do with the noisy world beyond his windows. True, the door to the studio could be considered a kind of border that he was forced to cross now and again, but he always returned to his photographic jungle.

"You photograph remarkably well – both you and your charming mademoiselle!" the old man complimented Samson, leafing through voluminous brown envelopes. "Ah, that's where you've been hiding!" he declared happily, extracting from one envelope a large double portrait and a pack of pocket-sized photographs on thick cardboard. "Do have a look for yourself," he said, handing everything to Samson.

The double portrait drew a tender smile. The Apache shirt came out black and made him look like a retired hussar or a gypsy, while Nadezhda in her sundress looked like a carefree, love-stuck lass at a summer cottage.

"I made three little ones for you," Leon Vishnevsky said. "You can give them as keepsakes."

Samson paid the old man and shook his hand. He caught himself thinking that he enjoyed the atmosphere in the studio, this sovereign realm of palm trees and photographic beauty. Vishnevsky's closed world seemed much safer than the open one outside the door.

"Don't forget, I'm always willing to come to your station," the old man reminded him. "Only happy people go to be photographed voluntarily, and there are surprisingly few of those around. Printing small cards for certificates and various documents is a boring task, painful for the eyes. So, taking portraits of your prisoners is the best option for me."

Back in his office, Samson couldn't resist showing off the photographs to Kholodny, who was delighted and immediately mentioned that he himself was planning to have his picture taken.

"The last time I posed for a photograph, I was still a priest," he recalled. "It's important for a person to see his face on cards at different stages, in order to comprehend the transience of life and to appreciate it all the more." He nodded as if someone else had just spoken the words and he agreed with them. "You and Nadezhda look better here than you do in real life! That old man is a true artist!"

"Oh, no," Samson said, shaking his head and looking carefully at the cards. "He didn't have to retouch these. It's the atmosphere, over there."

"What will you do with them?"

"The large one I'll frame and hang on the wall," Samson answered decisively. "Then, I'll inscribe one of the smaller ones and give it to Nadezhda. She'll give one of hers to me, and probably one to her parents . . ."

"You can't think in such small, ordinary terms," Kholodny said, his tone serious, meditative. "That's what a child or a peasant would do, but you're an educated person. And Nadezhda is no simpleton either – she's an employee of an important institution. You should arrange a solemn occasion, so that the memory lasts a lifetime. You are in love, aren't you?"

"Of course I am," Samson said, throwing a surprised look at his comrade.

Kholodny picked up the large photograph, in which Nadezhda and Samson sat beside each other on the couch, their shoulders touching but their hands apart.

"Such photographs are usually taken after the wedding, you know, but the old man managed to make one for you before you were married. While these little ones – they're of the appropriate, pre-wedding type."

"What's a wedding got to do with it?"

"Alright." Kholodny took a deep breath, as if he were preparing to launch into a sermon. "I can see exactly what's going to happen. I have a gift for these things – when I understand a person well. So, you'll sit down at the table, facing each other, and inscribe these images with ardent words. And then you won't be able to resist the urge to cling to each other, body against body. A magnetic force will draw you into each other's arms. Because an exchange of ardently inscribed photographs is the same as an exchange of rings at the altar. You understand?"

Samson considered the scenario. Kholodny's speculations began to make sense.

"You think ... the occasion should be more solemn? Maybe even a proposal?"

"See? You've figured it out for yourself. I tell you what – remember I told you about the chapel on the Dog Path? Where the anti-priest holds services? Why don't you get married there?"

"How?" Samson asked, taken aback. "We've rejected God."

"That doesn't matter. God doesn't reject anyone, even if they've rejected him. And we're talking about an anti-priest. He himself doesn't believe in God. He's been defrocked. So, this will be an anti-wedding, as if to spite God. To your joy, God be damned!"

"I've got to think it over," Samson responded absently. "I'll ask Nadezhda."

"No, no, no, that'll ruin everything! You just have to lead her there under some pretext. But, first, talk to the anti-priest. You've got to catch Nadezhda off-guard. If you confuse a person right before making them happy, they'll be thrice as happy. I can deal with the fellow myself, if you want. He and I went to the same seminary. I know him like a book."

Kholodny gave Samson a conspiratorial smile, but it immediately transformed into a frown. He undid the top three buttons of his tunic, reached inside, pulled out the silver cross, then reached in again.

"The burn itches," he explained, noticing his comrade's worried expression.

"Have you been applying the ointment the doctor gave you?"

"I thought it had already healed up, but the crucifix is heavy, keeps scraping off the scab ..."

"Then don't wear it."

"I have to." Kholodny lowered his head to look at the cross that now hung outside his tunic. "It's already saved my life twice. Look," he said, lifting it up. "Here's a mark left by a bullet it deflected, and here's a notch from a knife. How could I take it off, after that?"

“In that case, wind a handkerchief around it, or a footwrap, so that the silver doesn’t touch your skin,” Samson suggested.

“Now, that’s a sound hypostasis! I’ll do it,” chirped Kholodny, delighted with his comrade’s idea.

Chapter 25

The Saturday April sun turned out to be deceptive, but this only occurred to Samson when they had already walked half a mile from the house. He hadn't managed to lure Nadezhda to her own wedding secretly, but when the young investigator confessed to her about the true purpose of their stroll, her eyes lit up brightly and dreamily, like two polar stars. His father's beige summer suit, which Samson had donned for lack of a solemn one of his own, could not protect him from the chilly breeze. It brought to his cheeks and lips moisture picked up from the waves of the Dnipro. He turned to Nadezhda, who, unlike him, had managed to find among her possessions an item of clothing appropriate for both this personally festive moment and this not at all festive but in fact rather alarming historical moment: a long blue dress trimmed with white lace. Instead of a hat, which would have been a more suitable accessory in the old days, she had put on a blue beret, hinting, as it were, at the fact that she was not against participating in revolutionary demonstrations and rallies. In a word, her outfit was altogether appropriate. Even Kholodny glanced at her as they walked, with what appeared to be special interest or respect. The comrades had agreed that their attire shouldn't give the slightest indication of their belonging to the police force. As a result of this arrangement, Samson felt rather strange, ill at ease. Not only was he unarmed, but his father's suit hung a bit loose on him, making him doubly vulnerable. His appearance, he felt, was an affront to all passers-by, who did their best to look like grey, inconspicuous mice. It was, too, an affront to the memory of his father, since he had also pulled on, not without difficulty, the deceased man's summer shoes, which had been too tight even for him, although he had loved them very much. Once white, they now looked beige and seemed to blend with the colour of the suit, but walking in them proved extremely uncomfortable, and in fact painful. The edges of his big toenails were pressed into the index toes, which, in turn, were pressed into the middle ones. Samson didn't feel his ring toes or pinkies, so the shoes must not have caused them discomfort.

"I just hope mother and father find the chapel," Nadezhda said somewhat worriedly, looking at Samson.

So that's what was troubling her, he thought, and he gave her a reassuring smile.

"They'll find it," he promised. "We won't start without them."

"It's a sure thing. Every cabby knows the way," Kholodny added.

The breeze died down and they again found themselves on the sunny side of the street. The buildings of the Exhibition Grounds appeared ahead. Samson knew it was about a twenty-minute walk from there to their destination.

He asked himself why they hadn't taken a cab. And then he remembered what Nadezhda had once told him – that, when one reaches special moments in life, one must make an effort to remember the path that led up to them. This morning, their path ran along Zhylianska to Velyka Vasylkivska Street, and then past the foot of Cherepanova Hill, with its remnants of the formerly luxurious Exhibition Grounds which had adorned the city from 1913 until quite recently. After that, they would go through Oleksiivsky Park until they reached the "revolutionary" hole in the fence, which was as wide as the gate of a wealthy estate, and then proceed along Prozorivska Street towards the Dog Path.

Stepping onto the Path and hearing the suddenly appearing and soon disappearing murmur of the Klovski Stream, Samson felt a surge of excitement. It was as if he had left the real world and entered a fairy-tale kingdom, full of heroes and monsters.

The entrance to the Path resembled a funnel. It gaped from the bushes along the rapidly narrowing little track that led from the cobblestone pavement – a track trampled by thousands of feet. One felt, upon approaching it, that it would suck one right in, like a bog. After all, people only took the Path in one direction, towards the Monastery of the Caves. Indeed, as Samson, Nadezhda and Kholodny were approaching, a woman in monastic clothes ducked into this funnel-path, followed by an old man with a staff, and not a soul emerged from it onto the pavement.

Suddenly, Nadezhda stopped and looked down at her shoes. "Oh, no," she moaned. After only a few steps down the Path, the toes were smeared with wet clay.

She opened the purse dangling from the crook of her arm, pulled out a handkerchief and shifted her flustered gaze back to the shoes.

Samson squatted down at her feet and gave her a reassuring look, which seemed to promise that he himself would wipe off the clay. But, when he reached into the pocket of his suit coat, he found only what he had transferred there from his leather jacket: a few Kerensky and Soviet roubles. After a very brief hesitation, he took out a Kerenka, spat on it and began to scrub the toes of his bride's shoes.

Within a minute, it became clear that his work had been in vain. The stream continued to murmur somewhere nearby and – apparently, thanks to its effort – the Path was strewn with puddles that could not be avoided. Soon, his own formerly white, now beige shoes were brown with clay. He forgot all about their painful tightness. The only thing he could think about was propriety. One ought to marry in neat attire, not dirty and ragged. Nadezhda walked ahead, cautiously, holding up the hem of her dress with her left hand. Knowing how prone he was to clumsiness, Samson deliberately lagged a few paces behind, to make sure he didn't accidentally splash her with mud.

"How will my parents find the chapel?" Nadezhda asked,

stopping abruptly and turning back to Samson. "They'll never be able to walk this way."

A dog barked somewhere in the distance, and its call was immediately picked up by several more. Fear flickered in the bride's eyes.

"Don't worry, they'll be there," Samson assured her. "I sent a Red Army man with a note. They told him to tell me that they'd definitely come, as long as someone met them on Baseina."

"But who's going to meet them?" Nadezhda exclaimed in despair.

"I will!" Kholodny piped up from five paces ahead. "As soon as I get you to the chapel and hand you over to my comrade, I'll go back for them."

Soon, the dense thicket thinned out and vegetable gardens appeared on either side of the ravine. Samson had never walked here before. The Dog Path had a bad reputation and he and his friends had avoided it. That is why he now felt simultaneously like an adventurer-discoverer, with all the curiosity the latter word entailed, and like a frightened common man, consciously and submissively moving towards some unknown danger. Of course, he was at the same time moving towards his future family life. There was no guessing how dangerous this life would be – perhaps entirely free of danger, containing nothing but love and duty, till death did him and Nadezhda part. In any case, half-childish fears mingled with purely youthful expectations of miraculous happiness in his heart, and therefore he didn't so much submit to the Path as reconcile himself to it for the time being, expecting the events of the day to bring purely positive, joyful consequences.

About ten minutes later, a smaller path branched off from the main one and ran between the bushes to the right. Kholodny turned onto it, and Samson and Nadezhda followed.

Up ahead, a steel cross gleamed above the vegetation. A little later, the roof of the chapel appeared, and, after a few more steps, they came out into a clearing, where they saw the entirety of the wooden ecclesiastical structure, painted a heavenly blue. The path ran up to the wooden doorstep, which was also painted, but had been smeared with clay.

Kholodny walked to the door and gave two knocks. A latch sounded inside, wood scraping against wood, and the door opened slightly. A round, somewhat grubby face with a fleshy nose and fleshy ears emerged from the crack. It stared at the visitors with kind grey eyes. A smile formed on its thick lips.

"Please, come in, be my guests!" the man boomed as the door opened wider. He looked to be about forty years old, wore a cassock, and his bushy hair was uncombed and uncovered.

"I have to go and fetch the bride's parents," Kholodny explained. "They won't find this place on their own."

Samson and Nadezhda stepped inside. The chapel smelled of tobacco. Or perhaps the smell came from its inhabitant.

"My name is Mitri," the man in the cassock introduced himself.

"Dmitri?" Samson asked, assuming his ear had missed a letter.

"Mitri," the man repeated. "From the Sanskrit, *mitra*. It means 'friend'."

Samson introduced himself and Nadezhda, then asked, "How shall we address you? Father Mitri?"

The man shook his head.

"I'm not your father, I'm your brother. Brother Mitri," he said after a short pause. "We live in brotherhood now, and I'll call you 'brother' too, Brother Samson," he added solemnly, then turned his gaze to the young woman. "And you are Sister Nadezhda."

As Samson listened, he glanced around the room, noting an ordinary wooden iconostasis with its familiar saintly faces, a three-foot-tall candle stand, a couple of chairs against the wall on the right and, on the left, a bench and bedside table on which lay a book bound in black leather – probably Holy Writ. The space was a square, with each wall ten paces from its counterpart. Why, Samson wondered, would Kholodny call it an "anti-chapel"? Both inside and out, it looked to be an ordinary chapel. There were no posters proclaiming, *There is no God*, no red stars painted with broad strokes.

"Have a seat," Mitri offered, indicating the bench with his eyes. "Won't your parents be coming?" he asked Samson.

"They are no longer with us," Samson replied softly. "They were laid to rest in the cemetery on Shchekavytsia Hill, together with my sister."

"Then you must go to them afterwards, as soon as you can, to bow, share your news and ask for their blessing," the master of the chapel instructed.

"Yes, of course," Samson said, nodding. "I certainly will."

"It smells too much of tobacco here," Mitri said, raising his nose. "I'll light a candle!"

A match was struck and a single small flame appeared atop the candle stand, which could accommodate three dozen candles. The aroma of beeswax wafted through the air, sweetening the smell of tobacco.

"Before the sacrament, let me say this," Mitri pronounced, taking a chair from the other wall, placing it a few feet from the bench and sitting down to face the bride and groom. "Don't think that I am about to marry you in churchy fashion. I do not believe in God. I have my own views – more humane ones. I won't have people kneeling in this place, beating their foreheads against the floor. No, there will be no standing on one's feet all night, either. Humanity must be respected. We are given feet to travel roads, not to stand around and suffer. And so, I will marry you in accordance with the ways of the future. Without humiliation. Without driving fear into your hearts. You aren't afraid to get married, are you?"

Samson shook his head.

"No," Nadezhda whispered. "On the contrary. I'm quite curious."

"That's what I like to hear," Mitri responded. "I myself was afraid, the first time. And so was my fiancée, Masha. We were scared to get married, but also scared to go against the will of our parents. We passed through the wedding, one fear leading to another, and for this I came to hate the priest who married us, with a burning passion. I still feel anger towards him. I understand, of course, that he couldn't have acted otherwise. He didn't know any better. And neither did we or our parents. But now we can do things differently, in the new style. That's why the word 'stylite' appeals to me. Though I prefer 'brother'."

"You mean . . . you're twice married?" Nadezhda asked, not hiding the shock in her voice.

"Yes, twice," Mitri replied calmly. "But the second time I didn't marry a woman. I married an idea – the idea that everyone is equal and that the kingdom of God awaits us not beyond this life but within it. In order to attain it, all we have to do is to change human nature, change it beyond recognition. Because recognisable human nature is repugnant. It must be burned away, down to its roots, its very foundation, with fire and knowledge. I'll make you some tea while we wait."

Mitri disappeared behind the iconostasis. The young investigator heard water flowing. A rhythmic mechanical sound indicated that the master of the chapel was pumping the kerosene stove. Then, another match was struck and a flame flared up. Soon, the smell of tobacco grew stronger.

"I don't like it here," Nadezhda whispered directly into Samson's bare earhole.

Samson felt as though her whisper burned through his eardrum. He got up, moved to the other side of her and brought his intact ear closer.

"Whisper again," he asked, also whispering.

She touched his ear with her lips.

"I love you," she whispered.

He turned to face her, and his gaze came to rest on her lips. His lips soon followed his gaze.

"Have no fear – kiss! This is a temple of love!" Mitri's voice reached them.

Samson winced, as did Nadezhda. The wish to kiss sank back inside them, concealing itself among other hidden desires.

The tea smelled of hay. Dogs barked outside the chapel door.

"We've got feral dogs around here, some five packs of them," explained Mitri, who was sitting opposite the bench with a mug of tea in his hand. "Not long ago, two drunkards were torn limb from limb. I buried them behind the chapel. This is the only place in Kyiv where three elements meet: two dark and one light. The Path is a shortcut to the Monastery of the Caves, so pilgrims are always coming through – and dogs and bandits, they lie in wait. The bandits will sometimes rob and beat the pilgrims, but they tend not to kill them. The dogs might bite a pilgrim's arm clean to the bone. On occasion, though, a pilgrim will come through and the bandits will just step aside. The dogs, too. And, often enough, the dogs attack the bandits, maul them to death . . ."

Samson noticed Nadezhda cringing as she listened to Mitri. These stories must frighten her, he concluded.

"The dogs don't bother me," the anti-priest continued. "Neither do the bandits. I know them, now. Sometimes they come to me, to repent. Especially after they've killed someone. They're people, too, just like us. One used to teach at a secondary school – gymnastics and other sports. He said, one day, the bandits robbed and beat him, but afterwards they took pity on him and brought him into their gang. They didn't return what they'd stolen, though. They told him to take it from others, so that he'd see how unpleasant and toilsome their craft was."

"Is 'craft' really the word for it?" Samson asked, unable to hold back his disgust.

"Judge not, that ye be not judged," Mitri objected calmly.

"How can we not judge? Sergius and I are with the police, after all."

"The ways of the Lord are past finding out," Mitri pronounced. "You can jail whomever you like, but you shouldn't judge."

Realising that to dispute this might ruin this special day, Samson fell silent. He took a sip of tea and sensed the aroma of hay in his mouth.

"I'd like to have a smoke." Mitri glanced at the bedside table on which the book lay.

He rose and approached it, put down the mug, opened the book, tore out a page, placed it on the leather binding, poured out a bit of tobacco, rolled a cigarette and struck another match. Then, with the mug in one hand and the hand-rolled cigarette between the fingers of the other, he returned to his seat and breathed smoke into Samson's face.

"Interrogation course?" Samson unexpectedly asked, speaking largely to himself.

"What?" Mitri responded, before taking another drag.

"Never mind. I just remembered a course I took – in interrogation. They taught us to breathe smoke into the faces of detainees."

"I see," Mitri said. "You're a smoker, then?"

"No, just in the line of duty."

There was a noise outside. Someone had stamped their feet on the doorstep. Now, they knocked twice.

Samson followed Mitri with his gaze, taking note of the heavy wooden latch, which the anti-priest easily lifted out of the iron nailed to the door frame. Kholodny was the first to enter, followed by Nadezhda's parents, Trofim Sigismundovich and Lyudmila Nikanorovna. Their faces were fear-stricken. Lyudmila Nikanorovna seemed to have put on weight since Samson had last seen her.

"Not too late?" Kholodny asked.

"We wouldn't have started without you," Mitri replied. "Respect for the parents of the betrothed is a holy matter."

Lyudmila Nikanorovna forced a smile and began to pull off her drab, coarse, green hooded jacket.

"Help," she said softly, turning to her husband.

He did. And Nadezhda's mother's green silk dress emerged, its sleeves trimmed with dark green velvet.

"I told you to dress in the English fashion," she reproached her husband, critically surveying his altogether presentable brown woollen suit.

"You both look very smart," Nadezhda interjected, casting a nervous glance at her mother.

"Your daughter is right," Mitri added in his bass voice. "After all, you aren't promenading down a boardwalk past some ship-restaurants. You've come to give away your daughter."

"Yes, of course," said Trofim Sigismundovich.

"Forgive me," his wife added.

"Let us begin, then," Mitri pronounced. He walked over to the bedside table, on which he stubbed out his unfinished cigarette, leaving it there, and turned round. "Please rise. Do you love one another?"

The bride and groom rose to their feet.

"Yes!" Samson answered fervently.

"Yes," Nadezhda whispered.

"From this day forward, until the end of your lifetimes, you are obligated to preserve this love within your hearts and to sustain the red flame of the sacred family hearth, no matter how rich or poor it may be. Do you promise to forgive each other for sins great and small?"

"Yes, I do!" answered Samson.

"I do," whispered Nadezhda.

"Your family path will be strewn with joy and sadness, tears and hope. Only faith can help you reach its end with dignity. Faith in one another. From this day forward, until the end of your lifetimes, you will be each other's gods. Are you, Samson, prepared to recognise Nadezhda as your Goddess, whom you must always obey without question?"

"I am!"

"Are you, Nadezhda, prepared to recognise Samson as your God, whom you must always obey without question?"

"I am," whispered Nadezhda.

"Where there is faith and there are gods, there must also be evidence of this faith, tokens of love. Exchange them, but first inscribe them with oaths of eternal allegiance."

Samson understood what the anti-priest meant and drew two photographs from his pocket – one of himself, the other of Nadezhda. He handed the latter to his bride.

Mitri disappeared behind the iconostasis and reappeared holding an inkwell with two pens sticking out of it. He removed the black leather-bound book and the half-smoked cigarette from the bedside table, then commanded, "Sit down and write."

The bride and groom sat down on opposite sides. Samson was the first to pick up a pen. He froze, staring at the droplet of red ink that hung suspended from its tip before finally falling back into the mouth of the inkwell. Then, he raised his eyes to Brother Mitri.

"Red ink?" he asked, slightly puzzled.

"Red," the anti-priest responded. "Like blood. Oaths and promises ought to be written in that colour alone."

Samson gave a barely perceptible nod and lowered his eyes to the back of the photograph.

In an exquisite hand, he wrote out: *With devotion and love to Nadezhda, my dear wife, from her husband, Samson.* Then he added the date and *Kyiv* below.

To my beloved, dependable husband, Samson, from his faithful and obedient wife, Nadezhda, wrote his bride, her pen squeaking across the cardboard, and a smile appeared on her lips.

"Exchange the photographs and guard them carefully, forever – so carefully that your love becomes a legend among your grandchildren," Mitri intoned, his bass voice sounding surprisingly warm, as if he were sincerely moved by this solemn matrimonial moment.

After tenderly slipping the photos into their pockets, the newlyweds kissed and embraced.

Lyudmila Nikanorovna sobbed with happiness, her shoulders shaking.

Trofim Sigismundovich wrapped his arms around her and pressed her close.

"I congratulate you," Mitri said to the newlyweds. Then, he turned to Nadezhda's parents. "And I congratulate you." Finally, he gazed at Kholodny. "And you as well, Brother Sergius. I rejoice for your friend and for his happiness. And now we can honour each other with earthly delights. Thank you for acquiring and bringing them."

Samson threw a surprised glance at Kholodny, who bent down and gripped an iron ring attached to a square cut into the floor. This square turned out to be the cover of the entrance to a cellar, which had escaped the young investigator's notice.

"Let us descend for earthly delights, to mark this joyous occasion," Mitri urged Nadezhda's parents. Taking a burning candle from the stand, he led the way down the steep ladder.

Chapter 26

Although it had the same dimensions as the room above, the anti-chapel's cellar seemed more spacious – and this despite the three large barrels in the corner to the right of the ladder. Its inner walls were covered with white lime, which meant that they were made of brick or stone. There was dampness in the enclosed air, but it didn't hit the nose as strongly as the dampness in the cellar of Samson's building.

The young investigator was the second to descend. Meanwhile, Mitri had used the candle in his hand to light ten more in another stand, and this made the ceiling seem even higher. On a large oak table to the left of the ladder lay two weighty packages and a stack of newspapers pressed down with a long wooden-handled kitchen knife.

"Oh, how frightening!" Lyudmila Nikanorovna exhaled as she stepped down to the floor. "Do you sleep here?" she asked the master of the chapel.

He turned round. "No, I dine here. I sleep behind the iconostasis."

"He's got an alcove up there, big enough for two," Kholodny chimed in. Noticing Mitri's unkind look in his direction, he quickly added, "He's let me spend the night before. We slept there together."

"Why don't you lend me a hand?" Mitri cut in, indicating the packages with a nod. "I don't know what you've brought."

"Yes, yes, of course!"

Samson gazed around again. Now that there were six of them in the cellar, the sense of spaciousness was somewhat diminished. In fact, it felt crowded. Nadezhda's father shifted on his feet, glancing warily at the barrels. Nadezhda stood motionless, either in anticipation or in thought.

Samson looked at the ladder and shook his head, wondering how Nadezhda and her mother had managed to keep from falling. It was the kind they used in rural houses when it was time to get the hay down from the loft.

"I'll light the incense, make it more pleasant to breathe," Mitri announced, approaching the wall.

"What, may I ask, do you keep in the barrels?" Trofim Sigismundovich asked.

"In those two, gunpowder. In the other, pickled cucumbers."

"Gunpowder?" Nadezhda's father asked with fear in his voice, glancing at the lit match in Mitri's hand.

"Yes. They survived the explosions at the artillery warehouses. A man I know rolled them over, asked if I needed them. I told him, in times like these, I just might. It took a lot of work to get them down here."

"What would you need them for?" Nadezhda's father now sounded more surprised and curious than fearful.

"The monks from the Caves have been making threats. They think I've been luring away their pilgrims. If they try to burn me for my faith, I'll leave my door open, come down here and set the barrels on fire. It'll come down like the Church of the Tithes in Batu Khan's day."

"That was a bit different," Nadezhda's mother interjected.

"A bit," Mitri agreed, but his tone made it clear that he didn't wish to continue the conversation.

He took hold of a silver censer that hung on a long chain from a hook on the wall, lifted its lid, inserted the burning match and began to blow, enkindling the contents.

The pleasant, soothing fragrance of incense laced the air. Mitri gently let go of the censer and approached the next wall. Soon, all four censers were ignited, and with each breath the atmosphere in the cellar felt warmer, more churchlike.

Kholodny covered the table with newspapers, set out a few ribbed shot glasses, then took out and unfolded several paper bundles from the packages. These turned out to contain various smoked and dried meats, along with a quarter of a large loaf of rye bread.

"My goodness!" Lyudmila Nikanorovna exclaimed, clasping her hands in the air. "Where did you manage to find all these riches?"

Kholodny, who was already hacking at the smoked meats with a knife, turned round.

"Everything here was requisitioned from the Jewish Market. Where else? Our commander allowed it, for the special occasion."

The men brought two benches and a stool closer to the table. Nadezhda took a seat on the stool, and all the rest sat down on the benches. Kholodny filled the glasses with a dark liquid from a bottle.

"What is it?" Nadezhda's mother asked somewhat fearfully, trying to check the liquid's transparency by raising the glass and positioning it between her eyes and the burning candles in the stand.

"Made from oak bark," Kholodny answered, taking a sip. "Strong stuff."

"Do you have anything lighter? For ladies?" Lyudmila Nikanorovna asked plaintively.

"Mother, just take sips – you don't need to finish it," Nadezhda advised in a tender tone.

"But I must, I must . . . Otherwise, it wouldn't be a proper toast," her mother replied, confused.

"For ladies?" Mitri repeated, frowning. "You're definitely the first ladies I've had down here. To tell the truth, I never invite a soul into my cellar. But since you're the first . . ."

He got up and walked over to the leftmost barrel, then removed its wooden lid and lowered it onto a barrel of gunpowder. The smell of brine and dill was added to the air. Mitri rolled up the sleeve of his cassock, assumed the pose of a wrestler, slightly bending his covered knees, and placed his arm against the barrel so that his shoulder was level with its rim. This was a means of assessing how far down he could reach. He shook his head.

"Samson, your arms are longer than mine, aren't they?" he asked. "Come over here."

The young investigator's arms really were about an inch longer. Mitri helped him off with his jacket and shirt, asking the others not to look in their direction. Following the anti-priest's instructions, Samson lowered his hand into the cold brine, pushing apart the springy cucumbers. His armpit pressing against the rim of the barrel, he caught the neck of a bottle with his fingers and began to extract it.

Mitri spent a full minute wiping Samson's arm off with newspaper, then sniffed it and shook his head disapprovingly. He removed a censer from the wall and swayed it to and fro beneath the dried limb, to kill the scent of brine with incense. Another sniff elicited an approving nod. The anti-priest returned the censer to the hook on the wall and helped Samson back into his clothes.

Taking his seat next to Samson, Mitri raised his glass and boomed, "To the new family!"

"To their happiness and prosperity! May they be fruitful and multiply!" Nadezhda's father chimed in.

"To love!" added Lyudmila Nikanorovna.

"Drink up! Then a kiss!" Mitri rounded out the polyphonic toast.

The kiss was as strong as the oak-bark liqueur. Samson wanted to hold Nadezhda closer, squeezing her tight, but two obstacles stood in his way – first, their mutual shyness, and second, the fact that, in order to kiss his bride, he had to bend over the corner of the table, resting his left hip on it.

After the toasts, Mitri uncorked the green bottle Samson had extracted from the barrel. To Nadezhda's father's surprise, it was

French claret. The name of the wine could be read with both eyes and fingers; the beautiful Latin letters protruded in bas-relief from the glass. Lyudmila Nikanorovna took a sip and smacked her tongue. Trofim Sigismundovich had helped her empty her glass to make room for the claret, draining the liqueur in one gulp.

Time stopped. The aromas from the four censers infused the air with dreams and fantasies. The candles were bright, and it was strange to think that they burned not beneath the faces of saints, but before the faces of the living and thriving. There wasn't a single icon in the cellar, not a single holy image familiar from childhood. The censers smoked only for the living, only for those joyously celebrating the newly formed bonds of marriage. Brother Mitri might have been considered the only godly presence, had he not declared that there was no God, only faith. This meant that it wasn't God who had united Samson and Nadezhda up above, but other forces – new and revolutionary forces that transformed all that lay in their path, breaking and rebuilding, renouncing and educating. And this led Samson to reflect on the fact that he knew almost nothing about the new life and its rules. He didn't know where to get official confirmation of their marriage, how to declare his new status or what this declaration should and could bring them. After all, the rights of families differed from those of bachelors and spinsters, as did their responsibilities. Even in the directives concerning the requisition of property, the items were determined by numbers per family, not per person. He remembered reading one such directive, which stated in black on yellow – or rather, in grey on yellow – that *the permitted norm of furniture is one chair per family member plus one for a guest, one bed per person plus one couch per family, one dining table per family*, and so on.

Now, chewing smoked pork, he might not have been able to recall the exact contents of the piece of paper that was thrust under his nose when his father's desk was requisitioned for state needs, but that had been the gist of it. A family had more rights than a single person or a single family member – more rights pertaining to furniture and other matters. And that meant Nadezhda and he had gained better protection from the vicissitudes of life. Although, of course, their jobs at the Bureau of Statistics and with the police already exempted them from requisitions and from various duties, because, through their work, they were building the new, not yet wholly comprehensible life of the future.

They divided the uneaten meat equally, but left the unfinished liqueur and claret with Mitri. Darkness had descended outside the windowless chapel, which delayed the group's departure from this hospitable establishment. Lyudmila Nikanorovna was afraid to go out into the night. And then a pack of dogs began to bark nearby. Without hesitation, Mitri brought a revolver from behind the iconostasis and fired four shots in the direction of the barking. The dogs fell silent.

"Go now. Everyone who heard that will be hiding for half an hour. The dogs, too. They're clever animals – they know what a bullet is."

"But . . . in the dark?" Trofim Sigismundovich asked, still uncertain.

Mitri stepped away and returned with burning candles. He handed one to each member of the party, gently but rather insistently pushing them all out the door.

The latch sounded inside.

In single file, with candles in hand, they set off back towards town. The puddles must have dried up. The soles of their shoes neither smacked nor champed as they walked.

Early the next morning, Samson was the first to wake up. Tired after her wedding night, Nadezhda dozed peacefully with her left cheek pressed into the feathery pillow. Her round face radiated quiet joy.

Leaving a note with a promise to return by eight, Samson went out into the street and began to look for a cab. But the city was still asleep, with only obscure distant noises flying in the wind above the roofs of the houses.

He walked to the Jewish Market, and there, outside the Halytska bathhouse, spotted a cab. The driver was slumped in his seat, sleeping. The young investigator tugged at his long coat sleeve and the cabby shuddered awake.

"Where to?" he asked.

"The cemetery on Shchekavytsia Hill."

The horse's hooves clattered along the deserted street, through the sleeping city. This clip-clopping rose up to the lower sky, augmenting the morning's general soft hum.

At a certain moment, Samson thought that the cabby was asleep again. He seemed especially heavy, and his head drooped to his shoulder. Where would the horse take them on its own? The young investigator looked round. The street lamps gave no light, but the predawn greyness was bright enough to reveal the houses and corners. No, the cart was carrying him in the right direction – along Dmytrivska Street. Soon, they'd turn onto Monastyrska and ride over to Saksonsky Ravine, which was just a short jaunt from the cemetery.

Without noticing, Samson dozed off himself. The clatter of the hooves grew quieter, filtering into his dream. Other noises sounded – noises not from this life. Unfamiliar birds began to sing. Foliage rustled before his closed eyes, as if he were a small child making his way through dense thickets in search of some mysterious discovery. A sweet taste touched his lips, followed by the sting of oak-bark liqueur, and around him rose the aroma of an open barrel of pickled cucumbers. Then, closer than birdsong, came the dear voice of his mother: "Samson, darling, Dasha made a delicious paste! Make yourself a sandwich!" He realised they were at their summer house, outside Vasylkiv. These green thickets, then, were that wild, overgrown corner of the garden he alone dared to explore. There was a gargantuan anthill here, and nettles, and huge horseradish leaves. And soon their housekeeper, Dasha, would drag him out at his mother's behest, wash the grass and dirt off his hands and seat him at the table to drink tea and munch his snack: a slice of fluffy wheat bread, which he would have to smear with her paste. Not that he disliked this countryside treat. It was sweet – made of turnip flour with honey, treacle and nutmeg. Although, only the wealthy added the nutmeg; no peasant had ever heard of the stuff. Dasha added it, of course. When a peasant woman becomes a housekeeper for educated people, she herself gets an education. She begins to adopt and alter their recipes, and also to alter her own country recipes so that her educated employers can enjoy them. And so, with a few adjustments, Dasha's paste became quite toothsome indeed – sweet and savoury – good not only after a meal, but even instead of one.

In his dream, Samson licked his lips and sweetness spread over his tongue. It was the taste of Dasha's paste.

The young investigator's hand, however, suddenly grew anxious, reaching into the inside pocket of his jacket. It wanted to check whether he'd remembered to bring the photographs of Nadezhda and himself, both inscribed to his beloved late parents and sister. When it felt their cardboard backs, the hand relaxed and sank back down onto the soft, padded seat. While the cab kept rolling towards the cemetery, Samson remained in his dear, sweet dream of boyhood at the family's summer house. Only, now, as he drew closer to his destination, the birdsong was enriched by the cheerful, hungry, early morning caws of crows.

"Hey, citizen! We're here," the cabby shouted, shaking him by the shoulder. "Pay up, will ya?"

Samson gave the man his fare and the cab trundled away, disappearing from view into a nearby alley.

Slowly, somewhat distractedly and sleepily, Samson ambled towards the graves of his parents and sister, until his foot hit something soft. He stopped, rooted to the spot by a wild thought: what if he'd stepped on a corpse? This was a cemetery, after all. He was afraid to look down, but then he heard an animal's angry hiss and felt something dart from under his feet. By the time he managed to direct his groggy gaze at the receding rustle, all he could see was a red fox tail. He squatted down and looked closely at last year's leaves on the ground, at the new grass breaking through the dewy earth. And suddenly he felt the urge to stroke this pitiable grass, to comfort it, because it was forced to grow here, to nourish its life on someone else's death.

He reached down, tore off a blade of grass and brought it up to his eyes. It differed in no way from any other blade – neither those found here, nor those growing in fields and ravines elsewhere. He placed it in his mouth and bit down, paying close attention to the taste on his tongue. Was there a hint of death in it? No, he sensed nothing like that – only the usual dull flavour of grass.

He thought of his boyhood again, remembering how he and his friends had dared each other to chew grass in the Cadet Grove. Everyone had picked a handful, to see who could eat his faster – not simply swallow, but chew up and eat. He turned out to be the last, because the flavour of the grass interested him. He wanted to keep it in his mouth longer, in order to understand it better. It occurred to him at that moment that everything that grew on the earth retained the flavour of earth, adding to it something of itself – at times more, at times less. Potatoes added less, while apples added more. There was almost no earthy flavour in apples.

A fat Kyiv crow cawed overhead. Samson lifted his eyes to the crown of an old oak. The crow gave another caw.

The young investigator rose to his feet and dusted off his trousers, making sure his outfit was neat and tidy. After all, he was going to visit his parents, whose new address was permanent and inaccessible to the regular mail service.

It must be cold for them, he thought, again lowering his gaze to the ground. Glancing to the right, he saw an Old Believer-style wooden cross, with a little roof on top, painted blue. There was a paper icon where the main bars met, and under it was a tablet bearing a faded name. This, Samson reflected, was how time erased the presence of people. No wonder the rich paid to have the names of their relatives carved in stone, not painted on wood.

He sighed and moved on, passing by fenced and unfenced plots until he reached the part of the cemetery dear to him. There, he squatted down again.

"I've come to get your blessing, and to show you my bride," he whispered, looking at the slightly sagging elongated mound over which grass had not yet sprouted.

He took out the photographs and read the inscriptions aloud, so that they could hear them, if they could still hear his voice down there. Then he pulled from his pocket a sheet of newspaper and wrapped up the photographs, having placed them face to face, to protect them for as long as possible from the destructive subterranean forces of nature. He thrust his hand into the hard earth, driving it in an inch or two past his wrist, then drew it out and slipped in his gift to his parents. Once the gift was firmly lodged, he covered it up, smoothing the ground with his hand.

"There isn't too much water, is there?" he asked in a whisper. "We had a lot of snowmelt, and then the rains came."

As soon as he mentioned the rains, he thought he felt drops on his neck. Looking up at the sky, he saw no clouds. It was clear and blue, illuminated by the still-unseen sun, which would soon rise higher, warming all beneath it, drying the dew and the graves.

"I miss you," he whispered.

Looking up at the sky again, he thought about God – about the fact that God existed in people's minds so that they could avoid responsibility. He existed because He was responsible for everything. He existed for some, that is. For others, He didn't.

And others still didn't know or care one way or the other. But the word existed, didn't it? And behind every word was an object or a meaning.

A cold breeze that seemed to rise directly from the damp earth brushed Samson's face. Something flashed up above. It was probably just a bird, but it threw a scare into his mind. He looked up and at the same time leaned sideways, raising a hand to the sky. It seemed to him that a sabre had sliced the air overhead – that someone had tried to kill him again, as they had back in March.

It took the young investigator two or three minutes to calm himself. He kept panting, closing his eyes, remembering those terrible moments after the Cossack attack. He saw his father lying dead – first in his blue English shoes, and later, when Samson returned to the scene with Dr Vatrukhin, barefoot, someone having stolen the treasured footwear.

Slowly, peace returned to him – the kind of peace only found in cemeteries.

He sat on his haunches for a couple more minutes, then wiped his palm on the bark of a linden tree near the graves. Bowing to his family in parting, he turned back towards the entrance.

His palm still felt the chill of the morning earth. He wanted to wash it off with water, warm it. But where?

Lukyanivska Street was silent, unpeopled. He walked to Saksonsky Ravine on Solyana Street, then turned onto Monastyrska. Crows cawed at his back, distantly, as the tall hundred-year-old oaks receded behind him. Here, the trees were lower and younger, appealing only to sparrows.

Outside the barracks across from the Intercession Monastery, Samson spotted a wagon. The driver was adjusting the harness. In addition to money, the young investigator promised him a quarter pound of smoked pork – a good hunk to have with bread. He jumped onto the raised wooden side. The hay was soft but the wagon itself was rigid, springless. Luckily, it wasn't fast, either. They set off. Finding it uncomfortable to sit without a backrest, Samson threw his feet up on the hay and lay down. The grey-blue morning sky, gilded by the rays of the sun, floated above him. He felt like a child again. The walls and roofs of houses slid past.

His new life had begun, he thought. Then, for some reason, Dr Vatrukhin's face swam up in his mind.

He realised that the doctor didn't yet know about the big change.

Chapter 27

Samson strode off to the station, with a confident, unusually heavy step. He had the sense that, after the anti-wedding, he had gained weight. Perhaps this was due to the positive excitement and the worries about the future that were now mingled within him. Or maybe it was just the extra cup of tea he'd had over breakfast, when he and Nadezhda had informed Dr Vatrukhin, his face still wrinkled with sleep, that they were now married. Bewildered, the doctor had spread his arms wide, apologising that he had sat down at the table without a gift, then he jumped up from his chair and ran into the study. He returned moments later, smiling and holding a shiny object. "Please accept this," he told them. "I wish your family happiness for generations to come." He handed Samson a strange pair of steel scissors, which looked somewhat like tweezers. "Vera Ignatyevna Gedroits gave them to me, ironically, after we argued about the revolution. For some reason, she came to believe that I approved of that bloodthirsty uprising. It seems to me they'd make a much more suitable gift for you!"

Examining the surgical tool, Samson had asked, "What are they?"

Vatrukhin smiled again, only this time more significantly, and answered, "An umbilical-cord clamp!"

Nadezhda blushed and went off to the kitchen, supposedly to fetch some jam, while Samson had poured himself and the doctor another cup of tea each – their third round – as a sign of obligatory gratitude.

And now, turning onto Tarasivska from Mariinsko-Blagovishchenska, at the site of the recent tram accident, he shouldered this strange new sense of heaviness, unable to comprehend the nature of it in full. In every other way, he felt extremely well, and his thoughts flowed more vigorously than ever.

As he approached the station, his eyes lighted on a familiar face. Briskin's daughter Sophia stood about ten steps from the entrance. Once again, she held a bundle in her hand. The young investigator didn't need to enquire about its contents.

"For your father?"

Sophia nodded.

"I'll pass it on and make sure no-one takes it away."

She dutifully handed him the bundle, then gave him a pleading look.

"You can't see him today, I'm afraid," Samson said, realising what she wanted. "I'll be out all morning and afternoon, investigating a case. Perhaps tomorrow."

He didn't tell her that the case he'd be investigating involved her father, keeping the troubling thought to himself.

"You should go," Samson advised her. "This is not the best place to stand around."

His words led her to glance from side to side, and at that moment he noticed that there were a dozen more people standing nearby, motionless and confused, all holding bundles and looking for someone expectantly, searchingly, as if they had managed to convey their requests and were now awaiting a merciful response.

And, indeed, a Red Army man emerged from the station, found a young woman wearing a grey dress and a headscarf, took her bundle and went back inside.

No wonder things went missing, thought Samson.

In the station, he ordered the soldier on duty to bring Briskin up for interrogation. The room was empty, but a blotch of half-dried blood glistened on the floor beside the chained stool. The sight of it brought the taste of blood to Samson's tongue, as if it was his own lip that had been split.

He sat down and found that the table blocked his view of the stain, enabling him to put it out of his mind.

The Red Army man shoved Briskin into the room rather too roughly. Samson looked up and realised that the soldier was in a bad way himself. His bluish complexion suggested that he was either recovering from a night of drunkenness or slowly healing after a good beating.

"Stay by the door," Samson commanded, thinking that he now found it easier than before to issue such simple orders. He had grown in confidence.

Left alone with the detainee, the young investigator handed over the bundle. Briskin busied himself with it, unwrapping it on his knees. The two eggs inside elicited a smile, and this small, insignificant response revealed to Samson a change in the man's physiognomy: a new gap in his upper row of teeth.

Meanwhile, with trembling hands, Briskin peeled and ate both eggs. The plaintive look on the detainee's face told Samson that the second egg had gone down worse than the first. The young investigator summoned the soldier with a shout and ordered him to get a mug of tea from Vasyl.

Briskin drank the tea in one gulp as well, as if it had already cooled.

"How is she?" he asked, wiping his lips with his sleeve.

"Your daughter?" Samson asked to make sure, then, without waiting for an answer, continued: "She misses you, of course. Maybe you'll see her soon."

"So, you'll keep me here for a while yet."

Samson shook his head. "We'll issue a verdict in the next few days. We just have to question your Shura first."

"But no-one will harm her, will they?" the detainee asked with fear in his voice.

"I hope not."

"From your lips to God's ears," Briskin breathed out, then he looked down at the floor, noticed the bloodstain and gave a start. "Would you . . . honour a request?" he asked, and only then did he look into Samson's eyes.

"What request?"

"Will you bring my Sophia to Shura? She won't make it at home alone. God forbid bandits find out she's there by herself. Shura knows about her – she'll take her in. I want Sophia to be safe, to have enough food."

"Alright," Samson promised. "I'll do it. But only after the verdict and sentence are issued. I can't act before then."

"I understand. Please do hurry with the verdict, then," the detainee urged. "I don't know how much longer I can stand this. They beat me badly last night."

"Who? For what?"

"Merchants, just like me. Only there were three of them. I asked them, 'How can you approve of the new order? It's the new order that locked you up.' For that, they called me a counter-revolutionary and gave me a beating. They were drunk, of course. One of them had been passed a bottle of moonshine through a guard. They offered me some, but I can't stomach moonshine. My health won't allow it. I turned them down."

"That was probably the true cause of the beating," Samson suggested.

"No, it was politics. We argued about politics."

"So, you're against the new order?" Samson asked calmly.

Briskin thought for a moment, chewing his lips.

"No, I'm all for it, of course," he said at last. "But people need time to adjust themselves to any new order. They need time and clarification . . . It would help if the coming order were announced a few months in advance, not the night before it goes into effect."

Samson nodded.

"Alright, time to go," he announced as he rose from his chair.

He shouted to the Red Army man and ordered him to take the

detainee back to the basement. Then, he climbed the stairs and, before going to his office, looked in on Nayden.

"Comrade Commander, may I make a report?" he asked, noticing that Nayden was reading handwritten documents.

"Report," the commander responded, looking up from the papers.

"Nadezhda and I were married."

"My congratulations! Certainly the right move. In the right direction," Nayden clarified, a glimmer of kindness in his eyes. "What next?"

"I wanted to ask if I needed to get a document certifying this?"

"I'll write one out. Easy. We'll stamp it, too. I'll tell Vasyl to get everything ready," he said, then looked back down at the papers on the desk. "I'm racking my brains over this ... More curious thefts. Whoever's behind them is interested only in silver, leaving all other valuables behind. They've robbed the Monastery of the Caves and eight flats. You've already dealt with a case like this."

Samson nodded, recalling the German tailor's quarters on Baseina and the shoot-out with Jacobson, that strange, naive Belgian.

"I'll find out," he promised Nayden.

"Find what out?"

"Well, Jacobson's in prison, you know. I'll go and interrogate him. Maybe he knows something."

Nayden nodded. "Good thinking."

At his own desk, Samson again recalled his recent visit to the Halytska bathhouse, and how he had seemed to spot Jacobson through the steamy fog. But if the Belgian was in prison, then he couldn't have been let out for a steam. That was impossible.

He left his holster on his chair, looked into the corridor and summoned Vasyl.

"Nayden only just told me – I'll get the document ready," the old man said as he entered the office.

"This isn't about that. I want you to make a telephone call to

Lukyanivska Prison and tell them that I'm coming to interrogate a detainee named Jacobson."

"You'll need a telephonogram for that. Goes into the case file."

"How . . . ?"

"Simple. Write down your question and sign it. I'll call them and read it out. They'll prepare an answer and call back. I'll write that down, you'll sign the whole thing and we'll put it in the file."

Samson nodded and immediately wrote out his question. He handed it to Vasyl before the ink was dry.

Not three minutes after Vasyl's departure, the office door opened again without a warning knock. Kholodny entered, wearing not his uniform, but baggy grey trousers and a faded blue peasant shirt. Catching his comrade's bewildered look, he sighed heavily and assumed a guilty expression. The former priest kept that expression on his face and his eyes on Samson as he walked over to his desk.

"Unpleasant business," he said with feeling. "In the truest sense of the word. Got a bucket of slop on my head. I'd sworn off keeping close to the walls. Should've walked down the middle of the pavement."

"What happened, exactly?" Samson couldn't help but ask, noticing that Kholodny's hair was also wet and matted.

"After the skirmishes back in March, I started keeping close to the walls of houses when walking down the street, so I could duck and lie low in case anything happened. God helps those who help themselves, you know. Well, this morning, I was making my way to work along Karavaevska – and down it goes! A bucket of slop, right on my head, from a window up on the first floor. I couldn't very well show up at the station like that. My tunic stank something awful – hair, too. Had to go home and get water from the pump. Oh, it was ice cold! If this weren't Sunday, I'd have gone straight to the bathhouse, but no such luck . . . Washed up and changed into the only clean clothes I could find . . ."

"I'm sorry to hear that," Samson pronounced sincerely. "But you can't go out on official business like this. And where's your weapon?"

"Left it at home. Imagine putting a holster belt over this outfit. The Cheka would pick me up in a flash."

"You're right about that," Samson agreed. "Go and report to Nayden. But don't anger him with the truth . . ."

"What truth?"

"Tell him you were soaked by our foes, precisely because you were wearing a police uniform," Samson advised.

"Yes," Kholodny muttered after a short pause. "And you know what? Maybe that was why they did it," he added thoughtfully. "I remember the window. I'll go back and have a word with the bastards."

"When you see Nayden, promise him that we'll wrap up the meat case tomorrow. I'd hoped to get it over with today . . ."

"Listen, I'm sorry, but buckets of slop are unpredictable, like an act of God."

"I understand," Samson said, and nodded. "Just don't get him worked up by saying too much. Tomorrow, we'll question the last witness and put an end to this. Your uniform will be dry by the morning, right?"

"Should be. I hung it from the window and it's sunny out."

"You aren't afraid someone might nab it?"

"I'm on the first floor. Would be difficult," Kholodny said, frowning as he looked at his worried comrade. He was clearly a bit worried himself. "Maybe I'd better stop by later, take it in."

Kholodny left the office, but as soon as Samson turned his attention to the meat-case file, the former priest came back in.

"I can't," he whispered. "Looking like this? Even the soldier on guard downstairs didn't recognise me. Wouldn't let me in, for a while. My identification got wet too. It was in the pocket of my tunic. I left it to dry on the table at home – weighed it down with a mug, in case a breeze blew in through the window. Maybe you'll inform the commander for me?"

Samson felt no desire to disturb Nayden again, but he had little choice.

He walked over to the commander's office and told him about Kholodny's run-in with the slop.

"When will we put this meat business behind us?" Nayden almost shouted, though more in despair than in anger.

"Tomorrow – no question about it. We'll have the verdict by the evening," Samson promised.

"It's a good thing we don't have courts anymore," Nayden commented, shaking his head. "That we can judge for ourselves. Otherwise, we might as well snuff out the candles and go to bed, let the bandits and speculators run free."

By the time Samson returned to his office, Kholodny was gone. Sunlight poured through the window, falling directly on the former priest's desk. The desk wasn't as pedigreed as Samson's, nor did it bear any familial relation to Kholodny; it had obviously been requisitioned not from a professor, but from some petty clerk. There were no files on the desktop, no inkwell – only a book with a dark cover, almost at the very edge. Samson had hardly noticed it before, but now he felt the urge to pick it up. Opening it to the title page, he was stunned: could Kholodny really read English? The book was *The Wisdom of Father Brown*. Before the revolution, Chesterton had been much in fashion. Not a month went by without an article about the author in some popular journal, or at least a picture. His appearance simply begged to be caricatured. Nearly seven feet tall and three hundred pounds, he was more of a mound than a man.

To Samson's joy, he discovered that he hadn't forgotten his English. Chesterton's prose wasn't very complicated and went down smoothly. And then the young investigator's thoughts leapt back to his comrade. He wondered whether priests were taught English, in addition to the customary Latin and Greek.

He flipped through the collection and pressed his finger to the first page of a story he hadn't read before, "The Paradise of Thieves". A smile lit up his face at the word "Paradise". He could see why Kholodny might have been drawn to the book. The former priest saw himself as Father Brown – a clergyman who devoted his free time to unravelling criminal mysteries. Although Kholodny claimed not to believe in God, he still secretly wore a cross as he pursued Father Brown's path, investigating crimes.

Samson couldn't help but laugh, but a surge of fear quickly stopped him. If someone should hear him through the door, he thought, especially Nayden, they wouldn't understand.

Eager to return to a more sober state of mind, he left the book on Kholodny's desk and approached the diagram of pork cuts, frowning. Taking it all in with his eyes, he suddenly felt the heavy weight of responsibility on his shoulders and a degree of nervousness in his heart. Why had they dragged this case out so long?

He returned to his own desk, opened the file, spread the documents out before him and plunged into them as into an ice hole, head first.

Then came a knock on the door.

"Care for some tea?" Vasyl asked, entering the office.

But what he held in his hand was a piece of paper, not a mug.

"No, thank you."

"I've got the telephonogram here," the old man said, holding out the paper.

The document read: *We hereby confirm that prisoner Jacobson was released from Lukyanivska Prison by request of the Belgian consul.*

Samson raised his uncomprehending gaze to Vasyl, who was checking the evenness of his moustache with the index finger of his right hand. "Do foreign consuls really have the right to request the release of our prisoners?" he asked.

"We want foreign nations to recognise our authority," Vasyl

explained. “And so we respect their authority. And he’s no murderer, after all – just a petty swindler.”

“Perhaps not so very petty,” Samson said, then immediately added, “Of course, foreign souls are terra incognita. The real question is: how do we find him now?”

“I’m sure he’s still in town. Where could he run? War all around, bandits and hetmen. If you need to find him, write to the Cheka. They’ll track him down in two ticks,” Vasyl advised.

Samson shook his head.

“If they find him, we’ll never see him again,” he said with a dismissive wave of the hand. “You know, I think I’ll have some tea, after all,” he added, giving his interlocutor a pleading look.

“Glad to hear it,” Vasyl responded with a chuckle. “We’ve got bagels with pork fat to go with it. Local Armenian baker brought them in. He knows how to curry favour. Thinks we keep the bandits from his shop.”

Chapter 28

That evening, Samson left his place of work stealthily. He didn't want to run into Nayden, who would be sure to ask about the meat case. How would he have answered the commander? A bucket of slops had got in the way?

On Zhylianska, two blocks before reaching home, Samson spotted a lively crowd. They were gathered right at the intersection. Coming closer, he realised that nothing especially terrible had occurred – just an accident. A cab had hit a rural cart and turned over. The rather young, though already bearded cabby, who wore baggy black trousers and a long, torn Tatar shirt belted with a rope, was hurling insults at the other driver, whose cart was laden with sacks. The man was a typical villager, with a bowl cut and a moustache that drooped down as far as his chin on either side of his mouth. He was scared to death. The sacks must have been heavy, since the cart had remained standing. The onlookers were listening raptly to the cabby's tirade, but Samson saw right away that the man was exhausted and would soon fall silent.

"Hey, look, the police!" someone in the crowd shouted, and a dozen pairs of eyes were suddenly directed at the young investigator, causing him to stop in his tracks and twist his lips.

"Comrade policeman!" the cabby shouted. "Come over here, goddammit, and arrest this cretin!"

The last thing Samson wanted was to get involved, but his uniform, and especially his holster, made it impossible for him to walk away. Reluctantly, he approached the scene.

"I have no authority over matters of transport," he tried to pronounce as clearly as possible. "I deal with criminal matters."

These phrases had a strange effect on the cabby. His face showed fear, and his thick lips began to move silently, as if he were rolling as yet unspoken words over them.

"He said he'd kill me, the scoundrel," complained the cart driver, who wore crumpled canvas trousers and a warm shirt with an embroidered slit opening at the neck. "I'm carrying a load of salt from Vasylkiv for the ExProFooCom, and I was first at the intersection."

Hints of doubt sprouted on the faces in the crowd. Samson realised that, until he'd approached, the onlookers had been on the side of the cabby, but now their opinion was changing. They had either been pricked by the magic word "salt" or by the name of the formidable Soviet food institution.

"Alright, then," Samson almost shouted, pulling from his pocket a pencil and a folded blank piece of paper, both of which he carried on Vasyl's advice, in case he needed to hold an impromptu interrogation or take an unexpected statement. "Names and addresses," he barked, glaring at the cabby.

The man bit his lip and appeared to be thinking feverishly, trying to figure out what to do. He looked at his cab, lying on its side, then cast an unkind glance at the cart.

"The name's Pilip Porechka," he finally breathed out. "Left shed in the courtyard of the home of Mrs Katayeva."

Samson stopped writing and looked at the cabby in bewilderment.

"And what is the address of Mrs Katayeva's home?"

"How should I know? It's the green one, on the corner of Tyuremna and Korostyshivska Streets."

Samson sighed and finished writing, then directed his gaze at the villager.

"Petro Nadmogilny of Mala Soltanivka, Vasylkiv District."

"What about a street? House number?"

"What for? Everybody knows me, there."

The cabby grinned sarcastically at the villager, but then his dark-skinned face changed, filled with thought.

"What if he gives me a bit of salt? Could I drop my complaint?" he asked, narrowing his eyes.

"How could he do that, if the salt belongs to the ExProFooCom?" Samson responded sternly.

"Not yet, it doesn't," the villager said, perking up. "Only if they accept and sign for it."

Samson realised that the cabby's proposed solution appealed to the man, but its legality was questionable.

"Who owns the salt at this moment, then?" he asked.

"The Vasylkiv Cooperative Union."

"What would this union say?"

"Not a darned thing. I'm its head. Here, read this." The villager handed Samson a document. "I can give the scoundrel two or three pounds of salt, and nothing will come of it."

"Five pounds!" the cabby protested.

"Four!" the villager shot back.

"Deal!" declared the cabby, taking two steps forward and offering his opponent an outstretched hand.

The villager shook hands with the "scoundrel".

"Looks like I'm no longer needed here," Samson said cheerfully.

"Looks like," the cabby snapped back disrespectfully, without so much as glancing his way.

At the next intersection, Samson overheard an odd conversation that seemed to be taking place far from where he stood.

"I beg of you, don't give him the money in advance. It would be better if you agreed that your cousin pays him as soon as you get to Paris. Tell him you'll wire your cousin as soon as you arrive, and he'll come right over and pay."

"No, he demands twenty thousand at once," replied an anxious female voice. "I can't argue with him – I don't have the strength."

"I could go and see him, if you'd like," the male voice offered, sounding familiar, and after a moment Samson realised it was Dr Vatrukhin's. The doctor must have taken this lady into the study, close to the tin that held the severed ear.

"Please don't, Nikolay Nikolaevich – it's too dangerous!"

"You see, Natalya Andreyevna? You yourself admit it's dangerous, and yet you rush into the snare. Why not wait? Soon, the Whites will return and take power, put things in order, restore transport, and you'll travel to Paris with ease!"

"I'm afraid, Nikolay Nikolaevich, terribly afraid . . . He scares me, tells me that, if I don't leave immediately, I'll be arrested – that they'll take my house, requisition all my belongings. They know that my brother is with Denikin's troops."

"A brother is not a husband," the doctor objected. "If they come to question you, tell them that."

"If they come, I won't be able to get a single word out . . . You know my heart . . ."

"You cannot be so fatalistic," Vatrukhin said, trying to console the woman. "May I embrace you? You're trembling all over, like a lilac branch in a breeze."

The woman's deep sigh allowed Samson to guess that the embrace had been permitted. He also realised, standing there and eavesdropping, that it was both interesting and rather exciting to listen in on other people's conversations. It occurred to him that he had a right to do so, since the doctor had taken this lady into his father's study without seeking permission. For Samson, the room was the holy of holies, something of his own personal chapel. Perhaps that was why he paid such close attention to everything that transpired within, why he'd decided to place his ear there, in the bookcase. The ear was, after all, a part of him – flesh of his flesh, faithful servant of his hearing.

Approaching home, Samson saw a lady of about thirty in a simple black dress of the style usually worn by servants, only her face didn't match the garment in the least. Her profile was lovely and proud. She walked out of the building, glanced around and set off with small, nervous steps in the direction of the Provincial Bureau of Statistics and the Exhibition Grounds.

Over dinner, which was unusually rich thanks to the doctor's contribution to the culinary budget, Samson kept shooting enquiring looks at Vatrukhin, but he couldn't find the courage to ask about the lady visitor.

"Dear mate," Nadezhda suddenly addressed him in an odd, almost official tone.

"What is it, darling?" Samson asked with a note of fear in his voice, as if he expected to hear some terrible news. At this point, he also noted that his newly minted wife was dressed more solemnly than usual. She wore a long blue skirt and a yellowish blouse with long, puffed sleeves that tapered at the wrists, and there was a malachite brooch at her breast.

"Nikolay Nikolaevich was so kind," she continued, after a brief pause. "And I allowed myself to accept his wedding gift . . ."

"What gift?"

Nadezhda rose from the table, gracefully walked into her bedroom and returned with two blue velvet boxes on her open palm. She handed one to Samson. Lifting the lid, he saw a wedding ring glittering against a background of burgundy velvet.

The young man turned to Vatrukhin.

"Nikolay Nikolaevich, these are simply too valuable," he said in confusion.

"Samson, my friend," the doctor began with a smile. "When it comes to an event that, for the right kind of people, happens only once in a lifetime, the word 'valuable' means something completely different. It is you two whom I value beyond price, with your kind, tender Kyivan hearts. Please do accept my gift. What you hold in your hands is Nadezhda's ring."

Samson understood what needed to be done – yet his eyes fell on the half-eaten meal on his plate. It would soon get cold, and he hadn't had chicken breast in months. But the future would bring him more chicken breasts, he assured himself. And so he rose to his feet, assumed a solemn expression and directed his burning gaze at Nadezhda, who was standing beside her chair.

They slipped the rings on each other's fingers and kissed as Dr Vatrukhin watched them with a mawkish, slightly vainglorious look in his eyes.

"Now, you are like family to me," the doctor pronounced with genuine affection. "Just don't wear them outside," he advised. "Only at home. This is your matrimonial kingdom. Here, you are God and Goddess to one another."

That closing comment made Samson recall the words spoken by the anti-priest at their anti-marriage. It was strange that Vatrukhin had voiced the same idea – that he and Nadezhda were each other's deities. Maybe he too had visited the anti-chapel, or knew the anti-priest personally?

"Do you believe in God?" Samson asked him.

"I did, until 1917." The doctor nodded. "Since then, I've had my doubts. But I do think He's up there somewhere," he continued, glancing up at the lamp. "He's up there, looking down at us with a sly smile. My sense is that He withdrew from our little world on purpose, in order to show what happens when people try to organise their lives without divine supervision and mercy."

Samson agreed with these words. He returned to his chicken breast, which, to his joy, had not gone cold. The ring ceremony had taken very little time.

"Dear mate," Nadezhda said, addressing her husband once more. "I would like to ask you to allow Nikolay Nikolaevich to receive his patients in your dear departed father's study. That would be more proper, and more hygienic too. Otherwise, Nikolay Nikolaevich will be receiving them over there, in the corner, while we eat."

"Yes, yes, of course," Samson consented, albeit in a sad voice. After the gift of the rings, it was impossible to refuse the request, yet he couldn't help but regret the fact that Vatrukhin would now not only be allowed into the study, but would be setting up shop there. "Yes, certainly," he reiterated, as if trying to overpower these misgivings, but his voice still betrayed his true thoughts and feelings.

"Oh, and one more bit of good news!" Nadezhda added excitedly. "Nikolay Nikolaevich says I'm through with carbonated milk. He listened to my heart and said that everything sounded fine – that I'd recovered completely!"

Samson smiled, then shifted his gaze to the corner where Vatrukhin had been receiving patients. He noticed that the poster of Landolt's rings was gone. The doctor must have already rehung it in the study.

It occurred to the young investigator that he would have to remove his ear from the bookcase. He shoved the last piece of steamed chicken breast into his mouth. The delicate taste softened his thoughts and feelings.

"I'll put some tea on," Nadezhda declared, rising from the table.

That night, Samson awoke and, for a long time, just listened to the silence. At some point, he got up and tiptoed into the study. The moon shone bright. Its bluish light spilled through the window and over the parquet, conjuring an unusual, almost otherworldly atmosphere. Four abacuses lay on the floor by the wall. Somewhat confused, Samson raised his eyes to their usual hanging place and saw the poster of Landolt's rings. He was surprised that, even with such poor, odd lighting, he could make out, down to the bottom row, where each ring opened.

The young investigator stood still for a while, breathing in the air of the study, then went over to the bookcase to retrieve his ear. He returned to his bedroom, lay down again and slipped the tin under his pillow, covering it with his hand.

In the morning, after breakfast, he lowered the tin into his briefcase and set out for the station. He had decided that his ear should stay in his father's desk, where it wouldn't overhear any other stranger's personal secrets.

Chapter 29

Approaching the station, Samson again spotted Sophia Briskin. She stood a little further off this time, facing the entrance. As usual, she held a bundle, which surely contained two hard-boiled eggs for her father. Her face registered the dulling effects of shock and the sustaining force of hope. Nearby, but not too near, stood other petitioners, the relatives of other detainees. Closest to the entrance was a woman in a black headscarf. She was clearly in mourning, but there was no telling for whom – victim or murderer? Perhaps she had come to remind an investigator that the killer of her husband, son or daughter should also be killed. Or, on the contrary, she might have been the wife or daughter of the killer, come to plead pitifully for mercy. That kind of thing happened all the time. Be that as it may, Samson didn't recognise her and couldn't know why she had come. He could stand there all day, guessing at the reasons all these strangers had shown up at the station.

He approached Sophia and said, "Back again, are we?"

She lowered her gaze. He had the sense that she was about to turn away and cry.

"Don't worry, I'm kidding," Samson reassured her. "I know I promised I'd let you see your father," he said, reminding them both of his words. "What have you been doing with yourself?"

"Nothing," she whispered. "There's nothing for me to do. Maybe there will be when autumn comes, when the women at the summer houses in Pushcha-Vodytsia start making jam. I helped them last year . . ."

As Samson and Sophia were climbing the stairs, a guard down below tried to look up the girl's skirt. The long, grey skirt was topped by an austere black jersey, which had likely belonged to Sophia's mother, as it was still too big for her. The kerchief on her shoulders, too, was more suitable for an adult.

Samson rather roughly pulled Sophia to the right, closer to the wall, so that the wolfish Red Army men couldn't ransack her with their eyes. She hadn't noticed anything, but he managed to throw the guard a stern look, causing him to freeze, then turn away. At that moment, however, Samson realised he had a task for the man.

"You, there!" he barked. "Briskin! Interrogation room! Now!"

Three minutes later, Briskin was brought into the interrogation room. The detainee looked better than last time, and his face lit up at the sight of his daughter.

"You sit here," said Samson, showing her to his chair. "Your father knows his place. I'll be back soon."

Outside, Samson ordered the guard not to let anyone out of the room until his return. This was purely a formality. It was dangerous to leave Red Army men without orders to keep them busy.

In his office, the first thing he did was to extract the tin from his briefcase and conceal it in the depths of the upper left-hand drawer of his desk.

He thought about the day that lay ahead of him, which would include his final interview concerning the meat case, and wondered whether he might, at the same time, take Sophia over to this Shura woman. But he was almost instantly distracted by a clatter and indistinct cries outside the door.

He leapt out into the corridor and found himself nose-to-nose with Nayden.

"What's going on down there?" the commander shouted down the stairs.

"It's the Chinese!" someone shouted in response.

"What Chinese?" Nayden snarled, angrier still.

"Ours – Red Army – but they want something!" answered the same voice.

"Well, what do they want?"

"Haven't a clue! Whatever it is, they want it in Chinese!"

"Get down there and figure it out," Nayden ordered Samson.

On the ground floor, Samson realised that the Chinese were still outside, while the station's team of seconded soldiers were crowded at the entrance, as if preparing to defend it.

"What are they saying?" Samson asked one of them.

"God knows," a short, round-shouldered fighter answered. "Just keep yelling the same word over and over again."

"What word?"

"Somethin' like 'shanison'."

Samson shrugged and squeezed his way to the threshold. Directly in front of him stood two Chinese soldiers with worried faces. One of them was delighted at the sight of the young investigator.

"Sanson! Sanson!" he shouted.

Surprised, Samson came closer.

The soldier pulled a square of paper from the breast pocket of his tunic and unfolded it. He shot a quick glance down at the page, then handed it to the young investigator.

"*Gěi nǐ de xīn. Gěi nǐ de xīn*,"* he said, making a clarifying pushing gesture with his hand.

"For me?" Samson asked.

"*Gěi nǐ de xīn*," the soldier repeated. Then he showed Samson the pocket watch he held in his left hand. He shook it a bit, trying to draw the policeman's attention not to the object itself, but to the time it displayed.

Samson accepted the paper and stared with bovine incomprehension at the rows of Chinese characters that covered it.

"*Xūyào zhuājǐn*," the soldier said nervously. He shook the watch again. "*Li Yin Jun yǒu máfanle!*"†

---

* "A letter for you. A letter for you."

† "You must hurry." "Li Yin Jun is in trouble."

"This is from Li Yin Jun?" Samson asked, trying to make sense of what he had heard. "Where is he? Where is Li Yin Jun?"

The soldier shook his head, showing that he did not understand.

"*Xūyào zhuājǐn*," he said again. Then he turned to his friend. "*Wǒmen zǒu ba! Jíjiāng diǎnmíng!*"*

Both Chinese soldiers nodded to Samson and walked off to the corner of Karavaevska, where they turned right.

The young investigator returned to his office with the letter in hand. He lowered it onto the desk in front of him and stared at the characters, which told him nothing.

He concluded that something must have happened to Li Yin Jun, because otherwise the soldier would have come himself. But what had happened? Where was he?

The door swung open and Kholodny briskly entered the office. Stopping in front of Samson, he straightened the belt on his belly and the holster at his side.

"Shall we go?" he asked.

"Where?"

"To question the last witness. About the meat."

Samson stared at his comrade for a moment.

"Can you read Chinese?" he asked doubtfully.

"Odd thing to ask," Kholodny responded, and shrugged. "I can read Church Slavonic. English, too. But Chinese is Greek to me. Though, I can read a bit of Greek . . ."

"I assumed as much," Samson said. "It's just that I have an urgent letter here, and it's in Chinese." He held out the paper. "It's from my comrade Li Yin Jun – or about him. I have to find out what it says."

"Maybe Nayden can decipher it?" Kholodny proposed. His roving gaze slowly descended and settled on the diagram of pork cuts. "But he'll skin us alive if we don't close that case . . ."

---

* "You must hurry." "We have to go. The roll call starts soon."

"Why don't you go on your own?" Samson suggested.

"Alone?" Kholodny echoed, taken aback. "What if it's a trap?"

"What kind of trap could it be? It's just a woman named Shura, for whom Briskin appears to have feelings."

"No, I can't do it alone. The person under interrogation must be driven to distraction in order to reveal the truth. One interrogator isn't enough. I ask one question, you ask the next – like we were taught. Then, we light our cigarettes . . ."

Samson grimaced. He didn't enjoy the smoking component of the interrogation process, or tobacco in general.

"Then, perhaps you could wait?" he said, looking for another way out of his predicament. "Work on the documents while I find a translator, and then we'll go."

"Well, if that's your order, so be it," Kholodny said with a smile, sitting down at his desk. "Give me the file. I'll read everything over again."

Samson thrust the file into his comrade's hands and dashed out of the office.

He found Vasyl in the evidence room, reading a newspaper.

"Who can read Chinese?" the young investigator demanded.

"What you need is a Chinese fellow," Vasyl answered, slowly raising his eyes.

"But where can I find one?"

"At the Jewish Market," Vasyl suggested. "You can find anything over there. Anything and anyone."

It was as if a ray of sun had fallen on Samson's face. He lit up all over.

"You're right!" exclaimed. "I saw a Chinese merchant there – he interrupted the song about the tram accident! Kept shouting, '*Zhu-er-duo!*' Wonder what it means . . ."

"Go and ask."

"Thank you. I'll bring you back some gingerbread," Samson promised.

"You can keep your gingerbread," Vasyl chuckled. "Best get me an intestine pie instead. They go down easy with sweet tea, really hit the spot."

Samson shoved the Chinese letter into the pocket of his tunic and marched off to the market. It seemed to him that everyone was in a hurry that morning, and that the faces of the passers-by – especially of the better-dressed ones – were gloomier than usual. He remembered what Nayden had told him once: *When the enemy weeps, then we will smile*. But Samson didn't wish to smile. Besides, how could he determine, simply from the mood expressed on people's faces, whether they were his enemies or his allies? Didn't the commissars also say at their rallies that all men were brothers? Samson found that slogan to be somehow clearer, more to his liking. And, if all people were brothers, then one should, on the contrary, console those who weep. The ones smiling needed no help – otherwise they wouldn't be smiling.

The young investigator entered the market from Mariinsko-Blagovishchenska Street, passing the Halytska bathhouse. There weren't as many vendors and buyers about as there would have been on a Sunday, yet the hubbub – the music of the marketplace, in which none of the performers was obligated to hit the right notes – was as loud as ever. Samson could hear it especially well through his bare earhole. He adjusted his cap in order to balance the volume of the sounds that reached him from the left and the right. The closer he got to the vendors, the more these sounds filled his head and the easier it was to separate them into individual shouts and voices.

"Klaxon horns! Klaxon horns! Belgian klaxon horns for cabs and cars!" cried a resonant male voice, followed by the alarmingly sharp squeal of the object on offer. "Klaxon horns! Klaxon horns!" the voice called again, but it was quickly drowned out by a female shout: "Corn cream! Corn cream from Warsaw! Smear it on yer feet in the evenin' and yer corns'll fall off come mornin'! You'll be dancin' again in no time!"

Samson stopped. Movement made it difficult for him to concentrate. He listened out for something in Chinese, so as to know where to go with his letter. Soon, that familiar word – "*Zhu-er-duo!*" – reached him through the near and faraway cries and patter of merchants.

He hurried in the direction of the mysterious word – hurried clumsily, nearly overturning a table loaded with brass tea mugs.

Two minutes later, he stopped at a stall that displayed a mass of newspaper bundles.

"*Zhu-er-duo! Zhu-er-duo!*" the Chinese man behind the counter kept shouting, not paying the slightest attention to Samson.

Another Chinese man ran up to the stall. He and the merchant exchanged a few words, after which the merchant handed him a bundle in return for some money and began to search once more for buyers in the crowd.

"Comrade," Samson addressed him. "You read Chinese, don't you?"

Finally, the merchant noticed and looked up at Samson, who stood about a head taller than him.

"Yes," he said.

"Then I beg you to read this and translate it for me," Samson said, taking out the letter. "It concerns a comrade of mine."

The merchant adopted a more respectful attitude. He took the letter and, as he read it, Samson noticed his face darken and his thin upper lip curl somewhat haughtily towards his nostrils.

"What does it say?" the young investigator demanded impatiently.

"Do you know Li Yin Jun?" the merchant asked, staring into the policeman's eyes.

"Yes, he was of great help to me. He saved my wife."

"He was arrested. Tseka."

"The Cheka?"

"Like I say, Tseka," the merchant confirmed, nodding. "He needs help now."

"Does it say why he was arrested?" Samson asked.

"They write he killed two soldiers from railway."

Samson wondered whether this might have happened while his comrade was trying to retrieve his lost revolver.

He understood that it was difficult, almost impossible, to extricate a detainee from the grasp of the Cheka, but he had to try. Li Yin Jun was counting on him, otherwise he wouldn't have written.

"He needs help now," the merchant repeated.

"But what do I do?"

"Go to them. Ask them to free him."

"What if they don't?"

"You have to find the right people to ask, and have to ask them right, so they do it."

"I understand," Samson responded. "I'll go. What's your name?"

"Yu."

"How do you spell that?"

"One character."

"What does it mean?"

"Friend."

"A good name," Samson said, nodding. "We don't have one like that."

"Much you don't have. But now hurry. Help Li Yin Jun."

"Yes, yes," Samson murmured.

Feverish thoughts ran through his head like children lost in a dark wood, panicking, trembling with fear. Suddenly, he remembered the telephonogram from Lukyanivska Prison, which stated that Jacobson had been released by request of the Belgian consul.

"Is there a Chinese consul in Kyiv?" Samson asked Yu, staring hopefully into his eyes.

"Consul? There is. Fu Liwei. Lives in Holosiiv."

"He can help! We just need to write a letter and have him take it to the Cheka."

"Will you go, too?" the merchant asked.

"Of course," Samson confirmed.

"Good." Yu began to collect the newspaper bundles into a large paper bag. "I close up and we go."

After carrying the paper bag into a shed that leaned against a large storehouse at the back of the market, the merchant dragged Samson into the courtyard of the second house on the right on Zolotoustivska Street, which contained a stable and two unharnessed carts.

Yu shouted in Chinese. A young boy with a sleepy face peered out of the stable, answered in Chinese and, a minute later, led out and began to harness a dapple grey horse.

"Yu," Samson addressed the merchant, taking advantage of the pause. "What does '*zhu-er-duo*' mean?"

Yu cracked a barely perceptible smile.

"Dried pigs' ears," he said. "My product. I dry and sell. Only one in market."

The taste of dried pigs' ears reappeared on Samson's tongue – that unfamiliar Chinese flavour Li Yin Jun had acquainted him with.

"Did Li Yin Jun use to buy them from you?"

"Not buy. I give. He is a great man."

"Does the name Li also have a meaning?"

"Yes," Yu answered. "Li is strength. Also, sharp – and black."

The young Chinese driver had already taken his seat and was glaring impatiently at his passengers. Yu seemed to feel his gaze.

"We go," he urged Samson. "Hurry!"

He then said something to the driver, who gave the horse a command Samson didn't recognise, and the wheels of the cart began to spin towards the arched entrance.

"Does the horse understand Chinese too?" Samson murmured.

"What master speaks, horse understands," Yu pronounced firmly.

Chapter 30

Samson had never gone through Kyiv so quickly by cart. The young driver kept rising from his seat, shouting in Chinese to warn everyone to make way. Cabbies too cleared a path on noticing or hearing the cart rushing towards them, wheels clattering against the cobblestones – the ones heading the same way clinging to the right, those heading in the opposite direction moving to the left. The cart rushed past Samson's home and the Bureau of Statistics, then turned right.

Near the very place where Samson had lost his father and his ear, the driver seemed to slow down deliberately. Surprised, Samson leaned to the left and looked ahead. Several people were digging a pit in front of a two-storey house on that side of the street, tossing the earth onto the edge of the pavement.

After squeezing its way between a Red Army wagon loaded with furniture, driven by a soldier in uniform, and a Belgian truck, the cart speeded up again. Then, the driver turned to the left onto Nimetska Street, with excessive speed, and the display window of Samson's father's tailor, Sivokon, flashed by on the right. The glass was gleaming, and the young investigator took this as evidence that the tailor was alive and well.

The driver turned again, this time to the right. Three- and four-storey buildings gave way to two-storey ones, which were interspersed with vacant plots, some dug up for planting vegetables.

"Why does the consul live so far away?" Samson asked, turning to the Chinese merchant.

"Safer," he replied. "And cheaper."

"But this is completely untamed territory," Samson responded, again glancing at the street, where the two-storey buildings had now given way to single-storey homes and huts. "If someone were to attack him, no-one would come, no matter how much he screamed."

"Bandits do not attack Chinese," Yu explained calmly. "But, when power changes in Kyiv, always shooting. Dangerous. Shooting and robbing."

Samson gave Yu's words some thought. They struck him as perfectly logical.

"We have a saying," the young investigator began, after a pause. "Not my hut, not my problem."

"Good saying," Yu responded approvingly.

The cart shook. Samson looked back and realised that they had crossed a wooden bridge over a stream. On either side of the road – which, he immediately sensed, had ceased to be smooth – stretched countless vegetable gardens, some already turned up with a shovel or harrow, others lying dormant since the winter.

"Not far now," said Yu.

Soon, they pulled up at a structure that looked like a parochial rural school. In fact, a church stood behind the same picket fence, so Samson's guess turned out to be correct. Only, now, this school-like building played a different, residential role. On the left, on ropes stretched between two old cherry trees, hung drying shirts, trousers and footwraps. One piece of clothing among these everyday items attracted the young investigator's attention: a robe of blue silk, shining in the sun. What carelessness, he thought. It was sure to be stolen.

"I be quick," Yu declared, jumping to the ground. "He will write, and we will go."

"Tell him to take that robe into the house if he wants to keep it," Samson instructed, pointing to the object of his concern.

Yu responded with a nod.

Once through the gate, he went directly to the cherry trees, carefully removed the blue silk robe from the line and entered the house with it.

The cart's canopy kept Samson out of the sun, but he didn't want to sit idly in the shade. He stepped down to the ground and was struck by the silence of this largely unpeopled place. The road didn't look all that bad to the eye. It must have once been paved with cobblestones, which had then settled over the years, either from rain or simply with time. Later, it had been sprinkled with sand and broken bricks.

On the other side of the road stood a vacant lot with the remains of a collapsed hut. The age of the trees in the little orchard suggested that the hut had collapsed some two decades ago, which meant its owners had died even earlier. Further down, in the direction of Vasylkiv, the road began to resemble a proper street. Samson could make out rooftops and younger orchards.

The young driver, taking advantage of his short stature, curled up on his seat and dozed off.

Tired of looking around, Samson got back into the cart and pulled the canopy forward to protect himself from the sun as it moved towards the west. He tried to calculate how long it would take the consul to write the letter and get ready to leave, but he gave up halfway through and turned his mind to Nadezhda. She was more pleasant to think about. Had she changed since their anti-wedding? Had her attitude towards him changed? His attitude hadn't. His love for her had grown neither weaker nor stronger. It was a caring rather than a passionate love – calm and reliable, like everything done with the expectation of long service. The Germans, for instance, did everything with the expectation of long service, but at home only tailors and cobblers worked that way. For the rest, the results of their labour depended on their mood or on their feelings about their task. Could it be said, then, that Samson loved Nadezhda in German? Reliably, calmly?

Samson considered this. The idea of loving in German did not appeal to him. The world war that had ended the previous year gave it a cruel, bloody connotation.

No, he decided. He loved Nadezhda respectfully rather than calmly. While she loved him pityingly.

Samson recalled that, after the anti-wedding, he had suddenly become her "dear mate".

Then again, people did speak of "soul mates", and that had a more respectful sound to it. The thought was consoling.

He looked back at the house and, at that very moment, the door opened and an elderly woman emerged with a large empty basket. She took down the clothes and brought them into the house.

About five minutes later, the door opened again. Yu came out first, followed by the consul – a thin Chinese man of short stature, in a formal suit, holding a yellow leather briefcase.

When the three passengers were in the cart, Yu slapped the sleeping driver on the shoulder. The young man jumped up, chattering in Chinese – probably asking forgiveness.

The consul, who sat in the middle, introduced himself: "Fu Liwei."

Samson replied with his name. "Did you bring the letter?" he asked.

The consul opened the briefcase on his knees, pulled out an attractive red folder, untied its silk ribbons and withdrew a thick, yellowish-orange sheet of paper. He didn't hand it to Samson, instead bringing it close to the policeman's face.

At the very top of the sheet, in the centre, sat the bright emblem of the Republic of China. It looked like an old oriental jug, with a peacock clinging to one side of the neck and a dragon to the other. Beneath the emblem, embossed in gold, were the words, CONSULATE OF THE REPUBLIC OF CHINA IN THE RUSSIAN EMPIRE. The last two words had been neatly crossed out in the same ink used to write the letter below.

Samson stared at the orderly rows of neatly drawn characters.

"Mr Consul," Samson sighed. "I don't think they'll understand Chinese at the Cheka."

"I assure you that they will understand," the consul answered firmly, with barely a trace of an accent. "I will translate every word. Official Chinese documents must be composed in Chinese."

At the same time, Samson remembered that there were Chinese Red Army men seconded to the Cheka, and he calmed down.

The springs of the cart creaked as the road rose and dipped. Samson grew a bit queasy. The consul had slipped the folder with the letter back into his briefcase and sat in silence, his face as still as a sheet of steel and his unblinking eyes fixed on the driver's back.

They reached Sadova Street fairly quickly.

"We're going up to see your commander," Samson said sternly to the soldier on duty at the entrance. "The Chinese consul demands a meeting."

That was exactly what the consul had advised Samson to declare, and the young investigator uttered the phrase with surprising ease, although he well understood that the word "demands" lost all meaning within these walls.

A few minutes later, the consul and Samson were allowed inside. Yu remained with the cart.

On the first floor, the soldier guiding the visitors asked them to wait outside as he entered an office through tall double doors. But they didn't have to stand in the corridor for long.

"Come in," the soldier said as he opened one of the doors and stepped aside.

"Look who it is!" An excited and strangely familiar voice boomed in the spacious room.

About ten paces in front of them stood an enormous desk littered with folders and piles of papers and documents. It was a desk fit for a governor, perhaps even the tsar himself. Behind it, directly in the centre, yet dwarfed by its size, sat Nikanor Abyazov, without a cap, but in an ironed tunic.

"Comrade Abyazov!" Samson exclaimed. "I was worried about you – thought you might be . . . under arrest."

Abyazov rose to his feet, pushing away a heavy chair with a wide back upholstered in black leather.

"I was," he said. "And sentenced to death. But then they released me and assigned me to this post. So, you're now the Chinese consul?" Abyazov's eyes widened as an unkind, inquisitive smile spread across his lips.

Samson suddenly realised that the consul was nowhere to be seen. He looked round in fright and discovered that Fu Liwei was sheltering behind him.

"No, allow me to introduce the consul," Samson responded, stepping aside to reveal the important visitor to the commander.

The consul bowed, approached the desk, lowered his briefcase onto the chair for visitors, opened it and pulled out the red folder. Every one of his movements was markedly slow, emphatically ritualistic, as if there were special rules regarding even the subtle process of undoing a folder's silk ribbons.

At last, he extended the letter to Abyazov with both hands.

The Cheka commander also assumed an air of haughty importance and slowly raised the letter to his eyes. He immediately lowered it.

"It's Chinese," he said with obvious displeasure, giving the consul a cold, hard-hearted look.

"Allow me to read it to you," the consul suggested, transferring his briefcase to the parquet floor and sitting down in the visitor's chair.

Samson had never before been present at the official reading of a diplomatic document. The very tone of the consul's voice lent solemnity to the occasion. The man seemed to know the translation by heart, pronouncing each word clearly, with apparent joy, emphasising the significance, in both sense and sound, of each syllable, each letter. Abyazov, too, listened spellbound.

This, thought Samson, was how tsars and emperors wrote letters to each other.

"We therefore ask you to demonstrate good will and, as a sign of friendship between revolutionary Russia and the revolutionary Republic of China, to release Chinese citizen Li Yin Jun, closing all investigations into his actions and reversing all decisions and decrees restricting his freedom," the consul proclaimed, then immediately rose to his feet and stood motionless in front of Abyazov, who sat with his lips slightly parted, his face frozen in an expression of respectful awe.

"Does he mean your Chinese friend?" Abyazov asked Samson, as he emerged from his stupor.

"Yes, Li Yin Jun helped save my Nadezhda."

"Murat!" shouted the Cheka commander, and a swarthy soldier ran into the office. "Bring up the Chinese detainee Li Yin Jun. Not just any Chinese detainee, but Li Yin Jun – understood?"

Murat ran out.

"Alright, Comrade Consul," Abyazov began, staring thoughtfully at Fu Liwei. "I'll let your comrade go."

"I am deeply grateful, Comrade Commander," the consul responded, and bowed. "May I take him away with me now?"

"You may."

Soon, the doors opened, and a Chinese Red Army soldier was brought into the office. At first, Li Yin Jun's face registered nothing but cold detachment, but, when he saw Samson, he shook his head in surprise and joy.

"Take him away," Abyazov said to the consul. "I'll keep the letter. When our Chinese comrades make a translation, I'll affix my seal and place it in Li Yin Jun's file."

Samson felt as if he had sprouted wings. He couldn't believe his eyes and ears. Could it really be so easy to free someone from the Cheka? Even his own station probably wouldn't have released a detainee so quickly in response to a consul's letter. In fact, he couldn't even imagine how Nayden would have behaved in such a situation.

"Thank you," Samson exhaled, turning to leave.

But Abyazov's gaze suddenly stopped him, digging in like a fishing hook.

"You stay," Abyazov said in a commanding tone. "I've been meaning to have a chat with you."

The swarthy soldier led the two Chinese citizens out of the office. In parting, Li Yin Jun gave Samson a firm, manly handshake.

"Sit," Abyazov said, pointing to the visitor's chair. "We've had an unfortunate incident here, as a result of which I may be arrested again, or even shot," he continued in quieter voice. "Your thief Kosyakin has escaped. I can't understand how he managed it . . . From a locked, windowless cell . . . Nayden sent him here without a case file, so his presence wasn't recorded in our list of detainees. But I know he was here. And a few of the soldiers know it, too. If one of them talks, up there –" Abyazov quickly lifted his head towards the ceiling – "that will be the end of me. And Nayden won't get off lightly, either."

"Kosyakin's a circus performer," Samson explained. "From a circus family."

"I see," Abyazov responded gloomily. "I don't need him here, but if you could track him down and shoot him, I'd be much obliged. No-one upstairs can know that he ran off."

The Cheka commander stared into Samson's eyes so intently that the young investigator had no choice but to nod.

"Have you closed the books on the meat speculators?"

"We'll do it tomorrow," said Samson. "Or the day after tomorrow. No later."

"I'll stop by," Abyazov said. Noticing the look of confusion on his interlocutor's face, he added, "Since I helped open the case, it would be right and proper for me to sign the verdict."

The conversation did not last much longer. After enquiring about the general course of affairs at the Lybid station, Abyazov sent Samson on his way, citing the urgent need to draw up a list of detainees to be executed.

Only when he was out on the street did Samson recall that Briskin and his daughter were still in the interrogation room. He glanced around nervously in search of a cab, but none was to be found. Cabbies disfavoured and avoided this address, just as they disfavoured and avoided those who worked here.

He finally hailed one down on Levashovska Street, and, once he reached the station, raced up the stairs to the first floor. He stopped at the heavy door to the interrogation room and, gasping for breath, asked the soldier on guard, "Well?"

"Did as you ordered," the Red Army man answered. "They asked to use the latrine. I let the girl go, but not him."

The room smelled of urine.

"Sophia, go out and wait for me in the corridor," Samson commanded.

The girl obeyed.

"I'm terribly sorry, I couldn't hold it back," Briskin said plaintively.

"Don't worry, someone will clean it up," Samson assured him. "Kholodny and I will be going to question Shura now. A shame you wrote about her—"

"What did I write?" Briskin protested, scared. "I didn't write anything incriminating! Only that I sold her the heart for next to nothing."

"Next to nothing. Why not for nothing?" Samson asked with a metallic, slightly sarcastic note in his voice.

"She's a proud woman," Briskin justified himself. "She wouldn't have accepted it for free. I know her."

"I understand." Samson raised his hand in a calming gesture. "Forgive me. We'll go now. I can take your daughter with us and leave her there."

"I shall be grateful for as long as I live," the detainee declared, his voice trembling. He looked as if he was about to cry.

Samson nodded, opened the door and ordered the soldier to take Briskin down to the basement. Then, without particular haste, he made his way to his office.

Chapter 31

On the way to Shura's, bouncing along in an old, stiff, springless cart, Kholodny kept yawning and glancing somewhat reproachfully at Samson. He tried to ensure that his glances didn't land on the girl between them, who smelled of spicy salted herring. Samson hadn't noticed the aroma that morning, approaching Sophia in front of the station, nor had he noticed it later, when he let her out of the interrogation room. The odours on Tarasivska Street weren't especially pleasant to begin with, their main source being the horse droppings at the corner of the station, piled up by the yard-sweeper of the neighbouring building. And, in the interrogation room, the stench of urine had been overwhelming – not as bad as in the latrine, but close. In truth, Samson wouldn't have noticed the spicy smell even now, had he not seen Kholodny turning his fleshy nose out towards the street.

Their journey was a long one, all the way to Zakharivska Street, past Kyrylivska Square. It might have been faster to go through Lukyanivska Prison, but the cabby had decided to go through Podil instead. By the time they reached Zhytnotorzka Square, Samson too was yawning. Sophia alone sat with her lips pressed firmly together, gazing fearfully straight ahead, although her only view was the cabby's back. On the square, they ran into about a dozen wagons trying to leave the market. The trading day was coming to an end, and the first to go were those whose homes lay not one or two, but five or ten miles away. The merchants who lived in town usually stayed until closing time.

At last, the cab turned left onto Market Street, and from there onto Kyrylivska Street.

Samson thought back to his conversation with Abyazov. It would have been good to tell Kholodny about it now, but he couldn't do so in the girl's presence. Official conversations, even when conducted in a cab or out on the street, were not for the ears of outsiders. And so the young investigator had to mull it over by himself. They were about to conduct the last interview, the transcript of which, according to law, had to be included in the case file. There were already more than ten of these transcripts. If not for the conversation with Abyazov, Samson might not have added this one to the file. Now, however . . . He knew that Abyazov would come to help write the verdict. The Cheka commander would pore over every page of the file. He really seemed to suspect Samson of something – of having bungled the meat case in some way. One could hear it in his tone of voice. That meant he would come not so much to help as to nitpick, to find fault. Under these circumstances, it would be impossible simply to blot out Shura's name from Briskin's papers. And, if her name remained, they would need a transcript.

Samson bit his lip and glanced sideways at Sophia, whose face was still numb, free of expression. Like the two policemen, she bobbed up and down in the cart with every bump in the road, but she was motionless otherwise.

A cool evening breeze brushed Samson's face, bringing with it a pleasant, sweetly intoxicating scent. He looked to the left and saw that they happened to be passing Khryakov's brewery. Was it really open for business? And it seemed that a similar idea arose at that moment in the mind of Sergius Kholodny, too, because the two comrades exchanged surprised glances at the same time.

When the brewery was behind them, the intoxicating scent of malt vanished from the air. And so did the smell of spicy salted herring. Surprised, Samson twice surreptitiously positioned his nose near Sophia's hair, just to make sure.

Kyrylivska Street looked deserted. The squat houses and huts, with their gardens ready to flower behind neat, though not always freshly painted fences, caressed the eye. Looking around, one might believe that there had been no war, no revolution, no uprising of villagers in Kurenivka under the command of Hetman Struk. The road stretched away, free and empty, towards the horizon. No cart but theirs rolled along this road from the centre of Kyiv to its very outskirts on the holy hills. No other horse clip-clopped on the cobblestones, no other wheels creaked rhythmically on their axles.

Number 3 Zakharivska Street – which was actually more of a lane – turned out to be a hut with a green fence. A small booth to the right of the threshold made Samson stop outside the gate. But there was no dog. It would have come out barking.

The young investigator, briefcase in hand, went up to the door and knocked.

The woman who answered looked frightened to see him – apparently due to his uniform and wooden holster. Soon, she noticed the second, larger policeman, as well as the girl.

"What is your name?" Samson enquired politely, making no effort to enter the hut.

"Alexandra Ipatyevna Karyatis."

"Alexandra Ipatyevna, we would like to ask you a few questions concerning Moses Briskin. May we come in?"

She stepped aside.

Her rural living room was more reminiscent of an urban flat. The little bentwood table, with its convex sides, seemed to say: *You don't know where you've just set foot.* The large oval table couldn't have come through the narrow doorway in one piece. Its legs must have been unscrewed and brought in separately.

"And she—?" Alexandra Ipatyevna began, indicating the girl with her eyes, then cut herself off.

Something troubled Samson, but he didn't know what it was. He peered at the hostess's mass of light brown hair, her lilac sundress, her Turkish leather slippers with upturned toes.

She couldn't have been the Shura who'd bought a pig heart from

Briskin for next to nothing. To Samson, at least, a woman like this could never be a Shura – she could only be addressed formally, reverently. Shura was just too plain, too familiar. But perhaps Briskin called her that on purpose?

Surveying the room, Samson noticed that Kholodny, too, was eyeing the hostess, his mouth slightly open.

There were a few framed photographs on the wall, one of them depicting a handsome bearded old man.

"Who is that?" Samson asked.

"My grandfather, Herakleios Karyatis. He was Greek, from Thessaloniki."

"So, you're Greek?" Samson asked, surprised.

"Does it matter?" she asked in response. "What do you need?"

"Let us proceed in an orderly fashion," Kholodny cut in, his voice sounding both beautifully operatic and sternly police-like. "We need to question you. May I sit down?"

She invited the men to the table. Sophia also pulled out a chair, but Samson threw a glance to direct her to the couch in a far corner of the room. After taking his seat, he pulled an inkwell, a pen and two sheets of paper from his briefcase.

By habit, he removed the burgundy fringed tablecloth. One can't write so well on tablecloths; the pen pokes right through the paper.

As he was straightening the sheet of paper on the wooden table-top, he heard the strike of a match. Kholodny had lit a cigarette and now he extended his pack to Samson, who drew one for himself and lit it as well.

Somewhere nearby, a child began to cry.

"Is it a boy or a girl?" Samson enquired.

"A boy," she replied, rising to her feet. "Excuse me, I'll be right back."

The crying subsided.

"Odd smell," Kholodny commented.

Samson sniffed the air. The atmosphere was thick and warm,

somewhat reminiscent of the one he'd encountered in the basement around the corner from the Jewish Market, where sweets were boiled.

"Perhaps she's making dinner?" Samson guessed.

At the top of the sheet, he wrote out, *Transcript of the Interrogation of Alexandra Ipatyevna Karyatis*.

The woman returned. Looking her right in the face, Kholodny exhaled his puffs of smoke down to the floor. Samson kept turning, exhaling to the side. Eventually, he stubbed out his cigarette on the bottom of the briefcase, lowered it to the floor, and placed it beside the toe of his right boot.

She calmly answered the initial personal questions, but then Samson asked, "How long have you known Moses Briskin?" At this, she sank into thought.

The child began to cry again, and she jumped up from her chair. Samson followed her into the next room. She only noticed the policeman's presence after taking the boy out of his cradle.

The boy's face – the line of his brows, the eyes set somewhat closer than usual to the nose – looked familiar to Samson. He was the spit and image of Briskin.

"Please, go back," the hostess pleaded. "I'll be right there, just as soon as I calm him down."

"Moses Zelikovich is the father, yes?" asked Samson, already half-turned away.

She seemed to want to answer, but did not. Her face expressed her feelings more clearly than any words could have. At the mention of Briskin, her eyes glimmered with sweet pain and tender longing.

Samson returned to the living room.

"It's broth!" Kholodny exclaimed, almost coughing up the last word, as if he'd been waiting to share this conjecture for a very long time.

The young investigator shrugged. The air had indeed grown still richer, thicker, warmer.

*

"How long have you known Briskin?" he repeated when the woman took her seat, his pen poised to transcribe her words.

"It's hard to say. Maybe three years."

"Only three?" Kholodny asked doubtfully.

"Yes, three."

"When was the last time you saw him?"

"About two weeks ago."

"How many times has he brought you meat?"

"Several times."

"Can you briefly describe your relationship with Briskin?"

"It was good . . ."

Samson kept writing, but he felt increasingly nervous. He realised that the questions he was posing were somehow wrong, but the right ones seemed to be stuck deep inside his mind. Try as he might, he couldn't call them up. Nor could he understand why his hand was trembling. To his dismay, his penmanship, which had always been distinguished for its regularity and smoothness, was now uneven. His letters, too, seemed to tremble, bouncing slightly up and down. He bit his lip and turned to Kholodny.

"Would you mind taking over?" he asked, nodding at the transcript. "My hand is cramped."

Kholodny's face expressed displeasure, but he got up and the two investigators changed places.

"What are you cooking?" the former priest asked.

Alexandra Ipatyevna looked in horror at the pen clamped between his thick fingers. "What difference does it make?"

"I'm just curious," he answered coldly, but the look in his eyes was almost tender.

She read his gaze. "I'm making broth for the baby."

"Did you know that private trade in meat has been banned by the ExProFooCom?" asked Kholodny.

"What is that?"

"The Extraordinary Provincial Food Committee," Samson explained. "Like the Cheka, but for food."

Fear appeared on the woman's face. "I had no idea."

Kholodny took down her answer, then ran his eye over the whole transcript. He handed it to Samson, who took a careful look, noting with some relief that, even when they trembled, his letters were still much more correct and orderly than Kholodny's.

"Please write, 'Taken down correctly from my words'," he instructed the woman. "Then sign and date it."

Alexandra Ipatyevna took the transcript from Samson's hands. Her lips moved soundlessly. Reaching the end, she started over again. Her lips no longer moved, but her gaze grew sharper, more anxious.

Her anxiety infected Samson. The child in the next room began to cry again, but this time the hostess didn't budge. She was as still as stone.

"What on earth have you written?" she asked, staring at Samson the way a teacher stares at a poorly prepared pupil.

"What do you mean? Is there an error?"

"I didn't buy any meat from Moses," she declared. "I bought a heart."

"Are you joking?" Kholodny exclaimed. "Kidneys, liver, ears, heart – it's all meat."

Alexandra Ipatyevna threw an almost contemptuous glance at the former priest.

"Absolutely not," she exhaled nervously. "The heart – is not – meat." At this, she clutched her left breast with her hand. Her mouth contorted into a grimace of pain, but, by force of will, she managed to wipe it from her lips and turn to the open door through which the child's cry had sounded. It seemed as if she wanted the child to cry again, to give her cause to run out of the room and collect herself.

Samson felt his own heart begin to ache.

"Where is your kitchen?" he asked.

Transcript in hand, he followed her into the kitchenette, where a pot stood on a sooty kerosene stove, sending thick, heavy steam into the air. The smell of broth was unmistakable – and satiating in itself.

Samson placed a corner of the transcript beneath the pot. The document caught fire, and Alexandra Ipatyevna watched in fright as it burned in the young investigator's hand. When the blue flame reached his fingers, Samson released the remaining corner. It turned to ash on the wooden floor.

"I'll rewrite it," he said. "It was full of errors. The girl on the couch is Briskin's daughter, Sophia. Can she stay with you?"

"Of course," the hostess whispered.

"I apologise for the intrusion," Samson added.

"Why don't you sit for a minute?" Alexandra Ipatyevna suddenly asked. "At the table?"

Samson returned to the living room, where he lowered the inkwell to the bottom of his briefcase, then rolled the unused sheet of paper around the pen and placed them together in the briefcase's inner pocket.

Kholodny gave his comrade an enquiring look, sighed and jerked his heavy chin towards the window, as if to ask, *Time to go?*

Samson shook his head.

The hostess entered with two plates in her hands. She placed them in front of the investigators, along with two forks. Steam rose from small chunks of strange grey meat.

She went out again and returned with a wooden salt cellar.

Kholodny shrugged, forked a piece of meat, dipped it in salt and sent it into his mouth. After chewing it a while, he shrugged again.

"You know, I'd never tasted a heart before," Kholodny admitted when he and Samson were already on their way back. "She's right – it isn't meat," he said, twisting his lips. "Not at all."

"You won't tell, will you?" asked Samson.

"No chance of that. I had some, too, didn't I?" Kholdony responded with a faint smile.

After sending Kholodny home, Samson brooded over the meat case for another two hours, rereading the transcripts and trying to anticipate the questions Nayden and Abyazov might pose.

He didn't come home until midnight. To his surprise, he found Dr Vatrukhin at the living-room table, reading a book.

"Nadezhda is in bed. She couldn't keep awake," he said. "We heard gunfire nearby, so I decided to stay up and wait, just in case you were involved, God forbid . . ."

"Where was it?"

"God knows. Out there, somewhere."

"I didn't hear anything at all." Samson stood still for a moment, listening to the silence. "Nikolay Nikolaevich, I wanted to ask you something, concerning a medical matter."

The doctor assumed an attentive expression – the one he used with his patients.

"Do hard-boiled eggs relieve heart disease?"

"Nonsense, my dear Samson . . . You can't cure heart disease by rolling eggs over your chest," Vatrukhin answered condescendingly.

"No, I don't mean by rolling. I mean by ingesting, like pills."

"I'm afraid not. Eggs contain many elements harmful to the heart. Especially the yolk."

"We have a detainee whose daughter brings him eggs every day. He said it was doctor's orders."

"And you believed him?" Vatrukhin exclaimed, then immediately covered his mouth with his hand and glanced at the door to Nadezhda's bedroom. He continued in a whisper: "The fellow probably made it up so that the eggs wouldn't be taken away. And eats them to keep up his strength. Eggs are extremely nutritious, you know."

Samson pursed his lips.

Briskin had lied, he thought, both to him and to his own daughter, but the young investigator felt neither anger nor even resentment. A man under arrest must become something of a rat, he concluded. Otherwise, he would never survive among other prisoners.

Chapter 32

Abyazov was late for the sentencing. Samson regretted having hurried to the station in the pouring rain, dodging splashes from carts speeding through puddles and jets of water streaming down from leaky gutters. As soon as he entered, he folded his bamboo-handled umbrella and automatically looked around for where to put it, so as not to drip water on the stairs and in the corridor. But then he recalled that the station contained no such trifles as stands for umbrellas. Thank goodness that at least one relic from tsarist times, the boot scraper by the door, was dug deep into the ground and couldn't be easily removed. Unfortunately, the Red Army men still hadn't figured out the object's purpose and, in wet weather, simply pounded their boots on the threshold, trying to knock off the mud, or scraped their soles on the edges of the steps.

Kholodny and Samson waited for Abyazov in Nayden's office, sipping tea. When the Chekist finally arrived, he demanded another half an hour alone with the case file.

The two investigators went back to their office, where Samson turned his attention to the diagram of pork cuts. He felt rather melancholy. Up to the day before, they hadn't made much headway with the case, but now it was closed. The verdict and sentence would soon be issued, the file would be placed in the archive and Briskin would likely spend a couple of months in prison. So it seemed to Samson.

"Time to turn the page," he whispered to himself.

"I didn't catch that," Kholodny said, looking up from his book about Father Brown, the English priest detective. His face, too, bore a sour expression. He must have also felt idle, even somewhat bereft, now that the meat case was all packed up.

"I was just muttering to myself," Samson assured him.

Then, he took the diagram off the wall, rolled it into a tube and tied it with two laces that had come off an old folder.

Vasyl peeked round the door.

"Nayden's ready," he said. "More tea?"

Samson shook his head.

When they entered Nayden's office, Samson looked first at Abyazov. The Chekist's pale, firmly set face seemed to show that he had no particular complaints about the file.

"Come on, come on," Abyazov urged the newcomers.

"Sit down at the desk. You'll do the writing," Nayden commanded Samson.

Samson took his seat and looked at the sentencing form lying in front of him. On it were printed two empty rectangles, the left one headed IN ATTENDANCE, the right, SENTENCED BY. Below were spaces for signatures and stamps.

Slowly, Samson put down four names in the left rectangle, then turned to Abyazov, who sat nearby on the couch.

"So, how long should we lock him up for?" Abyazov asked, shifting his gaze to Nayden.

Pursing his lips, the commander replied, "Let's say a year and a half."

"But that's too long!" Samson exclaimed, unable to restrain himself.

"Too long?" Abyazov echoed in surprise.

Kholodny remained silent. He did not even seem to be listening.

"He has a heart condition," Samson responded, now more quietly.

"Briskin was speculating in meat even before the ExProFooCom issued its decree. We could give him more time. Two years," Nayden added in a judicious tone, cautiously glancing at Abyazov.

"But he sat on the Forage Committee, which means he voluntarily signed up to serve the Soviet cause," Samson cut in. "So, he traded in his spare time?"

"Not traded. Speculated," Abyazov sharply corrected Samson. His lips expressed displeasure – not sharp, restrained. His narrow eyes, meanwhile, betrayed thoughts rather than emotions. "If he had speculated during working hours, we could have given him five years. Under the present circumstances, I believe he deserves three." The Chekist pronounced the last sentence with a special degree of clarity and resonance, while prodding the others with an impatient glare. "Now, on to the second part."

"What second part?" Samson asked in confusion.

"What? Why, the heart of the matter!" Abyazov shot back, leaping to his feet. He picked up the file and quickly leafed through it. "Concerning Shpakevich, who established and maintained an illegal slaughterhouse. A much more serious affair than mere speculation. If it hadn't been for the illegal slaughterhouse, Briskin wouldn't have had any meat in which to speculate."

"But we didn't investigate him ... We only collected evidence against Briskin, and ..." Samson began to protest, but he stopped short, bumping up against the Chekist's cold, flinty gaze.

"That just shows how clumsy you all are. You questioned and released the culprit, then forgot all about him," Abyazov said through his teeth. "Yet his role in the case is correctly defined in the file: co-conspirator. Although, he isn't merely a co-conspirator, he's the prime instigator. Without him, there would have been no crime. Take down the verdict!"

Samson lifted the nib of the pen over the right rectangle.

"We have reached a decision," Nayden began to dictate, pulling the open file towards himself and finding the initial documents that indicated the names of the detainees. "For illegally trading in meat, Moses Zelikovich Briskin, born in 1886, of bourgeois origin, is hereby sentenced to three years in prison. For establishing and maintaining an underground slaughterhouse, Ivan Stepanovich Shpakevich, born in 1889, of bourgeois origin, is hereby sentenced . . ." Pausing, he looked enquiringly at Abyazov.

"To be shot," the Chekist calmly declared.

Nayden grew tense and even narrowed his eyes. Kholodny shuddered and also fixed his eyes on Abyazov. The pen quivered in Samson's hand, and, although no drop could fall onto the document from its nib, he nevertheless moved it to hover over the blue porcelain inkwell. He stared at the still-quivering pen, then lowered it into the inkwell and placed his hand on the desk to the right of the document, pressing it down with force, because he felt the hand wanted to rise up of its own volition, to tremble expressively before the eyes of all those present, betraying its owner's sudden nervousness.

Nayden gazed numbly at Samson's hand, then for some reason raised his own right hand to his face and examined his nails. Their tips were outlined by dark borders of dirt clogged underneath them. The commander looked both concerned and bewildered. He raised his fingers to his lips, as if he were about to bite off the dirty little arcs, but caught himself and lowered the hand to his knee.

"Well, shall we write it or not?" Abyazov asked in a threatening voice.

Nayden raised his head and looked at Kholodny – also rather sharply, angrily.

"Shall we?" He repeated the Chekist's question to Kholodny.

"Doesn't seem Christian, somehow," the former priest sighed. "Besides, it's a shed, not a slaughterhouse."

Samson gazed at his comrade with admiration, taking heart and swallowing the saliva that had pooled in his mouth.

"Since when do we pass sentences on the basis of Christian morality?" Abyazov shot back with steel in his voice, puffing out his chest and squaring his shoulders, as if he were preparing to take part in a parade right where he sat. "We will not turn the other cheek! Is it true, Comrade Kholodny, that you wear a cross under your tunic?" the Chekist asked, directing his piercing gaze at the former priest's eyes. "Is it?"

"Only for the purpose of self-defence," Kholodny answered, and, unable to bear the gaze, he looked at Samson.

"I see," Abyazov said, with a grin. "So, it works miracles, then?"

Kholodny didn't respond, but the Chekist hadn't expected an answer. He now stared at Samson.

"To be shot!" he repeated, indicating the inkwell with a glance.

"Let's go ahead and finish this," Nayden urged. "No more messing about."

Samson was still playing for time, although he sensed that it was in vain. The Chekist would never change his mind. The image of Li Yin Jun, whom Abyazov had set free with such ease, flew through his mind. In that case, a consul had intervened with an official letter. But Shpakevich had no consul, being a local citizen. For some reason, Samson especially regretted not having asked Shpakevich more questions before letting him go, not having learned anything interesting about the man and his life. Now, he was sentencing to death not an individual, with all his personal problems and habits, but merely a surname with an address.

"Sabotage?" Abyazov asked quickly in a low, menacing tone.

Samson lifted the pen, shook off a drop of red ink and brought it back to the document. The lines written ten minutes earlier had already dried. It seemed somehow excessive – violent, even – to continue an already dried sentence. His hand positioned the nib so that it would do so above the invisible bottom line of the preceding words.

"Tooo beeee shhhot," the young investigator repeated aloud, stretching out the words for as long as he could, then looked up at Nayden.

"Sign it," barked the commander.

Samson lowered the pen even closer to the paper, focusing on the spot where the nib would touch down and draw the first letter – but then his right hand flinched and the pen flew out, landed on the edge of the desk, rolled across a folder, leaving a trail of red ink, and fell to the floor. Samson jumped up to catch it, but staggered. To maintain his balance, he threw his left leg forward and immediately heard the crunch of the pen under the sole of his boot.

Abyazov's usually narrow eyes instantly opened wide and filled with hatred.

Dropping a regretful glance at the fragments of the pen, Samson returned to his seat and, seeing no other writing implements within reach, froze and held his breath, as if awaiting a miracle.

Owing partly to his paralysing sense of expectation and partly to the surge of mortifying despair brought about by the accident, Samson's body and mind grew weak. He hardly noticed Abyazov's left hand grabbing the porcelain inkwell and shaking out a few ruby drops onto the already stained folder – hardly noticed the Chekist's right hand digging into his palm with sharp fingers, forcefully separating the thumb, dipping it into an inky drop and pressing it into the rectangle for signatures. The firm red thumbprint looked strange in this rectangle, like that of a criminal.

Samson's thoughts were muddled. He pulled his hand away, looked at the red thumb and frowned.

Meanwhile, Abyazov had pulled the document off the desk. In one hand, he held the stub of an indelible pencil. After spitting on the pencil's tip, he lowered the paper onto a bare corner of the desk, leaned over and etched three words in poisonous blue: *To be shot*. The Chekist's writing was twice as large as Samson's, but what set the letters of the terrible sentence apart was not so much their size as their crude roundness. They looked as if they'd been put down by a diligent schoolchild from the countryside, who had yet to grasp the relationship between the beauty of his penmanship and the beauty of the written word. Abyazov's words were notable for their ugliness. Samson suddenly realised that he himself would never have been able to write them in a manner that would have corresponded so perfectly to their meaning.

Abyazov added his signature to the rectangle, part of which was already occupied by Samson's thumbprint. Nayden was next to sign. The last to confirm the sentence was Kholodny, who looked pale and acted as if he were hobbled like a horse, which was no doubt why he at first didn't manage to hit the right rectangle with the tip of the pencil.

Abyazov's signature turned out to be surprisingly neat. It was obvious to Samson that the man loved his name more than he did the terrible, ominous words used for sentencing.

The Chekist noticed Samson's interest in his signature, grinned contemptuously, then shook his head, turned round and left the office in silence.

Nayden, Samson and Kholodny also remained silent for a full five minutes, sustaining the heavy funereal atmosphere over their heads.

Eventually, Nayden came to life. He summoned Vasyl, ordered him to send a truck with Red Army men to pick up the second sentenced man and handed him the case file, so that he could copy out Shpakevich's address. He added that Vasyl should bring him "fresh crimes" by three o'clock.

Samson suddenly craved a smoke. He asked Kholodny for a cigarette and matches, went downstairs and walked to the corner of Karavaevska. The rain had stopped, but the clouds that hung over the university's botanical gardens promised nothing good.

After lighting up, Samson turned his back to the botanical garden and gazed at the street in front of the station. He saw a truck drive out of the courtyard and stop. Four Red Army men with rifles over their shoulders exited the building, cast disapproving glances at the sky, then climbed into the back of the vehicle. The truck drove away. The door to the station opened again and Briskin appeared on the threshold, accompanied by two soldiers.

He, too, looked up at the sky, then glanced around and spotted Samson. The prisoner stared in his direction but made no sign of greeting or acknowledgement. His hands were bound behind his back.

One of the Red Army men barked something at him. Briskin shuddered, shook off his outward calm and hurriedly set out in Samson's direction, the armed soldiers walking on either side of him.

The young investigator was surprised that Briskin was being taken away on foot. He stepped aside.

After watching them pass and move on, he wandered down Karavaevska.

"Someone came looking for you," the soldier on guard informed him upon his return. "Chinese."

"How many?"

"One. Left a package, with a note. It's in your office."

On his desk, he found a paper bag, smaller than the ones in which the merchant Yu had placed his bundles of dried pigs' ears. The opening was stitched shut with coarse thread, and a folded note was sewn to it. Samson tore it off.

In blocky letters, the note read: *Dear Comrade San Son, I will never forget the help you gave me. I wish you a thousand successes and I am ready to die for you. Your friend, Li Yin Jun.*

The familiar sour-spicy smell of dried pigs' ears hit his nostrils.

Samson took the bag over to the window and left it on the floor.

Back at his desk, he laid his head on his folded arms and dozed off.

Someone peeked into the office but did not enter. It was probably Vasyl. Perhaps an hour or two later, the door opened again. The stranger's initial steps sounded loud, but the thudding immediately stopped. Only the light scrape of a chair across the floor told Samson that Kholodny had returned.

Some time later, there was a shout – not in the office, but out in the corridor. Nayden was summoning someone. Samson listened without opening his eyes. The chair scraped again, and soon a heavy hand patted him on the shoulder. The young investigator raised his head and looked round. There were two glasses on the desk, filled to the brim. The scent of alcohol made him sneeze, bringing him to his senses.

Kholodny hovered over him.

"Shouldn't we drink to the verdict?" he asked.

"To the verdict?" Samson repeated haltingly. He gazed at his comrade in confusion. But then his eyes grew sharper and he raised his inky thumb to his face.

"To the verdict and to the condemned! See how it is? God is far more merciful than man."

"Does that mean you'll be going back to Him?" Samson asked.

Kholodny shook his head.

Samson sighed, reached for the glass and brought it to his mouth. The scent struck him again. He dipped his stained thumb in the alcohol, pulled it out and rubbed it on his tunic, but the ink wouldn't come off.

"It's made in England," Kholodny said bitterly. "Doesn't fade or wash away. Someone once gave me a bottle."

Samson's lips twisted, as if he were in acute pain.

"Try not to think about them. They are no longer of our parish," Kholodny continued, sounding more and more like a preacher.

"Three years . . . To be shot," Samson whispered distractedly.

"Anything might happen. You'll see."

"What will I see?"

"Maybe they'll run away. That's what your soldiers did, remember?"

Samson considered the comparison.

"But they were actually guilty of robbery."

"And they still ran away."

"I don't want to drink to this verdict," Samson declared, putting down the glass. "How could we?"

"Alright," Kholodny acceded, then picked up his own. "Let's drink to . . . to kindheartedness! It never triumphs, but it gives us hope."

After a moment's thought, Samson nodded, but his face grew no brighter. He emptied his lungs of air, drained the glass in one gulp and eagerly inhaled.

"Now, let's go. Nayden's waiting. He asked us to come as soon as you woke up."

"How did he know I was asleep?"

"He came in and saw you. The alcohol was his gift, to congratulate us on closing the case."

Wiping their mouths on the sleeves of their tunics, they entered the commander's office.

"There you are," Nayden said, looking up from the stack of reports on the desk in front of him. "This mess is giving me a headache," he confessed, nodding at the papers. "Some bourgeois louse's housekeeper stole his copper jam pot and now he wants her put away! I should put him away for filing this! Here," he said, pulling up a thick folder tied with blue ribbons. "These are more significant. Worth your time." He gazed intently into Samson's eyes, then into Kholodny's.

The former priest perked up and opened his mouth to speak, but then, through the half-closed door, came the sound of someone either running or leaping up the stairs. Nayden turned towards the noise. The door swung open, blasting them with a gust of air. On the threshold stood an unfamiliar soldier, obviously alarmed and struggling to catch his breath. His left cheek bore the scar of a sabre-cut.

"Quick! Quick!" he gasped. "Detachment's gone!"

"What squad?" Nayden demanded. "Where?"

"Escort detachment. Went into the bathhouse, left their uniforms in the changing room and just plain vanished. Washtubs, tokens, even the soap – all still on the benches!"

"Which bathhouse?"

"Halytska. We've turned the place upside down! It's like the ground swallowed them up," the soldier said, sighing. "Thought they might be hiding in the steam, but no . . ."

"What the hell is going on?" Nayden shouted indignantly. "An entire detachment? How many soldiers?"

"Twenty-eight."

The commander turned to Samson.

"Let's go," he snapped, then turned his gaze to Kholodny. "You too. Hey, Vasyl!" he shouted past the soldier on the threshold. "I want five Red Army men at the entrance, double-quick!"

Epilogue

Samson pounded on the front door of his building for no fewer than five minutes. Soaked through, legs wobbly with exhaustion, he waited and waited. After every few blows, he would turn his head to the right, to the kitchen window of the yard-sweeper's flat.

At last, the light came on and, a minute later, after making sure that the person behind the door answered in the familiar voice of a tenant, the widow pulled out the bolt.

"You're all wet," she informed him.

"I left my umbrella at work," Samson admitted.

"Let me pour you a glass. You might catch your death of cold. It's freezing – look, I've got goosebumps already," she said, raising the back of her right arm to Samson's eyes.

Samson stopped by her kitchen, but only for a little while. Either because of her words about the cold night, or because of the night itself, he had begun to tremble, and so he happily downed two glasses of home-made liqueur, one after the other.

"What's that on your thumb?" the widow asked.

"Ink."

"Had to leave a thumbprint?" she asked in surprise. "I coulda sworn you knew your letters."

"I do," Samson protested nervously. "It was an accident. I should go."

This time, no-one in the flat had waited up for him. Snoring sounded from behind the doctor's door, and silence reigned behind Nadezhda's.

Having pulled off his boots, Samson peeled off his wet tunic and trousers, hanging them on the backs of the chairs at the table.

He spent a long time in the bathroom, trying to wash his thumb clean. As the water poured and poured, he concluded he was too filthy to lie with Nadezhda in their marriage bed. When it seemed that the ink was gone, he went off to his old bedroom, climbed under the covers and froze in anticipation of surrender to long-awaited sleep.

Yet sleep was in no hurry. In its stead came images of the vain search that had ended an hour earlier – the search for the Red Army men who had mysteriously vanished in the bathhouse. It was as if Samson's thoughts hadn't actually left the establishment, in which he himself had bathed only recently. They kept scouring the corners, looking under the boards in the steam room. The air still retained the scent of steam, although the steam itself had long since evaporated. The washtubs and tokens still lay on the benches in the hall with the taps. The trousers, belts and tunics still hung in the changing room above pairs of boots adorned with footwraps. Personal military documents in the pocket of each tunic, neatly folded into small squares, indicated which was whose. But the men whom the documents identified were gone. And the young investigator's thoughts refused even to try to guess how a naked soldier might vanish from a bathhouse.

Samson closed his eyes, which didn't affect the colour of the ceiling above him. But then a strange noise distracted him from the bathhouse and from the darkness of the night. It was as if someone had pulled out a desk drawer.

"Look – remember?" said an unfamiliar male voice.

"Sure do," answered another voice, also male. "Kept an ear in there. Let's see."

The metallic screech of the Montpensier tin made Samson wince, as if it were being opened inside his head.

"Got another one!" the first voice exclaimed in surprise.

"And what are those?" asked the second voice.

Something clinked against the tin.

"Two bullets," the first voice responded. "Little ones. Mauser? Revolver?"

"Lady's pistol. I've seen the type."

"So, he's got a lady's pistol, has he?"

"Looks like it. Must have done the killing on the sly. If it were out in the open, he would've used a revolver."

"I just don't get it," the first voice complained. "I mean, I understand that he shot someone down with these bullets, then sliced off an ear – as a trophy. But to take out a bullet, you've got to dig around in the corpse's meat for a long time. Only a doctor could have pulled them out quick, but Kolechko's no doctor."

"What about that friend of his – lives in his flat? He's a doctor. Probably had him do it."

"He's an eye doctor . . ."

"Doesn't mean he didn't do it. If a bullet hit someone in the eye, then this fellow would take it out – and if he can get it out of an eye, he can get it out of anywhere."

"What's that? A map? Unroll it," the first voice ordered.

Samson heard rustling.

"See?" asked the first voice, sounding triumphant. "That shows how to cut up a carcass. Means he knows his way around a dead body. Could've got the bullets out himself."

"Should we take it?" asked the second voice.

"No," the first voice objected. "Let's just keep tabs."

"What?"

"Let's watch him a while longer, I mean. But write down everything we found. You never know . . ."

"Makes sense," the second voice agreed. "Back to the commander, then?"

"Nah, he's gettin' some rest – and he's a light sleeper. Might wake up and shoot."

The tin screeched again as it closed, and the two bullets rolled along its bottom. The drawer slid back into the desk and the night-time guests stepped away carefully, trying to make as little noise as possible. Samson didn't hear them leave the office. He heaved a sigh, recalling the first time his desk had been searched this way.

Samson had just enough time to wonder whether Abyazov had sent these men before a big yawn stopped his thoughts and slowed the flow of blood through his body. When the body wishes to sleep, it slows down all internal movements and halts external ones altogether. But these slowed internal movements brought Samson no peace of mind. On the contrary, they lured him into a trap of a dream – a torturous blind alley, from which one could only escape back into reality, never into another, sweeter dream. Morpheus drew him into a chapel dimly lit by candles, in the middle of which, on two low benches, stood an open coffin. In it lay a dead man in a suit and tie, his forehead bandaged. Blood seeped through the bandage. Samson himself was down on his knees, weeping. He would raise his hands to his face, then immediately lower them, because all his fingers were smeared with red ink, as if with blood. He knew it wasn't blood. The ink had a chemical scent. The red lines of the verdict issued earlier that day kept rising up in his memory, and a whisper from the darkness kept on repeating, repeating, "Samson, repent. Repent before it's too late."

In the end, unable to endure the torment, Samson awoke and wiped his wet cheeks with his hand. It turned out that he had been crying both in his dream and in reality. He walked barefoot into the living room and carefully moved a chair to a window overlooking the street. He sat down and fixed his gaze on the roof of the house opposite. At first, it was all but indistinguishable from the sky, but the longer he stared at it, the better he could discern the line separating the human realm from the heavenly.

New tears welled up in his eyes and rolled down his cheeks. Samson wiped them away again, sighing. He had lost all desire to sleep.

The end. But to be continued.

ANDREY KURKOV was born near Leningrad in 1961. After working as a prison guard and a journalist he found renown as a novelist with *Death and the Penguin*. Since the Russian invasion of Ukraine, Kurkov, whose novel *Grey Bees* is set during an earlier stage of the conflict, has become a crucial voice for the people of his country. He published his *Diary of an Invasion* in 2022 and also presented BBC Radio 4's Letter from Ukraine. His novels *Jimi Hendrix Live in Lviv* and *The Silver Bone* were longlisted for the International Booker Prize in consecutive years.

BORIS DRALYUK is an award-winning translator and poet. His translation of Andrey Kurkov's *Grey Bees* won the inaugural Gregg Barrios Book in Translation Prize from the National Book Critics Circle. His translation of *The Silver Bone* was longlisted for the International Booker Prize.